A Riddle of Stars

A
RIDDLE
OF
STARS

Pierce Butler

A novel

Z

ZOLAND BOOKS
Cambridge, Massachusetts

First edition published in 1999 by
Zoland Books, Inc.

384 Huron Avenue
Cambridge, Massachusetts 02138

Copyright © 1999 by Pierce Butler

PUBLISHER'S NOTE

This book is a work of fiction. Names, characters, places,
and incidents are either the product of the author's
imagination or are used fictitiously. Any resemblance to actual
events or persons, living or dead, is entirely coincidental.

FIRST EDITION

Book design by Boskydell Studio
Printed in the United States of America

05 04 03 02 01 00 99   8 7 6 5 4 3 2 1

This book is printed on acid-free paper, and its binding
materials have been chosen for strength and durability.

Library of Congress Cataloging-in-Publication Data
Butler, Pierce, 1952–
A riddle of stars : a novel / Pierce Butler.
p.   cm.
ISBN 1-58195-007-1
I. Title.
PR6052.U824R5   1999
823'.914 — dc21   99-29877   CIP

For Susan Holbert

THANKS TO

Bernie and Dick Smith of Valentia Island,
Co. Kerry, for "the old days."
Lane Zachary for perceptive reading and unfailing encouragement.
Susan Holbert, who helped in the writing of every page.

The real journey is the soul's.

WILLIAM BUTLER YEATS

Contents

A Riddle of Stars

A Green Monster

I T'S LOVE at first sight! I've never seen a motor vehicle like this before. Of course, I can't tell one American car from another. I'm just off the boat, as Rick keeps reminding me. But this is the one I want.

I never owned a car in Ireland, and I can't see myself in a shiny nine-days' wonder out of the showroom where Rick works. Whoever designs cars nowadays is in search of a spurious simplicity — with the result that even an XJ6 looks like a cucumber with square corners. Actually, it's an accomplishment to make a Jaguar look like a Toyota — but look at this beauty! The line of the trunk curves down from the rear window, comes to a point, then dives in under the car like the tapered fuselage of a jetliner. The hood — they call it the bonnet where I come from — is a noble straight line from windshield to headlights. And the thing has *hidden* curves: the lines of two perfect parabolas in raised profile behind the rear doors and above the front wheels. What modern designer would even think of it?

A Pontiac Le Mans. Strange conjunction of names, one French and the other — what? No matter. It's more like a boat than anything else. Look at the way the doors belly out like a hull. Maybe that's why I want it: a boat — to remind me of the Inish.

"They sure don't make 'em like this anymore," Rick says.

He's checking it out. That's what he's here for. If you're going to buy a used car, Lily said, take Ricardo with you. He knows about cars: he sells them. But that's not his only qualification. Rick has been around. He didn't come down in the last shower. According to Lily, he has pulled himself up by his bootstraps, from the streets of Medford, Massachusetts, to an apartment on Memorial Drive with a view of the Charles. I've only known him a couple of days, but in spite of his reservations about used cars he's willing to leave the showroom for an hour to help me — an hour during which he might well have sold a $25,000 vehicle! He's come in his suit — and his new white Infiniti. We're in a neighborhood of two-family houses in Watertown. Between Rick and his car, the whole street looks drab and uninteresting. Except for my Pontiac.

With the self-satisfied look of a magician who's about to make something disappear, Rick spreads a drop cloth beside one of its front wheels. He kneels, grabs hold of the tire — and tries to pull it off. Then he scurries around to the front of the car, leans on the hood, and bounces it up and down. Same for the trunk. He pinches the razorlike crease of his pant legs, hunkers down behind the car, and screws up one eye as though he's looking down the sights of a rifle, blowing on his hands because his leather driving gloves aren't warm enough. He moves the cloth, hands me his suit jacket, gets down on his back and peers in underneath the front bumper.

"Is it always parked right here?" he yells.

The individual who's selling it is a portly Armenian, of indeterminate age, with a crop of curly black hair and a huge Nietzschean mustache. His name: George Hagopian. He smiles a dazzling, childlike smile.

"Yes, right here. Right outside my house. Where else?"

Rick pulls himself out, stands up, flicks some dust off his shoes. "There's a lot of gunk on the ground."

George shrugs, spreads his arms out, palms up. "Get a lot of cars come by when I'm not here. What you gonna do? Is a public street."

"Can you start it up?" Rick says.

George gets in the car while Rick is under the hood. I stand behind him, trying to look knowledgeable.

"The transmission fluid is brown and smelly."

He holds up a metal rod, and I sniff it dutifully.

"What does that mean?"

He shrugs.

"Transmission could be shot," he pronounces, with an air of oracular doom.

Rick knows about things that are beyond my ken. What do I know about? Weather and tides and the shoaling of fish. A smattering of history. Not much use to me now.

"Does that mean the clutch?"

"I keep forgetting, Matty. Where you come from they don't have cars with automatic transmission, right?"

When I lived with my grandfather there were only a handful of cars on the Inish. The priest had one and the doctor and Shanahan who owned the hotel and the Knight of Kerry who owned everything else. It wasn't easy to get a car over there, before the bridge came. You had to wait for a calm day and a low tide, put planks across the gunwales of the ferry, and drive the car onto them. You put chocks behind the wheels to keep it from rolling off. Once the ferryman Jacky Bar (named for his fondness for drink) let me hold the tiller because he wanted to get a rise out of Shanahan whose new Morris Minor was on the planks. I was only nine years old, but I wouldn't have refused it for the world. To move my hand and feel the boat move in response — such joy. Shanahan sat in the car, a red face on him, doors and windows shut tight. He was going to go to the bottom with it, if he didn't have a heart attack first! But I brought him over safe and sound, and Jacky took the tiller out of my hand within a boat's length of the pier.

What does that old gobshite want with a car? my grandfather said, when he no more knows how to drive the contraption than the babe unborn! The old man had no time for cars — or for change of any kind.

"You want to drive." George smiles. "Here, come on."

He holds the door for me, as though he's ushering me into his house. I slide in. The seat is about as wide as a park bench. Rick is beside me, George in back, peering over the seat.

"It's OK," George says. "Drive."

"You see this stick here on the column," Rick says. "It's in park. Move it so the needle is at D. Then take your foot off the brake."

This is precisely the information I need. I shift to drive and move my foot from the brake to the accelerator. The incredible happens. This huge thing moves smoothly and almost silently into the street. I can't believe it. I'm so hypnotized by the sensation of a movement at once precise and fated that I almost forget to steer. Rick nudges me. I turn the wheel — which miraculously offers no resistance to my touch — align this green leviathan with the pavement, and squeeze the brake. The movement ceases. The hood stretches out in front of me, the raised portion in the middle converging like an airport taxiway. The thing is a monster.

"We drive on the right over here," Rick observes. "You got to get that down straight off. Then you'll be OK."

"Thanks, Rick."

"No problem. I promised Lily I'd look out for you. She'll have my head on a silver platter if I don't bring you back alive."

I crane my neck and guide the Monster across the street. I start to accelerate. There's something fluid and slightly unsteady about the suspension, and I find myself shifting a little in my seat, making those involuntary movements by which you compensate for the swell of waves underneath you. It *is* like being in a boat. I'm in the old currach my grandfather kept below on the strand. At any moment, I'll smell seaweed and salt, and the smoke of the old man's pipe from where he's hunkered down in the stern.

But there is nothing, save a street of tightly parked cars and mounds of dirty snow. It is a ridiculous idea, to think that this old car reminds me of the Inish. Besides, I do not want to be reminded. My hands tighten upon the steering wheel. Don't look back, is my motto.

I glance at the panel.

"It's got forty thousand miles."

"A hundred and forty thousand," Rick corrects me. "The clock's been around once."

"That's a lot?"

Rick shrugs.

"At least it means the odometer hasn't been tampered with. Does the heater work?"

"Heater's the best thing about this car," George interjects.

I have almost forgotten about George. Has my driving alarmed him? I glance over my shoulder. He is perched on the edge of the seat like a kid at a football match. His face has the rapt expression of a spectator, but the still and relaxed way he holds himself suggests detachment. When our eyes meet, his childlike smile breaks over his face.

I am about to smile back, but I remember Rick's warning that buying a used car is a tricky business. In fact, Rick wanted me to buy a new Infiniti on time, to prove I'd found my feet here. He tried to persuade Lily to consign a loan. The thought of a car like Rick's — the discreet elegance of the interior that insulates you from the street — gives me a little thrill. But the luxury of an Infiniti is not for the likes of Matt Quigley. And I wouldn't want to be beholden to Lily for so much money, even if she'd been willing to advance it. I don't even have a job.

"Relax," George says, beaming. "Drive. See if you like."

I drive around the block. There's nothing comparable in size with the Monster anywhere. I feel like Gulliver among the Lilliputians, afraid I'll smash something or someone and not even notice it. In a few minutes, I'm back where I started.

"I like it!"

"How do the brakes feel?" Rick says. "Spongy?"

"I don't know, Rick. They work."

"Is all right?" George says. "You want to take on the highway? I got time."

I shoot a nervous glance at Rick. I'm not sure I'm ready for the highway. And I need him to take charge at this juncture. Rick knows the ways of the world. Maybe some of his knowledge will rub off on me.

"Wait a minute," he says. "I think we get the general idea. What do you want for it?"

"Body looks great, huh? No rust."

"I've never seen this shade of green before," Rick says, glowering at the hood. "It's not a shop color."

"My brother did the paint job. He's a painter."

"What does he paint? Houses?"

"That's right." George chuckles. "How you know?"

"I don't care about the color," I say. "I like the shape."

I am flying in the face of a cherished superstition. I believe that green is an unlucky color, as did no less a personage than Charles Stewart Parnell, champion of Home Rule for Ireland, the Uncrowned King, the Chief. When he was arrested by the English on suspicion of inciting violence and conducted to comfortable quarters in Kilmainham Jail, he balled up the green tablecloth and flung it into a corner. But perhaps this superstition does not apply in the New World.

"That's right," George says, smiling his beatific smile. "First my brother drives in San Francisco, then he keeps in his garage. No snow in San Francisco, not like here. No salt in the road."

Rick is frowning furiously. "Can you turn down the heat?" he says to me. "It's like a boiler room in here."

George is ecstatic. "You see? You see?"

He leans over the seat, peering at each of us in turn. George's enthusiasm affects me in spite of my need to let Rick handle things. Nothing will do me but to buy this car. I feel as though I own it already.

"It's great," I say. "I won't need to wear a coat."

"The seats are torn," Rick says, peeling off a strip of duct tape. "The radio doesn't work. What good is a car without a radio? Looks like the windows don't seal very well either: the rubber is shot to hell."

George looks appalled, as though someone has insulted his brother. "Don't get wet in the rain. Not in this car."

"So how much do you want for it?"

"My brother wants five hundred."

"You've gotta be kidding me," Rick says. "Look, the transmission might have to be replaced tomorrow. That's at least five hundred bucks — that nobody's going to want to put into it. The brakes feel like they need some work; that could be another five hundred right there. Its days are numbered, whatever way you cut it."

George thrusts an arm between us, gesticulating.

"Truth," he says, "I don't want to sell. This car is in my family for years, ever since new. My mother gives to my brother when he comes over here, he gives to me. I feel for this car — like I feel for my own kids. Is truth! This car's like a good old horse, pull the load, always the same, give no trouble. You think is just a piece of tin, but when you got something do the job like this, you got to respect. You can depend on this car. No question."

His smile fades. His expression becomes pensive. "But my wife, she don't see that way, she wants a new car, something shiny and new, like you got right there."

He nods toward the Infiniti. "That's a nice car," he allows, looking at me.

It *is* a nice car. But where would you be going, a refugee from the Inish, grandson of a poor fisherman, driving around in an Infiniti?

A sly smile returns to George's lips. His right eyelid closes. He touches the seat back gently, almost reverentially.

"But I'd rather have a car like this got *character* than something shiny still smells like the factory."

"I'll take a factory warranty over character any day of the week," Rick says.

"But I know what you mean," I say to George. "I like this car."

Rick gives me a look. Suddenly I am afraid I have spoiled his strategy. But it's too late. George is looking at me with intense interest.

"Where you come from?" he says to me.

"I'm Irish. From Ireland. I just came over here — to live."

"Ah, Ireland," George says, twirling his mustaches. "Ireland very old country, very old. The English do bad things there. Truth? Just like the Turks in Armenia. So you all leave and come to America, huh?"

"That's right," I say, grinning.

"How long you been here?"

"Since Saturday."

"You come for Christmas?"

"To get away from Christmas, is more like it."

"What you want this car for? Christmas present?"

"He's going to live at his girlfriend's house in Walpole," Rick tells him, "and he wants a car so he won't be stuck out there in the boonies."

George's face bursts into a huge grin. He puts his hand on my shoulder and leans toward me over the seat. "Ha, ha. Only here three days and already has a woman. Just like an Irishman, eh?"

"That's right," I say, grinning like an imbecile.

Rick is laughing too. I'm relieved. I thought he was pissed at me for showing my hand.

George turns suddenly to Rick. "What about you? You're not Irish."

Rick's hand goes to his luridly floral tie.

"Second-generation Italian," he rattles off. "Grew up with my grandparents in a house where nobody spoke English. Had a hell of a time when I started school."

"Now you speak like Prince of Wales," George informs him solemnly. "Not like me. I never learn, no matter what happens."

"How long have you been over here?"

"Not long enough." George shrugs. "I tell you what," he says decisively, turning to me. "How much money you got to spend?"

I glance quickly at Rick. He has strictly admonished me to leave the bargaining to him.

"Three hundred dollars," he spits out.

"Three hundred dollars! To buy car, pay rent, take your woman to fancy Boston restaurant!"

"That's all he's got to spend on a clunker," Rick says. "And it's at least a hundred more than it's worth. He just needs something temporary, until he finds a job. Then he'll go out and get himself a real car."

George runs his hands rapidly through his hair. He looks genuinely concerned about my predicament.

"This car," he says, grasping the back of the seat as though parting with an old friend. "Three hundred dollars. All right? You take. If something goes wrong in two weeks — something you can't fix,

OK? — bring back to me, I give you money, tell my wife nobody wants, and sell for parts. A deal?"

"Wow," Rick says. He seems to be impressed. My heart gives a leap. Am I about to come into possession of the Monster?

"One other thing," George says, raising a chubby finger.

"Oh, yeah? What's that?"

"You got to eat at my brother's restaurant. Is on Mount Auburn Street, called Mount Ararat. Right? You won't forget: Mount Auburn, Mount Ararat. Great Armenian food, just like home. Cheap too. Forget about Boston restaurants."

"Matt?"

I realize to my dismay that the final decision is mine.

"What about your brother?" I say to George. "I mean, doesn't he own the car?"

George throws back his head, and the laughter comes pouring out of him. "What about my brother? Look, I tell my brother I sell the car to an Irishman for three hundred dollars. What's he going to do? Send me back to Armenia?"

I look to Rick. He permits himself a smile, but he has the air of a man who is not about to be taken in.

"You go to Mount Ararat," George says. "My brother is a happy man."

"Me too," I say, impulsively. "It's really just what I wanted."

Rick extends his arm in the jacket sleeve, exposing a gold watchband.

"I got to get back. Go ahead and buy it. If it lasts you six months, you'll have gotten your money's worth. I'm going to sell you a real car sooner or later."

"Deal?" George says.

"It's a deal," I say, reaching my hand back over the seat.

George grasps it and squeezes it. I turn to look at him. He's serious.

"Your friend thinks is bad you don't care about shiny new car," he says. "Maybe bad. Maybe not. I tell you something, Irishman. This country: no joke. Probably your girlfriend tell you too. But you just come here, don't know. Probably you have to leave something behind you: family, place you love, another woman. Truth? And you're scared. So you need a car. Drive around, feel better. Don't worry. This car a lucky car for you, if you treat like good old horse. Then everything is all right. You from very old country, don't know the ropes, like they say. You need some luck."

His eyes are very blue. I am surprised to find that he is actually looking at me, taking me in. This is different from Rick's interest in me, which is benign, almost avuncular, but derives first and foremost from my association with Lily. I sense that he does not approve of the Monster. But George is not just selling me a car, which may or may not be a dud. He is *giving* me something, an impulse of good-will, a wish for my well-being.

"Thanks," I say.

George shakes his head, grinning wickedly. "Don't forget look under hood sometime. And make sure you don't bite off more than you can chew!"

Suddenly becoming aware of myself as someone very much in need of goodwill, I experience a moment of panic. What in the name of God am I doing here?

Christmas Day in Walpole, Mass. Lily's Ireland photographs are spread out on the table. She is sitting on the other side of the room, with her feet drawn up beneath her, tense, expectant.

"I want you to tell me which ones are worth enlarging," she informs me.

But she wants more than that: she wants me to like them. Lily is a lawyer whose field is handicapped rights and access. She consults with firms throughout the state, and I have no doubt that she is competent. But photography is her passion. She lives out here because she likes the light.

I pace the length of the table slowly, trying not to let my feelings express themselves in my face. Lily's Ireland is full of light and space and sky. The slopes of meager hillsides catch the light and bounce it off into space. By squatting down before a five-barred gate and aiming at the sky she has managed to make the opening of a cramped little field seem like the gateway to eternity. The burial mound at

Newgrange seen through trees is like the bright green setting of an outdoor pageant. Even Dublin's grimy streets are filled with sky.

I know nothing about photography. But Lily's compositions are intriguing. Each framed scene seems to suggest something behind or beyond its bright surface. I never suspected that Ireland contained such splendor — or such depth. But it is not my Ireland.

"I like them all," I venture, stalling for time.

"What do you think of yourself in the doorway?"

There is one photograph of me, standing in the doorway of an old slate outhouse we came across on our way to Newgrange. As Lily pressed the shutter, a bird flew out of the door; it is captured as a blur of light beside my head. But all my attention is focused upon Lily, as hers is focused on me through the camera lens. My face is lifted slightly to catch the light, and there is in my eyes a look of trembling hope.

I find something preposterous in this look; it seems to be flaunting its happiness, to be asking for trouble. Only an *amadán*, a fool, would risk such hope.

"I don't recognize myself," I say. "Nor my country either."

"You don't think I've got Ireland?"

"It's too good to be true, Lily. You've made the most of every paltry gleam of sunshine. I suppose that's what you were trying to do. To me, Ireland is a gray country. And cramped. Great hatred, little room, as Yeats says. Where did you find all that space?"

I am trying to mitigate my criticism by teasing her. But she doesn't respond. She gets up and gathers the photos into an envelope. Her face, framed by its dark tightly curled hair, seems pale.

The dog pricks up his ears and follows her with his melancholy gaze. Cooper is a handsome cross between a collie and a Lab, with the collie's markings and coat and the Lab's congenial temperament.

"I thought you would enjoy looking at them," Lily says. "But I think they just made you homesick."

"I'm not homesick," I say, with a touch of vehemence that surprises me. "Sick of home would be more like it."

She leaves the envelope on the table and withdraws to the doorway where she stands looking at me doubtfully. She is dressed in her house clothes, faded jeans and white sweatshirt, an amusing contrast to the suits she wears to work. Energy seems to emanate from her body, from her large gray eyes that are fixed on me. This is one of the things I like about Lily, her animation, her sense of life. But tonight the atmosphere seems charged with tension. She must have guessed that I have something to tell her.

"Maybe you'd feel better if you'd had someone to celebrate Christmas with," she says. "But what can I do? I'm Jewish. Christmas irritates me."

"I don't have much time for holidays myself," I assure her.

But the truth is that I am disconsolate. Have I *ever* celebrated Christmas? Before my mother remarried, Christmas was a sad occasion that always reminded her of my father, who died when I was two. Christmas with my grandfather was a grim tête-à-tête over some leftover turkey Christine's mother sent us — and after she died we didn't even have that. Why should it be different here? The Christmas lights on the common opposite the Walpole town hall look like they've been hung by the inmates of a mental institution — but the sight of them brings tears to my eyes. The New World is not more surprising than the changes I continue to discover in myself.

"I don't begrudge Christians their celebration," Lily says. "But Christmas was forced upon me as a child. When my third-grade class sang 'Christ our Lord is King,' I sang along with them, but I felt like a traitor. I still resent it when I walk into a shopping mall at Thanksgiving and I have to listen to Christmas carols."

Lily and I are two of a kind, in spite of our differences. But I was hoping to celebrate Christmas with America, to be absorbed somehow into its sentimental warmth, and I have not found within myself a celebratory feeling with which to meet the day. I cannot even stay here with Lily — and Christmas has nothing to do with it.

"Lily," I say rashly, "I'm going to move to Cambridge."

Her eyes widen. "You're not going to live with me?"

My heart sinks. This is the responsibility of love, to know that what you do or say may hurt. I do not want it. But can one love without it?

"Rick has a friend who needs a roommate. I feel isolated out here when you're at work, even with the car. I'll be better off in Cambridge where I can walk to everything."

Lily's expression of surprise gives way to a shadow of hurt that is slowly absorbed until her face has lost its animation.

"We'll see each other on the weekends," I say with feigned cheerfulness. "You're busy working all week anyway."

"When are you going?"

"I told Rick I'd meet him there tonight. He wants to introduce me."

"You're leaving *tonight?*"

She turns and goes into the living room. Cooper gets up and trots after her. Appalled, I hear her light steps going away, accompanied by the scratching of the dog's paws. What have I done? I want to go after her, but I am afraid I will only make things worse.

Her steps return, and she reappears in the doorway. Her face is changed, suffused with silent tears. "I thought we were going to live together."

It is a simple statement of fact. She bears her hurt with dignity. But the knowledge that I have inflicted it twists something inside of me. I want to get away. It is painful to know that she is vulnerable to me.

"We will, Lily," I say. "But not now, not here."

"But why?" she persists. "I thought we'd picked up right where we left off in September — at least the first weekend you were here. We had a plan. What made you change your mind?"

Blissful reunion that enveloped me in light! Hours of lovemaking that restored me to my body. Only a week ago I felt like a human being. But since then I have paced the empty upstairs rooms of Lily's rented farmhouse and stared through glass wavy with age into the white fields. I have no function here, and I do not know what to do with myself.

But how did you think you were going to get off scot-free, Matty? It all came creeping back, the familiar gray fog of the Inish, the dim and cramped atmosphere of the old man's house, pursuing me across the Atlantic, a souvenir of Ireland: my Ireland, not Lily's. Now I am waiting each day for Lily to come home, but when she comes I cannot meet her with anything resembling gladness. I want to protect her from my gloom. Better that I should nurse it alone than that it should poison our relations.

"Maybe you'll move to town," I say ineptly.

"I noticed that you haven't been very cheerful for the last week — but I didn't think you were about to move out! Why didn't you *talk* to me before you made up your mind? We haven't really talked since you got here."

"I know. We'll talk next week. I want to. More than anything I can think of."

Last year in Dublin. We used to talk far into the night, make love, and talk some more. It didn't matter what we said: I lived for the first time in my life with my heart upon my sleeve and no fear of being slighted. I had looked forward to this, to being able to share my life with another human being, in spite of my anxiety that she might have changed toward me in my three months of silence. But how was I to know that *I* would change?

She watches me silently, as though to read in my face something I have left unsaid, to confirm some fear she has nursed from the beginning. But I have said too much. It will never be the same now. I have spoiled it.

"Do you want to take a walk before I go?" I ask.

"You're leaving right *now?*"

For an awful moment I think she will refuse me. Then she turns away. "Let me get my coat."

Surreptitiously I stow my suitcase in the Monster's capacious trunk and stand on the porch to wait for Lily, stamping my feet to keep them warm. The stars are very bright, even though Walpole is not far from the city. They seem very close at hand, embedded in a sky that is dense and solid, more like substance than space. How is it that these familiar constellations, more visible here than in the foggy winter night of the Inish, seem the stars of the New World: changed, alien, not mine?

Lily comes out onto the porch, in a huge parka with a fur-lined hood and mittens that make her hands look like pot holders. The dog rushes past her and bounds up to me. He pauses to sniff my hand and then races into the field, leaving a trail like a sled as he plunges through the deep snow.

Cooper reminds me of Finn, my grandfather's black Lab, who was prone to fits and almost drowned in the channel. The old man had always had a dog, but after Finn he would have no more. Too hard to part with, he said. There is something in that.

"I can't believe it," Lily commences, with a raw edge to her voice. "You just told me you don't want to live with me and you're going to get in your car and go without even talking about it."

"I don't know what to say about it, Lily."

"You're depressed. If it weren't for that, I'd have written you off when you stopped writing to me without a word of explanation. It's hard to accept a death — especially of someone like your grandfather. I'm trying to be patient. But I'd like to know what's going on with you. I think you owe me that."

She is upset, and she has a right to be. I am in a panic. I have given our relationship a mortal wound, and I must find a way to stanch the bleeding.

"I still feel the same as I did in Ireland."

"But you're *not* the same. Are you really bored out here? Or did you just decide you don't want to live with me? I don't want to spend another three months wondering if I'm ever going to hear from you again."

I want to reassure her, but words fail me. We trudge in silence past the Monster. Ruts of ice in the driveway make the walking slow and difficult. The house is on the edge of a large field that slopes down to a frozen river, and the wind comes out of the field with a steady unrelenting venom.

"It *was* hard while I was living in his house," I say. "I was carrying it around with me, like a huge bloody stone. But since I've been here, I feel like it never happened. It's like I never knew him at all."

"Doesn't that seem strange to you?"

"Lily," I say passionately, "everything here is strange to me! Even you."

This is a critical moment for us. I can tell by her hushed, expectant presence. There is a response she wants, a response I must give. I cannot leave her with the impression that I do not love her. But my heart feels like a closed fist in the middle of my chest. I seem to be paralyzed by the very thought of losing her.

"I wish I didn't feel this way, Lily. Truly. If I could do anything to change it —"

We come to the end of the driveway and stand beside the dark road. The wind gusts about us, and great skeletons of trees thrash about above our heads. I have no experience of this kind of cold. Here winter is trying to make a clean sweep, to burn everything that moves off the face of the earth. If there is life next spring, it will be new life, seeded miraculously in the warming air. Nothing could possibly survive this cold within the ground.

"I should have told you sooner. I'm sorry."

But I am not sorry, though I feel her distress. She is reproaching me for what I cannot help, and something within me resists her, with sullen, silent vehemence.

"What really happened to you in those three months, Matt?"

Fear creeps over me, worse than the most piercing cold. The New World can be lonely, no doubt, but it is not the loneliness of the In-ish, a loneliness to which the English word is not adequate, more truly *uaigneas*, a peculiarly Irish sense of desolation, with its echo of *an uaigh*, the grave.

"Lily. Have you ever had a dream in which you wanted to flee from some danger but you couldn't move because you were rooted to the spot? That's what it was like."

"But you *did* get away."

"Because of you! If it wasn't for you, I'd still be there on that bloody island in the middle of nowhere. That's why I'm here, to be with you."

"But now you're moving out."

"I'm moving because — I don't know why, Lily. You're right: it's not the same between us. But it's not *your* fault. I think I just need to be alone with it for a while. I know it seems like I'm walking out on you. But please bear with me. I love you, and I need your help."

Silence. A sigh.

"Let's sit in your car for a minute, OK?"

The Monster looks like an old shipwreck on an icebound beach. We get inside, and I start up the engine and the heater. George was right about the heater. In about sixty seconds, it's blowing out hot air, and the interior is almost tropical.

Lily pushes back the hood of her parka. Little eddies of chill air emanate from her. There is just enough reflected light from the icy road to see her, the heavy mass of her curls, the slight severity of her profile.

"It won't be like the last three months," I tell her. "I'll be out here every weekend — if you can stand to see that much of me."

"How will you find the time," she murmurs, "with all the plans Rick has for you?"

"I'll squeeze you in somewhere," I say, groping for something of Rick's bravado.

I notice that she is looking at me intently and that the expression of her eyes has become warm and distant. I lean across, and we kiss. Her breath is sweet, her lips and cheeks are cold. It is not like good-bye, this kiss. It is the beginning or the continuation of something, and with it I feel my body returned to me, once more a living organism that serves some useful purpose within the scheme of things.

There is a face at the window. I start up. It is Cooper, ears pricked, tongue lolling, smearing the glass. Lily slides away.

"You could still change your mind and stay," she says. "You didn't have your turkey dinner for Christmas, but I'll make you some potato latkes for St. Stephen's Day — even though you don't deserve it."

There is nothing left of Christmas, and tomorrow will not be St. Stephen's Day but the anonymous day succeeding Christmas in the saintless calendar of the New World.

"I told Rick I'd be there tonight," I hear myself say.

I put my hand up to my forehead and find it slick with perspiration. I realize that it's like an oven inside the Monster: the windows are fogged, and the fan roars like a brushfire. I snap it off.

"It's hard for me to leave," I tell her.

"It's hard for me too, Matt," she murmurs.

She opens the door and gets out. The dog prances about her,

barking. Cooper is a little wary of me and of my connection to Lily. Now he will have her all to himself. She has asked me to stay, and I have refused her. She has asked me to live with her, and I am moving out. This is the note on which we must part: an ill omen. I am superstitious about conclusions. I fear that a bad ending can cancel whatever good has preceded it. But I cannot mend it now.

As she moves away, she slaps the Monster's roof with her swollen mitten.

"Bon voyage," she says. "At least you have a car to come out here in. But my God! — it's like driving around surrounded by all the worst of America!"

I get on Route 1A and drive. There is no traffic, and I turn on my high beams. The branches of the trees on either side of the road are coated with ice: they rush by fantastically, like the icy pikes of a retreating army. The world has shriveled to the lighted cones of the headlights, and the only sounds are the hissing of the slipstream in the perished rubber seal of the windows and the crunching of the wheels on a fresh fall of snow.

Tomorrow *is* St. Stephen's Day; my calendar is still the Old World's. St. Stephen's Day on the Inish, very early in the morning, the Wren Boys, in grotesque disguise, used to come into the field and sing in rowdy straggling voices beneath the gable: *The wran, the wran, the king of all birds, St. Stephen's Day, was caught in the furze.* My grandfather would get up grumbling and fling them some change. He had no time for any customs save his own, but he regarded the Wren as sacrosanct: to interfere with it would have brought bad luck on the house. Since I was never entirely awake when they came, I remember them as voices in a dream, and they are forever associated with the deep silence of early morning on the Inish and the lassitude, the sense of depletion, that follows all occasions supposed to be happy.

To this must I wake tomorrow, sharing an apartment with a stranger, with nothing to do and the whole livelong day to do it. But I feel better in the Monster. I am warm and dry, I no longer sense the desolation of snowy windswept fields, and I am in motion, which allays my unease.

The Monster rolls easily with the dips and rises of the road, and again, as though in spite of me, my body remembers the impossible buoyancy of Granda's currach. Movement in one world inducing memory of another. What a strange and unlikely coincidence. Yet I feel the flimsy shell move with me, and I can almost see it moored on the calm tide, its black hull looking the same bow and stern, nudging the stones like a living creature, the water gently knocking against the tarred hull with a sound like fingers tapping a taut drum. Disarmed by this motion, I find myself again trying to imagine the old man as he used to squat in the stern, the pipe in his crippled hand, the other deep in a sagging pocket, his head cocked to one side like a bird's. . . .

But it's no use. I can't see him. In the place in my life that he used to occupy, there is only emptiness.

And yet I cannot believe in his death. Perhaps that is the explanation for those three lost months I spent in his house, unable to sleep, eating like a bird, hardly aware of day or night — I was waiting for him to prove he could defy the grave! They used to say that Parnell wasn't really dead, that his coffin was filled with stones. Is that what I thought? Or was I trying to make it up to the old man for my defection? Darkening days, clouds creeping down the hills, ceaseless buffeting of wind and sea. I sat there in the chimney corner, hour by hour, almost choked by the smoke of the fire, in which the physical world was dissolving. Intervals of deathly calm, the strand below the house shrouded in mist, every sound muffled. I was listening for his voice, straining to catch the cadences of those names he'd dinned into my head — Diarmat his favorite, Grania his nemesis, Mug Ruth the wizard of the Inish, Mananann Mac Lir the sea god. I felt myself draw near that Other World whose unseen existence he'd almost convinced me of. If I hadn't gotten the hell out of there, I would have ended up as odd as himself!

On the Jamaicaway there is more traffic. I cruise with one hand in my lap holding the wheel, my foot tapping the gas pedal. The stream of cars in which I am immersed coils and uncoils itself, a serpent scaled with light. It contracts at an intersection, and as I wait, I can see the expressions on the faces of people in neighboring cars: jolly, worried, indifferent, bored. Immobile, I feel my mind begin to seek its inescapable orbit.

To live alone in that house after you, old man — if that was what you intended for me — it was too hard. To make a life for myself on the Inish — that was all the home I ever had and yet I never felt at home there — too hard. I tried. There were moments before I left when I thought I'd actually die of *uaigneas,* as though it were a physical ailment, its tentacles wound about my heart. You gave twelve years on the Skellig before your accident, so I don't have to tell you that the winter nights are long. And I missed Lily. I never knew I had any heart in me at all until she made me feel it.

The light changes to green, the serpent resumes its mesmerizing progress, and I settle back into the movement, temporarily released. Once again I belong to this community of the road, I am swallowed up in it, subsumed in its anonymity, yet alive, separate, an observer capable of his own impressions, no longer obsessed. When I am in motion, I am able to believe that all may yet be well. That is why I need this car.

The city looms up ahead, a festival of lights. The traffic thins out and I breeze through the Fens and over Back Bay. The sight of the river and the lights of Cambridge give me a little thrill. This is another of my discoveries: I love to drive! The Monster is my boat, America my ocean. My real journey has begun.

I turn west on Storrow. I have half an hour before I meet with Rick, and a half a tank of gas. A sign for the Mass Pike flies past, and before I know it I am barreling around the arc that leads to the tollbooths. Without having made a choice, I find myself heading east. I pay my fifty cents and step on the gas. The highway is like a bowling alley. It stretches ahead of me, flanked on either side by high walls and buildings, a trench cut through the nighttime city. The lanes are narrow. I am in the middle, and there are cars and trucks streaming by me on either side. This is unnerving. I can either slow down or bring the Monster up to speed. Scared by my own daring, I depress the accelerator pedal. There is no perceptible change, save that a glance in the rearview mirror tells me I'm part of the flow again, the body of lights advancing as one.

The highway curves, and a tunnel rushes at me. Inside all is bedlam. Lights flash crazily on walls and columns, and the din is maddening. The wheel trembles momentarily, as though I am riding on cobbles, and I grip it tightly. This is excitement, this is life. No time to think of anything. My heart is in my mouth. But then we are out in the city night again, hurrying toward the Atlantic, my fellow travelers in this brave New World and I.

I choose north on the Fitzgerald Expressway and find myself in the heart of the city. There are great towers of light all around me, nudging the highway itself, and I can hardly breathe for a sudden joy. How strange that all this is here, the preposterous spectacle of the many living in the one place. People live cheek by jowl here, squatting one on top of the other in little boxes of light. But even you would have been moved by it, old man — the scale, the extravagance, the marvelous superfluity, this roadway raised above the roofs of houses so that your grandson can travel in view of the summits and the stars! That I should be here, embarked on this adventure, that the loneliness and silence of the Inish should be so irretrievably absent — I cannot credit it!

A sign for the Mystic Bridge — how can I pass it by? I round a corner in a ramp no wider than a roller-coaster track and see it ahead of me, a whalelike hump in the night. It is high and narrow, there are two decks, and the lights of cars crawl through it, winking as they pass the massive columns that support it. I ascend its mighty flank, and fields of light spread out on either side, all the unknown neighborhoods of the city, alight for the holiday, like a gigantic Christmas tree, spread-eagled upon the land. Angels and ministers of grace, it is a sight!

I roll down the window. The night air is both foul and salty, but I drink it in, as though it were the very essence of place. I can see starry roads winding over the face of the land and tiny two-eyed wanderers adrift on them. Oh, to be on the road, to travel without rest, with Rick or Lily or even alone, to leave all loneliness behind.

My eyes fill unexpectedly, and I feel a sense of well-being and an affection for all that I survey — and all beyond in the great American night. What a marvelous thing that in the world there should be a New World, a place where all rootless misfits such as myself can have a second chance.

But as the Monster approaches the crest of the bridge, my speed suddenly frightens me, and a shadow of doubt touches my joy. I press the brake, roll up the window, and start to descend. I do not know myself here, prowling the unquiet night of Boston, behind the wheel of this terrible machine. And the life that I know — is gone. I had no choice but to leave the Inish. It was not a decision so much as a necessity, and I can take no credit for it. I fled to Lily as to a last refuge — and now I have cut myself off from hope.

Do you know what it is, old man? I have escaped with my life, but not unscathed. I would have gone to the dogs had I stayed in your house, wasted away to nothing. But in order to tear myself free I have had to perform a sort of amputation, and God knows what infection may find me here. I even brought a piece of mortar from the chimney in my suitcase — in superstitious emulation of the famine emigrants. But I have left a part of myself in that house, and if I do not find a way to reclaim it I will never be whole.

A sign informs me I am in Chelsea. It is news to me that Boston has its Chelsea. God alone knows how I am to get back to Cambridge. I've heard that there are highways without exits for hundreds of miles! I'm driving in the wrong direction, and I'm going to be late for Rick. A tough station. But getting lost is the very least of it.

The Road to the Inish

AND AFTER THIS my exile — there is still insomnia. Suddenly I am preternaturally wakeful, and I know there will be no more sleep for me tonight. I turn on the lamp and try to read, but my head feels light and empty and I keep seeing the words upon the page, feeling the book in my hand. My mind refuses to be distracted from its strained awareness of itself.

I give it up, dress, extinguish the light, and walk through the kitchen, which is lighted only by the tiny flares of the gas stove's pilots, burning up death in the dark. Carrying my shoes, I hurry along the hallway. Jamie's door is ajar, and I can hear the patient sound of her sleeping breath. Gently I close the apartment door from the outside with my key, put on my shoes, and hurry down the stairs. It is breathtakingly cold on the street. I have not brought my coat, and it's more than my life is worth to go back for it. But I am not afraid of the cold anymore. It is a clean, unequivocal phenomenon, and it clears my head of the fumes of unremembered dream. Cold can kill you, but not unless you're a bloody fool. Memory is a more formidable adversary.

The Monster's seats have the very chill of the grave, but it starts at the first touch. I set the heater going, the fan on high, and before I know it I can smell the heat. My anticipation warms me, though the tips of my fingers are still numb. And when I pull away from the sidewalk and begin to roll on down the empty length of Cambridge Street — what blessed relief! I am in motion; therefore I have a purpose. A car emerges from a side street and accelerates ahead of me. I am overjoyed to see it, for now I am not alone. The city is not asleep, and I am no more of an odd fellow than the handful of others who are still wakeful at this hour.

I negotiate the underpass by Sanders Theater and slip through a ghostly Harvard Square. A digital clock mounted on the roof of the bank reads 2:55 in glowing red numbers. I approach the river on JFK Street, cross the Larz Anderson Bridge, and turn east on Storrow, heading for the Mass Pike. I am relieved to be driving, but I need an expanse of highway in front of me.

There is no one in the westbound tollbooth, and it takes a moment before I notice the ticket that the machine spits at me. I accelerate away from the booth. The lane narrows, then merges with the turnpike. Now I can relax. I feel as though I have navigated a boat through a narrow and dangerous passage. I have as much highway in front of me as my wakefulness could possibly desire. Like the ocean, it is not something to be taken lightly, but upon it I do not need to fear ambush.

I choose a middle lane and reach a steady speed. It's become my habit to note the odometer reading before I drive, to know the dimensions of my progress at least. Tonight I have already traversed the length of the Inish — seven miles — in not much more than seven minutes. How many islands could be placed end to end along this mighty western highway and the peregrinations of how many lifetimes completed in a night's unheedful travel? I marvel anew that there should be a country with room enough for such a road. But I am convinced that it traverses the void. The terrain on either side is an empty and unremarkable surburbia, unsullied by personal associations and history. Whereas every square foot of the Inish is saturated with the dense unseen life of ages, the air itself resonant with the hopes and fears of generations, with the still living breath of their unforgotten stories. On the Inish there is no escape from the past.

The regular passage of an occasional eastbound car, the unfolding roadway, the almost imperceptible vibration: all this is mesmerizing. I have no fear of drowsiness, but I roll down the window just to hear the sound of the rushing wheels, to feel the shocking bite of the freezing air. For a moment I am grounded, restored to myself. Then my mind begins to wander, to move in a familiar and unwelcome direction. Desperately I look around the interior, watch the glowing gauges, clasp and unclasp the wheel, run the fingers of my right hand over the smooth vinyl of the seat — just to remind myself of where I am, who I am, alone in a speeding car, crawling upon the eastern edge of the great continent of America. This is real — and this is enough. My sensations might be my salvation, if I could hold them. But the dream of the past is stronger.

Whenever I think of Dublin, I see not the gray stone buildings of the college, or the high vaulted ceiling of the Aula Maxima where I met Lily for the first time — at a lecture on Jack Yeats, the poet's brother, whose painting she admired — but the low houses along the Royal Canal, into one of which my mother and stepfather and I were unhappily compressed, upon our first arrival. And helplessly, as though there is some intrinsic connection, I recall a character of Beckett's who walks beside the Canal in despair, squeezing a little rubber ball in his hand. I feel myself once more within the city's dark miasmic hollow, surrounded by the ominous drumroll of black mountains; I cannot breathe.

I spent six wretched months in that house by the Canal. My stepbrother Brendan was born there, and my mother became so ill she could not travel to the Inish for my grandmother's funeral. I was lonely for the Inish, and I hated the Christian Brothers' school my mother hoped would make a young gentleman of me, since her own best efforts had come to naught. I hated the black blazer with red braid on the lapels, the mandatory participation in the barbaric melee of rugby, and most of all, the long snakelike leather strap the Brothers resorted to when pedagogy failed them. I did not want to be a young gentleman, if this was what it entailed. What I wanted was for my mother to take me back to the Inish — and to leave my irritable stepfather and the squalling Brendan behind!

Thus it is my departure I remember most vividly, the windy platform of Amiens Street Station and the pale and harried face of my mother as she lifts onto the train the battered suitcase bound with a leather strap that contains my worldly possessions. She is sending me back to the Inish — alone — to look after my grandfather. I am seven years old.

My mother bends and brushes my cheek with her lips. I inhale the medicinal scent of her makeup along with the interesting stench of the train. She hands me a package of sandwiches wrapped in foil.

"Don't be worried," she says. "You're not going among strangers. You'll soon get used to your granddad. He isn't the worst."

I enter the carriage and stand uncertainly in the corridor outside the compartments. The train is crowded with the supporters of the Kerry football team returning from a championship match: burly farmers in shabby suits with green-and-gold paper hats elbow their way by me, talking loudly and roughly. They smell of drink and sweat and heavy wet clothing. My stomach churns with fear and disgust.

I turn to the window. My mother is standing on the platform, regarding me. What is the meaning of her look? She tries to tell me something, but I cannot hear her. She motions me to come to the window, but the doors slam heavily, and people shout and run past between us. The train lurches and throws me against my neighbor. Then it moves, slowly and ominously and with increasing momentum. My mother raises her hand to wave — and disappears. I am left with the image of her pale distracted features. Then the platform and the waving laughing groups of people are borne swiftly away.

The train enters a tunnel, and an almost palpable darkness fills the corridor. The conversation ceases around me, then resumes with renewed bravado. I stand without moving, listening to the harsh clanking noises of the train, squeezing the handle of my suitcase.

"Jaysus, 'tis gone astray we are in the bowels of the earth," a coarse voice says. "I never knew the fucking thing to be so long."

"A pity herself isn't here for to grab ahold of," someone says.

"Keep your paws to yourself!" another shrieks in an absurd woman's voice.

Boisterous laughter. I am not afraid. I'm glad to be unseen. But light filters down the corridor, the train emerges into day, and the talk around me seems deafening. I watch the naked backyards of the terraced houses move past, a street full of cars waiting at a crossing, a still and filthy arm of the river.

A boy and a black-and-white dog appear, sitting close together atop a steep embankment. The boy's face is rapt, and I press against the glass as he and his dog wheel past, but he does not turn his head. Inexplicably, foolishly, I wish myself in his place, sitting alone with my dog above a railway track, staring after a hurrying train, waiting until it is time to go home. I have a lump in my throat, and I want to cry. But the thought of attracting the attention of the rough men around me makes me clench my teeth and blink back tears.

I stand looking at wet fields until my feet are tired. Then I walk slowly along the corridor, dragging the suitcase, looking for a seat in one of the compartments. I see an empty seat by a window and wrestle with the door. It transpires that the occupant of this seat has gone to the lavatory, but his friends make room for me and a red-faced man who smells of drink puts my suitcase on the overhead rack.

"Now you're laughing," he tells me.

The talk is about the football match. A bottle of whiskey is surreptitiously passed from hand to hand. I want to go to the lavatory, but not enough to thread my way through the drunken men in the corridor. I huddle against the window, my sandwiches in my lap, and follow the wooden electricity poles that whip past me until I feel dizzy. I close my eyes.

I awake in a panic. The train lurches, moves forward, then comes to a stop. Outside a voice shouts: "Limerick Junction!"

This is where my uncle is to meet me and help me to change trains. I get up hurriedly, ask for my suitcase, and struggle out of the train. I pull the suitcase across the platform, position myself against the wall of the station, and search the crowd anxiously. The people leaving the train disperse, the guard's whistle sounds, and the train begins to move. I am alone on the platform. I wait for a long time, walk up and down within sight of the suitcase, peer into the empty waiting room. Finally I approach the ticket office. I am afraid to say that there is no one to meet me — perhaps they will send me back in disgrace — so I ask for the Caher train.

"'Tis leaving! Run, let you! Go on!"

I run, as from the scene of a crime. I cross the tracks by an enclosed wooden bridge through which the wind blows. My suitcase seems to have grown heavier. I drag it up one side of the bridge, and it drags me down the other. A guard is walking the length of the train, slamming the doors. He thrusts my suitcase aboard and hustles me on after it. Gasping, I sit on the floor of the corridor. I have lost my sandwiches.

There are not so many football fans on this train, and I find a compartment with only one occupant, an elderly man in a shabby suit, wreathed in pipe smoke. I sit staring out the window at more fields and distant blue mountains. I have eaten nothing since breakfast, and I am weak with hunger and fear. There is probably a buffet carriage on the train, but it is more than I can do to make my way there. I am tired and frightened, and the motion of the train and the foul smell of the pipe have made me ill. I wait until I can endure it no more and make a rush for the lavatory. It is occupied, and I vomit on the floor of the corridor.

The train stops at a station, and I see a sign with the words MOUN-TAIN STAGE. When I get back to my compartment, the old man is gone. I go to open the window. It is raised and lowered by means of a leather strap, and as I wrestle it loose, it slips from my grasp. The window comes crashing down upon my hand and pins it against the frame. I stand there, in shock but feeling no pain. The cold air rushes into the compartment. I turn my head. There is no one in the corridor. I cannot bring myself to cry out for help. Above my door I see the communication cord which if pulled will stop the train, but this seems a rather drastic course, and besides I cannot reach it, tethered as I am to the window frame.

Outside the window, the train is traversing the side of a mountain. There is a steep drop to the ocean, and across a great expanse of bay a line of grim purple mountains. They run to the west and fall into the sea in great dark headlands. The sun is low in the sky, and there is a place where sea, sky, and land seem to come together. Something in this view quiets me. I stand by the open window, unmindful of the train's motion, the wind whipping my hair, my benumbed hand.

"Tickets, please!"

Someone comes into the compartment behind me.

"Jesus God, 'twould skin a brass monkey in here. Is it trying to petrify us you are?"

He stands beside me, but he seems far away. I do not leave off looking toward the misty confluence of the elements at the extremity of the bay.

"Are you stuck or what's wrong with you?"

He lifts the window, and I remove my hand. Sitting down, I see that there is a bright red bruise between thumb and forefinger; the rest of my hand is very white, as though it were dead. Then I feel the pain, and my head rolls back against the seat.

At once I am in a world of unimaginable clarity and peace. My eyes are closed, but even the darkness is benign. I wonder calmly why I have never experienced this peace before: it is so close, this other world, just behind my eyes. Nothing can touch me here, and I am not afraid.

I am bending over with my face upon my knees, and someone's hand is on the back of my neck. People are clustered around me. I can no longer see the window. I sit up. There's a murmur of approval, and someone hands me a glass of water.

"He's all right, he's all right."

"He's destroyed his hand. Look at the cut of it."

"He's all right. Are're you, boyeen?"

"Is your hand broken?"

My hand is not broken. At least I hardly feel any pain in it. I am strangely detached from the hubbub, not myself. I tell them I am going to meet my uncle Con O'Donnell in Caher, I accept their offer of a sandwich from the bar, and they withdraw, murmuring. I wolf down the sandwich. The ocean is no longer visible in the window. I stare at the blur of a green embankment, thinking of nothing.

At Caher the train empties. I walk out of the station and descend into the town, without even thinking of my uncle. My mind, like my hand before, seems numbed. I walk the length of a noisy and crowded main street. When at last I lift my eyes from the ground I find that I have walked out of the town into quiet fields. I can see an arm of the sea and distant hills. The silence has a quality I have forgotten in the city, like a single note sustained beyond the range of hearing. The spectral evening light on the sea makes me remember my loneliness.

I have lost my sense of direction. I ask a man sitting outside a cottage for the road to the Inish.

"Isn't it there in front you, boyeen?" he says, gesturing toward the sea with a dirty torn sleeve.

I walk down a long unnaturally straight road, dragging the suitcase, stopping frequently to rest my aching arms. The Inish disappears, then comes into view again, shockingly close. I pass between a house and a decrepit shed roofed with rusty sheets of metal. The channel looks full and threatening; a cold wind comes off it. A sloping pier points across the water to the houses of the Foot clustered about one steep narrow street. I'm no longer expecting to be met. I sit on my suitcase on the sheltered side of the pier, where the water laps quietly against the edge of the slipway. I sit there for a long time, trying to take some comfort in the gentle sound of the tide. The sun makes a brief appearance above the hills to the west, and then the light begins to fade out of the sky. I am too tired and desolate to hold my fear at arm's length. They have all abandoned me. How would they feel if I were to come to harm?

A car comes suddenly out of the dark and drives down the slipway. Blinded, I jump up and press back against the pier. The headlights dip and flash; the horn sounds a long drawn-out roar. The driver's door flies open.

"If that doesn't rouse the so-and-so!" a man's voice says from behind the lights. "How long are you in it?"

I recognize the voice of a farmer from up behind Caher, whose brother lives on the Inish. But I cannot remember his name, which embarrasses me.

"He's got his nose in his third pint by now," the man says. "And his feet to the bloody fire. I suppose you couldn't blame him. But when there's people still abroad that want to get home!"

The lights flash again, and the horn blares. Then the car reverses up the slipway and parks. The man's footsteps approach. His muddy Wellingtons come to a stop in front of me.

"That'll do the trick," he says with satisfaction. "He's coming down the pier beyond, cursing like a tinker, I'd say. But who have we here at all?"

He bends down to have a closer look at me. It's dark; I cannot see his face. His breath smells of drink.

"Matthew Quigley."

He whistles softly. "Oh," he says warily. "Where's your uncle from you?"

"I think I missed him."

He straightens up with a grunt. "Faith, it wouldn't be hard. He's slippery enough, the same customer. He must be at work by now. I'll take you round to him."

He peers in the direction of the Inish. The sound of an engine gradually emerges from the dark, grows louder, then shuts off abruptly. A boat rounds the pier and glides into the slip, a row of car tires hanging over the gunwale. The man beside me grabs a rope flung out of the dark, and the tires smack against the concrete. I stand up and approach the treacherous gap between the pier and the gunwale. The tobacco-stained hand of Jacky Bar grips mine in a vise and makes me step out and down into the well of the boat. My suitcase arrives beside me, unscathed. Then the engine is started up with a roar, and the two men withdraw to the stern. Deafened by the noise, breathing oily fumes, I huddle on the floorboards beside my suitcase.

But on the channel I breathe the salt air of the ocean, and something revives in me. I stand up and peer around the raised prow toward the familiar lights on the Inish, hanging dense above the floodlit pier and scattered throughout the dark. There is a sense of finality about this crossing. Dublin is behind me. I am separated from it by the trials of my solitary journey. I do not belong to my mother anymore. She has sent me away. Once I step out of this boat there will be no going back to her: I bite my lip and swear it.

The roar of the engine ceases, and a high pier slides by. This time I am lifted out onto the slipway, too tired to notice anything save the huge weathered stones that form its surface. But I am home.

The man who came in the car is carrying my suitcase, and I walk beside him, almost running to keep up. The channel is on our left, and we pass the church in its gloomy copse of trees. The massive stone buildings of the Cable Station are set back from the road; they are brightly lit and emit an eerie humming. I lived in one of the residences before my mother decided to move to Dublin, but I have never seen the machinery rooms where my father worked and from which this sound comes. We pass along a blank gable and halt in a dark porch.

"Wait here, boyeen."

I stand dumbly, asleep on my feet, but vaguely frightened by the humming, which seems to draw closer, becoming more ominous. Then there is someone bending down to me, shaking my limp hand. I catch a glimpse of my uncle's long owlish face.

"Where were you at all?" his distracted voice declaims. "Wasn't I there before you at Caher?"

"He went astray," the man who has brought me says.

I am too tired to experience relief. I want only to sleep, but my uncle takes my hand and I am dragged along, stumbling and falling against him. We pass a terrace of houses. Through tears of fatigue I gaze with longing at the lighted windows. I feel sure that life is happy in these houses, that there is shelter from cold and dark. Then the hedgerows rise on each side of the road: they seem to join above my head. My uncle keeps a tight grip on my hand. He is talking all the while in his odd musical voice, and I do not hear a word.

"Wake up, lad. Be a good boy now." He's shaking me by the shoulders. I slip between his hands. He raises me again and pinches my cheeks. "Come on, you're almost there. I can't carry you, you know. You're too heavy for me now."

The voice is pleading. I blink awake. The night is brighter, and I can see the tide at the bottom of a narrow lane. My uncle turns me toward a gap in the hedgerow and puts the handle of the suitcase in my hand.

"It's the house across the field there. Go on, let you. He's waiting for you."

"Who is?"

"Your grandfather. Go on now like a good boy."

He starts to walk away. My heart leaps in fright. He disappears from view. His voice floats back to me out of the dark. "Mind you tell him who you are now."

Then I am alone and wide awake. I feel the night around me, and it is not the bland night of Dublin, but a night of unfathomable depth, concealing the great ocean and the purple mountains I saw from the train. It seems to flow into me, filling my senses with darkness and cold. I sit down slowly, huddle against the suitcase, and begin to cry. I cry for my tiredness and hunger, for my mother who has disowned me, for the very strangeness of my native place. I cry until I have no more strength to expel tears. My fingers roll the dust of the road into little wet balls and crush them on the palm of my hand.

I stand up, lift the suitcase, and trudge across the field. Its surface is uneven, and I stumble and weave about like a drunk. The bulk of the house looms up against the sky. There is no light showing. Trembling, I approach the house. Suddenly an outbreak of barking freezes me to the spot. The door opens, but there is still no light.

"Stay back, Finn," a man's voice mutters. "Stay back, stay back now."

The barking ceases, but I hear the sound of the dog's eager panting and the flesh prickles at the back of my neck.

"Who is it?" the voice rises to a hoarse shout.

I open my mouth to say my name, but no sound comes out. If I were able, I would run, but not even fear can give me strength.

"Matthew Quigley," I manage.

"I can't hear you at all. Come up to the door. Come up, come up!"

Leaving the suitcase, I walk up a path and come close to him. I can make out only a dark composite form in the doorway. I hear the dog panting and thrashing about.

"Matthew Quigley," I whisper.

"God above!"

"Matthew Quigley," I repeat it like a mantra.

"Come in till I see you. Come in, boy. Come in!"

He withdraws into the house, and I step up warily. The dog rushes at me, and I start back against the door.

"Don't mind him at all," the voice says out of the dark. "You'd think he'd ate and destroy you, but he wouldn't maul a kitten."

The dog's wet tongue slobbers on my hands. He wants to jump on me, and I hold on to his coat. I'm not afraid of him anymore. I stand on the threshold, inhaling the smells of the house. It does not smell like any house I have ever been in. There is the smell of the dog's wet coat, of smoke and of fish, a sour bitter smell that reminds me of spoiled milk, and something else clean and penetrating that I know but cannot identify.

A match flares, and I see him all at once. He stands by a dresser, in a stained black suit and open shirt without a collar. His face is in shadow. He lifts a tall smoky glass and lights something with the match. The low flame glimmers on the glass and on the standing plates in the dresser, and the room is filled with a dim light. There is a blackened circle on the ceiling above the glass. I look at the dog. He is black and sleek with very white teeth and a pink lolling tongue.

"'Tis a long time since a lamp was lit in this house," the old man says. "I have no want of it at all. I work by the light of day."

The Cable and its residences have their own generator, so this is my first acquaintance with an oil lamp. I am fascinated by its mellow tawny light.

My grandfather wheels toward me. He is an old man, older than I remember. He walks stiffly, but with a little skip in each step, maneuvering himself with a stick. The fingers of one hand are strangely curled. He halts in front of me, leaning heavily on the stick, lowers his face to mine, and stares at me for a long moment. The skin of his face is not like skin: it looks like something dead and white, with blotches of red. His eyes are very bright, his mouth a humorless line. His ears are large and stick out so dramatically from beneath his cap that I forget my fear for an instant and I want to laugh. His breath smells of tobacco.

"I wouldn't know you at all," he says.

I am not sure if this is bad or good, so I hold my peace.

"What business have you walking abroad in the middle of the night?" he demands to know.

"My uncle brought me."

"Is it that fellow! If there's anything out of the way going on, he's the man will have a hand in it."

"He wouldn't come in," I volunteer.

"To be sure he wouldn't! A go-be-the-wall — for your life!"

I am afraid that his disapproval of my uncle will be transferred to me. He thrusts a pipe into his mouth and clamps his teeth upon it with a sudden violence that makes me start.

"Where's your mother from you? Does she think I'm a wet nurse or what?"

The tears start to my eyes, and my face begins to crumble. I see his look of derision, as he starts to turn away.

"Didn't she send me to look after you!" I blurt out, with the energy of despair.

He takes the pipe from his mouth and screws up his eyes. I stand there, still trembling with the shock of my own outburst, unable to tell whether it has done me good or harm.

"Do you tell me so?" he snorts. "Haven't I Pat-Joe? What can you do for me that Pat-Joe can't?"

"Whatever you like."

Pat-Joe is my tough unruly cousin whom I do not like. I want to say something disparaging about him, but I sense that this will not impress the old man.

"There's a boat falling to pieces below there on the strand with no one to mind her," he says. "But I suppose you'd be afraid of the sea."

"I would not!"

" 'Tis after your mother you take then, with your back answers. Can you ride a bicycle to fetch the water?"

"If my feet can reach the pedals."

"I'm afraid we'll have to stretch you a little bit first," the old man mutters.

He leans toward me again, opening his eyes as wide as the immobile skin of his face will permit.

"I suppose 'tis true for them," he intones. "My dancing days are done. A pity youth does not last. Though 'tis damn the thing your mother knows or cares about it!"

I do not dare to look at him. I think I am afraid that he will tell me something about my mother that I don't wish to hear. But even my capacity for fear has reached its limit.

"Well, come in and shut the door, let you," he says with a sigh.

"My suitcase."

"Go fetch it."

I step into the night. It does not seem so threatening. The dog comes with me and forages around while I wrestle the suitcase through the door. Looking up, I see that the house consists of a large open room, with a narrow stairs leading to a cleft in the low ceiling. The old man is standing behind a counter doing something with his hands. He is wearing glasses. There are tools and boots on the counter. I recognize the smell of leather.

"At least they don't expect me to clothe you," he mutters, eyeing my suitcase, "as well as feed you and keep a roof over your head."

Timidly I approach the hearth. There is no fireplace or grate. The chimney protrudes into the room, and beneath its hood are two low benches. I sit on one of these without being asked. I have come to rest here, for better or for worse.

The old man works for a few minutes in silence, then drops his tools with a sigh. "I suppose you'll be wanting something to eat."

Without waiting for an answer, he skips and hobbles to the dresser and brings back a piece of fish on a plate. He fills a tea-stained cup with milk from a tin canister and places it on the table. Tearing a hunk of bread from a loaf, he places it beside the plate. Everything is strange to me: milk from a cup and not a glass, a meal without knife, fork, or napkin. But I fall upon the food as though my life depends on its nourishment, and I do not notice the old man watching me from behind his counter until I have reduced the fish to skin and bones and wiped the plate clean with my bread. He has removed his glasses, but his expressionless stare is no less penetrating. I am wary of him, of his rough and unaccustomed voice, of what the voice may disclose. But there is also something reassuring in the attention with which he regards me.

Unaccountably, I begin to shiver and my teeth to chatter. The old man sighs again, stumps around the corner, and slowly lowers himself to his hands and knees. He moves so slowly that it is painful to watch him. Leaning on one hand, he pulls some sticks and crumpled scraps of newspaper from beneath one of the benches and arranges them on the hearth. I get up from the table and stand beside him. He fumbles in his pockets and tosses me a box of matches. I light the paper, and the fire blazes up, revealing the soot-caked wall of the chimney. The old man crumbles pieces of turf and feeds them carefully to the fire. Then, balanced on his stick, he drags himself onto the bench and sits there breathing hoarsely through the slit of his mouth. The fire leaps merrily, diffusing a fragrant earthy smell. He reaches beneath the bench and adds some larger pieces of turf. He straightens and leans his back against the wall, wheezing.

"'Tis destroyed you have me," he mutters. "How am I going to get my bottle of stout?"

"I'll get it for you," I say. "Where is it?"

"Put the poker in the fire first."

He gestures toward a metal poker standing in the corner. It is almost as tall as I am. Puzzled, I slide its tip into the fire.

"Put it where the fire is hottest. That's right. Now go look under the sink for my bottle."

It is a sink without taps! Beside a bucket full of water, I find a row of brown Guinness bottles. Most of the bottles are empty. I choose a full one.

"Hold the cap to the edge of the windowsill," the old man commands irritably. "Now hit it with the palm of your hand. Hit it!"

I try this, but the bottle almost slips out of my hand. I look at him for further instructions, but his head is turned away. We hear footsteps. The front door is pushed open until it sticks. For a moment I see no one, and then a pair of white hands emerges from the gloom, holding a package wrapped in newspaper.

"There you are, Christy," the old man says. "Good girl."

His voice has a softness that is new to me. It is Christine Sheedy, whose father ran away from her mother when she was a baby. She is about my age, but I do not know her except to say hello. She is wearing a man's sweater over her dress; she has no shoes on.

"Where will I leave it, Mister O.?" Her voice is high and clear, like a whistle.

"Leave it on the table there, Christy. What is she after sending me?"

"It's a piece of meat she bought above in town."

"Go to God! Tell her she shouldn't, Christy: she really shouldn't now."

Christine comes forward to the fire and slips onto the settle beside the old man. I am still standing by the sink with the bottle in my hand, but she does not look at me or say hello. Perhaps she does not even know I have been away. She tucks her legs beneath her on the settle and puts her hands into the sleeves of the sweater. Her knees are scratched and grubby.

I am sorry she has come in. She makes me uncomfortable. She is wild, like an animal, and I cannot take my eyes off her.

"Christy, girl," the old man says, "would you ever put out that lamp for me? I lit it for your man here, but it has me blinded."

Christine stands up beneath the chimney, ducks her head swiftly, and steps lightly as a cat across the house to the lamp. The light fades down and out, and there is only the unsteady glow of the fire.

"Would you ever do the needful while you're up?" the old man says. "He doesn't have the knack of it."

She comes and takes the bottle out of my hand, still without looking at me, and places it against the edge of the sill. At her first attempt the cap flies off miraculously, and a bubble of grubby froth emerges from the top of the bottle.

"There's a glass on the dresser. Let you watch her while she's pouring it now. Do you mind the way she holds it sideways? Don't fill it, Christy!"

Grudgingly I watch. Christine brings him the brimming glass.

"It's too full," he tells her with a malicious grin. "Give it here to your man and let him drink a little."

"I wouldn't like it."

"What's the matter with you, boy? It's only porter."

They are both looking at me. Christine's eyes are widely spaced. Her stare is vacant and intense. Flushing, I take a gulp from the glass. The sour taste stings my mouth. I swallow it down.

"It's vile," I say, using one of my mother's expressions.

"I have no *grá* for it myself," the old man says disgustedly.

"Alice used to say it was a great cure," Christine murmurs, as though repeating a line of verse.

"Aye. She'll lie easier in her grave if she knows I do have it."

"Who used to say?" I want to know.

"Alice! Your grandmother that was. But sure yourself or your mother couldn't even come to her funeral."

"I would have come if you'd asked me!"

I'm driven almost to impudence by Christine's presence. Who is she to know my family better than I do myself?

"If I'd asked you!" the old man says contemptuously. "Give me the poker there. Mind you don't burn yourself."

I hand him the poker. He brandishes the bright red tip wickedly before my face. Then, holding the glass between his boots, he lowers the poker into it. The stout foams and spills upon the hearth, and the poker rattles against the glass. He hands me the poker, picks up the glass, and drinks it off in one draft. Leaning back against the wall, he wipes his mouth with his sleeve. His eyes stare across the fire at the place opposite him.

Christine climbs back on the settle. I take my seat facing her and find that she is looking at me. I look back, but there is no acknowledgment in her eyes.

"Did you see herself today, Mister O.?"

"Oh, she comes in to me often and often," the old man murmurs.

"Who does?" I whisper, unnerved by the uncanny tone of his voice.

He stares into the chimney corner.

"She's very quiet altogether. You'd hardly know she was there. She sits on the settle beside Christy, and she has the beads in her hands, watching me. Sure 'tis still hardly a month since she was there in the flesh. Hardly a month. But by God, we'll be a long time dead."

He leans forward to the fire with his hands on his knees. The firelight ruddies his pale cheeks and casts the enlarged shadow of his cap on the chimney behind him.

"Alice, Alice, I says to her, but she just sits there with a sad look on her face, shaking her head over me, you might say. Is it so very sad where you are, Alice, and all the prayers you said before you went there?"

I stare wide-eyed at my grandfather. He makes a sound in the back of his throat that may be a chuckle. I look at Christine. She is playing with the hem of her dress. Beneath her shaggy curls, her expression is calm, almost bored.

"Not a sign of her today though," he says, with a shrug. "The dead do get sick and tired and have to keep to their beds some days like the rest of us."

He puts one hand in his pocket and pulls out a pipe and pouch. With quick birdlike movements, he knocks the pipe against his knee. Fitting it into the hand with the curled fingers, he rummages with the other hand in the pouch. Suddenly he gives a start and ceases to move, inclining his head as though to listen.

I can hear the hectic beating of my heart. I have been told that people who talk to themselves are mad.

"You were too easy with them two children, Alice," he says. "You never liked to hear a cross word spoken in the house. I'd have given them the edge of my tongue as soon as look at them, but you wouldn't leave me. And where did it get you in the heel of the hunt? Maura to marry out of the Inish and run off to Dublin —"

"I'd run away myself!" Christine pipes up suddenly.

"You wouldn't!" the old man exclaims.

"I would so!"

He screws up his eyes and regards her doubtfully. "Is it Paris you want, my dear?"

"I'd go to Paris, to be sure — or somewhere. Sure what is there here?"

I feel certain the old man will be vexed with her. But he only nods his head sagely.

"Aye, what is there here?" he murmurs. "All we have left are the fellows that can't find a place in the world. Like that son of mine in the Cable there polishing a chair with the seat of his arse and he an old bachelor that no one would have. I'll go into the Cable, he says to me, and I won't have to have the hard life, out on the face of the ocean in all weathers, the way you were yourself. Well, if 'twas a hard life, 'twas an honest one. But that fellow knows nothing of hardship — nor does he want to know! Holding up the wall outside Shanahan's bar night after night to see would someone stand him a pint —"

He starts to rise from the bench, his limbs trembling. "How was it I fathered him at all? He has no time for me — nor I for him! Ay, but that's the way of it. The child is the nemesis of his father."

I do not know what the word means, but from the irate glance he darts at me, as at someone possibly to be held responsible, I conclude that it is no good thing. He is immobile for a moment, as though listening, then slumps back.

"Ah sure, hush," he murmurs, the ire gone from his voice. " 'Tis true for you, Alice. I was, I was, I was so. 'Tis no use talking. 'Tis all a matter now."

I steal a look at him. He is staring solemnly into the fire. His eyes look white and unfocused, like the eyes of a blind man.

"You were always a sweet temperate woman, Alice," he says. "A sweet temperate woman. What was it possessed you at all to marry the likes of me?"

The fantastic thought occurs to me that it is really possible to communicate with the dead. I have returned to a world where inconceivable things can happen. Dublin is another planet.

My grandfather fumbles in the matchbox, strikes a match against it with the fingers of the good hand, and sucks the flame down into his pipe. The flame rises as he exhales; I wonder if he has breathed it into his lungs. As he bends forward, I see the finer, almost translucent skin of his forehead and temples, and beneath it a mesh of bluish veins. I breathe in the sweet tobacco smoke. His head comes up abruptly. "How's your mother keeping?"

The question shocks me into defensiveness. I take it as a challenge or a taunt.

"She is very well, thank you," I say coldly, with something of my mother's reserve and the genteel accent of the city she has begun to assume.

Christine is staring at me with her large expressionless eyes. The weight of my own strangeness seems to settle on me. I do not belong here. This queer old man before me is my grandfather — but what does that mean? I do not know him, nor this wild thing beside him who does not like me. The fatigue and anxiety of my journey rush over me. I feel the tears start to my eyes again.

"Oh, the women are trouble, early or late," the old man pronounces. "Did you ever hear about what happened to Diarmat?"

"Pardon?"

"Where were we at all, Christy?"

"The death of Diarmat," Christine utters in a rush, "who ran away with Finn's wife Grania on account of she tricked him with a riddle and he wanted her to go back to Finn but she wouldn't."

"The death of Diarmat O'Deena," the old man intones, "who wouldn't stand by his own people and came to a bad end — all on account of a faithless woman."

I am irritated by Christine's readiness to supply his answers, jealous of the relationship it implies. But the formal tone of the old man's voice arrests me. He turns the pipe to the corner of his mouth and sits motionless with the stick between his knees, looking at the fire.

"It was an autumn night like tonight, cold for the time of year, the air fresh and clean after the rain, and the sky a riddle of stars."

There is something priestlike in his manner that compels my respect and awe. But his voice has intensity and conviction — whereas all the priests I have ever heard were reciting words they had by heart.

"Diarmat woke in the dark with his wife beside him," he says, as though speaking of people well known to both of us, "the same Grania that he stole away from his kinsman Finn. He was wide awake and in a terrible fright for he could hear a commotion going on above on the mountain and he felt there was some heavy thing or creature itself sitting on his chest and crushing the breath out of him but he couldn't move or cry out to save his life. What is it, love? says Grania beside him."

The old man's voice turns shrill, and his lips curl in distaste. He does not like Grania.

"And didn't the thing leave him and he could breathe and move again. I hear the march of a company of men through the gorse of the mountain, he said to her. Sure, I hear nothing, *a croi,* she said, unless it's the lake water lapping the shore. And she turned over on her arse and went back to sleep. So Diarmat dozed off, but he woke again and it was still pitch black and he felt that his right arm was paralyzed beneath him and he would never have the use of it again. Grania, said he, I hear the cries of horses tangled up in a ditch of briars. Take your ease, love, said she. It's the wind in the reeds and the thistles. But Diarmat woke again before it was light and there was a cold sweat on all his flesh and he felt sure that a bad thing would happen that night and that it would make an end of him. Grania, he said, I hear the baying of the hounds and the sounds of the chase. Finn and my own people are abroad on the mountain. I must rise up and go. For it was one of his *geasa* never to hear the baying of the hounds without following the hunt."

I have heard of Diarmat and Grania as the insubstantial characters of a fairy tale. But this rendition has a shocking immediacy, and I listen to it with fierce attention, as though to an account of an experience that might well be my own.

"Don't go, my life, my love, cries the bold Grania. My apple tree, my brightness, don't go and leave me. For she knew she was to blame for the bad blood between him and Finn — and well she knew the bad thing that was to happen that night."

In the old man's mimicry, the woman's voice is uncannily real. I would not be surprised if she appeared beside him in the chimney corner.

"So Diarmat got up, and when he went to take his weapons he found that they had fallen from the wall. A servant offered him a cup of milk and it turned to a cup of blood in his hand and he dashed it to the floor. Then he saw two women washing a bloodstained shirt and he knew that it was his own. He went out and met Finn and the rest of his kinsmen waiting for him on the mountain. We're waiting for a man the likes of you, said Finn to him, to kill this boar for us. There's no one here the equal of it. And Diarmat thought of Grania grieving in the hall behind him and he knew for a certainty that his time was come and he went up alone to meet the boar."

There is a mist before my eyes, and I imagine in horribly vivid detail the iron of cruel weapons, the brimming cup, the soaked shirt. Something within me revolts.

"But why did he go," I hear myself say, "if he knew what was going to happen to him?"

He regards me silently for a moment, and I am afraid he will be angry with me for interrupting him.

"'Tis disgrace for a man to break his *geasa*, boyeen bawn," he says kindly. "Never to hear the baying of the hounds without following the hunt. Never to refuse the request of a kinsman — no matter what!"

But why? What are *geasa*? I cannot understand it!

"What was he to Finn?" I persist.

"What was he, Christy?" the old man asks patiently.

"Finn's sister's son," Christine pipes up. "Finn was his uncle so." As if I cannot work this out for myself.

"He went in fosterage to Finn," the old man says sternly. "Finn was like father to him. He bit the hand that fed him, like a cur dog."

The weight of his disapproval oppresses me. A sick feeling comes over me, a strange apprehension for Diarmat — or is it for myself?

My grandfather strikes another match over the pipe and breathes in the flame.

"Never to hunt a boar," he intones. "But Diarmat was not a coward, whatever else he was. He went away up to the boar, and the creature was as big as the side of a hill with eyes like buckets of fire in his head and bristles and tusks that'd tear the heart out of a man and hooves that'd trample him in the dirt. Diarmat killed him dead and came away safe from him without so much as a scratch. And Finn and the rest of them came up and stood around the beast laid out on the ground and Finn saw his chance. Will you walk the length of the carcass there, my little son, said he, for I think that I've never in my life seen a bigger boar. And Diarmat knew it was a treacherous request, but his kinsmen were standing all around him and he could not refuse. So he walked the carcass of the boar and one of the creature's bristles pierced the sole of his foot and he fell down bleeding in a faint. When he looked up, he saw Finn standing over him. For the love of Ireland, he said, would you go to the sacred well and bring me some water to close my wound, for my life is running out of me into the cold ground. Twice he asked, and twice Finn turned his face away. The third time Finn's heart was softened and he thought it was a shame for a fine man like Diarmat to die for want of a drop of water and for the sake of a treacherous woman and he went to the well and he came back carrying the water in his hands. But when he came up to Diarmat, he thought of Grania, her raven hair, her blood red lips, her snow white breast, and he let the water trickle through his fingers, and when Diarmat saw what he was doing he put his head back in agony and gave up the ghost."

I am squirming in my seat. I feel flushed, and my mouth is dry, as though I were about to expire of thirst myself within yards of a spring of cool water. I press my fingernails into the palms of my hands.

"Did he die?"

"Certainly he died! What would you have him do? Isn't that what always happens to those who turn their back on kith and kin?"

"What happened to the lady?" Christine says.

"Is it Grania?" the old man says scornfully. "No lady she, by God. She was back in Finn's bed before the corpse was cold. She knew which side her bread was buttered on, the little hoor!"

"No!" Christine cries crossly.

"Ay, that's the way of it."

I am amazed at Christine's impudence — and at the old man's patience with her. I pray that she will not make him angry.

"There 'tis for ye!" the old man says, slapping his knee with his palm. "That's enough now. 'Tis late."

He scatters the embers of the fire with his stick. It is very dark in the room. The dog makes a noise that is like a sigh. I hear my grandfather get up and go to the door. The dog follows him, its paws making a scratching noise on the flagstones. Christine remains sitting opposite me, like a statue or a part of the wall. I am glad that it is dark and that we cannot see each other. But I feel closer to her; we have shared an experience.

The door is opened, and the old man goes out. Cold air enters and a faint diffused light. Left alone with Christine, I feel a vague discomfort mount within me. I want to say something to dispel it, but I cannot think for the life of me. A faint trembling sound reaches us from outside. Suddenly Christine begins to chant in a mocking whisper:

"A riddle, a riddle, a riddle of stars! Mister O. takes a piddle outside in the yard!"

The sound ceases. Christine rises, a wraithlike shape, and flits across the house and out at the door. She does not say good-bye to me. Her indifference gives me a sudden painful smart.

"Go straight home, mind you," the old man tells her, "or your mother will skin me alive."

"Good night, Mister O.!"

Her voice floats back to me, like a birdcall. I want to call after her, to compel her to acknowledge me, but she is gone. I sink back against the wall, suddenly overcome by fatigue. The old man grunts and stumps back into the house. The dog nuzzles me with his cold wet nose. My eyelids are heavy, and I want to close them, to stretch out on the settle. But something in me refuses to yield to sleep. There is something I need to know before I can let myself fall into the darkness. But I do not know how to ask. I blurt out the first question that comes into my head.

"What does it mean, Granda? A riddle of stars?"

His footsteps come on, more slowly, as though he is tired. I sense that he is standing over me. I hear his straining breath in the dark. Will he mind that I have called him Granda?

"That's a riddle only God can answer, boyeen," he murmurs.

This is somehow soothing. I close my eyes. Immediately, I am aware of the ocean, the mountains I saw from the train, bathed in the light of stars. There is the feeling of peace that came over me after the window fell on my hand. My hand begins to throb, as though reliving the blow. I start awake, recalling where I am — and where I am not. The dog is licking my face.

"Come away, Finn," my grandfather mutters. "Come away now. Come."

"Did you know my father?" I hear myself say.

Silence. I am poised over the abyss of sleep. But I know that he is still standing there.

"Your father, God rest him, was a gentleman," his voice says. "The way he'd come in the room: he'd knock and put his head in first, before he came in. Not like the O'Donnells! They'd barge in on top of you, without as much as a by-your-leave."

I can entrust myself now, to sleep, to dark. I let go whatever it is that binds me to wakefulness. My grandfather's voice drifts on absently.

"He liked a good story, the same man. But I'm afraid he wasn't much of a hand at the telling."

I come back to myself on a westbound highway in Massachusetts. There is nothing but the sound of motion, the slight trembling of the wheel in my hands, the ghostly approach of oncoming lights and their whiplike passage. I feel empty, drained of identity, nameless and alone.

The Inish is where I was born and bred, my home for all of twenty years, and yet sometimes I think a mistake has been made, all my childhood is a dream my mother and grandfather have conspired to validate. What do I have to do with Pat-Joe and the fishing and the football and the Wren and the regatta and all the rest of it? It is to the world of the old man's stories that I really belong, to that imaginary island of night that he created in them, presided over by strange unknowable constellations.

But now that the old man is gone, no one will confirm that his island exists. I have severed my ties with the physical entity, the bare rocks and meager fields of the Inish, and I live in fear that there will never again be a place I can call home. What kind of life is possible in a place of exile?

Unless that place be Pontiac! The Monster is my home-from-home, my boat, my wandering rock. Its motion soothes me. There is nowhere I would rather make my bed.

I pull into a rest area and park behind a line of silent trucks. The cabs are all darkened; their drivers must be sleeping, waiting out the night. I lock the doors and climb into the backseat. I pillow my head against the protrusion of the wheel well and stretch out. The seat is so wide I scarcely have to bend my knees. I close my eyes. Sleep rushes over me like a wave.

Lost in the City

I UNROLL THE SHEEPSKIN and fling it upon the hearth in one movement, hoping for a dramatic effect. Lily's face registers only surprise. The dog slumps down beside it and sniffs it warily.

"It's for you," I say superfluously to Lily.

"Thank you."

"It wasn't expensive," I say, sensing a reservation. "There was a fellow selling them out of the trunk of his car by the side of the road. I couldn't resist it."

Lily squats down beside it and works her fingers into the thick short pile. Cooper rolls upon his side, growling softly, inviting play. She gets up abruptly.

"You don't have to bring me something every time you come out here," she says.

My expansiveness disappears like a punctured balloon. This is not a very good start to our weekend.

"I *wanted* to bring you something."

"But why, Matt? I think you do it because you still feel guilty about moving out on me. Or because you feel that we're not really getting along. I'm glad you're aware of that, and I appreciate the gifts. But they don't help."

I shrug. But I am downcast. I bring her things because that is what occurs to me to do. Obviously it is not enough. Her response throws the ball back to me; she wants me to examine my state of mind. I am not going to bite. I feel bad enough.

"Are you ready to go to the movie?"

"I'm ready. But we're spending a lot of time at the movies lately. I'd like to make sure we get a chance to talk afterwards. Is that OK?"

"Sure. Why not?"

There is a reproach here. And Lily does not even know the extent of my addiction, the number of movies I see during the week, alone. There *is* something wrong. We do not know each other's thoughts anymore, and for an instant I feel a shock of alarm: something must be done. But I am as weak as water, I have no force to do anything, and so I can only watch our difficulties as they unfold — fated, inescapable, preordained — as in a movie! I cannot even wish for the ability to change. Moviegoing and driving have become the poles of my life.

"I know why you want to go to the movies," Lily says lightly. "It takes your mind off feeling depressed. I use it that way myself. But it doesn't make for great communication. I'd rather do something more interactive in the future."

It's true that I want to take my mind off things. But what Lily does not know is that going to the movies is also the recapitulation of a childhood experience here in the heart of Boston. On the Inish I went to the flicks, as we called them, every week, to the Saturday evening show, since I disliked emerging into the daylight after the matinee. The picture house on the Inish was located on the pier, having formerly housed the lifeboat. Its wooden benches were like church pews, hard and upright, becoming progressively higher toward the back of the hall, so that the bench nearest the projector was level with the heads of the adults as they entered. The young fellows from the Foot went right to the front and horsed around if they were bored; my mother had thought them too rough for me, and I suppose they held this against me after she was gone. I sat by myself on this last and highest bench. I didn't mind, so long as the projector didn't break down. I was seeking escape and illusion, not companionship.

It wasn't until afterwards, when the film was over, walking home at midnight in the midst of a murmuring crowd, that I felt my isolation. But I consoled myself by remembering the old man's stories —

which interested no one but me — and I told myself that they constituted the *real* life of the Inish, the life of the Other World: a life that was going on all the time in the darkness, at a very little distance from mine, a distance that could more easily be bridged at night, after two hours of hypnotic devotion to the flickering screen.

Now in the darkness of buildings containing a half dozen theaters, each no bigger than the former lifeboat shed, I still seek escape, though without any real hope of attaining it. I no longer have an aversion to matinees. I now watch and listen with exclusive attention, aware of nothing but the illusion. I am no longer discovering a real life, but rather holding something at bay, an urban analogue of the dark life of the Inish, grown unfriendly. And when I emerge into the New World, I am at a remove from its bright and strangely artificial life. Everything is that much more incomprehensible to me, including that I am here at all — and that Lily is at my side. She is my assurance of safe passage, but I am convinced in my heart of hearts that I do not deserve such a companion and must surely lose her.

I am devoted to the classics of the American cinema — *The African Queen, Casablanca, Rebel Without a Cause, A Streetcar Named Desire, Long Day's Journey into Night* — and my ostensible ambition is to fill in the gaps in my cinematographic education. Today's picture — *On the Waterfront* — is in the city, a good half hour's drive. I am anxious not to be late. Lily asks me to drive — which is fine by me. When we go outside, it is snowing lightly. I am afraid that she will want to hear the weather forecast and decide we should stay at home. But she says nothing. We take the Monster. Some cars already have their headlights on; this makes the snow banks gleam on either side of the highway and deepens the half-light of the wintry afternoon.

"What's the latest on your job?" I say. "When are you taking the plunge?"

"Oh, God, I don't know. I have a dilemma."

"Maybe I can help you."

I'm relieved that Lily is going to talk about herself. Now I can listen and drive, which is what I most like to do.

"Here's the problem," she says. "I can't afford to live entirely off my savings. I need to freelance to pay my living expenses. But it will take time for me to get established as a freelancer. I won't be able to spend all my time on my own photographs and on putting together a show, which is why I'm quitting my job. So I'm wondering if it's more practical to stay on for another year and save more money. What do you think?"

I think of Lily's photo-collages, which are like artifacts from another civilization, or like reproductions of fossil shapes, framed in an irregular ellipse. Familiar objects and faces, rendered in sepia tones, peer out from behind the abstract forms. Some of these faces are like Lily's, a child whose features I know and yet do not know, a more dreamy, dark-haired Alice in Wonderland, wandering in the labyrinth of childhood. It gives me a little chill, this careful unveiling of the past — and it is not even *my* childhood!

I bring the Monster to a halt at an intersection. For a moment I feel the substance of our connection. It is still there, in spite of our difficulties.

"I'm hardly the person to ask for practical advice. But I think your collages are fantastic. They ought to be in the Museum of Fine Arts."

"Thanks, Matt," she says. "I want to do my own work, and I'm going to find a way. But I'm afraid that the reason I want to quit my job right now is just because my clients are driving me crazy. They hire me to help them comply with state regulations — and then they resent me for telling them they need to comply! I want to tell them to go take a hike."

I pull away from the intersection. Now this is better. I feel that I have a function: to help Lily believe in her future. It doesn't matter that I cannot believe in mine. One pessimist is enough in any couple.

"I don't know, Lily. For myself, I've never taken a decision in my life that wasn't forced upon me from outside. But I think you can do it. Why wait? In a year's time you might not feel the same way."

I glance at her. She doesn't seem impressed. I am negotiating a curve in the road, and I concentrate all my attention on maintaining an optimal speed. Suddenly I feel deflated. She has asked for my advice, but she values it no more than my gifts.

"When I do quit my job, I'm going to move back to Cambridge," she says. "I feel bad for Cooper. But if I have to schlepp my prints around to galleries and look for freelance work, it doesn't make sense to be way out in the sticks."

With that, she lapses into silence. There is surely a hint in this or at least an attempt to raise the subject of our difficulties. She expects me to be able to respond; that I cannot proves my deficiency. I rack my brains, but I know that whatever I say will only muddy the waters. It is hard for me to pay attention to driving, and I slow to a crawl.

"I discovered who Pontiac was," I say.

"Oh yeah?"

It is wrong to ignore it, to change the subject. But there seems to be someone else who speaks for me, who cannot face the present or the past, who would rather go to the movies.

"He was an eighteenth-century chief of the Ottawa tribe who organized an uprising somewhere in present-day Michigan."

"There's a Pontiac, Michigan," Lily tells me. "That's probably where he signed away the state to the white man."

"You know, I think that the Irish and the Indians have a lot in common. Both of them lost a language and a culture, had their lands taken away from them, their religion proscribed —"

"What a great idea!" Lily interjects, suddenly enthused. "Why don't you study *American* history?"

"I don't want to study anything right now."

"You don't have to apply to a degree program. You can start with a night class."

"I'd rather just go to the local library when the mood takes me."

My surly response casts a pall over us. We drive without speaking. Route 1A — the road to Lily's house — is not my favorite drive. The crash barriers that divide opposing traffic make the lanes seem terribly narrow, and the flow is constantly interrupted by intersections. Normally I take this as a challenge and shift from one lane to another, trying to make up time. But the snow has thickened, and everybody on the road is edgy. Besides, I'm back in the soup.

"I know you're not happy, Matt —"

"So who's happy?"

"I was — last year. So were you."

"What goes around comes around," I say, trying out an expression of Rick's.

"It's OK to feel bad," she says. "But I think it might help if you had an interest, someplace to go on a regular basis, something else to do besides walking around Harvard Square or driving in your car. Right now I'm the only person you know here, apart from Rick. That puts a lot of pressure on the relationship."

"Are you saying that you think we should see less of each other?"

"No! I'm saying that I'm concerned about you. Isn't there something you'd like to do? You could find a temporary job if you don't want to go back to school right away. You might find something you actually enjoy doing. Or if you didn't want a regular job, maybe you could do some volunteer work."

This suggestion strikes a spark.

"Lily, from the time I was seven years old I looked after my grandfather, all day every day, and I did that job as well as I could for fourteen years. So I don't want to volunteer right now — for anything. While I was going to school in Caher I worked weekends in a bar, and the year before I went to college, I worked the boat as well. I shelved books in the library in Dublin every minute I wasn't in class. I'm not looking for another menial job."

Lily is quiet for a while, and I sit there, glumly assessing the damage. I have spoiled our date, for sure.

"Are you sorry you came over here, Matt?"

It sounds as though she's afraid of what I might answer. I'm afraid of it myself. I cannot afford the luxury of being sorry.

"No, Lily, I'm not sorry. You don't have to worry about me. My grandfather left me some money too, so I can afford to do nothing for a little while."

The traffic ahead starts to accelerate and spread out. I step on the gas impatiently. But speed will not help. Figuratively, I am driving in a circle. I know that Lily is right: some sort of initiative is required, a new departure, a decision. But I pass the same exits, no one of them seems preferable to another, and the carousel of the New World takes me around again.

"I'm sorry to be so down in the mouth, Lily. I'll pull myself together by and by. I just need some time."

She does not respond. She has tried to help me, and I have rejected it. I no longer care about the movie; our discord will spoil it for me. But I've made this small plan for the afternoon, and something will not allow me to deviate from it, in spite of the catastrophe I feel gathering about me.

Route 9. Just as narrow but faster, with more traffic and ramps that disgorge entering cars directly into the speeding flow. I choose the outside lane as the one requiring least attention, but I'm driving too slowly and I get repeatedly honked at by cars wanting to pass. I grip the wheel and guide the Monster into the slower lane. It's all I can do not to compound our difficulties by driving into a car entering from the right.

The movie is at a theater on Commonwealth Avenue, a street admired by Winston Churchill (who had probably never seen the entire ungainly length of it). By the time I've found a parking place, we are more than fifteen minutes late. I slump over the wheel. Snow flecks the windscreen, quickly blotting out the view.

"Let's not go," I say. "I hate to miss the beginning."

"I've seen it. I'll tell you how it starts."

"You didn't want to go anyway. Let's find a nice quiet Chinese restaurant. In Chinatown. I'll take you out to eat."

"You can't afford it."

"Sure I can."

I am just grateful that she is still speaking to me. I want to do something for her.

"I'm not very hungry," she says. "Let's get a cup of coffee and have that talk."

She gives me an unsmiling look. Here is something else I could do for her, something she really wants. But my hesitation betrays me.

"If you don't want to talk, Matt, I can't force you. But I can't pretend that everything's fine between us."

"I want us to have a good time. What's wrong with that?"

She sighs. "If we're not going to see the movie and we're not going for coffee, why don't you just take me home before we get caught in a snowstorm?"

"Lily, it's Saturday afternoon, and here we are in the big city. There must be something we can do that won't make one of us miserable."

Lily is about to dismiss the suggestion, but she stops herself. "I could visit my father, since I'm here."

"Do you want to?"

"I can think of things I'd rather do. But it would save me a trip. And we seem to be at a loose end, don't we?"

"Where does he live?"

"The Financial District. He lives in his office."

"Direct me."

Everything will be all right. We have found something that Lily wants to do. I drive up Comm. Ave. into Kenmore Square. In the city, I do not mind stop and go. There is so much to look at, the crowds, the buildings, the vehicles. Just to be part of all this frenetic activity gives me a sense of importance. And now I have a mission: take Lily to visit her father.

"My father is a very eccentric person," she tells me.

"I like eccentrics."

"You haven't met my father."

I swing around the Public Garden and the Common and dive into a maze of back streets. Federal Street is narrow and filled with dirty snow piled on the parked cars and the sidewalks. On either side, walls of black glass rise to the towers that I have marveled at from the expressway.

"He lives in this building right here," Lily says. "It's really his office, but he's as thick as thieves with the janitor. Are you sure you don't mind?"

She seems to be of two minds about this visit, to lack her habitual easy confidence.

"I'm certain. I'd like to meet him."

"We won't stay for very long."

I drop Lily at the door and park in a garage on the next block. She is waiting for me in the lobby. She looks thoughtful, abstracted.

"I'm trying to get him to retire to a more benign climate," she tells me in the elevator. "The winters are hard on him, though he won't admit it."

We walk along a deserted corridor and stop before a door with a frosted glass panel. On the glass I read the ghost of two names: Golden & Taylor. The garbled sound of a TV or radio is audible from within. Lily taps on the glass with a coin.

"He can't hear us," she says. "He's a little deaf. I'll have to go down to the lobby and call him, unless his door is unlocked."

She tries the door, and it swings open upon a large empty office, lit by tall windows that face the harbor and the bay. There are only two objects in the entire space: a curved-back swivel chair strategically placed before one of the windows, and a bicycle on a stand in the middle of the stripped floor. The outlines of vanished filing cabinets and desks are still visible upon the walls.

"Let me see if he's decent."

Lily walks quickly over the floor and peers through a doorway in a corner of the office. "Turn off your TV, Dad."

"Oh . . . my . . . God," a hoarse voice intones slowly.

The TV is muted, but the noise of a radio persists. I walk to the window and look down ten floors into an alley strewn with refuse. Snow flurries whip by. The sky above the buildings is leaden, heavy with more snow. I feel a sharp longing for the darkness and security of the movie theater, the gentle hypnosis of the screen, and Lily's quiet nearness that for the duration of the movie I can take for intimacy. I am suddenly apprehensive, and I hope the visit will be a success. Lily and I have had enough trouble for one day.

Behind me, the radio is shut off.

"The top of the morning to you!" a voice croaks. "It's welcome you are to my humble abode."

I turn from the window to behold an aged man, dressed only in shorts and tennis shoes, though it is not warm in the office. He totters across the space that separates us, leaning heavily on a walking stick. I go quickly to meet him — for fear he will collapse — and he shakes my hand heartily, hunching over it, knees bent, back humped.

"I'm delighted to meet a real Irishman," he cackles in a rather unsuccessful brogue. "Sure I'm Irish myself, born and bred."

His limbs are slim and sinewy, and the hair on his mottled chest looks like cotton wool. His eyes are bright and mischievous, and he sports a luxuriant head of black hair that makes him look like one of the Three Stooges.

"I'm happy to meet you too, Mr. Golden," I say tentatively.

Lily emerges behind him and stands grinning against the wall. He retains his grip on my hand and taps about him with what now appears to be a broom handle.

"And what part of the old country do you come from?" he wants to know.

"The west — where they say that the next parish over is New York. And what part do *you* come from?" I say, deciding to play along.

He straightens up suddenly, lets go of my hand, and begins to sing in a powerful voice: "Oh, it's maybe someday I'll go back to Ireland, if it's only at the closing of my days!"

In one swift movement, he lets the broom fall, grabs the black mop of hair from his head, and flings it from him. Before I can assimilate what has happened, he whirls about and capers in front of me, crooning the rest of the verse:

"For to see again the moon rise o'er the Claddagh. And to watch the sun go down on Galway Bay!"

I've been had. In confusion I look around for Lily. She is bent double with laughter. The eyes of this suddenly youthful leprechaun before me all but disappear, and his toothless mouth chortles. "He thought I was Irish! Oh, God!"

"My father, Sam Golden," Lily says. "He likes to pretend he's an *alte kaka*. Here Dad, let me give you a hug."

Sam jogs in place while Lily hugs him, holding his arms outstretched. When she releases him, he starts to pace back and forth. I'm watching him carefully now — in case he's about to peel off his face and reveal the countenance of a thirty-year-old.

"You shouldn't leave your door open, Dad. What if someone came in and stole your bicycle — or your tennis racket."

"It'd be a sign from God. Listen, you don't stop playing tennis because you grow old. You grow old because you stop playing tennis. I haven't hit a ball in a week. I've watched my last Wimbledon."

"He plays against the wall here," Lily tells me.

A wavy horizontal line, approximately the height of a tennis net, runs the length of the blank end wall.

"This is my practice court," Sam explains. "It's not like playing a real game. But what else can you do in the winter?"

He really *is* an old man, I decide, as he stalks away to the window, almost as old as my grandfather was. But Granda seemed so much older, even when I first went to him, as though he'd wrestled with life and come off the worse for wear.

"If you moved to Florida, you could play out of doors all year round," Lily says.

"How would I get there? I can't walk, I'm not going to take a train, and I'll never get on a plane. There's only one way I'll ever be involved in an airplane accident — that's if one falls on my head. And anyway, the minute I set foot in Florida I'd turn into an old man. It's God's waiting room down there. Everybody you meet is senile."

"There's an old Irish story about someone called Usheen," I say. "He spent three hundred years with a fairy woman in Tir-na-nÓg, the Land of Youth, and when he came back to Ireland, he turned to dust as soon as his foot touched the ground."

Sam stops in his tracks and gives me a keen look. "Oh, boy. The Land of Youth. How did he get there?"

"On a horse that could gallop over the ocean."

"He should have stayed there," Sam says, resuming his pacing. "But it sounds like a good way to go. Dust to dust — instantaneously! Personally I plan to die of a heart attack on the tennis court. What the hell good is being ninety years old if you can't move a muscle — because you haven't got any muscles left! You're just an old sack of skin and bone! Believe me, there's nothing I loathe more than an old person."

Lily is right: her father is an eccentric. His attitude to death is a novel one. I admire it, yet there seems to be something improper about it. Death is a serious business — at least in *my* family.

"Matt will play with you, Dad. You have an extra racket, don't you?"

Sam swings around, his eyes gleaming. "He plays tennis?"

"Sure," I say impulsively.

I'm surprised that Lily has offered my services: it must mean that she still holds out some hope for me, in spite of our difficulties. If she wants me to play tennis with her aged father against the wall of his office on the tenth floor of a building in downtown Boston in the dead of winter — then I will do it. Why not? I like the old fellow. I suspect that we will be about evenly matched, given my inexperience on the tennis court.

"No, I can't do it," Sam decides disgustedly. "If you'd only come yesterday when I still had some zizzle. I'm not long for this world. Do me a favor, will you, Lily? If I get to be non compos, and those doctors are bending over me with their tubes and their monitors and their IV's — pull the plug. I don't care how you do it, just get me out of here, OK?"

"I told you before, Dad, I'd be perfectly happy to help you on your way, but it's too sticky from a legal point of view. The courts are not ready yet to acquit people who murder their parents, even if it's to put them out of their misery. Now, if you'd only make a living will . . ."

"I don't want anything to do with doctors or lawyers. It'll have to be suicide. I have no desire to be lying there like a human vegetable causing you grief and costing you money you could be putting away for your retirement, with my cerebellum gone south and a bunch of those medicine men poking me and prodding me and pronouncing me still alive."

He puts a brave front on it though: I'll give him that. I wonder how my grandfather took it. But I can never know that. I did my best by him for as long as I could — and then I failed him at the last. You get no second chance; that is all *I* know about death. Let me not think on it.

"Speaking of vegetables," Lily says, "do you need anything from the store? I'm going to look in your fridge."

She walks to the door in the corner, leaving us alone.

"Don't bother. I don't eat anymore. My days are numbered."

"I hope not, Mr. Golden," I say, surprising myself by my alacrity in contradicting him.

"I don't care, I've had a good inning. It's young fellows like you I worry about. It's a bad time to be an immigrant. Let me tell you, it's no longer bring me your poor, your tired, your huddled masses, yearning to breathe free, like it was when I came over here from Russia at the age of six months and three days. We're busy running up the biggest deficit in history. What line of work are you in?"

"I haven't finished college. Right now I'm half a historian."

"Ha, ha." Sam chuckles. "Half a historian. I hope you don't have to settle for half a loaf! But tell me: how do you like it here?"

"I'm just off the boat. I can't say yet."

"But are you having a good time?" he persists. "Are you enjoying yourself?"

He comes to a halt in front of me and stares at me closely. A penchant for asking probing questions runs in the family, apparently. But in Sam too it is an expression of interest, of acknowledgment.

"Sure," I say.

Sam regards me doubtfully, then paces off.

"Lily," he calls. "Are you showing him a good time?"

"There's no food in here!" Lily yells back. "I'm going out to the store."

Sam wheels around in agitation. "Don't go anywhere. Don't do anything. My digestive system is shot to hell. I don't want any food in this place. It'll only spoil and you'll have to throw it away when you come for the body. I'm not going to make it to the end of the week. I'm expecting every breath to be my last."

"Well, I'm glad we happened to be passing by, Dad."

He breaks into a jog and commences a circuit of the empty office. Lily and I exchange glances across the bare floor. I try to communicate that I like her father. I am happy that she wanted me to meet him, and I feel closer to her on account of it. I do not know what her answering look means; she seems amused and perplexed all at once.

"How's your back?" Sam asks her, coming back from the windows.

She makes a face. "Lousy. I have a chair I like at work, but my car is murder."

"What about this chair? Here, come sit in this."

Lily dutifully sits in the swivel chair. I come and stand behind her. The chair has a beautifully polished bentwood back, curved arms, and sculpted seat.

"It's a handsome piece of furniture," I say.

"It's not really comfortable for me," Lily says, getting out of it.

Sam stops dead in his tracks and looks at me in disbelief. "Oh . . . my . . . God. I have a daughter who's successful, happy, sensible, good looking, eats right, gets plenty of exercise, laughs at all her father's jokes — and do I thank God every day? No! I say to myself, She's her father's daughter, it's her genetic inheritance, what's the Almighty got to do with it? And now look what happens. She can't drive her car. She's an invalid. It serves me right."

"I'm comfortable in Matt's car. Maybe I ought to swap with him."

"You take his car," Sam pronounces, "and he'll take the chair. I've got to get rid of that chair."

The thought of exchanging the Monster for Lily's boxy little Geo appalls me. But I feel a surge of affection for her — and for her leprechaun of a father. I am empty, I am no one, I have no life of my own. I have put all that I know of family and home behind me. But perhaps I can be a part of Lily's life. Maybe that is what she is trying to tell me.

"It's really not so bad, Dad. If I didn't have to sit at a desk all day —"

"I can't understand it, Lily," Sam rails. "I'm as strong as an ox myself. Have you been taking the cod-liver oil I sent you? The condition that can't be cured by cod-liver oil hasn't been discovered yet."

Lily and I smile at each other. I feel a sense of relief, and a glimmer of hope awakens. Surely our difficulties can be resolved.

"I took it religiously, Dad. But I don't have any left."

"There's your problem right there. I'll go right out and get you some more."

He hustles into his room.

"Dad! It's twelve degrees out! Don't you listen to the news?"

Lily goes to stand in the doorway. Surreptitiously, I peer over her shoulder. Sam is pulling a pair of baggy blue sweatpants on over his tennis shorts. There is an unmade bed littered with newspapers. At the foot of the bed, two TVs, both on and muted, are stacked one on top of the other on a filing cabinet, their screens the only source of light. Seeing me, he grins scornfully. "I don't listen to the news. I *study* it."

In the corner next to a small fridge, a hot plate and a toaster oven are crowded together on a typewriter table, along with a radio with an earphone attached. A tiny sink is set in the wall. Affixed to the door of the fridge, a handwritten sign in large, bold characters that begins IN THE EVENT OF MY DEATH.

Sam surveys the wreck of the bed with a flashlight, unearths a red polo-neck sweater, and thrusts his head into it.

"Dad," Lily pleads. "Wait till next week. I can get by. It won't be so cold."

He opens a metal locker-room cabinet and rummages inside. "What do you think I am," he mutters, "an old man? The day I'm too old to run up and down the stairs carrying my bicycle, I'll take the elevator to the roof and throw myself off!"

He thrusts his arms into the sleeves of a green velvet jacket and completes the outfit with a red beret.

"At least let Matt go with you. Do you mind, Matt?"

"No, no. He doesn't want to go with me. It's too cold."

But I *do* want to go. It is something I can do for Lily. And for her father.

"I'll go," I say. "The cold doesn't bother me."

"That's right," Sam says. "He's an Irishman. Nothing bothers him."

He goes to the bicycle and takes it off the stand.

"And remember, Lily, if I do freeze to death out there, the number of the crematorium is on the door of the fridge, and the stocks and bonds are in the toaster oven."

Lily looks at me and shrugs. "What am I going to do while you guys are out there risking your lives? Oh, never mind. I'll think of something. Just make sure my father doesn't run over any pedestrians."

It is a side of her I have not seen, a Lily who shrugs and says, What can I do about it? It makes me feel even more fond of her.

I take off running after Sam, who is already on his way. He trundles his bicycle noisily down the ten flights of stairs and into the lobby. I follow anxiously at his heels, wanting to help but afraid to offend his self-sufficiency. In the lobby he breaks into a trot, rushing the bicycle across the marble floor. An incoming businessman in pinstripes steps aside in time to hold the heavy door for him, and when I reach the pavement he is freewheeling recklessly down the ravine of Federal Street, his smoky breath whipping around his head.

Distraught, I give pursuit, stumbling on snow and ice, propelled by a sharp wintry blast at my back. I feel sure he will speed into the middle of the traffic and come to a spectacular end. Lily has entrusted her father to my care, and I've blown it. I dart into the middle of the street and see him bring the bicycle to a sudden stop by placing both feet on the ground. He waits for me in the arctic shadow of the black Fiduciary Trust building. The rapid descent hasn't taken a feather out of him — whereas I'm gasping like a stranded fish. I want to tell him to take it easy, but I have to catch my breath.

He dismounts nimbly, and we walk side by side through the busy intersection and over the expressway. The sky has miraculously cleared to a cheerless winter blue, and the sun is about to sink out of sight behind the city. We cross a little piazza in front of the towering atrium of the Financial Center; the terrace is bare, and the café closed, its striped red-and-white awnings folded like the wings of a sleeping insect. I breathe deeply and feel that I am filling my lungs with great mouthfuls of an icy liquid. The facade of South Station faces us, pockets of snow nestling among its columns, the doorways shuttered with scrawled plywood. My fingers and toes are stinging, in spite of gloves and wool socks. I tell myself I probably won't get frostbite. But Lily's father is an old man; he shouldn't be out in this.

"How far do we have to go?" I ask.

"It's on Northern Ave. I'd be there already if I didn't have to watch out for the ice."

"What about going in my car?"

"No, no. I need the exercise."

He darts across the street, mounts the bicycle, and weaves along the pavement of Atlantic Avenue. I follow at a run, past the Trailways bus station. It's all I can do to keep him in sight. At least the pace keeps my blood circulating. Traffic rumbles in the canyon of the expressway, though the din seems attenuated in the cold dead air. On the left, the wall of the city rises, the new towers and blocks of glass distorting each other's reflections, dwarfing the staircase brickwork of the older buildings.

Ahead of me, Sam veers to the right. I reach the corner just as he enters the pedestrian walkway of a trestle bridge, pedaling feverishly. A gust of icy wind off the harbor tears through the lattice of the girders, and as I watch the bicycle slips out from beneath him. He comes down hard, on his tailbone, and continues to slide, sitting up, until he comes to rest against the bars of the railings, through which his legs protrude over the black water.

I rush up to him, trembling with cold or with fright, I don't know which. He does not look up but stares vacantly ahead of him. All I can think is that he has done himself a fatal injury — and I am responsible. What will Lily say? This is the end for us. I kneel beside him and touch his shoulder gingerly. "Mr. Golden? Are you all right?"

He does not seem to hear, but to my immense relief he tucks his legs under him and rises slowly, clinging to the railing for support. The entire bridge trembles as a truck rolls past. I stand behind him, ready to catch him if he should fall. He shuffles his feet tentatively and passes his hands over his limbs.

"All present and accounted for," he mutters. "Lucky I fell on my tush. But oh . . . my . . . God. How did I —?"

He puts his hands to his head and regards me with a look of horror. "I've lost my hat."

I see it floating beneath us, already sodden and sinking, like a small carcass.

"Here, take mine."

"No, no. You need it just as much as I do," he mutters vaguely. "You lose eighty percent of your body heat through your head."

I spot a smear of blood on his forehead. He sees my appalled look, removes his glove, and wipes the blood onto his hand.

"You're bleeding," I inform him.

"Am I not a man? If thou prickest me, do I not bleed?"

He walks stiffly back to the bicycle and spins each of the wheels in turn. Then he walks with it to the end of the bridge.

"Maybe we should turn back, Mr. Golden."

He stares ahead grimly, Peary or Shackleton contemplating the icy wastes. "At my age, there's no turning back."

The roadway broadens ahead of us into a bleak plain, with parking lots to one side and the blackened walls of factory buildings to the other. Sam mounts his bike again from the curb, wobbles erect, and bears down on the pedals. The wind comes at us steadily across the bright water of the harbor, and I run on his leeward side, keeping abreast of his uncertain pace, ready to support bicycle and all.

We pass an old A & P, its tiled front fading like a neglected fresco, Anthony's Pier 4 marooned in an icy parking lot, the World Trade Center. I am used to the solitudes of the Inish, where loneliness and desolation are natural conditions. But this arctic urban wasteland strikes fear into my soul.

Sam turns onto the Boston Fish Pier. There are two narrow blocks of stores and warehouses with classical pediments running their length. He dismounts shakily, leans the bicycle against the wall of the Harbor Lobster Company, and steps between pools of ice into the dim interior.

"It's over to the left here," he mutters to himself, "last on the left."

But the office is dark and closed. Through the window we can see a heap of empty boxes piled crazily upon the abandoned desks. Sam brings his face close to the dusty pane.

"Gone under," he mutters. "Bit the dust. After we came all this way."

He looks around cannily. There is light in a small shed on the opposite side of the building. He hurries toward it, slapping his hands rhythmically against his sides. His energy reassures me a little. But I will not be happy until I bring him back in one piece.

In the shed a beefy man in an oilskin apron stands with his back to us, washing fish in the stainless steel trough.

"What happened to Mr. Sandborn?" Sam says.

The man glances over his shoulder and then turns back to his fish, flinging a snake of water out of his hose.

"Went out of business. You're about the twelfth person this week come looking for him."

"You don't say. I didn't know there were twelve people in the entire city of Boston who cared enough about their health to look for the real thick Norwegian cod-liver oil you can't get in any of those so-called health-food stores."

"You're hooked on the stuff, huh?"

"Oh, I don't care about myself. I've lived long enough. It's my daughter who's got a back problem. Cod-liver oil is her only hope. We're going to have to go back and tell her we couldn't find any."

The man tosses a fish out of the trough. Its eye is a cloudy stone.

"Listen," he says. "I think Sandborn left some bottles behind. Let me go look in our office."

He steps heavily up an open stairway and opens a door. A light comes on, and we see him through the window barging about. Then he comes running down the stairs, a bottle in each hand.

"This the stuff you're looking for?"

"Oh . . . my . . . God," Sam says, accepting the bottles gingerly. "Two whole quarts. My daughter will be so happy. Here: what do I owe you?"

The man waves his hand dismissively.

"They're yours, bud, take 'em. Ain't no good to me. Just cluttering up the office."

He strides back into his cubicle and begins to throw fish into a crate. Sam stands for a moment in silent disbelief, looking at the man's fleshy back.

"I thank you," he says at last.

He carries the bottles out of the shed and places them tenderly in the basket affixed to the bike's handlebars. We walk toward the city,

Sam trundling the bicycle. I am relieved that we are on our way back. We cross the trestle bridge and turn onto Atlantic.

"This is like a Russian winter," Sam tells me with evident satisfaction. "It reminds me of the steppe."

"You were born in Russia?"

He grins wickedly. "I was born in the same village as Ivan Boesky. Yekaterinoslav, near Kiev. But I left when I was five months old. I almost didn't make it. My mother had to stuff me into the stove to hide me from the Cossacks. After that she'd had enough. My father was a big shot over there, owned a tailor shop and a cap shop, used to stop people on the street and tell them their caps needed mending. He was doing all right, he didn't want to leave. But my mother couldn't stand it."

I suspect that I may be the victim of another hoax. But I don't care. I will take an entertaining lie over a boring truth any day of the week. I find myself imagining Lily's father as a character from Chekhov, one of the peasants with whom Yegor travels across the steppe, or the old man whom Lipa meets after she has buried her child, who tells her that in spite of a hard life he does not wish to die and sings the praises of great Mother Russia.

"They had to travel all the way from the province of Kiev across Poland," Sam proclaims, "with three small children and me-in-the-belly, through Minsk and Pinsk and Dinsk to where that fellow Lech Walesa is now, Gdansk, to get to the boat. My father went onboard, and my mother went to follow him, with the three children and me-in-the-belly. Sorry, they said, you can't come onboard. Go away and come back again when you've had the baby, they said. Then you can get on. All right, said my father, rubbing his hands. Let's go home. But my mother wouldn't hear of it. You stay where you are, she said. *You're* not pregnant! So my father had to go, and my mother and the three children and me-in-the-belly trekked all the way back to the province of Kiev. When my father arrived at Ellis Island, they cut off his 'otka,' and inside two days they had him sweeping the streets."

I lean closer to him in order to hear above the noise of traffic.

"They cut off what?"

"His name was Goloborotka and they cut off his 'otka' and made a plain old Joe Golden out of him. I'd rather be back there making caps for the Cossacks, my father says to himself. So he writes to my mother to tell her he's coming back. I'll leave the key with the woman next door, she wrote back. I'll wave to you if our ships cross in the Atlantic. So of course he had to wait for her. She trekked all the way back across Poland through Minsk and Pinsk and all the rest of them and spent three months in steerage — can you imagine it? — with three young children and a squalling baby. What a woman, what a woman. I want my children to grow up American, she says. If it hadn't been for her, I'd probably be in Siberia today — if I was lucky!"

This open acknowledgment of a debt to a family member is strange and foreign to me. I have noticed that Lily does not scruple to tell me things about her father, both good and bad. Whereas I do not know what to say about my family, my mother and my grandfather, other than that they *are* my family. Where would *I* be if it hadn't been for my mother? To even pose such a question implies the possibility that she might have been different than she was — and that I cannot imagine. It also implies a connection between us that does not and can never exist.

But there is a connection between Sam and me — as though we are privy to a secret unknown to the rest of the world. We share the conviction that all will not be well, that all striving is in vain. The difference between us is that I am depressed by this knowledge, whereas Sam appears to take it as an incomparable jest on the part of the Almighty.

He gets on his bicycle again, but he doesn't take off through the grim-faced pedestrians as before. We retrace our steps along Atlantic Ave. and cross by South Station in a sudden flurry of snow. Ascending Federal Street, I take the bicycle from him, and he does not object. It is dark now. Ahead of us the hill is dotted with brilliant globes of light, alive with movement. The lights give the illusion of warmth, but the air seems to burn my lips, and I feel sure that my extremities have entered the first stages of frostbite. I increase the pace a little, with a wary glance at Sam. He is picking his way nimbly through the crowd. His breath seems more rapid, but he does not appear to be in distress. It looks like we're going to make it.

On the pavement ahead of me I see Sam's number, 176 Federal, in a circular bronze plate partly covered by ice. The lobby gleams like an aquarium through thickening snow. I lean against the heavy door — and we are immersed in a heady tide of warmth. Sam strides ahead of me to the stairs, then pauses and peers about him furtively. He turns to me, presses his finger to his lips, and, like a thief, steps across to the elevator and jabs the call button.

Lily greets us at the door. "I was getting ready to call the Boston Rescue Squad. They're gathering people into shelters in droves."

Flushed with success, I hug Lily, who gives me an astonished look. Sam puts the bicycle on its stand and settles himself in the swivel chair.

"I'm telling you, Lily, we're lucky to be alive. Your Irishman almost died of the cold, and I almost fell into the harbor. Mr. Sandborn has gone out of business, and his office is closed. But we didn't give up. We got two quarts — gratis. To get a gift of two quarts of Norwegian cod-liver oil! To survive a fall like the one I had! Oh boy!"

"Did something happen?" Lily asks me.

"He fell off his bicycle," I say sheepishly.

"That fall would have killed a lesser man." Sam chortles. "But I had the luck of the Irish. If your Irishman hadn't been with me, I'd probably be floating in the harbor right now. They'd never find the body — just like those two passengers who fell out of a jet into Boston Harbor on a subzero night in January. No hope. Dead as soon as they hit the water."

His face assumes a sly expression, and he leaps out of the chair. "But *he's* a lucky man himself to be hooked up with my daughter," he pronounces.

I glance across at Lily to see how she is taking this. She looks solemn, unsmiling, and a twinge of apprehension touches me, a rec-ollection of our conversation in the car. At least she does not jump to contradict him. I *am* lucky to have found Lily. Am I going to throw it all away?

"We're going to go, Dad. The snow's starting up again."

"Wait a minute. I want to give you something for dinner. Take him out to eat. He deserves it."

He rushes into his bedroom and emerges a moment later with some bills, which he presses into Lily's hand.

"Thanks, Dad. You want to come with us?"

"No. I have to listen to the news. You go eat, and I'll enjoy thinking about it."

He goes back in the room and turns on the TV. Lily takes the cod-liver oil from the basket and goes to the door. I hesitate, reluctant to leave, wanting to find a way to part from him that will express something of what I am feeling. But he comes running toward us again, through the ghostly space of the darkened office. "Don't forget the chair. He wants the chair. Take the chair."

"No, I can't take your chair," I begin.

"Take it! You'll be doing me a big favor. How do you think I got rid of the rest of the junk in here? I want to give away everything, so when I go Lily won't have to deal with it. Take it — or leave it. Whatever."

He turns on his heel and stalks back into his cave. I look at Lily. She shrugs. "Take it if you want it. That's my old man. He's never happier than when he can give something away."

"I want both of you to take that cod-liver oil," Sam yells as we leave, Lily with the bottles, me with the chair. "Health is the most important treasure in life. Money, fame, sex: what good are they if you don't have your health?"

We deposit the chair and the bottles in the Monster. Then Lily takes my hand and leads me through the snowy streets to a Chinatown restaurant. I cannot fathom her mood, but I decide not to worry about it. Maybe we can enjoy the rest of Saturday night.

I eat a lot of Chinese food and tell her the story of my expedition with her father, omitting no details. I even have a sweet Chinese beer to celebrate.

"I like your father very much," I tell her.

She looks at me seriously for a long moment, as though trying to fix what I look like in her mind. I feel myself becoming sober under this look. I remember my premonition. Something is coming.

"I guess you either love him or you hate him," she says.

"You don't get along with him?"

"I get along fine with him — but only because I play by his rules."

This brings me up short. I do not doubt that Sam is a difficult person, but there is something in her tone that seems to be directed against me.

"I enjoyed visiting him," I say lightly. "He's like a Russian peasant living in downtown Boston!"

"He's a rugged individualist all right, and he can charm the birds out of the trees. But try to talk about yourself. If you can get a word in edgewise, you're doing better than me."

I find that I want to defend Sam. Since this seems absurd, I say nothing.

"My father was always a performer," she tells me, "when he was at home, which wasn't very often. He was with his mistress, I know now. My mother cried and yelled at him, but she put up with it for years. And I just sat there and watched. That's what my collages are about: watching, trying to figure it out. You can observe a lot by just watching, as Yogi Berra says. But you get tired of sitting in the corner and feeling unseen. It makes me feel lonely just to visit my father. That's why I took you along. But it didn't help. I've felt just as lonely with you the last few weekends."

She bends over the table, eyes downcast, her face assuming the solemnity that I love.

"Matt, I know you don't want to hear this, but it's just not working out, is it? You're not really here anymore. You drive out to my house and then you want to turn around and go to the movies — and I'm the bag of popcorn you take with you! It's too hard for me to be with you when you're so withdrawn."

"What is it that you want me to do?" I say impulsively. "Tell me — and I'll do it!"

"I don't want you to *do* anything. I just want you to open up to me."

"You're telling me I should just shake this thing off and get on with it. Well, that's what I'm trying to do. It doesn't seem to make any difference."

"I'm telling you the opposite, Matt," she says, roused to vehemence. "You have to go through this, to feel what you're feeling. You can't ignore it or make it go away."

"But what *is* it?" I say. "I have no idea. Your unhappiness is articulate; mine isn't. If something is bothering you, you can put your finger right on it. For me it's all a great buzzing confusion in there. I don't know how to talk about it. To tell the truth, I don't think it's possible."

"It's not that you don't know how," Lily says. "It's just that it's difficult and painful. You're perfectly capable of understanding what's happening to you."

"Do you know how ancient Irish law used to punish murderers?" I say. "They were set adrift on the ocean in an open boat without oars or sail. That's the way I feel: I've done something irrevocable. I'm adrift, I'm out of sight of land; everything familiar has disappeared."

"You're not a murderer, Matt. You feel guilty because you didn't do what your grandfather wanted you to do. But he wanted you to go on living *his* life instead of living your own. You have the right to make a life for yourself, Matt, and you have to realize that. You can do it — if you want to."

This is what Lily says whenever difficulties arise. Can do: the hardheaded confidence of the New World. It is something that I *need* her to say: it is my lifeline. But then another voice within me speaks:

"My grandfather used to say, We are not our own men. It's foolish to make a plan and think you can carry it through."

"Do you believe that?"

My heart sinks. It is my creed. But does it mean I cannot care for Lily? How can I care for her when it is as much as I can do to look after myself?

"I don't know what to believe! I don't even know why we're having this conversation. What do you want from me?"

She takes such a long time to respond that I think she's finally gotten angry. But when she speaks, her voice is very collected.

"I want intimacy," she says deliberately. "I want to share the bad as well as the good with you, and I want us to be able to help each other. And I need to know you want that too."

What joy to be able to express what one wants so clearly and succinctly! For a moment I am rendered speechless by the simplicity of it. But I'm at the bottom of a well shaft, looking up at the tiny circle of light. Lily requires a clear and simple response — and I cannot find it.

"Do you understand what I'm saying?" she wants to know.

"Perfectly."

"Do you want to say anything?"

"No, Lily."

She's crying. I reach for her hand.

"I'm sorry."

"Don't. It's not your fault. It's just the way we are right now."

We sit there with the remains of the meal. The waiter comes with the check, and Lily pays him. I pass her some bills, but she waves them away.

"I do love you, Matt," she says. "But I was starting to tell you what to do with your life, and it was making you angry. It's no good to get my stuff mixed up with yours. We'll each have to find our separate ways through this. It's not what either one of us wanted. That's what makes it so hard."

The snow has ceased when we come out of the restaurant, and stars are faintly visible above the city's glow.

The drive back to Walpole in the Monster is long and bleak, not because we do not talk to each other but because we do — and all the time I know that the worst has happened and that things will never be the same between us.

When I stop in the driveway, I do not turn off the lights or the engine. I feel Lily's lips brush my cheek. She opens the door.

"I don't know what to say to you, Matt. I think I'll just say, Call me. But not until you know your own mind."

She steps out. The door slams. I see her shadow turn the corner of the darkened house. As I swing the Monster around, the headlights reveal the wide snowbound fields.

Ship of Death

NIGHT — or rather the early hours of the morning — the sky illuminated by an artificial dawn. Route 128, America's Technology Highway, a sign informs me. I know it from my maps as the route that curves about the city to the west, counterpart of the expressway — the Central Artery — that bears the life blood of traffic through the heart of downtown Boston. From behind the Monster's wheel, 128, or Interstate 95 — they coincide here — is a wide black river that streams by office buildings tiered like wedding cakes, with light blazing from their empty rooms. America is determined at all cost to keep the dark at bay.

I am always in the Monster now, it seems, day and night. I put on my coat in the middle of the afternoon and go downstairs to sit in it; I think I do this to escape from the telephone, which obstinately refuses to ring and bring me Lily's voice announcing that all is forgiven. I read, stretched out in the front seat, Yeats's *Autobiographies,* while keeping an eye on the bustle of Cambridge Street, registering the faces as they pass, their strangeness, their variety, their distinct, unassimilable features reminding me I am not at home here — or anywhere.

But I save my gas for the nighttime: nights when I cannot sleep, when I need motion like a drug, to wear out my restlessness. It works, but there is a cost. For memories always come when I drive.

I choose a middle lane and reach a steady speed. Route 128 is a different kettle of fish from the expressway or the Pike. At rush hour the traffic seems to move in a single melded block — at sixty-five miles per hour! This is terrifying at first, but shortly it becomes exhilarating; everybody tearing along, intent, focused; the knowledge that the slightest miscalculation can produce an appalling pileup. Route 128 is not for the fainthearted. Even at night there is always some activity, though the same ferocious concentration is not required.

I pass beneath an intersection, a great circle of access ramps, signs soaring above them like banners taut in a gale. So many roads, through the maze of which most of us come unscathed and some few come to grief . . .

When did I first notice that my grandfather was old? When did I start to think of him as the *old* man? When did my fearful apprehension of his death begin? It was the year Christine's mother died. I was nine years old, and I had been with him for two years.

Two years in which my mother sent cards at Christmas, Easter, and St. Patrick's Day, cards containing not a word of news or inquiry, signed by her on behalf of my stepfather and my stepbrother Brendan, whom I did not know except as a baby, and subsequently by another name, Teresa, "your new little sister." Two years in which my only entertainment consisted of the flicks on Saturday night (if "suitable," a judgment delegated to whoever sold the tickets) — and of course the old man's stories, Diarmat and Grania and all the innumerable hosts of others. Two years of nights by the fire while my grandfather recounted the events of his own life over and over again until I knew them as well as — or better than — I knew myself. Two years in which I discovered what it is to long for a place as I had longed for the Inish in Dublin — and then to find that it does not exist.

For the rest, it was a familiar life, and I fell back into it effortlessly. I returned to the schoolhouse, which I liked for the absence of both the pretensions and compulsions of the Brothers. I was already interested in whatever books I could lay my hands on — which confirmed my status among the young lads of the Foot as a "quare fella." If I did not go to mass on Sundays, it was on account of the intervention of Peg, my grandfather's elder sister. Peg was a widow who lived in her daughter's house in Caher. She'd never given me the time of day before I came to live with the old man, but she now conceived an interest in the welfare of my immortal soul. My grandfather would not enter the church because of a falling-out with the parish priest, and he thought that Peg should mind her own business. So I spent an hour each Sunday morning walking the strand or the heights of Bray, with the old man's tacit complicity.

Christine, though two years older, was my friend. She was always in and out of the house, and Granda thought the world of her. Then her mother had to go into the hospital in Caher, and she went to stay with her aunt Julia in Port, a bedraggled little mainland village at the narrowest part of the channel, where the new bridge to the Inish was to be built. Port and the Foot were at opposite ends of the channel; there was no ferry between them. The best way to go was by way of Caher, where if you were lucky you would meet someone with a car returning to Port. It was a long roundabout way, especially since the old man's house was plainly visible from the pier in Port. But I would have gone as far again, to see Christine.

It is low tide. Christine and I have followed the ebb down the strand, foraging among the seaweed, peering at bewhiskered shrimp with transparent bodies in the rock pools, clambering barefoot on miniature mountain ranges of rock that we have named for the great peninsulas of the West: Dingle, Iveragh, Beara. We sit on the rock that represents the Inish, feet in the water. The declining sun paints the low hills of the real Inish with a lonely light. We are both wet and disheveled. The day has been warm, but now I'm beginning to feel cold and weary.

"I have to go, Chrissie."

"Already?"

This is what she always says. It is a game we play. But I do not know when I will be able to come to Port again, and this gives an edge to our parting.

"Granda will want his supper."

"He'll have to wait for it, if you're depending on Con."

She is right. My uncle is in the pub, and it will probably be a while before he'll be ready to leave it, not to mind the driver of the car, a crony of his and a great drinker. The thought of the long road home, the ferry, and the walk back through the Inish depresses me.

"Stay here with me," Christine says. "We have the house to ourselves."

"Where's your aunt?"

"Above in Caher."

"Won't she be back?"

"You wouldn't know. Sometimes she stays in Caher with her friends. That's why she wouldn't take me with her to see Mammy."

She takes a strand of seaweed and puts it in her mouth. The little bulbs make a cracking noise as she bursts them with her teeth. Her eyes fill with tears. She sees me looking at her and makes a funny face. I want her to be happy. I am frustrated by my helplessness.

"I'd like to stay, Chrissie. But Granda will be wondering where I am."

"Couldn't Con tell him?"

She knows as well as I do that they're not on speaking terms. We look at each other, amused by the thought of it.

"I suppose he could. But he'd have to write him a letter: 'Matt is drinking stout beyond in Port. They'll be carrying him home by and by.'"

"Write him a letter." Christine grins. "And give it to the dog at the top of the lane!"

She starts up suddenly and curls her toes about the edge of the rock.

"I'll go away home with you!" she snaps. "I won't wait for that one. She'll be out all night."

She releases a shout of laughter. My heart gives a leap. It is what I love about Christine: she is never at a loss.

"I won't wait for Con either," she tells me. "To have to drive to Caher in the car with a smell of drink off them that'd knock you. I'd sooner swim."

To my amazement, she wades into the water. Her short dress is lifted and swirls about her waist. She turns her head and peers at me over her shoulder. "Come on, Matty. We'll be there in no time!"

She ducks her head and comes up gasping, her curls plastered to her neck. Then she lowers herself deliberately into the water and swims away strongly, kicking her feet. My heart is in my mouth. I cannot believe she will do it.

"Chrissie!"

As in a dream, I fling myself in after her. The water seems shockingly cold. I cannot do a stroke, so I paddle away for all I am worth. I shut my eyes tightly to keep the water out — and to keep myself from getting frightened. I am not a good swimmer, and I do not even like to go in the water. But I can't let her go on her own.

When I open my eyes, I see that Christine is almost at the other side. She has a short and rapid stroke, and she keeps her face in the water. I am out of my depth, and the shore is not yet close. Panic makes my limbs weak and rubbery. What if I get a cramp? I might drown — while people are drinking stout in Port and going about their business on the Inish. What is it like, to be snatched away from myself, from this sad bright evening, and all the days and evenings to come? Not to be here anymore. Panic rises in my throat, as though to choke me. But I see that the tide is no longer slack and the incoming current is carrying both of us toward the Inish. I take a breath, clench my teeth, and paddle on.

Christine is waiting for me on the strand. I come ashore in a flurry of strokes and stand up unsteadily, panting. Christine shakes herself like a dog and grins fiercely at me. I open my mouth to say something, and we both start to laugh at the same time.

"Come out of the water," she says. "Before you catch your death!"

She skips up the shingle, and I race after her, still breathless. Together we run through the field to the road. I am shivering with the cold, and the muscles of my jaw ache painfully. Christine scales a gate and peers into the road. "Not a sinner. We're golden!"

We run along the road, too breathless to speak. My clothes are heavy and wet, and make it hard for me to move freely. But I am no longer cold or tired. I feel a mounting sense of excitement that makes me want to run faster. I have escaped with Christine from that woeful place. She does not have to go home to an empty house — and I do not have to sit next to Con in the pub until my head falls off with sleep. To the devil with Port and everyone in it. We're free!

We race the last stretch of road and fling ourselves beneath the fuchsia hedge at the top of the lane. I want to laugh aloud for the pleasure of our escape, but I do not have breath enough. I nudge Christine to make her say something, and she grabs my arm and squeezes it. "Hush."

A thread of sound, growing stronger and continuous, the creaking of pedals and gasps of breath expelled. Then with a rush the bicycle passes the lane, and the sound dwindles away to nothing. We stand up and walk down the lane to the strand. The dog comes out to us, as soon as we reach the seawall. The old man is standing in the doorway, propped up by his stick.

"I saw ye!" he proclaims. "I saw ye!"

Christine's quiet giggle gives me courage. But we have to come under his eye. He leans against the door to let us pass.

"What were you thinking of at all?" he says to me. "Do you want to drown yourself? Do you, now?"

"If we'd stayed in Port, we'd have been drowned in porter," Christine tells him.

He opens his mouth to say something and snaps it shut again. Christine darts for the settle. I stand dripping on the hearth.

"Christy, take that towel and dry yourself in the room. Your man will give you some clothes. Go on, let ye — before ye quench the fire on me!"

Dry and meek, holding large slices of buttered bread, we creep back to the fire where the old man is sitting, motionless as a statue. Christine is wearing my school shirt and trousers. Her eyes are aware of the fun of it and dare me to laugh.

"*Oíche mhaith, a dhuine uasail,*" she greets the old man carefully in Irish. "Good night, noble person."

"*Mo bhláithín geal,*" my grandfather murmurs, as though to himself. "My little bright flower."

Finn comes and rests his muzzle on the old man's boot, subsiding with a sigh. I take my place in the darkest corner. Granda raises his head and looks at each of us in turn.

"I'll have to learn you to take the boat before you jump in the channel again," he mutters in my direction. "You're old enough — and bold enough!"

He reaches in his pocket for his pipe. Christine's face is serious and attentive in the firelight. We are home. We are to have a story.

Christine's mother eventually came home from the hospital. Christine stopped coming to the house, and I did not see her anymore except at school. After school she walked away quickly with girls from her own class, as though she didn't know me. I missed her. My sojourn in Dublin might have made me a celebrity, however briefly, but my association with the old man, himself a recluse who never left the house, isolated me. People came to see him, but they were mostly old and didn't pay any attention to me. I looked after the house, according to my lights, I fetched his water, I cycled to the Foot for his groceries and his stout, always alone, never joining the rest of the young lads, who loitered on the pier or among the empty porter barrels by the side of Shanahan's. It was not that the old man required a great deal of care; if anything, he resisted my attentions. He wished to look after *me*, in order to confound my mother's folly in sending me to him, and the only way he knew to do this was to have me under his eye or to know my whereabouts, my comings and goings, with tedious exactitude. I didn't resent this, at least not in the beginning. When I was away from him, I didn't know what to do with myself. I was as preoccupied with him as he was with me, determined to assume my role, to become the caretaker my mother wanted me to be. The old man's mood became the yardstick by which I measured success. For I had no doubt that I *could* ultimately succeed — until Christine's mother got sick.

The day begins with an ill omen. The old man is already in the shop when I come in from the outhouse. He has a pair of shoes on the lasts, and he is perched on a high stool over his work, pulling the twisted threads for the soles through a round ball of wax, spreading his arms wide as he does so.

"Is there any sign of old Finn out there?" he wants to know.

"I didn't see him."

"He has an old fit coming on him," the old man says disgustedly. "He was whining there by the door, so I left him away on out. Let you go look for him after your tea — before he does himself harm."

The dog is prone to fits, in which he foams at the mouth and chases his tail. It is distressing to witness, and I do not like to be reminded of it. I go to the stove and put on the water for tea.

Pat-Joe appears in the doorway, to my inexpressible irritation. Since I returned to the Inish he has been at me every chance he gets, finding material for taunts in my sojourn in Dublin: the Inish is not good enough for me and so on.

"Hello, Pakey," the old man greets him, with a cheeriness that makes me grind my teeth. "Come in and have a sup of tay. Come in, come in."

"I won't," Pat-Joe says stolidly. "I suppose ye heard the news about Christine's mother."

The old man sobers instantly. "No, no, we didn't. No. Save that she was under the weather. But that was awhile ago. Sure she must be over it by now?"

Pat-Joe's slouch in the doorway exasperates me. He has something to tell, and he wants to make the most of it.

"She'll be over it soon all right," he allows. "One way or another." He jerks his head at me. "Didn't your man tell you what they're saying in the Foot?"

"Sure he could go to the end of the world and come back without a word to say for himself. Did they say she was bad?"

Pat-Joe nods his head dumbly, his big stupid eyes gleaming. But before he can deliver his news, Mrs. Harty from the Foot, a red-faced old woman whose husband I have never known, appears beside him in the doorway. She is large and cheery, always with a ready smile, a particular friend of the old man's.

"Hello, hello, hello," he crows delightedly. "It's a power of visitors we have this morning."

"*Dia is Muire duit*, Bat," Mrs. Harty greets him. "God and Mary be with you. Good morning, young fellow," she says to me, peering about her as though she cannot make me out in the gloom of the house.

She slaps Pat-Joe lightly on the arm. "Let you go back to the trap," she tells him, "before the horse runs away with your grandmother and Julia."

Pat-Joe backs out, looking aggrieved.

"Sit down, sit down," the old man tells her, starting up from his stool.

"Don't stir, Bat," she says, reaching across the shop counter to touch his arm. "Sure I can't stop at all. We're on our way to Evelyn's. Pat-Joe is taking us in the trap."

He settles back on the stool and begins to work vigorously upon the sole of a shoe with the point of his awl.

"Who's outside with ye?" he asks warily.

"Your sister and Evelyn's Julia from Port."

Peg does not visit us, and we do not know Christine's aunt Julia. Mrs. Harty and my grandfather seem strangely ill at ease with each other. The old man bends over his work, and Mrs. Harty looks at the floor.

"She'll be well by and by," the old man says. "'Tis not the way she's an old woman."

"The priest went back to her yesterday," Mrs. Harty says.

I can feel the old man grow very still. Then he gives a little shrug of the eyebrows, which looks like indifference, but I know it to be a sign of distress. He lays down the awl, picks up a leather disc, and fits it into the palm of his hand. He works the bristle through the sole against the leather, draws the thread out to its full length, and inserts the bristle again.

"Do you want some toast?" I ask him. "Or fried bread?"

"But sure that fellow was only going to bring her the sacrament," he says coarsely. "And for the sake of what they'd feed him."

"Didn't he anoint her, Bat."

The old man lays down the shoe and the leather disc and sits very straight upon his stool, looking out the door.

"We're going up to the house," Mrs. Harty murmurs. "Come on away up with us now, let you."

He removes his glasses and waves his hand slowly back and forth in front of his face, as though to clear away something that impedes his view. "No, no," he says, frowning deeply.

"Don't mind Peg," Mrs. Harty urges. "She won't say a word to you."

"No, no. 'Tisn't Peg at all."

"Come on away, Bat. You might be sorry afterwards you didn't go. 'Tis a terrible thing."

The old man shakes his head emphatically, and I know that he will not be persuaded. He stumps out of the shop and settles himself in the chimney corner.

"God bless, so," Mrs. Harty says, withdrawing. "I'll send Pat-Joe back to ye if there's any news."

I take the butter from the cooler, butter a slice of bread, and place it beside him on the settle. He does not look at it.

"So that's why Christy hasn't been to see us this long while," he murmurs.

It occurs to me that he is right, and my spirits rise, in spite of everything. I had thought she didn't come because she didn't want to see me anymore.

"'Tis a con*trary* old life her mother has," he says. "You wouldn't wish it on your worst enemy. She'd have been better off to get away out of the Inish altogether while she still had her health. A lot better off, faith."

Though spoken aloud, this is not really addressed to me, and I am not expected to say anything in response. It is known to everyone, even to the likes of me, that Christine's father is not dead, that he went off to the mainland when Christine was a baby and never came back. Christine and I have never talked about her father. But since he is as good as dead, having been absent for so long, it is something we have in common, being both of us fatherless.

"And there was no one had a good word to say for her," he says, ire creeping into his voice. "You'd think that no one could reproach them for anything. By God, if all the things I know about the people of the Inish were known to the world! Whitened sepulchers, is what I call them. Fair on the outside and full of rotting bones within."

I scald the pot and add tea, chewing on a heel of bread smeared with marmalade. When I steal a glance at him, I am shocked to find that there is something more like fear than anger in his face. I bring him his tea and place it upon the hearth.

"Give it here to me," he says.

I place the cup on his knee. He grips it with his good hand and warms the knuckles of the crippled hand against the side of it.

"Eat your piece of bread," I tell him.

He does not typically respond to any request or directive, but he has conceded to me a certain authority in matters pertaining to his physical welfare. I take my tea and sit in the doorway, where the sun has warmed the flags. I cannot see him in the chimney corner, but I can hear him breathing. Every now and then he gives a short nervous sigh. His unwonted distress communicates itself to me. I've never seen anything disturb him like this.

The sound of a crash makes me jump. I get up and run back inside. The cup is in pieces at his feet and the tea splashed over the hearth. He is holding on to the poker as though in a gale, sitting bolt upright against the chimney. I gather up the pieces of the broken cup.

" 'Tis you'll have to go for me," he says quietly.

I look up from the floor, apprehension dawning. "Go where?"

"To see Christy's mother."

"Why don't you go to see her yourself?" I blurt out.

He does not answer or look at me. I am in a panic. I want to see Christine. But I am afraid to go into a house where there is someone dying.

"Let you go, boyeen bawn," he murmurs in a strange cajoling voice. "Let you do this for an old man. Let you go — and I'll buy you a brand-new German sprat for to fish off the rocks with."

He has the force to command me, and I am almost ashamed to hear him try to win me over with presents — or refer to himself as an old man.

"Be sure you see her," he tells me. "Don't be said by anyone. Tell her I sent you."

I hurry out, for fear of further instructions. I have never been to Christine's house, but I know it well enough. Christine and her mother live in a barrack of houses built for the lighthouse keepers and their families. Her father was a keeper, and they occupy the house on sufferance, having no relatives on the Inish to take them in should Irish Lights reclaim it.

I go by the higher road, to avoid the Foot. I climb the hill that leads to the heights of the island, and the open sea comes into view. It is a deep windblown blue, wreathed in places with a corona of spray, and I can see the arm of the Dingle Peninsula and the Blaskets huddled around its tip like sleeping whales. There the great ships of the Spanish Armada foundered and went down, while the English soldiers stood on the cliffs and forbade the Irish to save a single man of all the Spaniards from drowning. The sea looks cold and implacable, but it is warm and windless between the high hedges with their red and purple pendants of fuchsia.

The road descends to a crossroads, and I take the right fork and go down through trees that conceal the Knight's estate and the cove of Glan. I come within sight of the Foot without encountering a soul.

There are some people on the road ahead, and I cut across the fields to come to the back of the lightkeepers' houses. I stand by the corner of the warm whitewashed wall. Couldn't I go back and tell him that I saw her or that they wouldn't let me in? He had no business sending me here in the first place. But I remember the strange way he was with Mrs. Harty, and I feel sorry for him — for perhaps the first time since I came to him.

I go up to the porch. The door is painted a crude red, the same color as the railings leading to the beacon above Glan. I lift the latch and step into the porch. The house door is ajar, and I hear a murmur of voices from inside. I tap lightly on the open door; nobody comes. I step into the dark windowless hallway and tiptoe toward the stairs.

Suddenly I find myself standing in the doorway of the kitchen. Peg and Mrs. Harty are sitting around a table with a group of women from the Foot. Their heads are turned toward me. Peg is stiffly erect. She is lame from birth and wears a shoe with a raised heel, which rests on a small footstool beside the table. Her sparse gray hair is piled upon the back of her head, and she has exchanged her everlasting housedress for a severe black gown shiny with age. With the exception of the ruddy Mrs. Harty, they look at me severely, as though I have interrupted a profound and gloomy colloquy. I want to announce my errand boldly, to tell them that my grandfather has sent me. But no words will come.

"It must be Christine he's looking for," Mrs. Harty says.

A younger hard-faced woman whom I do not know rises briskly from the table. She is tall, with very dark eyebrows and dark impatient eyes.

"Christine," she calls. "Christine!"

She comes to the door and peers into the corridor behind the stairs. "Christine!"

"What, Aunt Julia?" Christine's distant voice calls from the back of the house.

"There's someone here to see you!"

She goes to the table. The women talk softly together, ignoring me. I want to see Christine, but I must see her mother first. The stairs are in front of me. I feel sure that is where Christine's mother is. I move away from the kitchen door and place my foot tentatively on the first step, my heart pounding. But a door opens behind the stairs, lighting up the hallway, and I step back quickly. Christine comes in. I see her face before she catches sight of me. She looks like someone woken out of a deep sleep.

"Oh," she says, as though startled.

She smiles, and then the smile leaves her face and her eyes wander, as though she's forgotten me. She makes an awkward motion with her hand and walks back down the corridor. I stand there, unsure of its import.

"Who is it, Chrissie?" says Pat-Joe's voice from within.

"It's Matt," she says brightly.

I follow her into a bright room filled with furniture: a dining table and chairs, armchairs, a sofa. A window in the back wall is open, and the room smells of the fields. Pat-Joe turns from the window, scowls at me, and goes up to Christine. "Are you coming outside?" he says.

Christine shakes her head. Pat-Joe stares, then stalks out of the room without a word. Christine stands still for a moment with her back to me, then she steps awkwardly around the table to a door that opens into another room. She seems to have lost her catlike grace; her movements are ungainly and sudden. She stands very still at the door for a moment. Then she comes and stands next to me, her head averted. "We can't go in. The priest is with her."

Her voice has the urgency of confidence and a suppressed excitement. I am delighted to see her, and I do not care about anything else.

"I missed you, Chrissie. So did Granda."

She stares at the floor, distracted again. She is wearing a clean Sunday dress, and she has a ribbon binding her unruly hair.

"Let me show you the garden," she says.

There is something formal and adult about this invitation, as though she is repeating something she has been told to say. She leads me through another door into a tiny overgrown yard. We are quite alone here. But Christine is not herself. She does not seem to know me. I feel suddenly awkward, and I remember why I am here.

"Granda sent me," I bring out.

Christine fixes me for the first time with her wide gray eyes.

"This is her garden," she tells me seriously. "Of course, she hasn't been out here in a long time. But she'll be out again soon, please God, before the warm weather is gone."

She talks like an adult, like an old woman. It must be because her mother is dying. I want to let her know that I am aware of this, to help her somehow. But I can see no sorrow in her face, and I am afraid to say anything that might make things worse for her.

"We were wondering why you didn't come to see us," I say.

I regret this immediately because it is not what I mean to say. Christine frowns and seems puzzled. A sleepy droning voice comes to us through the open window. "Lamb of God who takest away the sins of the world."

"Would you like to see the flowers?" Christine asks.

She leads me along the narrow gravel paths and points to each cluster of flowers in turn: pink and white carnations, snapdragons with dumb toothless mouths, foxglove, lupine, a net of sweet pea against a white sunny wall.

"It's up to me to look after them," she tells me fussily. "But I don't have green thumbs like Mammy. These are the roses. They're supposed to be in a circle."

She steps around the circle for me. The center is overgrown with weeds and grasses. I spy Pat-Joe standing in a corner. When he sees me looking, he turns to the wall, as though shielding something with his body. Christine ignores him, to my shameful satisfaction.

"Montbretia," she says conscientiously, pointing to a delicate orange-colored flower in a mound of greenery. "But of course that grows wild all over the Inish."

She is looking at me expectantly, and I nod to humor her. It is our custom to name things for each other: plants, birds, the people of the old man's stories. But this is just a shadow of our game. I know that Christine's heart is not in it.

Abruptly she looks away, and I follow her glance to the lace-curtained window of the sickroom.

"He's gone away," she says. "Come on."

My heart pounding, I follow her to the door. I do not want to leave the garden, where it is safe, to go into the sickroom. But I cannot fail the old man.

In the room with the furniture, Christine stops and turns to me. "You won't know her," she says in a whisper. "She hasn't eaten this long time, poor thing. It's in her throat, you know. She can't swallow anything. The nurse feeds her through the bag."

The house is perfectly still, save for a sniffling sound from behind the open door. My own body seems fragile, threatened, prone to a multitude of calamities.

"And she suffers, God help her," Christine says, in a trancelike voice. "I heard the nurse say she was allergic to the medicine that they give her for the pain."

She turns and goes to the door. I hang back; she beckons urgently and silently. I step forward to the door. At first I cannot see anything but white: white walls, white curtains, white sheets of the bed. The room is very bright; it is a sort of converted porch, and one wall is glass partially screened by lace. Sunlight pours in upon the red linoleum, which shines with an unnatural brilliance. The walls are clean and bare; they seem to shimmer, themselves a source of light. Above the bed there is a picture of the Sacred Heart with a night-light on a little shelf beneath it.

I force myself to look down at the bed. Christine's mother is lying on her side, with her knees drawn up. There is something childlike, almost playful about this position that cheers me. She cannot be so sick if she can lie like this in bed: dying people lie upon their backs and stare at the ceiling, whence death comes to them.

Christine steps forward and kneels by her mother's head, as though to pray.

"It's Matt Quigley, Mammy," she says. "He came to see you."

The woman in the bed gives no sign of having heard. Christine motions me forward, nodding encouragingly. Suddenly I see that the side of her mother's face is all red and swollen, one eye practically concealed. I am frozen on the threshold. I must announce that my grandfather has sent me, but fear rises from my stomach to my throat and renders me speechless.

Christine gets up and takes me by the arm.

"She wanted the window open and a bee came in and stung her. Come over here where she can see you." She tries to draw me with her. I cannot move. The bright air of the room seems to vibrate with an unseen energy.

"What are you children doing at all?"

Christine's aunt is standing behind us, blocking the door. Flushing, a thief caught in the act, I look to Christine.

"He came to see Mammy," she says, suddenly tearful.

"Come on away and let her sleep. Isn't she tired after the priest?"

"My grandfather Bat O'Donnell sent me, Mrs. Sheedy," I announce in a loud, unnatural voice.

"Will you hush, for the Lord's sake!"

She pushes Christine and me before her, hands on our shoulders. In the hall, Christine breaks away, bolts up the stairs, and slams a door. I am in shock. I feel sure that something dreadful has happened, and that it is my fault. Mrs. Harty emerges from the kitchen and quietly ushers me out.

"She's not herself, God love her," she tells me. "With her mother the way she is, she has no heart to play."

She comes to the gate with me and stares down the road toward the Foot, as though expecting someone. I look up and find to my consternation that her plump ruddy cheeks are wet with tears.

"Tell your granddad I'll stop in later on," she says, with a catch in her voice.

I take off running without a backward glance.

I do not go home to the old man. Instead I wander back the Inish, past the last houses, to where the road becomes a turf cutters' track that fades out in a plain of bog before the sea. The place is called Paris, on account of an attempt by one of the Knights to relieve overcrowding on his estate. When his people were reluctant to move to this lonesome place, he had the priest harangue them from the pulpit: Is it Paris ye want? The question is now asked sarcastically of anyone who wants to leave the Inish: Is it Paris you want?

The people had the right of it: this Paris is a desolate spot, even in summertime. The coast descends in flat shelves of rock to the sea, and I walk along the cliff, looking down. There is a big swell below me; the noise of the waves breaking against the rock is almost constant. The day is turning cloudy and dark.

This is what it means to die: to lie in a white room and to be unable to move or feed yourself, to be stung in the face because you cannot raise your hand to brush away a bee. Christine's mother is dying — and she is not even old. I remember that Granda is old, suddenly, inexplicably old. What if he gets sick and takes to his bed? What if he begins to die? What will become of me when he is gone?

An eager snuffling sound makes me turn. Old Finn has found me. He comes bounding over the heather, contorting his sleek and powerful body like a fish. I take him by the ears and roll him onto his back. He bares his teeth, mock-snarling, and takes my hand in his mouth. There's nothing wrong with him; he's as strong as an ox and full of mischief. We tussle for a while, and then he leaps away and starts for higher ground. At the top of a rise he stops and looks back for me. I allow him to lead me to the house.

"May the devil mend you," the old man mutters when I come in. "I thought you were gone into the ocean, yourself and the dog."

I can tell by his tone that he is more relieved than angry. But I do not care what he thinks. I sit opposite him on the settle and spread my hands to the fire. I am not cold. But the chill of *uaigneas* is in my bones, and the fire looks like something that might drive it away.

"Did you see her?" the old man says.

I nod without looking up.

"Well?"

I want to tell him that Christine thinks she will get better, but when I meet his eyes a lump rises in my throat and I cannot speak. We sit in silence. Outside the wind has picked up. A sudden draft blows smoke into the room.

"She was as much and more to me than my own children," the old man says. "But that's the way. 'Tis death that'll find us all, late or soon. How can a man escape the day of his death? There is a time marked out for each of us, and when that time is come, if you went into the bowels of the earth itself, death would find you out. We have only the time of our lives, and young or old a man must go when death calls."

He delivers this warning in a sort of chant. The vague but dread image of a personified death fills my mind. I imagine a fatal footstep, a midnight knock at the door, a fearful summons.

"That's what the old people thought anyhow," he mutters, as though admitting a shadow of doubt. "Did you ever hear what they used to say about the Skellig rocks outside?"

I shake my head.

"That the souls of all the dead must go there when they die — and stop there some of them for all eternity! I gave five long years on the Great Skellig, minding the old monastery, and I'd as soon stop there as any place. But to be a ghost there, not to be able to touch the stones or to feel the wind on your face, never to draw breath or to have living speech with a Christian, but to be forever wandering over it, voiceless and alone, without the poor shelter of human flesh, through wind, rain, and storm . . ."

But it does not seem to bother him. He is himself again. It is well for him. I wish I were an adult too, with the magical power to keep loneliness at bay. And to think that loneliness persists after the grave, that the souls of the dead are drawn to high lonely places, there to keep a cheerless disembodied vigil with no hope of release. It is too much!

"Will Christine's mother have to stop there, Granda?"

A still attentiveness creeps over him, as though if he listens he will hear the answer murmured at his ear.

"'Tis only the souls of the damned must stop there, so they say. God knows she had a hard enough life, poor soul. Her journey will be short."

I have heard about the afterlife from the pulpit; it is a remote and abstract world, nothing to do with me. But what the old man says about the Other World has an uncanny power of conviction. My curiosity gets the better of my fear.

"What journey is that, Granda?" I say.

He is silent for a while. Then he sighs, as though coming to a decision.

"There's a journey after death, boyeen, for those that can make it. The old people say it's like a sea voyage by night, out beyond the Head and the Seal Rocks, out beyond the Skelligs, to a sea that has no shores. Some souls go astray and never find land, some come to shore after storm and wreck, some sail straight and true into the harbor of the blest. You can be on that voyage for a day, for a year, or for a thousand years —"

"How do you know how long it will take you?"

"There's no living creature can know a thing like that," he says impatiently. "The old people used to say you could shorten the road in death if you made the pilgrimage to the Skellig in life and climbed up to kiss the cross above the monastery. They used to say long ago that if you were courting and you wanted to make sure your girl would have you, you had to go to the Rock. That was when I did it, when I was a young man courting a girl outside on Inishvick."

I have heard this story time and again, but I cannot stop myself. "Did it help you, Granda?" I say.

"It didn't," he snaps. "Christine's grandmother it was, that married a Yank in the end. And there lies the root of all my trouble. But sure it was my own fault and no one else's."

I bow my head, blink back tears, and bite my lip. He has no time for me really, save to go to the Foot for him and to listen to his stories.

"The sure way to shorten the road is to have your fill of suffering," he murmurs. "'Tis only a disappointed man will want to leave go of the world."

There is a finality in his voice that makes me feel even worse. I turn my head to the chimney so that he will not see me cry.

"You didn't see Christy at all?" he wants to know.

"I did."

He starts to speak and then checks himself, as though he doesn't know what he wants to say. I realize that he misses her too.

"She doesn't have any heart for the stories, Granda, with her mother that way."

He nods solemnly, as though I have said something profound. But somehow knowing that he feels the same as I do only makes me feel worse.

"Did you have bite or sup?" he says.

I shake my head.

"There's bread and cheese on the counter."

"I'm not hungry."

"Have some milk then, let you."

Stifling a sob, I get up and pour milk into a cup. His concern cheers me a little. I take a piece of bread as I pass the dresser. I feel him watching me as I eat.

"What's the matter, boyeen?"

"I'm lonesome."

He leans toward me and grips my knee stiffly with the bony fingers of his good hand. Then he straightens up against the chimney with a sigh.

"I suppose this is a lonesome place after Dublin," he says. "I don't know what they were thinking of at all, sending you to me."

"I don't like Dublin," I say vehemently. "I don't want to go back there."

"What do you want so?"

The crisis of tears is past. Dry eyed, I try to think about this, as though if I can answer he will grant my wish. I want to go away from here. I want to have a proper home and a family. But I cannot tell that to the old man.

"I want — not to be lonesome."

"Sure it's an odd heart that is never lonesome," he says gruffly.

Abruptly he gets up and stumps over to the stairs. I want to ask him what is the matter, but I am a little afraid of him and I let him be. I hear his footsteps overhead, the creak of the bed, and presently a series of deep rasping sighs, as though he is trying to expel something from his lungs. Then he is quiet.

I sit on the settle until there is no more warmth in the fire. Then I go upstairs and climb into bed in my clothes. But I cannot rest. The moon rises, near to full, and I follow the outline of the window frame as it crawls upon the floor. From below, the scratching of Finn's paws upon the flags and the lapping sound as he drinks from his water bowl. From without, an occasional squall of wind. When I try to close my eyes I have the impression of moving at speed. The night races past me silently; collision threatens at every moment.

I get up, wrap a blanket around my shoulders, and sit on the floor in front of the low gable window, looking out upon the moonlit sea, clasping the blanket tightly around me to keep from shivering. The Skelligs are like scraps of cutout cardboard pasted on the immense horizon, their shiplike shapes leaning into invisible waves. To think that the monks lived there, fed and sheltered themselves, survived the seas of winter and the Viking raids! And before that — thousands of years before the monks — the ancestors of all the people of Ireland made landfall there, buried their dead there so as not to carry a sickness into the Inish, gave Ireland its name: Eire. I murmur their strange names the old man has taught me: Amargin, Eremon,

Eber, Donn. They could be out there on the Skelligs tonight, by the look of the place. Maybe they still live beneath the earth, like the Danann or the Shee, and come out only by night. That is the Other World, the underworld, the world of the dead, as close to ours as the image in the mirror, as the vein in your neck, so Granda says.

I clench my teeth to keep them from chattering and stare out at those unearthly rocks, as though by dint of staring I will see — what? Something that will scare the life out of me? I am no longer afraid. My loneliness has withdrawn to a great distance, and I feel myself filled with a strange calm, as though with a clear cold liquid. Skellig of the Specters: it *is* the Other World, but close, so close now, in the livid and ghostly light of the moon, that there is really nothing to be afraid of. I feel myself drawn to it, drawn out of my body almost, longing to be one with it, to know it — and to leave death and separation behind.

I sit looking out, watchful, immobile, until the moon is down and the peaks of the Skelligs are merged with the night.

Low tide and the channel as flat as a sheet of glass. I spend a long evening scalloping on the strand, stooping and kneeling in the mud until the light fails and the tide comes in. Then I walk to the Foot, dragging the dead weight of the scallops after me in an old sack, and deliver my catch to the hotel. It's dark by the time I get back to the house.

When I come in, my mother is standing by the hearth. She is holding a dark-haired little boy by the hand. She looks as though she would like to sit down but there is nowhere for her to sit that would not soil her clothes. There is something different about her appearance that I cannot put my finger on. Her features appear blurred. But she gives me the same pleading and distracted look that she wore on the platform at Amiens Street, before the train pulled away.

"Matthew?" she says, as though she's not quite sure it's me. "This is your little brother Brendan."

I hesitate for a moment, and then I walk to the back door, where I rinse some of the mud off my hands in a saucepan of rainwater. I am shaken to find her here, but I feel obliged to behave as though it's the most natural thing in the world. I look around for the old man. He is in the shop, bent over his leathers. He does not look up.

Finn lumbers in and rushes up to Brendan. He sideswipes him with his large wet flank before my mother can intervene. My little brother tumbles on the dusty hearth and commences to wail. Finn noses about him, tail lashing eagerly. My mother scoops him up. He buries his face in her shoulder and continues to cry loudly.

"Can you put the dog out?" she says to my grandfather.

He continues to work without looking up. Her eyes turn helplessly to me. Before I know what I am doing, I have grabbed Finn around the neck and led him to the door. He thinks it is a game and squirms joyfully. I close the door upon his quizzical expectant look.

"He's been dying to see you," my mother informs me. "Say hello, Brendan."

He steals a look at me and cries louder. The imperative note in his crying irritates me. I stand by the door, wanting to ignore them, but unable to. I envy the old man, who seems oblivious to everything.

"Little lamb," my mother murmurs, as though to herself. "My own little lamb."

Brendan stops crying. My mother's attention returns to me. She looks me up and down, her face assumes its harried look. I realize that I am barefoot and covered from head to toe with the slime of the strand.

"I suppose you have him scalloping at all hours of the day and night," she says to my grandfather.

It is more of a remark than a complaint, an attempt to open communication. My grandfather's hands are hidden behind the counter, and from where I am standing I cannot see what he is working on. He bends his head further to examine his work.

"'Tis himself wants to be out after the scallops," he says, without looking up. "I have no *grá* for them at all, nor for any creature come out of a shell. They're dirty things, is what I say."

"You don't want to be like those ragamuffins from the Foot," my mother says plaintively, "thrown out of the house every day at the crack of dawn and gallivanting around the island until dark. It's a wonder they don't come to harm, the way they're allowed to carry on."

I stand without speaking, frozen into my body, my face burning. The truth is that I would give much to be like those ragamuffins, the children I go to school with. But they have perceived too that I am not one of them. My absence in Dublin must be to blame. And my mother's poor opinion of them, which they are well aware of.

"It's all my fault," my mother says. "I knew I should have found someone else to look after you, Daddy. You've let him run wild."

"Yerrah, there's no fear of him," the old man intones calmly. "No flies on him at all. He takes the scallops above to the hotel there and sells them to old Shanahan and hides the few shillings he gets in an old tin upstairs. Old Moneybags, I call him, he's that careful of his threepenny bits and his tanners."

My mother turns to me, grasping the sniffling Brendan in her arms. She looks as though I have done her a mortal injury.

"Why do you want to have anything to do with that fellow Shanahan? I wouldn't be under an obligation to him for the world, with the type of people that stay in his hotel. And what do you need to sell scallops for? Shanahan is probably telling the whole village that we're no better than paupers. Isn't the money I send you enough for you?"

"Faith and that goes into the tin too," the old man says. "It's all grist to his mill. He must be saving up to build the bridge for us, so we won't have to take the ferry anymore."

I feel humiliated and betrayed, beset on two sides. Next they'll be telling me that I haven't looked after Granda.

"Does he go to mass and the sacraments?" my mother asks.

She is determined to know the worst. My heart is beating wildly. The old man's face assumes a canny secretive look. "Is it me that could take him, that can hardly get as far as the outhouse there?"

"Couldn't you get Peg or Con — or someone?"

He sniffs contemptuously, as though my mother ought to know that there is no question of him asking Peg or Con to do anything. He still has not looked at her: he keeps his eyes fixed on his work. It is as though he is talking to someone on the other side of a door.

"He goes away on out anyway, wherever he goes," he tells her. "He could be walking the heights of Crom, for all I know. But I suppose he knows to do what his mother tells him as well as the gorsoons at the Foot."

I am furious with the old man. He has justified himself, while obliging me to lie.

"You go to mass like a good boy, don't you, Matthew?" my mother pleads.

They can both go to the devil, I think blasphemously. If I am damned, it is their fault. Why is she asking me anyway? She knows I don't go.

"I haven't gone to mass since I went in Dublin."

My mother stares at me. Then she gives a start, utters a little exclamation, and to my horror her face crumbles and she begins to cry. She sets Brendan down in the ashes, reaches behind her for the settle, and rummages in her handbag, sobbing jerkily.

"God help us," she mutters, in a broken voice. "Where did we get you at all?"

The old man continues to work and pays no attention to her. Brendan wanders aimlessly for a moment, then buries his face in her shoulder and sets up a wail. She ceases to cry abruptly, gathers him in her arms, and rocks him until he is quiet. Then she glances quickly at each of us in turn.

"I wouldn't doubt you anyway, Daddy," she says with a pathetic gaiety.

"What did you think when you sent him here?" the old man says deliberately. "That I'd school him in the catechism and the rosary and the stations of the cross? That I'd be at him to do things I have no time for myself?"

"You'd think the teacher would have said something to him," my mother persists. "Or the priest."

"The teacher minds his own business like the quiet private man he is. And there hasn't been a priest next or near this house since Alice passed away." He puts some vehemence into this assertion, and my mother grimaces unhappily.

"It's a sin," she says. "Three years without mass or the sacraments.

I'm sure it gave the old ones below in the Foot plenty to talk about — and to think that no one would do anything about it! But it's all my fault."

I am afraid she is going to cry again, but she shrugs and rises from the settle.

"There's no use crying over spilt milk," she says. "I was telling your grandfather before you came in. Jack and I are going to London."

All of a sudden I feel the cold of the flags rising through the soles of my feet, mounting in my legs, filling my body.

"And Brendan," my mother adds with affected cheeriness. She shifts him in her arms with a playful toss of her head. "And Teresa your little sister. We came to get you."

I want to fly, but I cannot move. I am cornered. I glance at the old man. He is still bent over his work. He has abandoned me.

"Jack has a new job," she announces. "We'll have a nice house. We'll be a family again. With a new baby brother or sister. An English baby it'll be, God help us."

She flushes as she says this, and I realize what is different about her appearance. She has come to get me. I am to leave the Inish. For an instant I feel a surge of excitement — and then I remember that house on the Canal, my stepfather, the Brothers. To live with them in London, with Brendan and my little sister Teresa — and another baby. It is a family all right, but it isn't really mine. I don't believe that she wants me to come anyway. I think she's only saying it.

"It's too much for you to have to look after Grandad all on your own here," she says. "I should never have sent you in the first place. Peg will come. She'll be able for it, if anyone is."

She sounds impatient. She's annoyed because I won't answer her. She turns to the old man. "You'll be better off with Peg here, Daddy. It's the house she grew up in. She'd rather end her days here on the island than with her daughter."

The old man does not move a muscle. His voice seems to come effortlessly out of the air. "She'll not come into this house until I'm ready to be carried out of it."

My mother sighs shortly.

"I'm not going to argue with you. The two of you are a disgrace the way you carry on with each other. Why don't you let bygones be bygones? You'll have to have someone come in — unless you want to go to the Infirmary above in Caher."

The old man lets out a dry chuckle.

"I am an old man," he tells her. "I don't have to do anything. I'll please myself from here on out."

"It's news to me if you ever did anything else!" my mother retorts.

She turns her back on him and faces me. "You're not going to stay here and turn out a ne'er-do-well like Pat-Joe Duggan, are you, Matthew?"

What choice do I have? I'll have to go with her if she says so. I had to go to Granda's house when she told me to. But I will not speak to her. I will not say yes.

"Don't you want to make something of yourself, Matthew?" she pleads. "Don't you want to make Jack and me proud of you? Don't you want to grow up to have a good job and a nice place to live, instead of this —" She gestures vaguely at the hearth with her free hand. Brendan stirs, and she strokes his hair.

"Brendan says he wants to be an altar boy when he's old enough," she tells me. "You could be an altar boy too if you wanted to. You're not too old."

An altar boy! This is too much for me. "I'd rather be a corner boy!" I shout tearfully.

My mother takes a step backward, her eyes widening.

"A corner boy," she flings at me. "That's you all over, and you'll never be anything else! Whether you come to London or you stay here, it makes no difference."

"I don't want to go!" I shout, beside myself.

"Go on, let you," the old man says. "Now is your chance. Sure what is there here?"

"No!"

A terrible silence falls. I cannot look at either of them. I have done something irreparable. It was not my fault, but that doesn't matter. I'm to blame for it just the same.

"Suit yourself," my mother tells me in a tired voice. "You're always the same. If there was ever something a body wanted you to do, you had to go and do the opposite."

It must be true. There is something wrong with me. That was why she sent me away. And there is no help for it. I have a lump in my throat, and I am biting my lip to try to hold back my sobs. Then I look at her, and I see that she is crying herself.

"I tried to do my best for you, Matthew," she weeps. "It was so hard after your poor father passed away. I didn't know what to do. It was your friends were a bad influence on you. It was the likes of Pat-Joe Duggan. I should have asked the priest to speak to you. I should have sent you away. But I could hardly afford to put food on the table with your father's insurance money, not to mind send you to boarding school."

I listen to this dry eyed. Her imaginings have so little to do with my life that for a moment I feel stronger than she, capable of opposing her will.

"I never wanted anything but to make a proper home for you," she tells me tearfully. "God knows it's true. That's why I went to Dublin with Jack. How could we have any sort of a life in this place? I never meant to send you back. But you were so bold in Dublin, with your back answers to Jack. Still, I thought it'd be only for a little while. It wasn't my fault that Jack never took to you —"

She presses the back of her hand against her mouth and shuts her eyes, while her shoulders shake silently.

"Go on away, boyeen," says the old man gently. "I have a crow to pluck with your mother."

I spring to the door and step outside, closing it swiftly behind me.

"Matthew!" my mother calls in a cracked and husky voice.

"Let him stop there awhile," I hear the old man say. "'Tis to the dog he's going."

Finn is beside me at once. I kneel down to him, and he thrusts his wet nose into my hand. Blindly I burrow the crown of my head into his flank, and he squirms away, trying to lick my face. I get up and run to the seawall. He follows, bounding with excitement. I get down onto the strand and walk quickly away from the house.

It is twilight, but not cold, hardly a puff of wind. As I walk I stoop to pick up thin pieces of slate and skim them upon the flat surface of the tide. Finn follows each stone into the water, up to his shoulders, barking. Then he turns back, shakes himself dry, and scurries ahead of me. I am glad of his company. I want to walk until it is dark, until I have exhausted myself, until I am too tired to think of anything. I do not want to go with my mother. I do not want to go back to my grandfather. I do not want anything.

It happens all of a sudden. At one moment Finn is beside me on the strand, shaking himself all over me; then he is in the water again, swimming away from me, his black head thrusting eagerly, the muscles of his shoulders working as he paddles with his legs.

I whistle and call. He keeps on going, as though drawn by something I cannot see.

"Finn! Come back here! Finn! Hi!"

Fear tightening a knot in my stomach. Finn is a great swimmer. But if he has a fit while in the water, he will drown. So Granda has told me. And it will be my fault for letting him go.

The wake of his progress divides upon the tide. He is still swimming away from me for all he is worth. I wade into the cold water, up to my waist, my armpits. I shout after him. My voice floats out over the channel, blaring shamefully in the stillness of the evening.

No use. His head becomes a black dot; it disappears in the gloom of the channel. I cannot find it through a mist of tears. I stumble up the strand and scan the water again. I have lost him.

"Matthew!" my mother calls faintly. "We're going. Come say good-bye to Brendan."

I hunker down on the shingle, out of sight of the house. She calls again more faintly. Then silence. Darkness thickens around me, like smoke emanating from the ground. I hold my breath, the better to hear, but there is not the faintest sound, not even a movement of the tide upon the strand. Has he stopped swimming? The thought of it terrifies me: he is alone out there in the dark, with the depth of the channel beneath him, not knowing his way home.

I sit until it is completely dark, straining my ears for the sound of paddling feet. My wet clothes seem to be growing heavier and colder.

The strand is unnaturally still. I am waiting for the moon to rise, so that I can see the channel again. But the night must be overcast: there is no moon. I try to imagine Finn, his sleek wet body emerging from the water, the fan of spray as he shakes himself, the wet dog-smell of him — as if by wishing I can bring him back. He does not come. I will never see him again. I will never see my mother again: she has gone away. I will have to go away myself and leave the old man. I cannot face him with the news that I have left Finn drown.

A frantic pattering upon stones, panting, a shape blacker than the night rushes upon me. I grab Finn around the neck and hold him until he is quiet. I bury my face in his sopping fur and cry in little whimpers that sound strange and alien in my ears. Finn squirms free, shakes himself and drenches me anew, returns to me. I hold on to him for dear life, shivering, my teeth clenched to keep them from chattering.

"Old Finn," I try to tell him. But I have no voice, save a whisper. My throat is on fire after all my shouting after him.

Suddenly the road ahead is lit up, the blackness pierced by darting lights. I slow down and pass an accident, a litter of glass, a jeep with a shattered windscreen facing the wrong way, a Honda with its passenger door sheared away, all in the brilliant glare of an unnatural light brighter than that of day. And in the corner of my eye as I go past, I see someone lying in the road, attended by kneeling figures who cast long long shadows, as though on a backlit stage.

Flickers of fear arise and subside. I accelerate, grateful for darkness, for soundness of limb, for breath of life. In the rearview mirror the bright scene of the tragedy folds in upon itself, wavers, and is gone.

To the Cape

IS THERE SOMETHING in me that drives people away? This thought strikes me like a blow, on Massachusetts Avenue, in Cambridge. I am only a couple of blocks from my apartment, but for the moment I am stunned, I feel that I cannot take another step, some help must come to me now, this instant, or I will give way here in the street, under the sheer weight of my misery.

My distracted gaze alights on the sign: OLD CAMBRIDGE BAPTIST CHURCH. It is a stone edifice, which reassures me. What refuge can be found within a church made of wood? I hurry down a narrow path toward the door. In the porch there's a notice board cluttered with colored posters. I step inside: a low drab vestibule; a smell of cooking emanating from a stairwell. The odor of sanctity is distinctly lacking. But I am relieved to be off the street. The moment has passed, though I am aware that I am still holding something at bay. To my amazement and confusion, a long-forgotten invocation comes to me: *Jesus mercy, Mary help.*

I go down a corridor and pass through a wooden door marked SANCTUARY. The interior is high and vaulted, with tall stained-glass windows. But the dusty wooden floor is bare, save for some scattered folding chairs — and instead of an altar there is a stage.

Some tentative hope is crushed by this discovery, and fear takes its place again. I am in need of sanctuary. But the world and its concerns permeate this place. The stained glass has a purely geometric pattern: no images of Christ or the saints. Instead of candles and flowers, a mop and broom in a corner, children's toys scattered about the stage, faded backdrops. Sacred and profane cheek by jowl, the church and the playhouse. But somehow I feel I have only myself to blame. What sanctuary can there be for the renegade?

I sit on one of the chairs, for want of knowing what to do. I have the place to myself. I have the whole of the New World to myself: save for Lily and Rick and my roommate Jamie, whom I never see, there is not a single person in all this vast continent who knows my name. The thought suddenly frightens me. On the Inish I knew everyone — and no one. Everyone knew me, and no one had the slightest idea who I was. But there is comfort in an identity, even if it is a false one. I feel threatened with extinction as I sit here. So this is the loneliness of the New World, the other face of the anonymity I sought in coming here. Or is it *uaigneas* in an urban guise, the dead hand of Ireland reaching across the Atlantic to blight my puny hopes? Or simply this: I cannot bear my life without Lily.

But it is no wonder she has given up on me. This demand of hers, this insistence on introspection, has always existed between us, like a bad debt, and now she has come to press for it. But you cannot dun a man with empty pockets. I am not equal to it, I do not have it in me to give her what she needs, and so she has cast me off like a crooked penny. And I could not be more completely alone.

I raise my eyes again to the high windows. The light they admit is bland and unsanctified. But what is it that you want, Matty? The consolations of religion are denied me; my mother and grandfather between them made sure of that. How then to acknowledge the mysterious, the ineffable, that which determines fate? I want to sit on top of the Head and look out at the Skelligs. But I have ceased to acknowledge the existence of that Other World — or anything outside of myself that can help or console.

Someone enters behind me and crosses the floor, footsteps clattering irreverently on the bare boards. Hastily, I get up, as though caught in the act, and turn to leave. A man is standing by the stage, making a pile of the toys. As I pass him, he turns to me a bored face, devoid of greeting or acknowledgment. But it is Jack's face I see in his surly features — Jack, my mother's husband, my putative stepfather who did not take to me, who was not sorry to see me go back to the Inish, who did not even come to the station to see me off. And I remember in an instant the expectations I had of Dublin before we moved there — and the longing for the Inish with which they were replaced.

In a daze of pain I push the door, walk back down the corridor, and step out into the porch. The noise of the street rushes at me. I turn my back on the church and walk down the path. So much for that. How can I bear it, the empty day, my need, my lack of aim or plan — that Lily calls hopelessness?

I remember my car, and against all sense and reason my spirits are suddenly lifted. The Monster is my sanctuary. Therein lies my hope.

It's already dark when I get to the dealership where Rick works, and I manage to park outside the showroom. The lights are out, save for a glimmer from the offices in back. But Rick has left a door unlocked for me. I walk across the darkened floor, skirting the sleek shapes of the cars, my feet making no sound on the carpet. As I pass, the bodywork catches and distorts a gleam from the streetlights. It is strange to be here at night, as though among the discarded carapaces of some long-extinct creatures, frozen into beauty by the passage of aeons.

A crack of light issues from Rick's door. He's at his desk. He puts down the phone as I enter and rushes around the desk to shake my hand.

"Did you make the sale?" I say.

"You bet," he says, grinning hugely. "My third this week! So how're you doing?"

"I'm OK."

Or at least not quite as wretched as I was before he called. He was concerned about me, wanted to know why I hadn't seen Lily. I told him it was a long story; he insisted on hearing it, as soon as he'd nailed down his sale. I'm grateful for his call. He has saved me from another gloomy evening.

"I'm taking you out to dinner, Matty. To celebrate my best week since I started in this business. Then we'll have a serious talk, man to man. Love and work, Freud said. We've got to straighten out your love life and your work life. But first, a little drink."

He indicates a chair, and I sit while he extracts a bottle and two glasses from the drawer of a filing cabinet. In spite of myself, his company cheers me. Rick has an incorrigibly positive attitude toward intractable problems. Although I'm afraid this facile New World positivism may deprive my predicament of its significance, for tonight at least I'm willing to play along.

Rick pours from a dark bottle into an enormous brandy snifter.

"Fine old Armagnac," he says, handing it to me. "Fifty bucks a bottle. You can really tell."

I have never drunk Armagnac, and I take almost half the contents of the glass into my mouth. It is sweet and fiery at once, and I swallow it down recklessly. I am in need of what comfort it can give. Rick pours a generous measure for himself, loosens his tie, settles into his chair, and props his feet on the desk.

"Why don't you just call her?" he says.

"She doesn't want to hear from me," I mutter gloomily.

"That's not what she told me."

"She said she feels better when she's not with me. She thinks I'm depressed, and she doesn't want me to call her again until I get over it."

"So what?" Rick says lightly, swirling the amber liquid in his glass and bringing the rim to his nose. "She's going to tell you what she wants, not what she's willing to settle for. That's the way the game is played."

"How can you call it a game? It's so cold-blooded, so calculating. I can't just go to Lily with a list of what I need from her —"

"Why not?"

I'm stymied. This is a novel way of looking at things, a possibility that hadn't occurred to me.

"Besides, I can't give her what she needs," I say. "I don't have anything to offer. She wants to feel close to me, and she says I'm keeping her at arm's length."

"That's what women are like," Rick says. "They want you to put your cards on the table, but they're willing to play even if you don't. Call it a dialogue if it makes you feel any better about it. You're going to sit down and talk it over. And then you'll do a little horse trading."

I sit there, placated by his reasonable tone, incapable of discovering my objections. I only know that the Armagnac tastes as good as any spirits I have ever had. I drain my glass with a clumsy flourish, and Rick immediately replenishes it.

"You'll work it out, Matty. You've just got to get over the idea that there's something wrong with making a deal."

Suddenly I remember my last tête-à-tête with Lily in Chinatown, her sincerity, her conviction. I cannot bargain with her, or treat her as an opponent. Besides, she is right about me: I'm not fit company for a corpse.

"It's no use. We've already talked about it, and she gave me an ultimatum. You know Lily. She won't back down."

"I've known her since the sixth grade! She knows what she wants, but she's a reasonable human being. Don't be afraid of her. You've got to say, What do *I* want out of this situation? Right? You've got to have a plan."

My heart sinks at this news. This is my weakness, my fatal flaw, the impediment to my success in the New World. I do not have a plan.

"I wish I did, Rick. It seems to me I had a plan when I lived with my grandfather on the Inish — to get out of there by hook or by crook. But as soon as I got to college in Dublin, things started to go wrong. I had a stroke of luck when I met Lily. I never expected to meet anyone like her, much less to spend the rest of my life with her. In a way, it was too good to be true. Now I just sit around my apartment all day. It's beginning to scare me. The only time I'm happy is when I'm driving my car."

Rick drains his glass, pours again, leans toward me across the desk.

"Yeah, I know what you mean," he says sympathetically. "I've been there too. You're seeing me at my peak. But it wasn't so long ago I was going nowhere fast, driving a cab for a living, hardly making enough to pay for the medallion, sleeping until noon every day — and if I opened the fridge on Sunday and there was no beer, I'd drive three hours to New Hampshire and back just to buy a six-pack. Ask Lily; she really helped me figure it out. Had to hit bottom first though."

He grins, and his eyebrows rise incredulously. It's hard for me to imagine Rick driving a cab. He seems to belong behind the wheel of that white Infiniti. But I am grateful to be taken into his confidence.

"Come on," Rick says, coming around the desk. "I want to show you something. Bring your drink."

He opens the door and moves white-shirted among the cars. I am suddenly struck by the outrageous extravagance of America, in which there can exist a veritable supermarket of cars, each one with a price tag that would buy you a couple of houses on the Inish. Rick stops by one, stoops to glance inside, then swiftly opens driver and passenger doors.

"This is the model up from mine," he informs me. "Probably be my next car."

Hand on my shoulder, he ushers me into the passenger seat. He closes the door, walks around the car, and sits in beside me.

"Mr. Quigley," he commences. "Now what will it take to get you into the driver's seat of this car?"

I open my mouth to protest, but he raises an admonitory finger.

"Let me show you some of the features, Mr. Quigley."

He turns the key in the ignition. The engine starts up, then subsides to a whisper. There is not the faintest tremor to indicate that it is running. Rick turns on the parking lights. They create a halo of light on the wall in front of us and illuminate the instrument panel, which casts a Mephistophelian glow upon his features. The interior is permeated with the opulent fumes of the Armagnac. I am a little drunk, mesmerized by the dials and pointers of the panel, my body cradled by the cannily sculpted contours of the seat.

"Leather seat covers," Rick assures me. "Feel them. That's optional, of course, but nice. Six independent seat adjustments. Count 'em, six! Heater inside the cushion on the driver's side to warm up your tush on a cold morning. Fantastic AC, absolutely frigid. Separate front and rear controls, automatic settings, temperature display. Stereo CD or cassette player; not a luxury, if you ask me. Keyless entry. A frill, but hey, it's part of the package. Light group; overhead stays on until you insert the key in the ignition. Power doors and windows, goes without saying. All doors lock automatically when your speed reaches fifteen miles-per-hour: good security feature, especially if you're in a bad neighborhood. Believe me, this car has a mind of its own."

I run my hand along the seat. It has the feel and texture of flesh. I lean back against the headrest and close my eyes. The glass is round and warm in my hands, and I am floating, insulated from all discomfort and threat.

"I know you don't care about the specs," Rick says. "But this car gets from zero to sixty faster than anything else in its class. You're driving around in a dinosaur right now. It's the difference between night and day."

This gratuitous insult to the Monster rouses me. I sit forward again, shake my head. I feel a little nauseous. I have had too much to drink.

"I'm glad you called, Rick. I feel a lot better. But I can't believe you're serious about selling me a car. I don't even have a job."

"That's the next thing I want to talk to you about. I know the manager in the Burlington dealership. He's looking for a floor salesman, strictly commission. That means you have to sell cars. But don't worry; you'll knock 'em dead, with some pointers from yours truly. All you've got to do is to show up wearing a suit and tie. And don't bother to mention your college career. You're overqualified for the job; that's your only problem."

"I don't even *have* a suit and tie," I protest.

Rick reaches into the backseat and tosses a package into my lap.

"A suit that's just a tad too small for me. I've only worn it twice. A couple of shirts, one dress, one casual. Go on; take a look."

I draw out a suit jacket with wide lapels, light gray with a white pinstripe, and a silk shirt, a subtle watery green in the overhead.

"You can wear it to work," Rick says. "But it will really look fantastic on a date."

A date? I see myself as Rick, stepping out of a white Infiniti, immaculately suited. The woman's evening gown is black, tight, slit to the thigh. She is tall, curvaceous, suntanned. I do not see her face. But it is not Lily's.

"Thanks," I say. "I appreciate it. But —"

"They'll probably give you a deal on one of last year's floor models," Rick interjects. "And you'll be on your way: job, car, apartment. But you don't have to tell me right now. Think it over, OK? There's something else I want to run by you."

He snaps off the lights, turns off the engine, but remains sitting beside me. It is eerily quiet now, without the faint purr of the engine. Cars pass soundlessly in the street, as though in a silent film.

I cannot see myself selling cars. But I need to listen to Rick's propositions. Can I put on his knowledge with his clothes? Perhaps his example will magically rejuvenate my scattered will.

"Why don't you go out with Erica?" Rick comes out with. "She likes you. She was saying the other night she'd like to get to know you."

"Isn't she your girlfriend?"

"This is true," Rick says with a grin. "But hey, it's a free country. Now Erica and I have a deal. We're committed to having fun together — but we still go out with other people every once in a while."

He makes it sound like it's the most natural thing in the world! Suddenly I realize that Erica is the woman in the sleek black gown. Her blond hair falls to her bare shoulders, and there are diamonds at her throat. Rick has told me that her family is well off. I've only met her a couple of times — at Rick's apartment — but I would have to be a blind man not to want to get in bed with her, and I am amazed to think that it is possible. She's nervy, high-strung, hardly introspective. But an American beauty — who is interested in *me!* I feel a rush of excitement.

Rick grins sheepishly and passes his hand over his carefully barbered hair. "Let me come clean about this," he says. "This woman I just sold a car to; she's got class. Sat down and wrote out a check — for thirty thousand bucks! Didn't bat an eyelid. I felt like she was coming on to me a little, so I asked her for a date. I can't believe I actually did it. She's a little out of my league, a stockbroker, works for a big New York house, got an apartment in Manhattan. Ricardo Cozzolino from Medfo'd, hobnobbing with a New York broker!"

He stops and looks at me. "You're not shocked by all of this stuff, are you? I mean, it's probably not what you're used to."

His worried expression makes me laugh.

"Knowing you has been an education, Rick."

He chuckles, drains his glass.

"I'll turn you into a man-about-town before I'm through," he assures me. "Now listen: everything is aboveboard. Erica is cool. But it would make it a lot easier if she had something going on too. You know what I'm saying?"

I nod sagely.

"So here's the deal," he says. "I have a date with this woman next weekend. I fix you up with Erica for the same night."

"You mean a double date?"

"Ha, ha!" Rick gasps, slapping my shoulder. "You're a card, Matty. Wouldn't that be fun! No, I go out with this woman, you go out with Erica. If you guys hit it off together, we can just take it from there. What do you say?"

I take a breath to say, Sure — and then I stop myself. What am I getting myself into? What about Lily?

"What have you got to lose?" Rick says, as though reading my mind. "You're not seeing Lily, you don't have anything else to do, and you're lonely."

"What are you going to tell Erica?"

"I'm going to say, I told Matt you were interested in getting to know him and he'd like to get together with you. That's it. She won't think you're head over heels in love with her, if that's what you're worried about."

I am in love with Lily. But everything has become complicated, obscure. I cannot give her what she wants. I have not been able to meet the obligations of love. But this would not be love.

"You don't *have* to," Rick says, frowning.

The truth is that I *do* have to! I'm a desperate man. I cannot spend another night alone in my apartment, trying to infer the rules of baseball from the arcane patter of the TV announcers. How can I refuse a woman like Erica? This is a chance of a lifetime.

"I want to," I hear myself say.

"Great! Erica's been a little depressed lately herself. But you guys will cheer each other right up."

Rick takes the glasses back to his office, locks up, and together we walk to his car. He refuses to ride in the Monster, which irritates me a little. But tonight I am grateful to him for — everything. I still feel a little shaky, like a man who has narrowly avoided an accident. But the prospect of Erica, wanton, long-legged beauty, hovers before me in the night, investing the darkened street with mystery, making my flesh tingle.

"This woman gave me a stock tip," Rich says. "I asked Lily to lend me some money, so I could buy in. I'm kind of miffed at her for refusing. But I have another source. Wish me luck. If this pans out, I might be moving up, to the next model, the next level. Who knows? Stick around. Someday I'll be coming by your house to pick you up in a Bentley."

We're standing on either side of his car. He leans on the roof, twirling his keys, pensive. "But there's many a slip," he murmurs. "It's a high-stakes game. Listen, Matty, if it doesn't work out, we can always take a trip together. You'd be up for that, wouldn't you?"

"Where would we go?"

"We could swing through the Southwest. I have some friends in Paris, Texas — and in Taos, New Mexico. We could go through the badlands, the desert. That's really something if you've never seen it."

Visions of the desert of New Mexico unfolding on either side of the Monster's elongated hood, the grotesque shapes of cacti, strange purple skies, flat-topped mountains streaming by in the haze. The road to Nowhere.

"I'd like to," I say.

But these visions fade, giving place to that of Erica. Her figure merges with the sensuous lines of the cars in Rick's showroom. Her boudoir is lit by the discreet light that emanates from the instrument panel. Her perfume is the clean scent of soft new leather. She is what I need, my assurance of success.

Can it really be that this blond goddess of the New World will take to the likes of Matthew Quigley? I have Rick's word for it. I do not want to go anywhere. For now, all roads lead to Erica.

The Toyota pulls onto the pavement opposite, and Erica slips out, blond hair gleaming in the early slanting sun. She crosses the street, checking for traffic with quick darts of her head. She looks like a thoroughbred racehorse, with her almost impossibly slender and fragile limbs. I've been watching for her for the past half hour.

The doorbell rings below. I press the release and hear her rapid footsteps resounding in the stairwell. I try to breathe deeply while she ascends — I'm nervous as a cat. She is taking me to the Cape, where her family has a house. My agitation when she phoned made it hard for me to listen, but I seem to remember her saying that the house is empty and that we can stay over if we wish.

"Hi," she says brightly.

She's wearing a brilliantly white blouse with a wide collar, like a peasant's smock, and a pair of spotless denim jeans that fit her to perfection. There is nothing of the peasant about her, even in jeans. Her hair is piled elegantly on top of her head, giving her an extra inch of stature, and the tiny unobtrusive studs in her earlobes have the look of diamonds.

"Nice apartment," she says, though all she can see of it is the hallway. "You ready?"

I gesture toward the door and wait for her to precede me.

"I'm planning to go in the ocean, if it's not too cold," she says. "You might want to bring a suit."

"I'll just sit on the beach and watch you swim."

This is not what I mean to say, and it embarrasses me. She shrugs and turns away. I follow her down the stairs and out into the street. She is about to cross to her car.

"Do you want to ride in *my* car?" I say, indicating the Monster.

Her face betrays her anxiety. I suppose she thinks that this old crock won't make it to the Cape and back. But I don't want to ride in her Toyota. I cannot allow myself to be separated from my only source of security.

Erica shrugs and tosses her head. "Let me go get my stuff."

I watch her in the rearview mirror as she crosses the street, carrying a shoulder bag. She slides in beside me.

"Where the hell did you get this thing?" She giggles.

The Green Monster has broken the ice! I am intoxicated by her smile, which relieves the severity of her deeply tanned face, her high, aristocratic cheekbones. I believe she likes me. My confidence is magically restored.

"A fellow sold it to me for three hundred dollars. He said he'd give me my money back if anything serious went wrong with it."

She shakes her head, as though such arrangements are not part of her experience. I pull into traffic and point the Monster's regal bonnet — must I call it a hood? — down Broadway. We roll as smoothly, as whisper-quietly as any Bentley.

Erica is struggling with her seat belt. She doesn't know that you have to draw the belt out in one continuous movement and hook the shoulder strap before it will engage. The Monster was built before mandatory seat belts, and this system is something of an afterthought.

At a traffic light I lean across her and fetch the troublesome shoulder strap. She smells of sun and perfumed soap. I reach into the seat to find her buckle and touch her hip as I do so.

"Thank you," she murmurs.

Her voice makes my stomach turn over. It's low and husky, a little stagy — but definitely friendly. Elated, I step on the gas. The Monster responds like a flying bomb. What joy! A car, a woman, and the road to the beach. Now *this* is America!

I weave my way through the columns of the T at Lechmere, fly past the spire and dome of the Science Museum, and skirt the Charles River Dam. In a moment we are zooming up the expressway ramp with the Garden rising in front of us like the Great Wall of China. To the left, the skyway stalks over the streets like a many-footed beast toward the great hump of the Mystic. I feel myself imbued with power and choice, clad in the bright metallic armor of the New World, in hot pursuit of happiness with this American beauty beside me. Here in the heart of the city, at the confluence of asphalt rivers, borne up by the strength of great hoary girders, I am no longer lost and alone.

"It's about two hours to the Cape," Erica informs me. "I can probably drive for a little if you get tired."

"I love to drive."

I round the corner and ease into the southbound traffic. To my left, glimpsed between the buildings, a pale sea-bedabbled sky; to the right, rooftops and attics; ahead, the towers of the Financial District. I remember Sam and his office, and my speed involuntarily slackens. Is he prancing back and forth across the empty floor, belting a tennis ball against the wall? I liked Sam. Will I ever see him again? What will Lily say if he asks about me?

Without warning the lanes curve and fall away and we dive into the earth with a hundred fleeing beasts whose baying rebounds from the walls and rages in our ears so that we are deaf and dumb in this tunnel of babel until as quickly we emerge into the light and lo! the city has vanished and we fly over the rooftops unfettered.

But the thought of Lily casts a shadow across the bright roadway and the gleaming river of cars. Perhaps I *will* visit Sam and play tennis. We have something in common, the two of us: we have failed to make Lily happy.

"Have you ever driven on the expressway before?" Erica wonders.

Is my driving making her nervous? It's hard for me to talk and drive at the same time. But we are strangers. We need to get to know each other.

"What do you do for a living, Erica?"

"I work with horses at a stable in Lincoln," she says eagerly. "We give riding lessons. I'm not a riding instructor, although I love to ride. I give the horses a rubdown after they've been ridden, make sure they've got feed and water, clean out their stalls. It's not a full-time job, but I'm there just about every day. I love to be around horses. Probably more than I like to be with people," she finishes with a nervous laugh.

While I consider my response, the sea appears on our left, the darkest blue. A cluster of red-brick buildings on a little peninsula spins past, like a latter-day fortress. Two massive gas tanks, crazily daubed. Erica slides down a little in her seat, propping her knees against the glove compartment. I have the strange impression that she is trying to make herself as unobtrusive as possible.

"You must know about horses," she says hopefully, "coming from Ireland."

I don't have the heart to tell her that I did not belong to what my mother with more than a trace of envy called "the hunting, fishing, and shooting crowd," the tweedy Anglo-Irish types who were the Knight's guests on his tree-screened estate above Glan, nor to the racing set in Dublin, who own and train racehorses with fabled names for steeplechases at home and abroad.

"I've placed a few bets," I say, "on the Grand National and the Derby. But I've never been to a race — or sat on a horse, for that matter. Does your family own horses?"

"My family owns property," she says shortly.

"Did you grow up around here?" I ask, trying to ignore the tone and wishing I had changed the subject.

"Sherborn. It's a rural town, not far from here. My parents still live there. I mean, it's perfectly nice, but I don't even like to drive through it. I didn't have a very happy time growing up there."

The atmosphere within the Monster has suddenly become charged with her emotion. I'm a little taken aback. I want to get to know Erica — but not quite so quickly.

"I'm sorry," she says. "I guess I'm kind of down on my parents right now. They don't like Rick. Can you imagine?"

"What don't they like about him?"

"They think he's not really interested in me as a person," she whispers. "My parents are kind of uptight. They don't appreciate his joie de vivre. Rick is a little too . . . uninhibited for them. But they'll come around. They'll have to."

This has an ominous sound. The tone in which she speaks about her parents makes me uncomfortable. It's inappropriate: I hardly know her.

"Rick is such an *interesting* person," she persists. "Don't you think so? He knows about so many different things: cars, clothes, good food and drink. You'd never know he came from Medford! I lived a very protected life, growing up in Sherborn — and where I went to college it was more like a snooty finishing school and I felt like I was still living at home. Being with Rick has really opened me up to things. He wants me to go to Europe with him, to visit Italy. I've never been to Europe. I'm really looking forward to it."

It strikes me that Erica's conception of the relationship is not the same as Rick's. At least he hasn't mentioned a trip to Europe. But that is no business of mine. I just want to enjoy Erica's company. I still cannot believe that I am here with her, that she has invited me to spend the entire day with her — and the night as well?

The highway narrows, and there are trees on either side. Now there are trees in the median strip, and you can't see the oncoming traffic. There's a nice cozy feel to this road, two lanes going in the same direction, nobody out to break records. It feels like a road that goes to the sea.

"What do *you* do?" Erica wants to know.

"I drive around in my car."

I am determined to show her that the Monster is no crock. I check the mirror, peer swiftly over my shoulder, and pull out to overtake a Rabbit. What a name for an automobile. The Monster wants to roll right over it, to leave it squashed flat on the steaming roadway. But we pull abreast of it smoothly, as it putters along with angular determination, and then I step on the gas, and it disappears. A moment later, it wobbles into the rearview mirror, receding in the Monster's speedy wake.

"Nobody can spend all day in a car."

"I read. I watch baseball on TV."

"I grew up with three brothers," she tells me. "Sports was all they ever talked about."

"To tell the truth, I'm not particularly interested in sports either," I hasten to add.

But I need a substitute for the movies. I feel too lonely to sit alone in the dark of a movie theater without Lily. The meaningless geometric ritual of baseball, the rigidity of the camera angle, the stylized commentary: all this has a soothing, not to say mesmeric effect. A brief thrill when the ball is actually hit, the misery of the pitcher, the anxiety of the fielders. They must each of them be thinking, What if the ball is hit to me? What if I make a mistake? Better that it should be hit to someone else. And then back to the incomprehensible pas de deux of pitcher and catcher, their cruel teasing of the awkward and vengeful batter, the twitching of fingers and nodding of heads before the slow motion of the wind up — and the sudden violence of the pitch.

"They were into dogs too," Erica says. "They bred greyhounds. One of them bit me twice. And my father refused to have it put to sleep."

"I'm sorry."

She puts her hands up to her hair, shakes it down onto the seat back in a flood of gold, puts her head back and laughs. "I have to stop complaining about my family. Let's go to the beach!"

To the beach! Her laughter ringing in my ears like gold, I veer into the passing lane and overtake a calvacade of desultory motorists dreaming of stocks and bonds, of mortgages and marriages, of anything but the golden sands, the royal blue of the ocean. An arc of steel girders rises above the trees ahead.

"That's the Sagamore Bridge," she says. "We're almost there."

The Sagamore turns out to be not quite as good as the Mystic. There's a rotary in front of it and then a steep climb like a roller coaster. The Monster has no trouble accelerating uphill, but the lane is narrow, and I can't take it as fast as I would like. There's a fine airy feeling on top, with the canal and another bridge on one side and the bay on the other, everything shading off into a hazy blue in both directions. But an evil-looking factory or power station on the bay side, with a tall blackened chimney, spoils the effect. The descent begins too soon. As bridges go, I've seen better.

"We have to go to the national seashore," Erica informs me. "The beaches around here are so rinky-dink. Not the *real* Cape."

I have studied my maps, and I know that the national seashore begins at the elbow. Route 6 is real enough, if unexciting, a narrow highway bounded by trees and scrub. There's sand along the shoulder and not much to see, apart from occasional glimpses of the sea. After a stretch of divided highway, we pass another rotary — which

is a challenge for me because in Ireland the traffic flows clockwise —
and there are houses and little lakes at intervals, then a wider margin
on either side and rolling hills. Apparently the Cape is not so narrow.
Looking at the map I'd imagined riding along the top of a sand dune
with the bay and the sea visible at once.

Directed by Erica, I turn off the highway, and soon we're in the
narrow sandy streets of Wellfleet. The buildings are like dolls'
houses, even the church looks like a toy, and there's nowhere to park.
The Monster feels like a bull in a china shop, and I keep expecting it
to go rampaging through a picket fence and smash somebody's
white clapboard summer house into a million matchsticks, ending
up with its noble grille wreathed in wild roses.

"Do you want to get something to eat?" Erica asks.

The rumble of my stomach almost drowns out my assent. But it's
early in the season, and the sandwich store she takes me to is closed.

"I really want to get to the beach," she says, a touch of anxiety in
her voice.

Who needs to eat? I'll survive. We pass a small harbor and a row
of shuttered summer houses on bleak sandy lots. Following the road
through high dunes, we cross an arm of the harbor, then turn onto
a narrow spit of land that stretches away into the bay. I park between
a pair of cars in an otherwise empty lot with a view of the beach. Erica sits still for a moment, her face pensive. We haven't talked since
the bridge, and I'm getting a little anxious myself. But maybe if I say
nothing she will just come into my arms.

Some hope. She flings open the door, runs a couple of steps
toward the bay, and then turns back to me. The wind catches her
hair and whips it across her face.

"Isn't it fabulous?" she demands, swinging her arm grandly
toward the horizon.

I look about me. Fabulous? No, not fabulous. It's all golden and
blue and milky white: a land that hasn't dreamed of disaster — all
surface, pastel sky, pristine sands. The little white houses across the
harbor are safe from memories of harm. The sea is an untroubled
blue; the clouds, high and white, look as though they could never
bear the burden of thunder and rain. A far cry from the Inish: sev-

ered promontory; bleak, glaciated land. There the ice rent and tore and left the bones of the earth exposed: here it ground everything to sand. Suddenly, in an instant, I am painfully lonesome for Lily.

"This is my special place," Erica tells me seriously. "Probably the only place where I really feel at home." Her eyes express a kind of plea.

"It *is* special," I say.

It is an appropriate setting for her, I am thinking, containing the gold of her hair, the blue of her eyes. She is a sight for sore eyes. But she is not Lily — who knows my thoughts before I utter them, who is truly interested in me, who has a wisdom beyond this woman's ken.

I lock the Monster, just in case, and follow Erica, who walks a little ahead of me, barefoot, carrying her towel. The beach is deserted, and as soon as she reaches the sand, she spreads the towel and sits on it. I squat down beside her. We stare wordlessly at the illimitable object of our quest, our great sweet mother, at last within reach. What now?

"Do you want to smoke some dope?" Erica says. "I brought some joints."

She sees my hesitation, and she turns toward me, rolling on her hip, smiling up at me, brilliantly. Do I want to smoke? I'll do anything for that smile.

"Sure," I say.

She sits up, reaches into a pocket of her skirt, and fishes out a crushed cigarette package and a book of matches. Inside there are three slim, tightly rolled cigarettes. She holds one between her lips and cups her hands awkwardly around the matchbook. After a few tries she gets the tip of it lighted. She puffs on it, so that the tip reddens, swallows the smoke along with a gulp of air, and hands the thing to me. I take it gingerly between my fingers, but I do not carry it to my lips.

"Have you never smoked?"

I shrug. I am loath to admit it.

"It's easy," she assures me, serious again. "Take a little smoke into your mouth. Then take a deep breath and hold it. You've got to do it quick while it's still burning."

I breathe out strongly. Then I take a little puff, followed by a deep breath. I'm surprised by how easy it goes down. Erica breathes out smoke with a sigh and takes the joint from my fingers. She glances quickly up and down the beach. She looks worried. But there's no one in sight.

"I don't feel anything," I tell her.

She folds her legs into a half-lotus and lights the joint again. Her cheeks are hollowed as she puffs, and her tanned face looks grim. I take the joint from her hand. I draw in more smoke this time and hold it down a little longer.

"It takes a little while before you feel the effect. The guy who got it for me said it was a sleeper. That means it creeps up on you."

She rolls away from me and lies on her side, presenting me with the shapely curve of her hip, upon which her arm rests loosely, her fingers cupping her thigh. She is waiting for me. This is the moment. Heart pounding, I reach for her. My hand falls upon her shoulder. It is an innocent, friendly touch, devoid of what it is intended to convey. But she turns and slides into my arms. Her body is firm, almost hard. I can hear her breathing slowly and carefully, and I imagine that her eyes are open. The shock of physical contact is not unpleasant, but neither is it warm. Is something the matter?

I tighten my arms around her. With a sudden jerk of her head that takes me by surprise she brings her mouth to mine, and our teeth click together. I move my hands to her shoulders. She kisses me energetically, and I kiss back, my hands in her hair. This is more like it, I am thinking — and yet it is not enough like it, or I would not be thinking at all. The pleasure I expected to feel is strangely lacking.

"Maybe I should seduce you right here," Erica murmurs.

But her voice is calm and self-possessed, the voice of calculation, of one who weighs the pros and cons. She's not exactly carried away either, is she? She presses her face against my shoulder and gives a long, shuddering sigh. I loosen my embrace, and we fall apart like unbound sheaves and sit up in the same motion, side by side on the towel.

"I'm sorry," she says. "I'm a little weird today."

That's when it hits me! One minute I have my arms around her — but I'm not really there. And the next minute, wham! I'm right here with a vengeance, I'm so intensely here, it's astonishing, it's scary, and I want it to stop. Suddenly I am thrust into my body, into my senses. I'm in the present moment, on the very cutting edge of time, but so unrelentingly, without a fraction of a second's absence, that I want the ground to open and swallow me, to drown this slow explosion of consciousness in the dark womb of earth.

"Uh-oh," Erica says. "I guess you're stoned."

How does she know? I close my eyes — and the process is reversed. The world rushes at me in a soundless implosion. I am the black hole of the universe, and I'll suck everything into myself and drown the world of phenomena if I'm left unattended. Help! I snap my eyes open. The world is still there: intensely, brilliantly, painfully there.

"I'm stoned too," she says.

She's turned toward me, feet folded under her. For an awful moment I think she's going to cry. She reaches out and takes my hand. Her touch communicates a wave of sensation, an impossible intensification of the already too intense.

"I have something to tell you," she says calmly, looking down at our hands. "I should have told you this morning. I'm ill. I have lupus."

Lupus? Good God. The very light seems to have taken on a different quality, as though the sun has been eclipsed. I am afraid to look at her.

"Are you going to be all right?"

"I don't know," she says, pathetically chirpy. "I just found out."

I turn my head warily, like a drunk carrying a brimming glass, until she comes into my field of vision — and in an awful instant I feel her presence, I see her for the first time, not her impeccable clothes, not her perfect body, but the essential person that she is. I see the fear in her eyes, the nervous trembling of her lips, the imperceptible shrinking of her slight frame, as though from a predator. All that she is is there, nothing added or removed. Suddenly clairvoyant, I see that house is Sherborn on its acres of lawn, the patrician father and pale wilting mother, those three brawny lumps of brothers, the reptilian head of the greyhound, its tiny sharklike teeth. Erica, haggard and drawn, pursued, running a gauntlet of males, stricken with the awareness of her body's flaw, surprised in youth by the wolf of mortality. She is alone. I feel her loneliness and her fear, as though they were my own. Does she see *me* like this, turned inside out, the inescapable present agglomeration of all the moments of my past?

A shameful consciousness of my own position comes over me. *I am the predator.*

"Is it OK for you — to be at the beach?" I manage to say.

"It's OK," she says, withdrawing her hand. "I'm on medication."

"I'm sorry," I stammer. "I wish I'd known. Rick didn't mention it."

"Rick doesn't know," she informs me. "Rick doesn't *want* to know. So please don't tell him. OK?"

Love of Jesus! I take her hand again. I am about to say something, but it eludes me. Her eyes have the look of a creature expecting a blow. I see through the envelope of skin, through beauty of flesh and muscle, to bone: the tense sickle of the jaw, the high ridges of the cheekbones that seem to compress and narrow her eyes, her domed forehead with its gleaming sheath of flesh. Her bronzed hand that holds mine is an intricate structure of interlocking bones, her shoulders an architectural achievement, her half-lotus a miracle of statics. It dawns on me — as an experience of the senses, not a thought — that our bones are all we have to hold us erect: without them we should be as limp as jellyfish, hopelessly intelligent invertebrates, incapable of coupling, of anything deserving the name of love.

"I hope you'll be all right" is all I can come up with.

"I hope so too."

I might as *well* be a fish, for all the interest I now have in love — hand, act, or part. My God, maybe she's dying! I feel cold, cold as a fish, a stone, touched by the passage of an icy wing. I am actually shivering.

I withdraw my hand from Erica's and stand up in a fright. Or rather the intricate machinery of the body demonstrates that it still remembers how to turn the trick. What new wonders and terrors await me now that I stand erect upon the earth? I take a step and I am instantly plunged in it, the overwhelming world of sensation, the squishy sand beneath my shoes, the scratch of the shirt against my chest, the belt's clasp about my waist. Let me out of here!

"I'm going back to the car," I say.

I don't know how to explain to her that I need to be in my car.

"I'm sorry," she says. "I guess our trip to the beach is shot."

She gathers the towel, and we walk abreast, though separated by a couple of arm's lengths. Suddenly I am wary of her. What will I do if something happens to her? I will be responsible.

The Monster is now alone in the lot. Where are the other cars? Perhaps there's been an emergency and the Cape has been evacuated. Erica and I are the only two left. I walk quickly over to the Monster. If I put my hand on its familiar hull, I'll be myself again. But the first thing I see is a spot of rust on the roof. I run my finger over it and chip off a flake of paint. The idea takes root, like an evil weed: the Monster riddled with tiny buboes, swelling up with rust, shedding its paint like a diseased skin, feeding upon itself — until it crumbles at my feet in a heap of green rubble.

"Can you unlock the door?" Erica calls.

I let her in, and we sit side by side, as though stunned, looking out. The dune grass shudders in a freshening wind. The harmless-looking puffy white clouds have been knitted together into a high screen that dims the sun's light, and the face of the ocean is darkened by squalls.

She turns to me, her smile conspicuously absent. Instinctively I place my hands on the wheel. All of a sudden I am myself again. That extraordinary hypersensitive self has packed up and left: I know it with a heavy complacent certainty. The world is just the world again, nothing to get worked up about. And Erica is just Erica, though no longer quite so golden. She still looks desirable — but what is that to me? I just want to get her back to town before a medical emergency overtakes her.

"Why did you want to go out with me?" she says.

I look away, out to sea. There is an ominously dark mass of cloud on the seaward horizon. Its components seem to be all drawn to a point, like sails attached to the crown of a masthead. I was an idiot. I thought I was going to jump into bed with you, no questions asked. Nothing is that simple, not if people are to treat each other as human beings.

"I was lonely. What about you?"

Her lips start to tremble, and she clamps them together. "I wanted to make Rick jealous. I know what he's up to this weekend. I'm sorry. I feel bad that you had to get mixed up in this."

"That's all right," I say. "I saw the Cape. It was better than sitting alone in my apartment."

"I just want to go home now."

And I to take you there, to hand you over to Rick. But her eyes are filled with tears. Her perfect mouth is twisted by a sob.

"I'm afraid," she says brokenly. "I don't know who's going to look after me if I get sick. I can't move back in with my parents. I can't tell Rick. He'd think it was such a bummer."

I put my arm around her, and she weeps with her face pressed against my shirt. I am tense, exhausted, anguished. Is this part of her deal with Rick? I promise not to bother you if I contract a life-threatening illness? What sort of a deal is that?

She draws away, wipes her eyes with a sleeve. Her appearance unnerves me. Her eyes are wide and fearful, her features pinched and tired. Is this the same woman who stepped out of her car in front of my apartment this morning? So much for appearances. She is unhappy — just like everybody else. Suddenly I know that she has never offered me refuge or escape, save in my dream of a New World that has made her a prize and denied her vulnerability. I know too that I will have to go back to Lily, if she will have me. Lily is the real thing, no false hope, no fantasy. I should never have listened to Rick.

"You have to tell Rick that you're ill," I say.

Her eyes widen incredulously. And yet I can tell that she wants to be convinced.

"If you don't tell him, I'll tell him myself."

She sniffs, bows her head. "You're right. I'll tell him. How can I keep it from him? It's crazy."

I look out to sea. The storm is passing by. It trails sheets of rain over the bay, with faint rumbles and brief lightning flashes among the clouds, becoming more remote and subdued even as I watch.

"Rick is a decent person," I say. "He won't let you down."

I start the engine and drive through the lot to the road.

"I'm sorry if you got the wrong impression," she says. "I do like you —"

"I think we're even on that score, Erica. I like you too."

She takes my hand and squeezes it, hard.

"Thank you," she says quietly.

For what? For sending you back to Rick, where you belong? For some small modicum of hope? Physician, heal thyself.

I stop at a superette on Route 6 and buy a quart of milk and a chocolate bar to take the edge off a ravenous hunger. Erica does not want anything to eat. She closes her eyes, and she's asleep before I pull onto the highway.

It is dark by the time I reach the city. Its skyline appears before me, defined by a myriad of lights, rising like an array of crystals in a jar. The Monster roars up the middle of the deserted expressway, past a four-chimneyed power station and a desert of warehouses. The towers of the city rise higher, drawn by a mysterious force, the turning of the earth, the puppet strings of the gods. Perhaps they are not really there, perhaps this spectacle is nothing but a cloud of brilliant fireworks, fixed by some pyrotechnic miracle, a ghostly holograph projected out of the night upon the Monster's windscreen, signifying — and encompassing — nothing.

No, they are real enough — and I must make my life among them. But there is no sanctuary, here or in Ireland. I cannot make the act of faith that prayer requires, nor imagine what might constitute help, in the absence of belief. I have been barking up the wrong tree, with my dream of a joyride with Erica — in a white Infiniti! I must turn again to Lily. I am connected to her in a kind of kinship that could never exist with Erica. It will not be plain sailing. But as the old people of the Inish used to say, *Is fearr an troid ná an t'uaigneas.* Strife is better than loneliness.

A Prospect of the Sea

WHEN IN DOUBT — drive.
Interstate 95 connects the Canadian border with the southern tip of Florida — New Limerick, Maine, with Key West. I've found a long, wide stretch of it, north of its junction with Route 128, eight broad lanes with plenty of room on the shoulders. Here the rush-hour traffic has miraculously melted away, the median strip is as broad and flat as the highway, and I can see for a good mile or more fore and aft. The Monster devours this ruler-straight ribbon of road, mile after mile, yet it replenishes itself at the top of each gentle rise, another asphalt mile to be traversed, gleaming black in the hard sunlight, interminable.

I am driving north to Plum Island to look at the ocean. I did not really look at it when I went to the Cape with Erica; I was too distracted. I feel guilty, since Lily once suggested that we should go together — and I have not called her yet. But I want to be alone with the ocean. I am hoping to find some comfort in it, the comfort I sought in vain in the Old Cambridge Baptist Church — OCBC! — and the courage to call Lily. But I must not hope for anything quite so definite. It will be comforting enough — though an unconscionable extravagance — to drive there and back.

The asphalt shimmers in a heat haze; the car I am approaching floats above the surface of the road like a boat. I am cruising at sixty, and I glance warily in the rearview mirror. No vehicles in sight: an inexplicably empty highway, bright and desolate. I glide by the car in the outer lane, wait for its reappearance in the rearview mirror, and ease back into the middle. I roll the window up, and the din of the wind ceases. Nothing ahead but the next rise of the road against a cloudless sky, nothing behind but the narrowing highway. What else is there but memory?

My mother did not come to see me anymore, but her greeting cards now contained a few scrawled lines, ritually deploring our separation. I wish we could be a family again, was her habitual refrain. It was my fault that we were not, as the advent of each holiday reminded me.

The school on the Inish was a primary school only. My mother informed the old man I was to go to school in Caher. So I went back to the Brothers there. They did not have the arrogance of their city counterparts, and in a larger school, with school fellows I did not know, I felt less of a misfit for my interest in my schoolwork. Each morning I rose at six o'clock, laid out food for the old man, and cycled to the Foot, rain or shine. I lowered my bicycle into the ferry, dragged it out again at the other side, and attacked the long uphill road to Caher. I was back on the pier again at four o'clock in the afternoon, often wet and cold, waiting until Jacky Bar saw fit to come and get me. With luck I would be home by six; it was usually later. The old man would be waiting for his tea, and then there was homework to do. It was a long day, but I did not really mind it. Caher was a godforsaken place, with every other building on its single street a pub. But I knew that street led to roads that traveled over the length and breadth of Ireland, whereas every unpaved boreen on the Inish led only to a prospect of the sea.

Old Finn did not succeed in drowning himself. But he grew sick and infirm and had to be put down. The old man did not want to part with him. But I couldn't bear it any longer, watching the dog drag his emaciated body about the place, refusing food, gasping for breath. I asked Doctor Gleason, who doubled as vet, to come; it was the first time I'd directly crossed the old man. When the doctor came in the house, Granda had been sitting with Finn for hours, his hand on the dog's neck, muttering to him in Irish. He got up and went into the room, smashing his forehead against the door in his haste. I held Finn while the doctor gave him the injection; at one moment his eyes were alive and fearful, then he collapsed as though he had been shot. Pat-Joe and I buried him in a corner of the field behind the house, sobered by the task, our dislike of each other temporarily in abeyance. The old man took it quietly enough. He only swore that he would never have another dog in the house. I mourned Finn in secret for weeks, until his presence — about the house or at my heels upon the strand — ceased to be palpable.

Christine was living with her aunt Julia in Port. She went to school to the nuns in Caher, but I never saw her there. She resumed her visits to us after her mother's death, but she came rarely during the school year. I looked forward to the summertime, when I was not in school and could expect to see her more often. Since she always left us before it was dark, we no longer listened to the old man's stories together. He did not talk to us about his life anymore, and under no circumstances would he tell one of the old stories while it was light out. As often as not he would go in the shop and ignore us. Christine and I became a little strange with each other. Sometimes I did not know what to say to her, and I found myself longing for the old days. But when she wasn't there, I always missed her.

I come downstairs after helping the old man to bed. Someone is sitting by the embers of the fire. There is no other light in the room, and I advance warily, my heart in my mouth, until I see that it is Christine.

"We were expecting you earlier," I say. "How are you going to get home in the dark?"

She gives me a little wan smile and shrugs. She is sad about something. She will tell me by and by. I sit opposite her on the settle. I am very glad she has come.

"You can stay the night," I tell her, "if you don't mind sleeping below in the room with the lobster pots."

"I'd love to," she says wistfully.

"Why don't you then? Granda will get such a surprise when he sees you in the morning."

"My aunt doesn't know I'm out."

"Why didn't you tell her?'

She doesn't answer. I reach under the settle and throw some pieces of turf on the remains of the fire. It flames up, and I see Christine more clearly where the firelight touches her, the dense tangle of her hair, the side of her face, her shoulder, her knee.

"My aunt wouldn't like me to stay here."

"Why not?"

She gives me a long look from her widely spaced eyes. The freckles on her broad cheeks seem to run together in the ruddy light, making her face dark. She is serious tonight, as though she's thinking about something else. I want to draw her out, to make her laugh.

"Because I'm already sixteen, and you're almost fourteen, Matt. She thinks it isn't right, even with Mister O. here."

I want to assert that I cannot understand this objection. But I do not really want her to explain it to me. Besides, something tells me that Christine will not stay no matter what I say.

"Not that I give a tinker's curse for that old one!" Christine brings out suddenly, flashing a mischievous grin.

"Is she at you again?"

It is one of our pleasures to make fun of Christine's aunt Julia and her friends.

"She's always at me, boy! But it's all a matter now. I'm going away. That's what I came over for, to tell you, before you heard it from someone else."

She is looking at me as though pleading with me not to say anything. I feel that my face is flushed, and I turn my head. How can she be so matter-of-fact about it?

"Aunt Julia is sending me to London. She has some friends there who need someone to look after their children."

The word London strikes my ears like a knell. It has all the awe and force of death. If Christine goes off to London, she may as well be dead.

"But you're not finished school," I protest.

"If I don't go now, Aunt Julia's friends will find someone else. I can always finish school in London anyway, I suppose."

I am angry with her, and I know that I cannot hide it. But I will not speak to her.

"I don't mind it, Matt," she says. "It'll be all right, one way or the other."

"But do you really *want* to go?" I blurt out.

She is quiet for a while, sitting with her hands in her lap, as though waiting for something. I begin to wonder if she is going to answer me at all.

"I suppose Aunt Julia's friends can hardly be worse than Aunt Julia herself," she says. "And I'll have a few shillings in my pocket, which is more than I'll ever have here."

I am bitterly disappointed that she does not value our friendship more than a few shillings, and I want to tell her so. But before I can say anything, she reaches swiftly across the fire and grips my hand.

"You're the only person I'll miss, Matt. Yourself and Mister O."

I smile back at her through my tears.

"And I'm going to London," she notes carefully. "It was to London that my father went, you know."

She bows her head, but keeps holding my hand. We sit for a long time like this. Above us the old man snores faintly. Apart from that, it is absolutely quiet in the house, the quiet that has replaced old Finn's characteristic sigh, the scratching sound of his paws upon the flags, and his muffled bark as he pursued some creature in sleep. But I want this silence to continue. I am holding my grief at bay, and I want nothing to disturb my concentration. First the dog, and now Christine.

Christine disengages her hand and leans back into the chimney corner. She clasps her shoulders with her hands and rocks herself gently. "How's himself these days anyway?" she murmurs.

"He's like a bear," I say, "he's that cross. He hasn't touched a piece of leather in ages, and he won't let me tidy up the shop. Sits in the corner talking to himself by the hour. No one comes to the house anymore. He doesn't want anyone, save for yourself and Mrs. Harty."

Christine gives a start. "God above, it must be all hours! Tell him I was asking for him, will you?"

"Won't you be over again before you go?"

She shakes her head slowly, her eyes pleading with me again. "I'm taking the train to Dublin on Saturday."

She gets up and stands by me, as though waiting for me to give her leave to go. But I will not make it easy for her. "What will I say to Granda?"

She twists her hands awkwardly together in front of her. "Give him my best." She moves toward the door. I want to get up and go to her, but my body feels as heavy as lead. I can hardly lift my head.

"Good-bye, Matt."

She opens the door. I leap up and cross the room to her.

"I'll walk a bit of the way with you."

"Do," she says.

We walk up the lane between the high hedges of fuchsia in the dark. I feel her take my hand again. She holds it loosely until we come to the road. Then she turns to the left, toward the Head.

"Why aren't you going to the Foot?"

"I'm going to swim over to Port — like we did long ago. Remember?"

I cannot see her face in the dark. Even her voice sounds blurred.

"I'll swim across with you!"

"Don't be mad. How would you get back?"

"I'll stay beyond in Port. If your aunt won't give me a bed — I'll sleep in the porch of the church."

Her laughter rings out. It is good to hear, on this most miserable of nights. I have to laugh a little with her myself.

"Oh, Matt," she says, when she gets her breath. "You and the rest of those poor goms who're too drunk to go home to their wives. I'm only codding you. I'm sorry. I took Dennis Mac's punt. He's in the pub, legless, and he doesn't know I have it."

"Even so," I tell her severely. "The tide must be nearly full. You could be swept out of the harbor before you knew it."

"I don't care what happens," she says in a cold voice that frightens me. "So long as I get away from Port."

We walk in silence. I can feel Christine's distress, and I want to say something to ease it. But no words will come. Presently the village of Port is below us, a straggle of lights in the dark. Christine climbs a gate and slips down into the field beyond. I follow her through the wet grass to a rocky foreshore. Here she stops and waits for me. I can hear her breathing rapidly, as though she has been running.

"I won't always be looking after someone's children," she tells me. "I'll go back to school over there, as soon as I find my feet. I'd like to go to university too someday. And maybe I'll meet my father. You never know."

It is painful to hear the note of hope in her voice. Christine has never in her life been further away than Killarney. I have been to Dublin, where you could lose yourself in no time, and I know that London is an even greater city. She has no more chance of meeting her father there than I have of meeting mine walking the roads of the Inish.

We step over a barbed-wire fence and descend to the strand. It is a very dark night. Christine cannot find the punt, and we wander up and down, the stones clacking loudly beneath our feet. She gives a cry and then a shout of laughter. I hurry in her direction. I see the dark mass of the punt, and I hear her laughing, but I cannot find her in the dark. I lean over the gunwale, and she puts her arms around my neck and hugs me tightly. She isn't laughing anymore; I feel her tears on my neck.

I want her to be gone. I cannot stand it much longer. I drag the punt down to the water. It slides easily on its flat bottom over the stones, making a hollow cavernous sound. I place the oars in the rowlocks for her.

"Get in," I tell her. "I'll push you off."

"Don't get yourself wet. I can do it myself."

We both get behind the punt and push it until it floats free. We are standing knee-deep in cold water.

"Get in, Chrissie, for the love of God," I say, my voice breaking shamefully.

"Listen," she says, gripping my arm. "You'll come to London too, that's what you'll do, as soon as you're finished school. I'll have a place of my own, I'll show you around the town, such a time we'll have. Won't it be grand?"

My shoes are full of water, and my feet are thoroughly chilled. My entire body is becoming cold and numb.

"Promise me you'll come," Christine whispers, squeezing my arm.

"The tide is turning, Chrissie."

She drops her hand and slips into the punt.

"You'll come," she tells me, as she flails the oars. "It's only another three years until you're finished in Caher. What is there here for you then?"

I swing the stern until the punt is pointing toward the lights of Port, bend my knees, and push. The punt and Christine in it immediately disappear.

"Chrissie!"

I hear the rhythmic sound of the oars for a couple of strokes — and then nothing more than the wash of the ebbing tide.

The old man is standing at the foot of the stairs, and I am crouched above him with a candle, ready to ascend backwards and light his steps as I go. He holds the banister with one hand while he feels with the end of his stick for a purchase in the corner between the first step and the wall. But instead of making the sudden lurch with which he negotiates the steps, he raises his head, and the candlelight falls full upon his upturned face. There is something in his face, seen in this dramatic light, that gives me a little shock. His eyes are blank, like a blind man's; perhaps he is blinded by the light. But it is the haggard look and expression of angry surprise that gives me a turn.

I place the candle on the top step and go down to him.

"I'll walk behind you, Granda," I say. "There's plenty of light."

I'm afraid he will insist that this is an unnecessary precaution, but he looks past me.

"If I climb that stairs again, I won't come down out of it alive," he mutters.

So there is no help for it. At ten o'clock of a fine August evening, I begin to dismantle his massive ramshackle bed, aided by incoherent shouted instructions from the foot of the stairs. I do not resent this task: I am too frightened by its implications. For a long time now he hasn't been further from the house than the storm wall overlooking the strand, and that with my assistance. Now he can no longer climb the stairs.

In an hour I have the bed in pieces, and I slide the unmanageable mattress recklessly down the stairs. By midnight the thing is re-assembled in the shop — he refuses to be confined to the room — and I go to bed tired to the bone, leaving him surrounded by the discarded tools and the dry sheets of leather curled at their edges. It is strange to be upstairs without him — almost as if he had died.

He appears to be sleeping when I leave early next morning to take the boat and check the lobster pots. It is calm and mild on the channel, with a light offshore wind bearing the scent of freshly cut fields. I must take advantage of a good day like this, but I am working slowly, clumsily, the light reflected off the water dazzling my sleepy eyes. I haven't slept, for thinking about the old man's refusal to climb the stairs. It oppresses me still, a portent lurking in the bright air.

I spend the day in the boat and take my catch to Shanahan at the end of it. He is paying me a pittance for my lobsters, and we both know it. I would get more for them in Caher, but it is a long pull up the river in a currach, and there are many tides and winds in which you could hardly get there at all. Since Christine left, I feel the need to earn and save as much money as I can. But I try to conceal this from the old man.

When I come back in the evening, the house is dark. The old man is in bed in the shop, lying very still. I have a moment of fear before he speaks.

"There must have been great fishing outside," he remarks. "They say the sea will be a dry cow before the world's end, empty of fish entirely. Faith, 'tis a prophecy that hasn't come true yet. But at the rate you're going after the lobsters, you'll hasten the evil day."

I light the oil lamp and carry it into the shop. My anxiety for him makes me irritable. "Did you get out of bed at all today?"

He covers his eyes against the light. His cheeks are pale with an untidy stubble. "I did. And then I came back to bed. 'Tis all a matter, whether I'm up or down. Would you ever take that light away?"

I carry the lamp into the kitchen.

"I'm going to make supper. Will you come to the table, or will I bring you something in bed?"

"Let you make it for yourself," he tells me vehemently. "Don't mind me. I had a few spuds in the middle of the day. I'm all right."

I am hungry, but I cannot be bothered cooking a meal for myself alone. I take some cheese from the cooler, and bread, and I sit at the table with my back to the old man's bed in the shop.

"But I suppose they'll be a dearth of fishermen long before they've farmed the ocean dry," he says. "They'll be all gone to America; that's the way with the Inish anyway. My father, God rest him, remembered when there was no thought of America any more than this bed I'm lying in — and they were fine happy days too."

I take a deep breath. I must say it before I lose my nerve. "I'm going to buy an outboard for the boat, Granda."

"Jesus, Mary, and Joseph! What do you want with an outboard?"

"To take my lobsters to Caher. I'll get a better price for them from the fish merchants there. That fellow Shanahan is cheating me. I can pay for the motor with what he puts in his pocket."

I do not mention that I also plan to set some pots outside the harbor, in places where it is dangerous to take a currach. The old man is quiet for a while. I am tempted to believe that he is not going to object.

"It's good for a young lad to keep himself occupied," he says at length. "But I declare to God you live in that boat. If I didn't hear you coming and going, I wouldn't know you were here at all. What do you want with all that money anyway?"

"I might need it in a couple of years' time. When I finish school."

"What will you need it for?" he insists. "You're not planning to take unto yourself a wife, are you?"

I get up, open the door, and look out over the seawall. The interminable summer evening is still poised on the brink of dark, and the channel has the gloomy air of a deserted church. There is neither comfort nor mystery in it, nor even loneliness and longing. I am oppressed by the tedium of it, by its immutability, by its intolerable sameness.

"I suppose you're lonesome after Christy. That's why you haven't a word to throw to a cat lately." He says this innocently, as though he himself has no feeling about her. I feel the blood rush to my face.

"It'll be the same with her as with all the rest of them that leave the Inish," he says with sudden bitterness. "No thought for the people at home no more than for the stranger."

I want to speak up for Christine. But it is true we have not had a letter from her. I suppose she is busy. Still, you'd think she could have scribbled a postcard, if only to let us know she is safe and sound.

"If you want to go, you may suit yourself," the old man murmurs. "I have all I need now to see me out."

That he knows what is in my mind infuriates me.

"I'm not going anywhere!"

"Pat-Joe will go to the Foot for me and bring me the water and the milk. Sure what else do I need? He's the boy that will stop at home here, if anyone will."

As though Pat-Joe has ever done more than to bring him the Sunday paper, which he does not read, and to sit there for an hour smoking Granda's tobacco. I have a mind to tell him so, but there is a note of dejection in his voice that distresses me. He is not himself tonight. It occurs to me that maybe there really is something the matter, something that requires the doctor. But I am afraid to suggest it.

I decide to sit with him and keep an eye on him for a while, though God knows I would rather be in bed. I close the door and go to the chimney corner, where I stretch out upon the settle.

"The story of Diarmat and Grania," the old man chants quietly from the shop. "If there be a lie in it, be it so! 'Twas not I who made it or invented it."

I am encouraged to hear him begin a story. It would be strange if he did not. There cannot be too much wrong with him then.

"Grania was the wife of the chieftain Finn. It was an unlucky hour that her father gave her away, for she hated Finn so much she sickened of it."

I watch him out of the corner of my eye. He is lying on his back, his hands clasped upon his chest beneath the bedclothes. He is not looking at me, and I think he doesn't realize that I can see him. But his voice seems to seek me out, to demand my attention.

"At her bridal feast she cast her eyes around, and who did she see but Diarmat, one of her husband's kinsmen, who was as fair and handsome as a woman. I'd give my dowry, says she, for a long lustful look from that one, my soul to the Devil for a night of lying beside his smooth body, though Hell is a great privation for all eternity. She could not take her eyes from him all through the feast, and when he got up from the table to make water, she followed him out and went up to him as bold as you please though he was uncovered and laid her hand upon his thigh. I swear to God above I never saw a man like you, she said, and I put my *geis* upon you now to take me away with you this night and to return my love."

His voice is soft and secret now, as though such things are scarcely fit for my ears. I am no longer sleepy. I feel agitated and restless. I would like to go out and walk on the strand. But I cannot interrupt the story.

"Diarmat felt his heart sink down to the soles of his feet as he stood there uncovered before her and she looking at him without shame. Aren't you Finn's wife, he said, and I his warrior and kinsman? He hasn't had me to bed and bolster yet, said the bold Grania, and I wouldn't give a snap of my fingers for a wedding night with an old man the likes of him. Here is a riddle for you, said Diarmat, for he was at his wit's end. I will not take you by day, says he, and I will not take you by night; I will not take you clothed, nor will I take you unclothed; I will not take you within, and I will not take you without; I will not take you in company, neither will I take you on your lonesome. Grania had no answer to this, and Diarmat covered himself and got away from her."

I have heard this riddle before without giving it a thought. Why does it trouble me now? It is only nonsense. He was telling the same story the night I came here: he will be telling it until the day he dies. Christine came in to us and sat on the settle opposite me. I remember her grubby knees peeping out from under her dress. Maybe that is why she doesn't write: because I did not promise to go to London. I always thought she was more at home on the Inish than I was. Now she is gone out of it — and I am still here.

"But when Diarmat went to his tent just before it was day, he found Grania there before him. She was all dressed in the sheerest fairy stuff so that he could see every inch of her, and she was mounted on an ugly old buck goat that she had stationed with his forelegs outside on the grass and his hind legs inside the tent. I have not come to you by day, she said to him, and I have not come by night; I am not clothed, neither am I naked as I was born; I am not without, I am not within; there is no one with me, but I am not alone. You must take me away! When Diarmat heard this he knew he would never again have a moment's peace, and without a word of good-bye to friends and relations he took her away with him just as she was."

The old man raises himself suddenly in the bed and stares indignantly into the kitchen, where the lamp is standing on the table.

"For it takes a woman like that to come between a man and his own people — between a man and what he knows is right!"

There is an angry look in his eye. He is angry with Christine because she went away without saying good-bye to him. Now I think I understand why she did not want to see him. I am afraid of this look. It is the same look he gave me yesterday when he could not climb the stairs. He is angry with *me*.

"Diarmat and Grania were pursued by Finn throughout the length and breadth of Ireland, but when they lay down together for the night, Diarmat used to put a long rough stone between them, and whenever they stopped to eat, he would leave raw meat behind them as a sign to Finn that his wife was still untouched. One day they were fording a stream upon the Inish of the Oak Trees when a little wave of the stream splashed Grania and drenched her from hip to knee. Diarmat, she said to him. You're a great man for the hunt and for any sort of a fight, but when it comes to women you're as weak and spineless as a newborn baby before its mother gives it suck, and I think this little wave of the stream that's after wetting my thighs is worth more than you are. Diarmat turned around with the bitter word on the tip of his tongue, but when he saw her there with her skirts lifted up to her waist, he forgot the sound of his own name and everyone that was ever dear to him. He went into the stream after her and took her into the bushes and made a wife of her. That night they cooked meat in the glen, and they left it untasted as a sign for Finn."

Why is he telling me these unmentionable things? He does not like Christine anymore. He does not like me. But he will keep me here with him, and he will make me say that she is not my friend. He will be a hundred years dying — and I will never get away from him!

I jump up from the settle. The old man gives a start and jerks his head toward me.

"I suppose you'll be telling me next that Diarmat and Grania are real people and that the whole thing happened here on the Inish when you were a young lad!"

For a moment he looks bewildered and unwell, as though I have given him a fright. He lowers himself down in the bed.

"That's what the old people say," he mutters. "If you climb up the side of Crom you can see one of their beds in the rock, where they lay down to rest in their flight from Finn."

"What old people? I never heard anyone say it but you."

If I had any sense, I would go to bed. But I am beside myself. I feel harassed and put-upon, and I want to say something hurtful.

"Sure how could you? The likes of the old people will never be again. The old days are gone. But there was magic in them," he says quietly.

I stride into the shop and stand at the end of the bed, confronting him. My heart is thumping like a live thing in my chest.

"What is it you're calling magic? Is it your *geasa* that can make people go out of their minds? Is it a riddle that makes no sense because it has no answer? Is it swords that jump out of your hand and cups of blood and bloody shirts? Is it a boar with poisonous whiskers the like of which never was in this world or any other? It's a poor sort of magic — that only a fool would believe in!"

The sight of his appalled face terrifies me. I turn away and run to the stairs.

"Wait now, wait now," he calls after me hoarsely. "Come here, I want you."

I halt on the dark narrow stairway and lean my forehead against the crumbling plaster of the wall. My head is pounding as though something is about to burst in it. I want to ignore him and go upstairs. But I cannot. I step down and walk back into the shop as though in a dream. My hands are trembling by my sides; my body feels almost weightless, insubstantial.

"What do you want the money for?" he insists. "It isn't to buy an outboard."

I have a sick, helpless feeling. There is no escaping him. I will have to tell him. "I want to go away," I blurt out. "To go to university in London."

My voice is louder than I intend. I try to read his reaction in his face. I am tense, as though ready to ward off a blow. But the old man looks genuinely puzzled. "To go for a scholar, is it?" he says. "What do the Brothers have to say to that?"

"One of them gives me books — about history — that he wouldn't give to the fellows in the Leaving Cert class."

The old man's eyes narrow. He draws the bedclothes up around him. "Are they right and suitable for a boyeen of your age?"

"Why wouldn't they be?" I say, advancing a step toward the head of the bed. "They're not suitable for anyone else. Who else would look at them? I'm the only one who would open a book outside of the schoolhouse. What do the rest of them want with books? All they want to know is who plays center field for Kerry and who won the seine boat race in last year's regatta."

I stop short. You may praise God or the Devil around here, as the humor takes you, but you must never say a good word about yourself.

"There were good men came out of the Inish school," the old man tells me grimly, "and never felt the need to go to Caher. They settled down here on the Inish, to live their lives and look after their families. It's the least you could do, to give a couple of years, to look after the house and the land, your family's property that will come down to yourself in the end. 'Tisn't everybody has to be told. Look at Pat-Joe and the way he looks after his grandmother since he came out of school. He doesn't go around looking down his nose at people either, just because he goes back the Inish for her and brings her a few sods of turf."

The heavy certainty of his conviction oppresses me. It will crush my petty hopes — if I do not fight it for all I am worth!

"Does Pat-Joe have time for your stories?" I shout. "Does he?"

"Faith, if he doesn't, I don't hear him opening his gob to give cheek to his elders!"

"It's all right for Pat-Joe to spend the rest of his life digging turf. He doesn't care — so long as he has a bit of amusement on Saturday night! He doesn't know any better. He doesn't *want* anything else."

I am standing over him, trembling, frightened by my own words. He is a sick old man, lying there in the bed, but he still has the force to keep me from what I want. My anger leaves me, and I feel ashamed. I am a worthless creature, to be talking like that about my own cousin. I want only to get away, to hide, to sleep.

"And who's going to pay for you to go to university?" the old man wants to know. "It won't be out of your own pocket, no matter how many lobsters you bring to Caher."

"I'll earn more," I inform him. "And there is such a thing as a scholarship."

But even as I say it, I feel the improbability of my plan. I will never have enough money, even if I am good enough at school to be able to go. I will have to stay here and look after the old man anyway. There is no help for it.

He folds his hands upon the bedclothes and closes his eyes, as though ready to go to sleep. He seems to have forgotten about me. I stand there, waiting to be dismissed.

"And to disturb the house with your shouting and roaring while I was telling a story," he murmurs. "You'll never have luck."

There is something in his aggrieved tone that touches me unexpectedly. The stories mean more to him than anything else in the world, and I have told him that I do not care about them. I did not mean to say it. It is not what I really think.

I come forward and get down on one knee beside the bed.

"Listen, Granda," I say. "I don't want to go for a while yet. Not for another two years."

He fixes his eyes on me fiercely. "Am I supposed to give up the ghost to oblige you?"

I stand up and back away from him, my face burning.

"You're a very clever lad when it comes to the books," he says slowly, clipping his words. "But you don't care about anyone but yourself. You're like your mother that way. When it comes to your own kith and kin, you have no more nature in you than a stone."

I run across the house, throw the back door open against the wall, and dash through the garden and into the field. The night engulfs me like a shroud.

On Christmas Eve, I meet the postman at the top of the lane. There is something from my mother, the expected card. But it must also be a reply to the letter I wrote her in September. I take it onto the strand and hunker down out of sight of the house. I asked her if I could stay with them in London, if they would help me find a job there and apply to a university. I did not want to ask her, for fear she would refuse. But I want to go away from here, and there is no one else I can ask. I do not want to stay with them, and they probably do not want me either. But I will put up with them, to get to London. They are supposed to be my family, so my mother keeps telling me.

I tear the envelope and take out the card. My fingers are trembling. It has taken her a long time to write, and I am convinced that this is a bad sign. I open the card. Clipped to one side is a ten-pound note — instead of the usual five. The other side is signed at the bottom of the page: *Love — the O'Brien family.*

This is her reply. At least it is not a direct refusal. But I am so cast down I cannot move to rise. My body is heavy with defeat.

I lift the note. The page is half covered with my mother's illegible handwriting, beginning *Dear Matthew,* ending *Love — Mam.*

Wouldn't it be lovely to be a family again.

I raise my head and look out at the channel and the mist settled heavily on the hills above Port. Unwillingly my eyes come back to the card.

We'd love to have you come for a visit, maybe at Easter or for a week during the summertime — if you can get someone to look after Daddy while you're away. But I don't know where we would put you for any longer than that. Jack thinks maybe you'd be better off where you are. The devil you know is better than the devil you don't. Anyway, I hope you won't ask Jack for money to go to the university. It's frightfully expensive, and we couldn't afford it at all. Hope Daddy is keeping well. Tell him we were all asking for him.

I didn't ask her for money! I asked her for help — but it doesn't matter. I was a fool to write to her, and I will never write again. Ten pounds! I have a good mind to send it back to her. But it doesn't matter. There is nothing that matters. I knew it when she didn't write. I knew it all along.

There is no London for me, nor Paris either. I will never meet Chrissie there nor go to the university. I am stuck here on the Inish — for the want of a few hundred pound.

On St. Stephen's Day the Wren Boys wake me early with their rowdy, irreverent singing. Downstairs in the shop the old man does not stir or make a sound, and after a few hopeful shouts they leave, their voices fading across the field. The Wren is an old tradition, according to Granda, and the goms who go out nowadays are only making fools of themselves. Here at least is one subject on which we see eye to eye. They dress up as women or tramps with masks covering their faces and play their tin whistles as the humor takes them. But they're only out for drink — and for playing the fool with the women.

I get up, light the fire, bring the old man a cup of tea, and then I go back to bed, where I read until late in the afternoon, one of the books that Brother Lyons has given me, a history of Ireland by the Christian Brothers that the class will use next year in preparing for the Leaving Certificate. I am determined to finish it just because Brother Lyons believes me capable of it, but I do not like it. There is nothing in it but names and dates and battles: from reading it you would think that the people long ago never lived at all. I would rather listen to one of the old man's stories, but I know there must be somewhere a history that is *real*. This is a history for children, who do not know the difference between Finn MacCool and the Great O'Neill. At the university there must be a different kind of history, a history that tells you what people thought and felt about the things that were happening to them. But I will never get there now, neither in London nor anywhere else.

In the evening I walk to the Foot, to get the old man his stout. I take the Lower Road and meet no one; they are all in Deasy's pub by now and in Shanahan's with the Wren Boys. I don't want to talk to anyone, so I leave the road by the church and cut across the fields. At the back of Deasy's I pass through a stinking yard where the toilet is, a strip of painted wall and a drain. A door leading to the bar is open, and I can hear them at it inside and smell the heat and the drink.

I go into the grocery and signal to one of the family behind the bar. There is a great commotion going on, music and singing and shouting. From the shop I can see people dressed in straw masks, with football shirts and skirts over their clothes. It is well for them with their masks: they can do what they want and nobody knows them. I remember that I wanted to put on a mask and go out with them when we lived at the Cable Station — but of course my mother wouldn't hear of it.

One of the young girls serves me. She forgets to give me a bag, and I cannot get her attention. I take the stout in my arms and hurry back through the yard. Two fellows come rushing out of the bar ahead of me. I move to step around them, and one of them staggers into me. He stands still for a moment, his back to me, as though he's so drunk he doesn't even know what has happened. Then he turns and brings his face close to mine. My heart jumps, and I start back, the bottles rattling in my arms. It is a hideous waxen face with thick arched eyebrows and heavy frozen jowls. But it's only a mask. The fellow starts to laugh. He's one of the Wren Boys.

"Oliver Cromwell," he says gruffly. "At your service."

His voice sounds familiar, but I cannot place it. The other fellow comes over, and together they lean toward me silently, with their huge grotesque heads behind the masks. I see by the light from the open door that the second fellow is wearing a straw skirt over his trousers and a pair of Wellingtons; his mask is like a skull, all twisted to one side in a wink. I am not afraid of them.

"Money for the Wran," the Skull croaks.

"Christ, man, I can't hold it in no longer," says Cromwell.

He starts to piss against the wall next to me.

"Get out of my way!" I shout.

I try to shoulder my way past. The Skull stands his ground. He chants in a stupid drunken voice. "Here comes I, the Devil himself, if you don't give me money, I'll break all your stout!"

"Or drink a bottle with us, for the love of Jaysus," Cromwell says, still pissing. "Don't be sneaking off to drink it on your own."

I know who it is! A clot of anger rises in my throat.

"It's not my stout, Pat-Joe," I say. "It's Granda's, as you know damn well."

"Who's Granda?" the Skull asks. "I don't know any Granda. That's my friend Oliver Cromwell. And I'm Beelzebub. I'm the Lord of the Flies."

"You're black enough anyway," Cromwell chortles.

I am sure it's Pat-Joe. He couldn't pretend to save his life. But they are both drunk, and I want to get away from them.

"I don't care who you are. Let me pass!"

Beelzebub slaps me lightly on the side of the head. I am holding the bottles, and I cannot avoid his hand.

"Stay and have a drink with us, why don't you?" he cajoles. "'Tisn't afraid of the stuff you are, is it?"

Behind me Pat-Joe guffaws. "He's afraid it will burst his bladder!"

I remember my mother's unreasonable dislike of Pat-Joe, and an expression of hers floats unwanted into my head.

"I'd sooner sup with a tinker by the side of the road," I say slowly and deliberately, "than sit down and drink with the likes of you."

Beelzebub catches me by the shoulders and pushes me back against the wall. "Listen to me, you little fucker. 'Tis time you packed your bags and took to the road yourself. The people are sick and tired of you and the way you're getting to be a head above yourself."

I feel suddenly sick and weak, as though he has actually struck me.

"Give him a box," I hear Pat-Joe urging him.

"I wouldn't give him the steam off me piss!"

He releases his grip on my shoulders and steps back. I turn to Pat-Joe and tear the mask from his face. But it is not Pat-Joe. It is one of my schoolmates from Caher, to whom I've never even spoken; he is a class ahead of me. I am dumbfounded. I want to apologize and to demand an explanation all at once. But before I can say anything, my legs are knocked from under me. The stout goes flying with a clatter, and I am lying on my back in the filthy yard.

The two of them go arm and arm to the door and shut it after them, leaving me in the dark. I get on my knees and fumble about for the stout. There is broken glass everywhere, and I cut my hand on a piece of it. The smell makes me gag. I get up and stumble out of the yard.

I strike out across the field, running as hard as I can in the dark. I stumble through a tangle of uprooted furze bushes that block an opening and come out onto the Upper Road. My trousers are wet to the knees from the grass of the field, and my hand is stinging painfully. I run for a long way upon the road. Occasionally I pause and walk a couple of paces, but then I see the masks, I hear the taunting voices, and I find myself running again.

The moon rises; it is as bright as day. I pass the lane that leads down to the house and keep on toward the Head, toward the mouth of the harbor and the Skelligs beyond, great dark spikes in a sea that looks like a shield of beaten silver. I leave the road and start on up the slope. I do not stop until I have climbed halfway up the side of the Head. I have a stitch in my side, and my breath is being dragged in and out of my lungs like a mad thing.

There is a sharp wind off the ocean up here. It chills the sweat on my face and neck, and I begin to shiver. All around me on the slope are the remains of ancient stone huts, or *clocháin,* as they are called, vivid in the moonlight, some shattered, some buried in the earth. I walk into one of them. It has lost its roof, but when I hunker down and wedge myself into a corner, I am out of the wind. The pressure of the walls against my shoulders is comforting. The stones are large and remarkably smooth; there are even little cubbyholes and shelves where people must have stored things, time out of mind. The wind rages high above me, with a sound like the shaking of a sail, drowning out the noise of the sea. The rasping of my breath grows quiet; the aching muscles of my legs are eased. I put my head back against the stone and close my eyes.

The people are sick and tired of you. Well, if they are, I'm sick and tired of them — and of this black hump of a benighted rock! If it weren't for the Cable there would be no one and nothing here save the gulls to shit upon it. Christine had the right of it, to get the hell out of the place while the going was good. God above, any self-respecting person would take the ferry as soon as he had the sixpence for the fare. Look at the ones that stay behind, the old man that's as odd as two left feet and Con that'd be lost anywhere else — and the likes of Pat-Joe! To hear Granda: *Is it Paris you want?* It's because he's too uncouth for any place but a bloody rock in the middle of the sea. He should have stayed on the Skelligs, so he should, that was the place for him all right — with his specters. He doesn't really care what I do. How many times have I heard him say it: *Sure what is there here?*

My hand throbs painfully in the cold. My mother wanted to be shut of the Inish too — and who can blame her? That was why she sent me back, so she'd never have to set foot in the place again. You'd think she would help me to get away myself to London, but I suppose it is because I refused her once. Or maybe there is really no room in the house; there must be at least four or five of them by now. They are no kin to me really. I'd be no better off with them than among strangers.

I stand up. The brilliant light of the moon lies on everything, the scattered stones of the *clocháin*, the hills of the mainland, the Skelligs and the sea. It would drive you crazy to look at it, so beautiful and so lonely. But what is it really but a heap of old rocks and stones? There is no magic in it, no Other World, no ghosts and specters. There are only old stories that Granda tells himself to keep from going mad. I'm already a little bit mad myself from having to listen to him.

"I'm going away," I shout into the wind, "whether you like it or not. I'll go to Dublin anyway, before I stop. I'll get into the college there, by hook or by crook. I'm not an *amadán*, you know."

There is a sudden lull in the wind. I stop short — to see if I will be struck down on the spot. The hills and fields gleam in the dead light of the moon. There is only the distant sound of the waves below me and the sighing of my own breath.

"And do you know what I am going to do there in the college?" I say, appalled and fascinated by the raw sound of my own voice. "I am going to study the *real* history of Ireland. Your old fairy tales are only fit for children — and for old men astray in their wits! You may go to the Devil and take them along with you!"

I drive through the pretty town of Newburyport, cross a bridge over a narrow snaky river, and I'm on the island. It does not feel like an island, and I am unaccountably disappointed, almost sorry that I came. On one side of the road there are sand dunes, on the other a marsh that stretches to a horizon bounded by a line of trees.

I drive on mechanically. The road turns into a dirt track. I slow down, open the window. Heat fragrant with the scent of the marsh, which is brown and purple and yellow, restful to look at. But empty.

I drive until I come to the end of the road and park in a lot surrounded by masses of beach roses. A boardwalk through the dunes; my eyes narrow against the powerful glare of the sand. Unbearable heat, a little rise — and then I step into coolness, as through an invisible doorway. I am looking down on the ocean from the height of the dunes. The beach goes off on either side as far as I can see. I come to myself, with a little shock of pain.

This is as close as I can get now to the Inish, as close as I want to get. All of that is gone, over and done with. But I cannot convince myself. My past seems to be invisibly present on this Atlantic beach of the New World, defining my every word and gesture with its subtle, ghostly influence.

Love and Work

I CANNOT call her.

I am terrified of the telephone. I'm afraid to hear her voice in my ear telling me I've waited too long. I cannot bear to think of myself standing with the receiver in my hand after she has hung up, listening to the fatal buzzing of the dial tone. Therefore I will have to drive out there to see her. If only to say good-bye.

It takes me a week to reach this decision, and then I wait another couple of days for a Sunday. A reasonable person might call first, to establish a time convenient for her and obviate the need for guess-work. But since I cannot call, I settle on late afternoon, remembering that Lily likes to go to bed early before a workday. Will she think I am inviting myself to dinner? Or if I arrive after dinner, to stay the night? Perhaps our interview will be short and sweet. I cannot help my foreboding.

I drive without paying much attention to where I am going. The Monster seems to know the way. It is a cold pristine evening, light draining out of the pale cloudless sky, the kind of sky that arches over the sea, that contains a faint melancholy intimation of the sea's rich blue. I am already behind schedule, which must be significant. I am afraid to face her. I am afraid of the reflection of my own state that I will receive from her. But I am more afraid of that state itself, whatever it is, of going deeper and deeper into it, alone.

Enough! I turn into Lily's driveway. From the road there's no light visible in the house, but it's dusk, so she may not have felt the need.

When I round the slight bend, I see that her car is not here. My heart sinks.

I park in Lily's place by the kitchen window, shut off the engine, and sit for a moment, breathing deeply. Then I open the door and step out. It is clear and cold with a full moon; across the field, darkness has gathered beneath the trees marking the course of the stream. The field looks naked without its immaculate blanket of snow, and the air is raw, smelling faintly of rotting leaves. The moonlight falls full upon the front of the house, making it shimmer uncannily, as though the clapboard is wet. It is like a ghost house.

I walk up on the back porch. I could let myself in — I know where the key is — or leave a note. As I pass the kitchen window, I see a cone of light falling from a floor lamp in the living room beyond. I lean back against the porch railing and look into the house. There is something at once welcoming and sad about a lighted room viewed from without, the promise of warmth and shelter, and the awareness of encroaching dark. I shiver a little. I should have come this morning — or at any time during the last month. I am too late.

Lily passes the kitchen door with the cordless telephone held to her ear. My heart surges, as though I have seen a ghost. She comes back in a moment and enters the living room, where she sits in the chair beneath the lamp. Her expression is intent and serious. She opens her mouth to speak, but continues to listen. Then she speaks, with animation and energy, but no word carries to where I stand. I am fascinated by her. She seems more desirable than I have ever known her, and more remote, existing in her own circumscribed world that no longer contains an awareness of Matt Quigley and his vexed fortunes. I cannot be part of that world; it was a mistake for me to think I could be. This is what she was trying to tell me, as gently as she could. She will find someone who will talk to her, and I will certainly be the better for having known her. I will stand here and watch her for a little while — and then I will go away.

She lets her hand hang loosely over the arm of the chair, an uncharacteristic gesture. She laughs a little, then talks seriously again, pushing back the dark mass of her hair. Who is she talking to? It is none of my business. I can feel her withdrawing into her own life, becoming a stranger. A sense of loss wells up in me; tears come to my eyes. I must go away, now, while she is still on the phone. But I remain standing in the dark, watching her through the glass.

She presses the off button on the phone, places it in her lap, and stares ahead of her. She is looking straight at me, but she doesn't see me. I turn and walk down the steps.

I hear a rapid scratching on the gravel, and the dark mass of an animal rushes past me. I start, and then I recognize Cooper by the white markings at his throat and the tip of his tail. He wheels and leaps up to plant his forepaws against my chest, his tail lashing. At the same moment the porch light flares on, and Lily is standing behind the screen door. She raises her hand and peers into the dark. I step back into the light, the dog squirming about my feet.

"Hi, Matt."

"I'm sorry if I frightened you."

"If Cooper doesn't bark, I know it's a friend."

"I thought he might have forgotten me."

"He may not have forgiven you, but he hasn't forgotten you."

Her tone is light, wry, faintly regretful. She has made up her mind.

"I didn't think you were home," I say. "Where's your car?"

"In the shop. I had to take a taxi home from the train station on Friday. Aren't you going to come in?"

She holds the door for me, and I step past her into the kitchen. Her proximity, the perfume of her hair, thrills me, and then she steps away. She is wearing her faded house jeans and an oversized sweater, but she looks eminently desirable for all of that. The sight of her brings back all my feeling for her. But now she is beyond me, as her quizzical, distant manner makes plain.

I sit uneasily at the kitchen table. Lily leans against the stove, hips thrust slightly forward, watching me, unsmiling.

"So how are you?" I venture.

"I'm OK. I just got off the phone with my father."

"I hope he's well."

"Actually, he called me up to complain about his health. He's having some difficulty urinating. He has to go for some tests."

This news disturbs me. I feel a burgeoning apprehension. "I'm sorry to hear that. I hope he'll be all right. I like your father."

She gives me a clear unsmiling look.

"He liked you too," she says. "He asked about you. I told him I hadn't seen you."

There is a question here — or an opening for what I have to say. But I draw back from it involuntarily. How to begin? I realize that I do not have a plan, in spite of my best intentions. And I am concerned about Sam. I didn't know I felt so attached to him.

"Maybe I'll stop by and see him next time I'm downtown," I say.

"You should. He'd really like that. He seemed fine the last time I saw him, when I went by with you. But he says he hasn't been out-of-doors for weeks, which is not like my father."

"I'm sure it's nothing serious," I feel obliged to say — with the uncanny sense that I'm just whistling in the dark.

"You can never tell with my father. He's been predicting his death since before I was born. One of these days he's going to be right. My father thinks that if he drops his guard for one moment and concedes that he just might live until tomorrow, God will strike him down. Personally, I'd rather be hopeful in my ignorance."

"You mean you'd rather not know?"

"We all know we're going to die, don't we? But my father is depressed. When I call him on the phone, it's like hearing a voice from beyond the grave. That's his way of dealing with it. Go and see him. It'll cheer him up."

There is something in the prospect of Sam's death that concerns me deeply. I want to go, but I wonder if I can. I was concerned for the old man too — before I abandoned him.

Cooper sidles up to Lily and nuzzles her hand. She makes him sit. He regards me expectantly.

"Rick told me you went out with Erica."

This takes me completely by surprise.

"We went to the Cape," I stammer, as though this is an explanation.

Her expression of composure gives me no clue to her feelings. The dog moves to rise and come to me, but she holds his collar, and he subsides, placing his muzzle on his outstretched paws, his great soulful eyes still seeking mine.

"Lily," I say. "I was lonely."

"Why didn't you call me?"

"I didn't know what to say. Until now. I have something to tell you."

"You've found true love with Erica!"

Before I can respond she releases the dog, gets up, and walks into the living room. Cooper raises his ears and thumps the floor with his tail. I get up and go to the door. She is standing in the bay of the window, facing her reflection in the glass.

"Lily, I haven't seen her since. It was sort of a one-night stand — not that she spent the night or anything. You're the only woman I'm interested in."

She keeps her back to me. I come and stand behind her, keeping my distance.

"Rick is such a jerk sometimes. You and Erica. What a stupid idea."

"He told you about . . . fixing me up with her?"

"He feels guilty about it — especially since he found out that she's sick. He should have known better. But that doesn't let *you* off the hook. What were you thinking of? *Gentlemen Prefer Blondes?*"

"I couldn't care less if I never see the inside of another movie theater. I'm sorry, Lily."

She turns around abruptly, and I have to step back.

"What *did* you come out here for?"

Her eyes flash at me. Inexplicably, I feel myself becoming calm.

"I came out here because I love you and I don't feel alive without you."

She sighs and lifts one hand to her hair, not looking at me. "You don't seem to feel alive *with* me either."

Something in the casual way she says this gives me hope. I take a step closer to her. "If I felt it last year I can feel it again. Right now I feel — frozen. But you're right: I've got to face it, to go through it. The trouble is that no one in my life ever told me that it's possible —

until you came along. I want to believe it. But I can't do it without you."

We are standing very close in the window bay, the room dimly lit on one side, the dark pressing on the glass from the other. But she no longer feels closed to me, though her face is slightly averted from mine.

"Come on," I murmur. "Give us a hug."

I put my arms around her. She feels soft, familiar, friendly. I experience a powerful sense of elation. She steps back, and I let her go.

"But are you really going to talk to me again the way you used to in Ireland?"

My heart rises within me at her tone.

"Lily," I say giddily. "I'll do anything you want. Talk to you? You'll be sorry you asked. I'll talk to you till the cows come home, I'll talk your ear off, I'll tell you my life story over again, with all the unflattering details I left out first time around. I'll tell you the history of the Inish and of my family unto the seventh generation, I'll tell you every one of my grandfather's interminable stories, I'll recite the genealogies of the Irish kings, historical and mythical, all the way back to Maolsheachlainn the Great, contemporary of Noah, I'll talk away all the nights from Samhain to Bealtaine and back again, I'll talk until you beg me to stop . . ."

She puts her hand over my mouth. I lead her to the couch, where we sit side by side, turned toward each other, our knees touching.

"Why don't you start by telling me how much you've missed me?" she suggests.

I feel the warmth of affection emanating from her. We slide into each other's arms.

A loud plaintive whine comes from the doorway. We turn around together. The dog is sitting there on his haunches, ears erect, head tilted quizzically to one side.

"He needs to go out again," Lily says. "And I need to think about going to work tomorrow. Have you had anything to eat?"

I shake my head. I'm not particularly interested in food. I reach for her again, but she gets up and opens the back door for Cooper. We are kissing in the kitchen when he scratches on the door to be let in. Lily goes to the fridge and produces some leftovers for me. I eat without taking my eyes off her. I am lucky she did not turn me from her door, and I feel very grateful to her. But am I entirely forgiven?

"You could do me a favor," Lily says suddenly. "If you wanted to stay the night."

My heart gives a little flip.

"I could?"

"You could drive me to the garage in the morning, and I'd be able to pick up my car. Otherwise I'll have to take off early from work."

"I'd be happy to."

"You don't have anything planned?"

"Lily," I say, amused and dismayed by her punctiliousness. "What do you think?"

"But on the couch, OK?" she says, with a tight little grin.

I am content. And as it turns out, Lily relents and comes downstairs in the middle of the night, and our reconciliation is complete. When I wake, at some ungodly hour of the morning, she is in the shower. I come into the kitchen, still stupefied with sleep and happiness, to find her bustling about, dressed in a dark green suit and lacy white blouse. She kisses me briskly on the cheek. "You need to hurry if you want to have breakfast."

"I'll wait until I get back to my apartment. It's too early for me to eat."

I walk out into the crisp morning air. The sun has not yet cleared the trees at the bottom of the field, and the sky is clean and cloudless, pale at the zenith, deepening to black in the west. I watch the smoky plume of my breath diffuse in the cool air and listen to my feet crunching the gravel. I am momentarily at peace with myself and the world. I have mended my fences with Lily. I did not do it with efficiency or with style, but I regard it nevertheless as a small accomplishment. It gives me a reprieve, a space in which to breathe.

I start up the Monster and turn to face the road. Lily comes running from the house with her briefcase and slides in beside me. It gives me a little thrill to be setting out with her early in the morning, engaged on the world's business, if only for an hour. She is dressed to face the world, all fragrant and new, but I remember our lovemaking of last night, the marvelous shock of it after weeks of loneliness, and I hold the memory to myself with secret pleasure.

"I'm finally going to do it," Lily says. "I'm going to give them a month's notice. Today!"

She sounds excited. It is a pleasure just to hear her voice, to have her in my life again.

"Congratulations! When did you decide?"

"A few minutes ago."

"Really?"

I glance across at her. She seems to be amused about something.

"If I'm doing what I want to do with my own life," she tells me, "I won't take your coming and going so much to heart."

"Lily! It won't be like that. Believe me!"

"I missed you, Matt. I'm glad you're back."

I drive, Lily directing me. I am savoring this time with her, knowing that it is brief, knowing too that nothing untoward can happen.

"Do you see much of your roommate?" she asks.

"No. And from now on I'll be seeing even less of her. She's moving out."

"She is? What are you going to do?"

"I'll have to find a new roommate or get a job and pick up the extra rent myself. To tell you the truth, I'm thinking about getting a job."

I am a little surprised to hear myself say this. Yesterday I had come to no decision; both alternatives seemed equally unpalatable. But I seem to have discovered resolution overnight. Isn't it amazing what a little happiness can accomplish?

"I thought you didn't want to work right now," Lily says.

Something in her voice causes me to remember our testy exchange about work the last time I saw her. But we are safe now. I do not need to fear.

"My money's not going to last forever. And I like the apartment. I'd rather pay the extra rent than move to a smaller place or have to live with someone I don't know from Adam."

"Lots of people have roommates. You just interview until you find someone you like."

"Interview? I can't do it. I'd feel I had to give the room to the first person who called. I'd rather work."

I'm surprised that Lily is not more enthusiastic about my decision. It seems to me that she wanted me to get a job, if only so that I wouldn't be so depressed.

"You'll have a lot more room," she says.

"Maybe I'll turn Jamie's bedroom into a study, though what I'd study in it I don't know."

"This is the place," she tells me.

We are passing a Geo dealership. I pull into the lot. I am suddenly tense, not knowing how to take my leave of her. She sits quietly for a moment.

"Listen," she says. "I just had an idea. Maybe I'll move at the end of the month. Cambridge would be great for me. If you had someone to share the rent, you could be a little more relaxed about getting a job. What do you think?"

She turns to me, her eyes alight, and then the animation drains out of her face as she reads my consternation.

"But I thought you moved out because you didn't want to live in the country," she begins. "You even *suggested* I should move to town."

I sit there, helpless, unable to utter a word.

"Well, it doesn't matter what I thought," she says. "You don't want to live with me. That's the bottom line."

"Lily, it's not that I don't want to live with you —"

"You don't have to say anything. It's all perfectly clear. Now I have to go to work. Thanks for the ride."

She opens the door and swings her legs out.

"I'll call you," I say desperately.

She walks briskly toward the service entrance, carrying raincoat and briefcase, leaving me sitting there with the door open and the engine running, amid the ruin of my new hopes.

My first day — or rather night — on the job: I am to work the night shift at Carr Fasteners in Kendall Square, a ten-minute drive from my apartment. I have been told to report to work at 9:00 P.M. for a shift that lasts until 6:00 A.M., with two ten-minute coffee breaks and a half hour for "lunch." So I have a job — and an excuse to call Lily.

I leave the Monster in a vast vacant block that serves as a parking lot. The building runs the length of the block. It is five stories, of red brick with large windows of what looks like black opaque glass and steps leading up to three cavernous porches. I am fifteen minutes early. With my stomach twisted in a knot of excitement and fear, I cross the lot slowly and stand in one of the porches, trying to look as though I belong there.

My interview, which took place in an office building in Kendall Square, was perfunctory. I was confronted by a portly gent in a white shirt who scribbled on the forms scattered about his desk and did not appear to listen to my answers. Rick had enjoined me not to mention my abortive college career or my lack of a work permit. I wasn't at all sure I'd be able to lie, but it turned out not to be necessary. One glance at my physique seemed to tell my interviewer all he needed to know: two arms, two legs, not disabled or infirm. I took his taciturn manner for dissatisfaction and had resigned myself to the continuation of my search when I heard him announcing time and place and hourly rate in a monotone, still without looking up from his forms. I left in a euphoric daze, without knowing precisely what would be required of me, save that I was now employed on the floor of a parts factory. What kinds of parts? What difference, so long as I am considered capable?

Nothing remains of my euphoria as I stand before this cheerless edifice. It is one thing to interview for a job, quite another to perform it. But perhaps my duties will distract me. I've brooded about Lily all week, unable to sleep, restless even in the Monster. To have come so close to a reconciliation — and then to have it snatched away. But what could I have said to her request? It must be true that I do not want to live with her. I am a creature who requires solitude, as much as I suffer from it. But that does not mean I do not want to see her.

Men, dressed mostly in overalls, begin to pass me, singly or in twos and threes, and climb the stairs into the building. I notice that most

of them are wearing boots, which makes me wonder about the suit-
ability of my sneakers. At five minutes before the hour, a bell sounds
somewhere in the depths of the building. Ask not for whom. I pass
through the high doors. The staircase is metal and makes a faint
ringing sound beneath me. As I go up, another group of men comes
bounding down, and I step back against the wall. The entire staircase
trembles, and from behind the huge metal doors on each landing
comes a vague roaring sound. I ascend to the fourth floor and open
one of these doors. The sound hits me like a physical blow, like a
solid substance blocking my way, and for a moment I can only stand
on the threshold, almost senseless, incapable of taking in what I see.
Someone pushes by me. I step inside and close the door after me.

The room is vast and cavernous — it seems to extend farther than
I can see — and filled with large machines, taller than any of the
workers that attend them. At first I cannot believe that these machines, which appear perfectly motionless, are the source of the appalling noise and vibration. But then I notice that they are all trembling slightly, that something snakelike is being fed into each of
them and that something else — pieces of chopped-up snake? — issues from the other side. In the center of each one, something is
moving so rapidly that it's hard for the eye to register. It is this something that produces the noise and the vibration. The attitude of the
workers attending the machines is shockingly casual. They stand
very close to them, apparently unconcerned, occasionally stooping
to peer into this central area where the most ferocious action is taking place, or reaching down to grab one of the little pieces that the
machine spits out. Now I see that some few of the machines are actually immobile. A man stands before one of them, delving in it with
long slender rods that resemble knitting needles.

I notice a brightly lit office off to one side, so I go and stand in the
doorway. A man wearing an oil-smeared cap emblazoned with a disheveled *B* looks up from a newspaper on an empty desk.

"I'm Matt Quigley," I begin.

The man says something, but I cannot hear him on account of the
noise. He may be introducing himself, but from the sour expression

on his face I am inclined to doubt it. I close the door to shut out the noise.

"I'm supposed to start tonight."

"There was supposed to be two of you," the man in the cap says irately.

His finger marks the place in the newspaper column where he has been reading. For a moment, it looks as though I cannot begin work because there are not more of me. But then he gets up abruptly, or rather he unfolds himself from his seat and comes around the desk. He is extraordinarily tall — and as thin as a rail. He jams the filthy cap down upon his forehead, stoops to avoid knocking his head in the doorway, and stalks out past me. I'm not sure what he intends, but I decide that my best course of action is to follow him.

The Cap strides down the main aisle of the room, between the rows of pounding machines. His overalls flap loosely about his legs; he is nothing but skin and bone. He takes a sudden left and comes to an idle machine in the corner. Without looking around to see if I am with him, he bends from the waist, quickly lifts, and throws a circular object onto a low circular tray beside the machine. He peers at me over his shoulder, while maneuvering the object into place, and speaks. I cannot hear, and I place my hand to my ear.

"Don't cut the wire till you've got it on there!" he yells.

He produces a wire cutter from somewhere and snips three pieces of wire. I see that the object is a large coil of metal tape. With swift jerky movements, like a wind-up toy, he peels the edge of it off the circumference, squares it with the wire cutter, leads it through a guide, and into the machine. Then he motions me over to a control box, upon which there are two switches, a light, and a red button. He hits the on-off switch; the light comes on, but nothing moves. He points with the wire cutter to the other switch, auto-manual. It is set at manual. He presses the button next to the switch. The machine makes a sudden thump, and I jump back. Frowning, he motions me forward. He takes a pair of needlelike rods, dons a pair of goggles, and pushes the tape onto a narrow set of rollers in the empty center of the machine. He presses the red button. I am watching this time, and I wince as a part of the machine crashes down upon the end of the tape and swiftly withdraws, leaving a slight indentation. He peers in, adjusts the position of the tape with the rods, and presses the button again. The heads of the machine crash down, a second indentation appears, this one a little deeper than the first. He prods the tape, jabs the button, holds it down. The noise becomes continuous, the heads crash up and down, the tape advances. A tiny piece of it shoots out into a metal crate. He picks it up, pushes back the goggles, and eyes it skeptically. Then he hands it to me. It is one half of a snap fastener, the kind you see on denim shirts, the part with the little protruding nipple that snaps into the other part. I am astonished that this simple object is produced by such a complicated machine. But did I think they grew on trees? I have a strange feeling of satisfaction, to be in possession of this arcane fragment of knowledge.

The Cap taps my shoulder with the wire cutter. He presses the button and holds it. The motion of the heads accelerates until I cannot see them, the tape moves swiftly beneath them, and fasteners are spewed into the crate. He snaps the second switch to auto and takes his finger off the button. The machine has reached a steady pitch; like all the others it seems motionless, except for the noise — which drowns out even the surrounding racket — and the blur of movement of the heads. I smile my comprehension at the Cap. He doesn't acknowledge it. He hands me the rods and the goggles, gestures down the row of machines, says something I do not hear, and walks away.

I stand in front of the machine that has been entrusted to my care. I'm a little apprehensive, but it seems to be doing just fine. The tape is peeling smoothly off the coil, the heads are drumming evenly, and the little pieces are making a mound in the crate. I stroll out to the main aisle and look around. There are men loitering beside machines. No one looks at me, and conversation is impossible because of the noise. That's fine with me. I ought not to have worried. There's no question of my ability to carry out this job. Perhaps I'll bring a book tomorrow night.

I wander back to my machine and watch the coil get smaller and the pieces accumulate in the crate. I shut the power off just as the end of the tape passes beneath the heads. There is a small chewed-up piece of tape left in there. I put my hand in and pick it out. Then I pick up a roll of tape. It's heavy: how the Cap lifted it without breaking himself in half is beyond me! I try to stand it on edge, but it starts to come apart, so I pick it up and throw it onto the feeder just as I have seen the Cap do it. Next: cut the wire. I see no wire cutters, and after a perfunctory search I go to look for the Cap. I run into him almost at once, bearing down on me with his lanky, loose-limbed stride. I make a snipping motion with my fingers, pleased to have adopted the language of the floor. He ignores me, strides up to my machine, and picks the wire cutters off of the shelf that held the rods and the goggles.

"Sorry," I mumble into the din.

Suddenly the Cap is yelling at me, waving his long arms, and gesturing down the row of machines. I am in shock. I cannot hear what he is saying, and I do not know what to do about it. He goes over to another idle machine and thumps the control panel with his fist. He kicks the heap of coils with the toe of his boot. He glares at me. Has he lost his mind? Is this one of the effects of prolonged exposure to this noise and the vibration? Then he comes back to me, holds up six skeletal fingers, shakes them in my face, and turns on his heel and walks away.

I am trembling with frustration and embarrassment. I want to go after him, to find a place where we can talk without this infernal din in our ears, so that he can tell me what he wants me to do, instead of engaging in this ridiculous pantomime. Suddenly a little man in overalls, with silver hair and gold-rimmed spectacles, materializes beside me. He points to the pocket of his overalls upon which his name is embroidered. Al. Thank God for a civilized gesture.

"Matt," I yell in his ear.

He nods seriously, puts his hand on my shoulder, and speaks at my ear in what sounds like a remarkably penetrating whisper.

"You have to operate six machines."

I feel like an idiot. I turn to apologize to Al, but he's already in motion. He moves the length of the row, smoothly slinging coils of wire onto the feeders. I want to help him; he looks more like a watch-maker than a factory worker. Can he really be strong enough for such work? But he's got five coils in place, and he snips the wires on one of them and tosses me the wire cutters. I go down the row, snipping the wires. By the time I'm done, Al has got a machine up and running, and he's on to the next one. He makes a brisk gesture in the air with his hand, and I understand immediately that he wants me to trim the tapes and lead the edges into the machines. I do so. Al has three machines running; he starts in on the fourth. I go back to my original machine, and by the time I have tapped the tape through the heads and am ready to switch to auto, he has five machines going. I hit the switch, determined to show I'm good for something, and the tape immediately crinkles up and is crushed beneath the pounding heads. Al turns it off. I reach in to clear the heads, and Al knocks my hand aside.

"Use the rods," he hisses in my ear.

He deftly extracts the damaged tape, taps a new length through, and works the machine up to speed. He hands me a wad of grubby cotton wool and indicates his ears. Before I can yell my thanks, he's slipped away, leaving me with sole responsibility for six pounding and, as far as I can tell, perfectly functional machines.

I spend the next four hours of my shift running from pillar to post. I anticipate a respite before my machines run out of tape, but things start to go wrong long before that. The tape gets jammed or warped or unhitched from the feeder, and each of these calamities takes me completely by surprise. No sooner have I cleared away the mangled tape and gotten the machine up again than another one is down or has reached the end of its run. I rush to the end of the line and crouch over the coils, already aware from a subtle difference in the infernal din that yet another machine has ground to a halt. Sometimes I cannot restart a machine, in spite of my best efforts. Al materializes from nowhere with a handsome-looking chap whom he introduces as Mario. He yells the name in my ear, steps back and grins at Mario, who is wearing a set of headphones and a beatific expression. I understand that Mario's function is to service recalcitrant machines; he opens a toolbox and goes to work. He sings along with the music, but no sound issues from his mouth. All too soon, he's tapping my shoulder: the machine is ready to be added to my burden.

Al comes down the line and shuts off all my machines one by one. For a moment, I'm afraid I'm about to be fired.

"Break time," he says cheerfully.

I pull the cotton wool out of my ears, and I become aware of the uncanny silence. It makes me feel slightly giddy, this silence, as though I had forgotten its existence. I want to take advantage of it, to sing aloud, to whistle, to shout.

"Coffee truck's downstairs," Al says. "You can get a sub."

I follow him down the staircase. The distant roar of machines sounds from the other floors. My body is numb, but I sense the awakening of unaccustomed aches and pains, and a not unpleasant feeling of fatigue. My thoughts return to me too, as though from a great distance: I remember Lily and the uncertainty that surrounds our relationship. But my troubled ruminations of the past week do not enmesh me; I can recall them, but my fatigue keeps them at bay. Perhaps this is the advice I have so often heard tendered to the distraught: keep yourself occupied. The Devil makes work for idle hands. I have done well to find a job — if only it does not kill me.

The truck is parked opposite the porch. There is no one in line — apparently I have worked part of my break — but when I turn around I see a row of men squatting against the outside wall of the building, smoking, drinking coffee, and talking. I take my place at the end of the row. How pleasant it is just to sit! I wolf down a meatball sub, something I would never dream of eating in the normal course of events — but I may need some red meat to get me through the night. It's hot. I want to sprawl full length on the pavement; I feel as though I can sleep. Al comes and squats down beside me.

"You Irish, Matt?" he says.

"How did you know?"

He grins secretively. "I'm from the old country myself."

I can't decide if he is serious or joking. Everybody here is from the old country if you go back far enough. I cannot hear any trace of Ireland in his accent, which is flat and hard.

"What generation?"

"Now you've got me." Al chuckles.

He steps around me and squats down on the other side. "Get yourself a decent set of earplugs," he admonishes. "Or you'll end up like me, deaf in one ear. You a student, Matt?"

"I quit school."

"What you want to do that for?"

It is a fair question, though not one you expect a stranger to ask. But I like Al. There is no nonsense about him.

"I wanted to come over here," I say. "To be with my girlfriend."

It is probably tempting fate to assert that I still have a girlfriend. But my answer has satisfied Al.

"I gotcha!" he says, with evident approval. "You're just here at Carr temporary-like."

"I'm here for as long as I can put up with it. If I don't work, I'll be out on the street."

This may not be entirely true, but it gives me satisfaction to say it. I am a working man. I am earning my living by the sweat of my brow, I am an immigrant who has made good, albeit illegally.

"I've been here twenty years," Al says. "Mostly night shift too. I don't get to be awake much during the daytime, except I'm on vacation. Twenty years. How'd you like that? Night in, night out for twenty years."

"I'm just hoping to make it to the end of my first shift without do-ing anything else wrong."

Al nods sagely. The streetlight winks on the lenses of his spec-tacles.

"Don't let Ed Lunt bother you," he says. "The guy with the Red Sox hat."

"I didn't know his name."

"They call him something else around here, four-letter word that rhymes with his last name. He has new fellows come in here all the time, can't be bothered to tell them to be careful, and then he won-ders why he has so many accidents on his floor."

"Accidents?"

"Yeah. Carr is real generous with their workmen's comp. They'll give you fifty bucks a joint."

He holds up a thumb that seems abnormally short — and doesn't have a thumbnail. The sight of it makes the tips of my fingers ache strangely. Al flashes a wicked grin.

"It don't make no difference now. I ain't nothing for the women to look at. Five more years and I'm out of here — with three-quarter pension and social security — and then Ed Lunt and all the big muck-a-mucks in the office can kiss my derry-air, if you'll pardon my French. I'll be sitting at home nights drinking Irish whiskey instead of riding those frigging machines."

He gives me a nudge and a wink: we both know that drinking Irish whiskey is the pinnacle of worldly pleasure. Then he hoists himself slowly to his feet, leaning against the wall, as though he's feeling those twenty years — or the five still to go. I start to rise, but he puts his hand on my shoulder.

"Just sit," he says. "I got to get back and make sure Ed Lunt ain't fouling up my run with bum parts."

"Would he do that?" I say in astonishment.

"Don't trust no one, is my motto," Al says. "Not even yourself. And keep your hands out of those machines — or you'll be coming in for a bonus you don't want."

The rest of the night wings by without incident, apart from a brief run-in with the Cap. Out of nowhere, he's towering over me, thrusting a part under my nose. I take it and examine it. The little nipple is all skewed to one side. The Cap shuts off the machine and gives the crate a kick. He stalks away.

"You got to keep checking 'em," Al hisses at my ear. "If they weren't too cheap to buy new machines, the job would run straight through and the stock wouldn't get screwed up all the time."

This is the final lesson of my first night: Keep checking 'em. My speed in loading increases. I can't match Al, of course, but I manage to have no more than one machine down at a time. And I'm beginning to hear the subtle shift in sound that indicates that a machine is spewing out defective parts. When I hear this, I shut the machine off before I look in the hopper. It's easier to start it up again if the tape hasn't gotten mangled.

Wonder of wonders, when the day shift arrives, all my machines are up and running. I beam at my replacement and float out of there, high as a kite — or delirious with fatigue, I can't tell which. An early morning peace lies over the parking lot. Rush hour hasn't yet started in Kendall Square. The voices of the night shift and the slamming of car doors seem to resound in empty space. I slide gratefully into the Monster and start it up. It roars like one of my machines. I put it in drive and let it roll out of the lot. I have survived the worst. It's plain sailing from here until Friday.

In Kendall, I inadvertently take a left and find myself heading for the city by way of the Salt and Pepper Bridge, speeding toward the two towerlike edifices at midspan. The sun is just above the horizon; its light catches the roofs of Boston, the black glass of the Hancock, the golden dome of the State House. There's no one ahead of me on the downslope, and I step on the gas, borne along by a wave of elation. I have a job. I have a function in the New World, although a small one. I must be back at my station by 9:00 P.M. this evening or the Cap will have a fit.

And I must call Lily. To give her the news, to discover if she is still speaking to me. I will invite her to dinner — in the apartment I have refused to share with her. What have I got to lose?

I jump when the bell rings, even though I've been waiting for it impatiently. I rush into the hallway and press the intercom and the door release at the same time.

"Hi, Lily."

"Hi."

I could not infer her attitude toward me from our telephone conversation. At least she accepted my invitation. I throw open the apartment door and step out onto the landing. Lily comes unhurriedly up the stairs. She is wearing a black blouse I haven't seen before with her blue jeans, and a wide silver chain at her neck that gives her a touch of formality and elegance. I scan her face for a sign. She seems composed, detached.

"You look great," I say.

"Thanks. It looks nice in here."

I've done my best for the occasion. The table is spread with a white linen cloth, two long-stemmed crystal wineglasses, antique dinner plates with Chinese scenes, and a pair of matching brass candlesticks, all from the local Goodwill store. I have a twenty dollar Chablis in the fridge and a pair of two pound lobsters squirming in the kitchen sink.

"Would you like some wine?" I say, hoping to start the evening on a cheerful note.

"I want to apologize for asking to move in with you," she says.

My heart contracts. I had hoped to avoid this subject. What good will it do to talk about it now?

"It's I'm the one who should apologize, Lily."

"No," she says reasonably. "You want your own space, to go through whatever it is you're going through. You need to live alone right now, and I shouldn't have asked you to give it up for my convenience. I know better than that."

"You mean you're really not upset about it?"

"I felt a lot worse last month when I thought you weren't going to call me."

It dawns on me with a new clarity that Lily is attached to me, that she wants to be with me, that I am not merely a difficulty she longs to be shut of — in spite of my withdrawal from her.

"I have my own *mishegoss*, Matt," she says lightly. "You told me you wanted to make it work, and so I thought, Well, maybe it will be OK to live together after all. It wasn't a good idea. You haven't come to terms with your own stuff yet. We'd end up right back where we were at Christmas — and then one of us would have to move out again!"

"We *will* live together sometime," I begin.

"You don't have to say that. Let's see what happens. I'm still afraid you'll drift away from me into your own world — or go back to Ireland. That's my shtick: I want attention, I want to be sure. It comes from being my father's daughter, from wanting his love and attention — and never really getting it."

Something else is dawning on me. It is possible for me to discover what I want, to articulate my needs, even to oppose them to Lily's — and still be loved by her. An extraordinary thing!

"You've got *my* attention, Lily. I'm glad we're back together. I don't know how you put up with me. But I appreciate it."

I move to embrace her. She brushes her cheek against mine.

"I'll take that glass of wine now," she murmurs.

The meal is an unqualified success. The Chablis is perfectly chilled, and Lily is willing to hoist the lobsters into the pot, sparing me the sight of their contortions. For all the lobsters I have pulled out of the sea, I have never cooked and eaten one. But I produce the nutcrackers I have remembered to buy, and Lily gives me a lesson in how to open the formidable red and horny carapace and to extract the succulent meat inside. She is most thorough, teaching me to suck the legs and the tail, to break open the body and discover pockets of meat among the sinews, urging me (in vain) to sample the roe, which she claims is a great delicacy and even conducive to sexual prowess. I want to interpret this last remark to mean that she intends to stay the night, but I have a feeling that I am not yet out of the woods.

She carries her coffee into the room overlooking the street and lies on the couch. I sit on the floor with my back against a chair. I am happy to be here with her. I am grateful to her, and I want to tell her. But suddenly, inexplicably, I am moved almost to tears, and I am afraid my voice will betray me.

"It *is* a nice apartment," Lily says. "But I don't need to move to the city to start my business. I'll use the telephone. Besides, being out in the country is good for my work: that's why I moved there in the first place. I won't have to set up a new darkroom, and I can start right in on the dozens of rolls of film I have waiting to be developed. I still have more Irish photos I want to show you."

"I didn't give you a very encouraging response to the first batch. I'm sorry. You know, I *did* like them. But I think you were right; they made me homesick."

As soon as I say this, my emotion acquires clarity. It is a sadness, a regret, a longing — but for what I cannot tell. Lily gives me a searching look.

"You know what my father said when he heard I was quitting my job? My daughter starting her own business: it's like a virgin going out with Frank Sinatra. He just likes to worry. But that's *his* problem. At least he wants the best for me — I'm not sure your family always wanted what was best for you."

"What do you mean?" I say coldly.

"Your grandfather didn't want you to leave the island. He wanted you to put aside your own life to look after him and his house."

I am beside myself. I feel that she is attacking me for no reason. But I wait until I can control my response.

"It's a different culture," I tell her. "Family members look after each other. It's more than expectation. It's an expression of feeling."

"Matt," she says seriously, "your mother abandoned you. She sent you back to the island when you were seven years old — and she never took care of you again."

At this moment, an extraordinarily vivid image comes to me. As in a waking dream, I see my mother standing on the platform of Amiens Street Station after she has handed me and my suitcase onto the train. She looks at me through the glass, that distracted look a child could not understand, but which was received as blame.

I am standing in the middle of the room, but I am dissociated from it. I am filled with an inexpressible sadness, with an awareness of bonds from which I can never untangle myself. I feel with the immediacy of this present moment the helpless apprehension of a child before the rigors of an unknown journey, the pain of loneliness and abandonment. Tears blur my vision.

Lily is standing in front of me, holding my hands. "It's true, Matt, isn't it?"

I feel like someone advancing in the dark with arms extended. I am in a familiar place, but I am afraid of what I may find.

"It would have been a mercy for her to have gone with me on that train," I say.

"That is the very least she could have done for you," Lily says.

"But what's the point of blaming my mother now for something that happened fifteen years ago?"

"It's better than blaming yourself."

Suddenly I know what my mother's look means, I know it contains *her* distress, which has nothing to do with me. I know that she cannot see me, no more than if the sheet of glass between us were a mirror — and I know why I do not like her. Anger comes rushing in, like the hot blast from a furnace door. It was not my fault, Mother, I want to say. It was not my fault that you couldn't find someone to look after my grandfather, to do the work no child should have been sent to do, that you could hardly look after your own new baby, not to mind Jack and the house. It was not my fault that Jack didn't take to me. I was only a child.

Then everything falls to the ground and is swept away. I am sobbing violently, and Lily has her arms around me. I give myself up to it: I am too surprised to do anything else. It seems to last for a long time. When it is over, I feel relieved, and embarrassed. I step back.

"I'm sorry," I say. "I don't know where that came from."

"It came from you, Matt. It's the way you feel about what happened to you, except that you're not always aware of it. You can bury things, but they're still there, buried alive."

"Maybe it's better not to disinter such things."

"I know it's hard," she says quietly. "But every life has its own suffering, and there's really no way to avoid it. It's like a boil — expressing it is the only way to get relief! The Sufi poet Rumi says, Those who go into the water come up in the fire. And those who go into the fire come up in the water. You just went into the fire. Sooner or later, you'll come out the other side."

I walk over to the window and look out, to hide my tearstained face. The mist of sadness has withdrawn to the periphery of my awareness. In the foreground there is something I did not know before, a feeling more solid than any memory of my mother, more telling than mere fact. It is a feeling of anger: fire. God knows I have some reason to be angry, but somehow it has taken me by surprise. I do not want to burn with anger, to be consumed by it, much less to use it against my mother. I do not have to. I am here with Lily. I am safe — for now.

"Are you all right?" Lily asks.

I turn from the window. "I'm a new man," I tell her, with as much cheer as I can muster. "New job, new life — and a girlfriend who's worth crossing an ocean for. How can I possibly go wrong?"

Happy the Corpse

MONDAY AFTERNOONS, before my first shift of the week at Carr, I drive into the city and pass two or three hours in the Boston Public Library. I eschew the air-conditioned comfort of the new building for a few moments' pause in the deeply shaded courtyard of the old library, with its pool and trees and the tall, dark windows. Then I climb the wide stairs to the reading room and establish a base for myself at the corner of one of the oak tables. There is peace here, if not respite from the heat, with ineffectual fans turning in the high vault of the ceiling, the dark wainscoting and the brass lamps mounted on the tables, the drab solid walls of books. I am content to sit for a while, watching the bowed heads, listening to the discreet murmuring from the tall and ornate librarians' desks, breathing in the atmosphere of reasonable and unhurried diligence. The room has a soothing effect on me; it promises and demands less than a church. There is a place for me whenever I want to avail myself of it, a little niche in the city's harsh facade, and no one knows or cares whether I am of studious intent.

Of course I cannot help but read: the habit of years dies hard. The name of Pontiac has spawned a research of sorts, a paper trail of revelations about a world I know only through the so-called westerns I saw in the old picture house on the Inish. I am acquiring a detailed knowledge of the history and culture of native Americans, from the ancient ceremonies of the Hopis to the latter-day depredations inflicted by the U.S. Cavalry upon the Sioux. In this history I recognize something of the weary tale of cultural conquest and eviction in Ireland. To hell or to Connacht: that is our Trail of Tears. But there is something more personal in this recognition, or I would not feel so drawn to it. The loss of language, of immemorial custom, of land itself: that is my predicament too.

My afternoon is punctuated by excursions into the sweltering street, where I surreptitiously feed the Monster's meter. And thence back to the mystic visions of Black Elk, the assassination of Crazy Horse, the heartbreaking odyssey of Ishi, last of his tribe. But this identification is no more than a feint, useless to hold memory at bay. It is the old man's stories I find myself longing for, with their shadowy intimation of betrayal and loss. They seem closer and more comprehensible here in the formal atmosphere of the BPL, but this is an illusion, the last vestige of my scholarly ambitions. The stories have refused to disclose their meaning to the blunted knife of scholarship, and I cannot find in my imperfect recollections the magic I repudiated as a child and now long for in vain.

I glance up at the great clock high above the entrance. My hour has come. I am cast out from my sanctuary. I bring my books to the return cart, go slowly down the shallow steps, and walk with reluctant tread to the Monster. I know what is going to happen. The seat is hot and sticky, and I can hardly touch the wheel. As soon as I pull out onto Boylston Street, it begins. My drive to work is only a short hop on Storrow and then the Salt and Pepper Bridge — but it is time and enough for memory to reassert its claim.

To school in Caher for another two years. On Fridays and Saturdays I worked behind the bar in Dennehy's on Main Street. They made up a bed for me above in the house, and I did not get back to the Inish until Sunday morning. When the results of the Leaving Certificate examinations were made known, I had done better than any student who had ever attended the school — though God knows I did not have much time for study. Brother Lyons contrived to get me a scholarship to the college in Dublin. He had been exiled to Caher for some breach of the order's rule, but he still had friends in the city. He was a cultured and sensitive man; I can now see that Caher must have been torture for him. He dedicated himself to helping me escape, and I was beside myself with joy — until I realized that I did not yet have enough money saved to live in Dublin. Thus checked, I discovered that I was afraid of the city too, afraid of being alone there.

Another miserable year, during which I worked day and night, in the boat, in the bar, in the fields during the haymaking. I felt that the delay would somehow prove fatal to my ambition — and if I hadn't been so intolerably miserable, perhaps it would have. The old man and I were at daggers drawn, or so I imagined, since we didn't speak to each other except when it was unavoidable. I frequently spent the night in Caher after a long evening behind the bar and left him to shift for himself. I did not like to be in his company — and not just because of our falling-out. He seemed to be withdrawing into himself, severing his connections from the living, developing a hard and impenetrable shell, within which to die unseen. I did not like to imagine what he thought about as he sat in the chimney corner throughout the livelong day. I repeated to myself his own wisdom: It's death that will find us all, late or soon. How can a man escape the day of his death? I told myself he was reconciled to it, and I believed this. But I knew that I was hastening the evil day by leaving him. That was what he resented: that was the reason for the remarkable rigidity that had descended upon him, like a bodily manifestation of his thwarted will.

I went to Peg to ask her to look after him. Couldn't you stop with him for another year? she wanted to know. It was all she could do to keep from flying out at me. I put the question to myself; in a way it would have been a relief not to have to face the unknown. But I had no choice. Another year like this and I am done for, I said to myself. Peg wouldn't give me an answer. But I knew she would go to him. She had no choice either.

I worked with the energy of despair — until the day I walked out the door to go to Dublin. He refused to say good-bye to me. By his stiff and silent manner he seemed to repudiate the sense of what I was telling him: I'm leaving now, Granda. I'm going to Dublin, to the college. It didn't make a lot of sense to *me* at that moment; I was convinced it would end badly. I'll write to you, I said. I'll come down to visit. He pretended not to hear.

Two years at the college. Be sure to write, Brother Lyons said, as he saw me onto the train in Caher, and tell me what you think of the place. I did not write to him, and I'm sure I have compounded the bitterness of his isolation. But I didn't have the heart to tell him that the college was not a sanctuary for me, nor the home from home I wished for. How could I have explained it? My grandfather believed passionately in the personages of his stories: they were as real for him as the people of the Inish. The people of the college, professors and students alike, did not seem to believe in the reality of historic figures. The students believed in nothing, as a matter of principle, and the professors in ideas only, in method, in the writing — as opposed to the flesh and blood — of history. To listen to them you would think that the real subject of history is history itself — and not the lives of those who have lived before us. And so I did not find my real history here, except in a few scattered images: the great Hugh O'Neill on his knees before Elizabeth's envoy in abject surrender, not knowing that the Queen was already with the angels; Parnell dying in a hotel room in Brighton — and all because he forgot to put on the pair of dry socks his good wife had provided him with.

The scholars had a name for Granda's stories about the Skelligs: synthetic history. If only he could have heard them! They wondered if Diarmat and Grania were derived from Tristan and Iseult — or vice versa. They noted that both Arthur and Finn liked to hunt boars; they discovered an Irish King of the Boars, and a Welsh king transformed into a boar. I learned from them that poor Diarmat was killed by a magical boar who was really his foster brother, a variant the old man had never heard of. They remembered that Adonis was killed by a boar — and they wanted to know if Irish girls would give themselves to strangers at the beds of Diarmat and Grania the way women did at the shrines of Aphrodite.

What was the meaning of Diarmat's riddle? According to my learned sources, it absolved him of his guilt, for if he didn't take Grania by day or by night and all the rest of it, then he didn't really take her at all; that is to say, he didn't do what he did. Most enlightening.

But why did he come to a bad end? They informed me that the hero of Gaelic myth dies when he has violated his *geasa* and that his death usually has something to do with a woman. The unfortunate king of Caher is slaughtered while he lies sleeping with his head in his un-faithful wife's lap. Fergus is speared while swimming in a lake — with the redoubtable Maeve wrapped around him like a fish! And Diarmat, his riddle notwithstanding, is caught between two incom-patible obligations: he must not hunt a boar, nor refuse a kinsman's request.

These answers were of no use to me. Diarmat was not a real per-son, but his predicament was real. I wanted to know why he was obliged to love Grania, why her invitation proved so irresistible and fatal. It was the same question I'd asked the old man the night I first heard that story from him: What is a *geis*? It did not occur to anyone at the college to ask that question. So I made do with what they had to offer. I learned to classify the cycles of stories, to enumerate the motifs, to point out parallels with other mythologies. But I felt like an archaeologist, laying out potsherds, sticking labels on them, mak-ing conjectures about a life that I could not imagine. It was not what I thought the college would be.

I might have left, but I did not know what else to do. I didn't write to the old man because I didn't want him to know about my disap-pointment. I did not go back to the Inish at Christmas, and I told myself it was because no one invited me. (Was I expecting an invita-tion from Peg?) I did not go back the following summer because I found a job in the library that was more congenial than tending the bar in Dennehy's and because I did not want to lose my tiny flat off Baggot Street. But really I think I was afraid that if I did go back there, I would not have the force to tear myself free of it a second time.

And then — Lily! For all the time she was in Dublin I refused to think about her return to Boston. On the day she left I wanted to leave with her, to turn my back on the Inish and the college, to be shut of everything at once. But we both knew I could not arrive in Boston without having something to do there — or escape the Inish without some kind of leave-taking. So I told her I would stay for another year, to continue my disillusioned studies while applying to schools in Boston, and to break the news to the old man.

September: Lily is gone a week, and I have not heard from her. Lectures have not yet begun. I walk through the quadrangle of the college in a daze, feeling more estranged than ever, inhabiting a virtually posthumous existence. The gray stone buildings have a cloistral atmosphere without the bustle of students. I am thinking of Lily, trying to picture us together in Boston, that far-off and unimaginable place. I am waiting for the courage to go back to the Inish. I cannot hold Boston and the Inish together in my mind: they are like oppositely charged poles that repel each other violently. They do not seem to be part of the same world. If we only had Old Ireland over here, is the exile's futile lament. But I do not have to meld Boston and the Inish together. I only have to choose between them, to ratify the choice I have already made.

There is a telegram lying in the hall when I open the street door of the flat. I pick it up and carry it inside. It has become very quiet and still all around me. I have no thought save for Lily as I tear it open. What if something has happened to her?

BARTHOLOMEW VERY BAD, it reads. PRIEST CALLED. TELL YOUR MOTHER. No signature.

I stand there with the paper in my hand. I feel a sense of loss that is not grief or the apprehension of grief but the loss of time, of opportunity. I should have gone sooner, last month, last week, when I still could choose to go. Now it is too late for choice.

The telegram is from Peg. Nobody else has ever called my grandfather Bartholomew. I go out to the pay phone in the hall and place a call to my uncle Con. The switchboard on the Inish takes a long time to connect me, and then the line is very bad. This compounds my anxiety. My uncle comes on at last. His voice is scratchy, impregnated with static. There is a faint cloudy roaring in the background. I imagine him sitting on a wave-swept rock, clutching the telephone for dear life. From the remote perspective of Dublin, anything is possible.

"I'd say there's no fear of him," he protests.

"Did you *see* him?"

"I haven't laid eyes on him in donkey's years, boy. You wouldn't want to mind Peg. I think she wants to get rid of him, the way she goes on."

"I'll be down tonight," I tell him.

"Sure there's no need," he grouses.

Con regards the telephone as an agency of disaster. This is probably the only reason he keeps it, to be informed of deaths and wakes. But his manner is belligerent and incredulous, as though this will ward off evil news. He tries to make me feel that my call is a frivolous and unnecessary expense. How is it I do not know that everything is as it should be?

"I was thinking of coming anyway," I say.

"Suit yourself, boy."

I send a telegram to my mother. I spend a long time over it and end by mitigating somewhat the effect of Peg's bluntness: PEG SAYS GRANDA SICK. GOING DOWN TONIGHT. What else can I say? I do not know anything.

I am too late for the evening train. I leave my flat and walk down to the Canal, where I jog beside the water until it gets dark, in the hope of tiring myself. In vain: I do not sleep.

At some indeterminate hour of the night I think of calling Lily — it is Saturday morning over there. I get out of bed and turn on the light, but I do not have enough coins for the phone. This seems an absurd reason not to call her. I could reverse the charges; I feel a need to speak to her that almost warrants this drastic measure. But I allow myself to be ruled by my scruples.

As soon as it is light I walk along the river past the quiet formal elegance of the Four Courts to Connolly Station. There is very little traffic and no one on the quays. The city has a serenity that it lacks by day, and I remember that Lily liked it. I sit in the empty, noisome station, thinking of her, wishing I had called her. The time seems long until the train arrives, screeching and hissing like a demon. I walk through the carriages until I find an empty compartment. The train enters the tunnel that leads out of the city, and the darkness presses closely about me.

While the darkness lasts I am that child again, traveling alone, torn between longing for the Inish and the pain of a separation he does not understand, going into the unknown, into the dark. I try to shrug it off. All is for the best, I assure myself. I need to tell the old man that I am going away. There is no danger here: this is my opportunity.

Out of the dark and swiftly through the outlying suburbs: I find myself expecting to catch a glimpse of the boy and the dog I saw on that first journey back to the Inish, as though they have been trapped these many years in a sliver of stationary time. The train rushes on through fields, tears by stations without stopping, and I occupy myself by trying to catch their names as the signboards fly past: Sallins, Newbridge, Kildare, Monasterevin, Portarlington. The names themselves mean little to me and conceal less; it is the succession that is significant, every step of which is a removal from the civilization of Dublin and its bland hinterland — and a penetration into something more essential and profound.

But what does it have to do with *me?* I am committed to Lily, to flight. I feel that I am going into a trap.

The palms of my hands are damp with sweat. The train stops in Portlaoighise, and I want to run out of the compartment and jump down onto the platform. I stand up to do it, my heart thumping. But the door is drawn back, and two people enter, a countrywoman and her teenage daughter. I sit down abruptly and close my eyes. I feel weak, disembodied, not myself. The train bears me on.

I try to resign myself. He is old and sick, and it is the least I can do, to tell him I am going away and to say good-bye. There is no escaping it. I will never have any peace in the New World if I do not see him one more time.

Templemore — the great temple — and Thurles. I change trains at Limerick Junction, where once I waited in vain for Con to meet me. It is a bad place for a child to be lost, an isolated station without a town, owing only its name to Limerick proper. After the Junction, the names of the stations become more intriguing: Rath Luirc, Buttevant, Mallow, Banteer, Rathmore. Perhaps it is the echo of the

Gaelic names, the rumor of a subterranean life beneath the bland Anglo-Saxon veneer. Or else it is the ominous presence of mountains away to the left, the Galtees and the Ballyhouras, rolling precursors of the ranges of the west, haven of the dispossessed who emerged from them with mouths stained green from eating the grass of the fields, to burn Spenser's castle at Kilcolman and send the poet packing, back to London to die.

But what will I *do* over there in the New World? Will I be any better off at an American college, as Lily promises? Surely historians are the same the world over. I have failed to interest myself in their enterprise. I do not know where else to turn for a profession and a livelihood. Maybe the Inish is all I am good for.

The train stops in Killarney. I sit there without moving while passengers come and go and the heavy doors slam. My anxiety increases until the train begins to move again. Through Farranfore and Killorglin: this is the West proper, rocky fields and mountains, a landscape stripped of trees, the ever-present sea. Mountain Stage: a bleak empty platform, where the window fell on my hand and caused me to faint. I look out the window at the expanse of Dingle Bay — and my hand begins to ache! This bodily recollection unnerves me. I get up and step across the carriage. The sea is gray, the peaks of Brandon black and forbidding against a low sky. Gingerly I check the window to make sure the frame is secure. But there is no strap, and it is no longer possible to open the window. I slump back in my seat. Here, mercifully, sleep releases me. I know and feel no more until the train lurches to a halt in Caher.

I walk out into the bland evening, feeling refreshed and calm. The houses of Caher seem shabby and diminished, and this somehow reinforces my composure. I will not be here long. I will see him, and then I will go away. There is nothing here that can touch me. I cannot come to harm.

I take a taxi from the town. The bridge is completed now, and it connects the Inish to the village of Port. The neighborhood of the old man's house is now more closely connected to the larger world than the Foot. This seems a kind of violation of the natural order, as does the bridge itself. It looks just like the roadway, with the addition of an ugly white railing, already rusting. Before I know it, the taxi has spirited me over. I am back.

At the cross the tarred road ends. The driver rolls down the window. I breathe in the cold, moist air of the evening and look back at the bridge, a huge and ominous shadow in the dusk. No doubt it is a great thing for the people. In the old days, if you were taken ill in the wintertime and the weather was bad, you might die before they could get you to the hospital in Caher. Even in good weather people used to complain about Jacky Bar and the way he ran the ferry. But you might as well complain that the earth is not flat. The Inish is no longer really an island, and for some reason this does not please me. The threat that I feel emanating from it does not reside in its isolation.

The dirt roads are still hardly wide enough to allow two cars to pass. I ask the driver to leave me at the top of the lane. I need a moment to collect myself. The taxi drives away, and the silence reconstitutes itself around me. Across the field the house looks smaller, more sharply defined against the water. But there is a stack of turf against the gable, and smoke rises placidly from the chimney. The air is chill, the tide hushed, and the mountains of the mainland are circled in the dusk like a great amphitheater. Nothing is out of place here. Everything is as it was, as it will always be. So why does this peace and silence seem like a pit yawning at my feet?

As I walk slowly down the lane, I see the red points of lighted cigarettes in the dark and become aware of figures standing against the ditch.

"*Dia duit,*" a voice murmurs deferentially. "God be with you."

If there are people waiting here, it can only mean that my grandfather is not long for the world. Panic grips me. I run heavily along the foreshore, moving in a dream, hardly aware of the impact of my feet on the uneven stones. I clamber onto the seawall and rush up the gravel path. There is something odd about the house, but I cannot say what it is. I reach for the latch of the door, but there is no latch. I find the handle, turn it, and push with my shoulder, expecting the door to stick against the flag, as always. But it swings open freely, and I stumble into the room.

The first thing I see is that there is no bed in the shop. The shop itself is still there, but everything else is changed. The old dresser has been replaced by kitchen cabinets; there is a new stove and sink. A lightbulb is hanging on a long wire from the ceiling. Electric light!

I take a step into the room. There is a group of people sitting around the fire, their heads turned toward me. It is dark beneath the chimney, and I cannot make out their faces. A man gets up and comes toward me, squinting in the harsh light of the naked bulb. He puts out his hand, and I take it involuntarily.

"You were always great with him," he murmurs. "He never had any time for me."

His bleary tear-filled eyes plead with me. It is my uncle Con.

Peg walks stiffly out of the back room, glances at me without surprise, and goes to the sink, where she stands with her back to me. If I am not mistaken she is wearing the same black gown that she wore to visit Christine's mother. This recollection brings it home to me: I have come too late.

"Where is he?" I blurt out.

"Isn't he in the room?" she murmurs.

I move away from the fire. Con is still holding on to my hand, his eyes fixed on my face in an intense pleading stare. "Let you stop here a while," he says. "The women are with him, to lay him out."

With this, all volition leaves me, all feeling, and all need. The world has come to a stop, and still I am living and breathing. This is the event I feared for all the years I looked after him. And yet it has taken place outside of me, I cannot touch it, I cannot grasp its substance and its significance. It is happening in an unfamiliar place, to a person I do not know. I stand there unmoved, in the eye of the storm.

Later, fortified by a hot whiskey, I approach the door of the room, escorted by Peg. It is open. I can see the oil lamp lit upon a chest of drawers at the foot of the bed; apparently there is still no electricity in there. Involuntarily I come to a stop. Peg limps past me into the room, moving with the same characteristic jerk of her right hip.

There is a murmur of conversation, and then another old woman, red-faced and breathless, comes out.

"I'm sorry for your trouble," she murmurs, taking my hand in her limp moist grasp.

It is Mrs. Harty, Granda's particular friend. She holds my hand and gives me a sorrowful look — or is it a look of reproach? I want her to tell me something about the old man's last hours, but she turns away and walks back to the fire with slow and painful concentration.

I stand by the door. I feel the weight of my body as an awkward superfluous mass. To have a body seems a gross unnatural thing: that it should end in death is only right and proper. But is it natural to feel no weight upon my heart, no overpowering and liberating flood of grief?

I hear a sound from the room, and I step across the threshold. I am standing by the head of the bed, and I see him lying in it, out of the corner of my eye. The sight of him is a shock. His features seem to have been erased by death; it could be any old man lying there in the bed. His mouth has lost its firm intolerant line, the lips collapsed upon themselves, the lines above his brows dissolved.

But then his appearance suddenly comes into focus, and I see that it is himself and no other, with his large ungainly ears and flat gaunt cheeks. His narrow head is propped up by two large immaculately white pillows; his hands rest on a spotless bedspread that is stretched taut over his meager body and tucked beneath the mattress with a vengeance. He is wearing a nightshirt, but the old cap that never left his head is missing, and without it his scant silver hair looks pathetic and defenseless. The skin of his face has a yellowish sheen in the unsteady light of the oil lamp. But the awful thing is that he appears neither dead nor at rest. It is as though he has taken a vow of silence and immobility in return for our fearful obeisance.

Peg is sitting on a chair opposite me. She is almost as rigid as the old man in the bed, and her face is hardly more animated. She does not look at me, but there is a reproach in her downcast eyes and reverential demeanor. I walk to the foot of the bed and turn to face him. I have the unmistakable sense of his presence, of an energy still la-

tent beneath the pall of death. I feel certain that his eyes are alive behind closed lids, that he continues to regard his life, as though unwilling to allow its elements to be dispersed. He is not ready to join
the hosts of winged souls at their aerial rendezvous above the crags
of the Skelligs, to pursue the journey of death across a shoreless sea.
Something detains him here, though it chills my flesh to think so.
Something that has to do with me.

"I made up a bed for you upstairs," Peg mutters.

I go out of the room quickly and turn to the stairs, without looking toward the group around the fire. I enter my old bedroom. There
is still some light from the window, and I see the bed standing alone
in the middle of the floor. My bookcases are gone, my table and
chair too. I grope around, but I cannot find a light switch or a lamp.
It will be a long night.

I sit on the bed in the dark. It is nonsense to think that the old
man's influence should survive him. I have had a shock, and I am
not the better of it. I try to think of Lily, but her image has no substance. She does not know I am here, and it now seems a fatal mistake not to have called her before I left. But I cannot call her now. I
still feel the old man's presence in the house, and it seems to negate
even the thought of flight. I do not have to tell him I am leaving, but
that gives me no relief. It is as though he has anticipated me — and
cursed me with his dying breath.

I take off my shoes and settle myself with my back against the
headboard of the bed, to wait out the night. The wake will be tomorrow and the funeral the day after. It is only two days and two
nights — and then I will cross the bridge and never set foot in the Inish again. But I am afraid of the place, as though its very air can
transmit a contagion that will prevent my escape. If only I could
sleep.

When I come downstairs in the morning, there is a coffin on the
floor outside the room where he is and two men I do not know
standing in the kitchen with cups of tea in their hands. Peg is at the
stove and nods her head to the table, where a place is laid for me. But
I have no stomach for breakfast — and I cannot sit here and eat
while they are putting the old man into his coffin.

I walk out of the house and realize all at once what is different about it. The house was built with thick slabs of slate from the quarry here on the Inish, placed one on top of the other so that their cut edges formed the uneven face of the walls. Peg has had the slate cemented over and the cement whitewashed, so that the walls look smooth and bright. But the cement bulges in place, the corners are not vertical, and the whitewash is spattered about the gravel and on the glass of the windows. She has spoiled the house: it is no longer a part of the landscape. I wish I had never seen it like this.

I walk up the lane. It is a raw misty day, and my face and hands are soon chilled. I have forgotten my coat, but I refuse to go back for it. I come to the road and turn toward the Head. I feel numb, and I am almost grateful to be incapable of thought, to listen vacantly to the sound of my footsteps and the wind in the hedgerows and the empty fields, and to know nothing else.

I turn into a path that skirts the bulk of the Head and leads to the cliffs beyond. It is a very old path: the old man used to call it *Bothar na Scairte,* the Road of the Cataclysm. It passes below the *clocháin* and then climbs steeply to the edge of the cliff, where it comes to an abrupt end. I pause to get my breath and look back. From this height I can see how the Inish extends the contours of the mainland; they find their final expression in the peaks of the Skelligs, as though the landscape has really been formed by some unimaginable upheaval. This strikes me as uncanny. The very rocks and fields confirm the old man's fantasies.

There is a ruined tower house overlooking the ocean, a relic of the English fear of invaders from the sea. It is a gloomy old shell, framed by walls that bear the marks of vanished joists and a carved stone fireplace that seems to hang in the air above the piles of slate from the fallen roof. The threatened rain commences, and I enter this roofless shell and squat down among the high weeds, my back wedged into a corner. There is no shelter here, and soon I am wet through. But I do not leave. I want to hide myself from all company, from all thought and feeling, from awareness itself, as though there is some omniscient and all-pervasive accuser that seeks me out.

*   *   *

It is evening when I return, chilled to the bone. The house has been transformed by the preparations for the wake. The chairs have been pushed back against the wall and a long plank set up on crates to serve as a bench. A second table has been placed end to end with the kitchen table, both of them covered with a long white cloth. There is a barrel of stout by the back door and bottles glimmering on the counters.

Peg and Mrs. Harty are bustling about. They take no notice of my entrance. I trudge across the clean-swept hearth and stand in the door of the room. I am prepared for the sight of the coffin, and I force myself to step inside. Then I see that my grandfather is clothed for the grave in the dark brown habit of a Franciscan monk, complete with scapulars and a rosary entwined in his horny fingers. This is another shock. The hood is raised to frame his head, which has taken on a rigid, hieratic dignity. I advance a step, scarcely breathing. Traces of powder and even rouge are visible on the face, but no expression. He is really gone now, absent, departed. I no longer have the illusion of his presence, but what remains is somehow more awful. In this grim habit he has become the calcified ghost of himself, the very embodiment of authority and inflexible will. People called him a hard man. He is still unbent, even in death.

I stand there, mesmerized, robbed of will. I want to apologize for leaving him, for coming back too late. But the enormity of what I have done paralyzes my mind. I want to take my leave of him, to say good-bye, to go away and have done with him. But he will neither leave me go nor acknowledge my presence.

Someone touches my shoulder, and I give a little start.

"Excuse me, love," Mrs. Harty murmurs. "Lord God, you're wet! Wouldn't you change your clothes before you catch your death?"

I go out of the room. I feel that I have done myself some violence, that there is something torn inside me, and I want to go back, to stand in front of him until I reach some kind of resolution. But it is no use; it is too late. What is lying in the coffin is not my grandfather. You cannot say good-bye to a stone.

I walk into the shop. It is the only part of the house that remains untouched, and I find some comfort in that. I stand with my back to the rest of the house, fingering the stiff dry sheets of leather, the dusty tools and the lasts, the miscellaneous clutter of his workbench. I open a drawer and find his pocket watch. I take it in my hand. It is gold, heavy, large as an egg. One of his sisters sent it to him from America, but he never wore it.

"The place is full of his old rubbish," Peg says. "He wouldn't let me get rid of it. If you want to have anything for a keepsake, you may take it and welcome. It'll all be thrown out as soon as the funeral is over."

I put the watch in my pocket and gather some of the lasts and tools on a sheet of leather, along with an old brass bell, a worn tobacco pouch, a discarded pipe, some coins and yellowed papers. I walk up the stairs holding the sheet of leather in front of me. I intend to sort through it, but instead I sit on my bed. I feel weak and tired, and my clothes are wet, but I am incapable of helping myself.

I am aware that time is passing by the steadily increasing murmur of voices from downstairs. But I am still sitting in the same position when I hear a footstep close at hand.

"Peg said to tell you the priest is here."

Pat-Joe is standing in the doorway. I look up. There is something different about him, a sort of apprehension beneath the bluff good humor of his expression.

"I'll be down in a few minutes," I tell him.

He continues to stand there, looking awkward and embarrassed, as though reluctant to leave me.

"You're above in Dublin, I hear," he says with affected cheerfulness.

"That's right."

"How do you like the Big Smoke?"

Pat-Joe has never asked me a question in his life. I do not know what to make of it.

"It's not like the Inish," I say warily.

"'Tis true for you!" he says eagerly, his accent broadening. "This place is lonely enough, especially in the wintertime. You'd want the old bit of fun!"

Suddenly it occurs to me that he is lonely here, with only his jovial manner to defend him, and I wonder why I never thought of it before. There is no reason for me to be wary of him. He is only trying to be friendly, after his lights. But I do not know what to say to him.

"I suppose you'll be going back after the funeral," he says, as though anticipating happier days.

"I suppose so."

"Sure what is there here?"

The old refrain. In Pat-Joe's mouth, it smacks of humiliation and despair. I feel sorry for him.

"I'm sure it's what you make of it," I say.

"You're right there, Matt," he says with sudden energy. "You never said a truer word."

He rushes back down the stairs. There is something pathetic about his jauntiness: it is not convincing. He is a disappointed person, who does not even know the cause of his unhappiness. I feel none of my childhood animosity toward him, but I do not want to talk to him. There is something about his predicament that touches me on the raw.

I remove my wet clothes and put on my one and only suit and the white shirt Con has loaned me for the funeral. Then I slowly descend the stairs. The house is blazing with light. In addition to the single lightbulb there are candles set in saucers all about the room; their images are reflected in the dark of the windows, in the glasses on the counters, in the eyes of a crush of people standing and sitting so close together there is hardly room to move. A great fire roars up the chimney, and it is oppressively warm, in spite of the doors standing open to the night. I am perspiring copiously in my suit and shirt, but I feel cold at the same time. I am certainly feverish, on top of everything else.

I have made an unobtrusive entrance, and I stand by the foot of the stairs wondering what to do with myself. My life is sundered from the people here. They think me a quare fellow, and I do not know how to talk to them. They have come to pay their last respects to the old man and to sympathize with his family. But Peg is the one they feel sorry for. They know that she looked after him in the end — and that I ran off and left him.

I cannot stand here all night. I need air. I take a step toward the door. My body feels weightless, as though the force of gravity has been reduced. The thought occurs to me that I am about to faint. Among the people lining the wall by the front door, I see a woman with Christine's eyes and hair, holding a little boy by the hand. Her eyes meet mine, and a shock passes through me. It is one of Christine's relatives from Port — or else it is a hallucination! I move in the woman's direction, as though in a dream, until a black-suited figure comes between us.

"I'm sorry for your trouble, Matthew."

I allow the priest to take my hand and shake it.

"Father Carey," he says apologetically. "We haven't met. I must have come to the Inish about the time you left it."

Father Carey is a thin smooth-faced young man with a shock of red hair barbered above his ears. I know as well as anyone that he has been here for three years. I haven't met him because I am not a mass goer. He seems as embarrassed by this fact as I am.

"I have a little duty to perform for the family," he tells me hastily. "Your grandfather's will is in my possession. Mr. Dwyer the solicitor gave it to me because he had to go up the country to a funeral of his own."

He pauses, as though to give me time to react to his explanation.

"I see," I murmur, inadvertently conveying a disapproval I do not feel.

"I'm not sure I'm the man your grandfather would have chosen for the job. I'm afraid he didn't have much time for the church."

"Is that so?" I manage.

"But if you'd like to stop at the house tomorrow," he says hastily, "on your way home from the graveyard, I'll read the will to all concerned. Or would some other time be more suitable?"

"No, tomorrow will be fine. Thank you."

"I thought it would be best to have it done as expeditiously as possible, if you follow me."

We stand in silence for a moment, and I wonder how I will get away from him. Then Mrs. Harty appears and seizes my hand. "Isn't it strange that it's poor Bat laid out below in the room and I to be left here behind him?

She looks like she is going to cry. But she stiffens suddenly and gives my hand a jerk. "But that's the way," she says sharply. "Let you come in to the fire."

She draws me through the crowd, my hand held tightly with both of hers. There is a row of people sitting on the plank that runs the width of the house; they are turned to each other in twos and threes, like an audience waiting for the start of a show. People are gathered around the food too, and Pat-Joe is standing by the barrel, dispensing stout. Cigarette smoke floats in a blue cloud beneath the ceiling.

A steady stream of visitors moves in and out of the room where the old man is laid out; I can see the sheen of candles on the open door.

I allow myself to be led to the hearth. Hands squeeze my hands, pat my arms and shoulders, make way for me. Sympathetic eyes peer into mine; it is impossible to doubt their sincerity. "Sorry for your trouble," I hear from all sides.

I am delivered to an empty seat on the settle, among the old folk. It is unbearably hot and stuffy by the fire; my shirt is stuck to my back. Someone is talking urgently at my ear, but I cannot sort it out from the general hubbub.

"Ah, sure he's *dazed* with grief," my uncle Con explains to the company.

There is a murmur of approval. Con is beside me on the settle, in the grubby suit that he wears to work in the Cable Station, a shapeless fedora covering his knee.

"Didn't he go quick enough in the end though?" he says.

"That's the way with death," Mrs. Harty says.

She is huddled in the chimney corner, bent over the fire, as though drawing life from it.

"He was a fine, free, and eloquent man," she proclaims. "You couldn't look for a better. It was an education just to listen to him."

Con retrieves his glass of stout from beneath the settle and takes a long pull. He takes the hat in his large palm and bends his pate to it, molding it to the shape of his head, leaning back against the chimney. Then he covers my knee with his hand. "There's only one of us he ever had any time for, and it's that boyeen here."

"What age was he at all?" Mrs. Harty asks me.

"He was a good eighty if he was a day," Con snaps, as though he is angry with someone, with death perhaps.

"He would have been eight-four in March," I inform them automatically.

Con leans toward me confidentially. The smell of drink on his breath makes me nauseous.

"Did he ever tell you what he wanted to do with the house?" he murmurs at my ear.

I shake my head.

"I suppose your mother would have no use for the place, living over there in London."

"I have no idea," I say, without turning to look at him. "You'd have to ask her."

He gives a little snort, snatches the hat from his head, and returns it to his knee. I become aware that Mrs. Harty is watching me intently. When our eyes meet, she leans forward and touches my hand. "Didn't Peg make a lovely job of the house?"

She beams at me, red cheeks dimpling. I nod and smile like an idiot. I feel sure that she has somehow divined my disapproval.

"And the trouble she had to go to for the water and the light." Mrs. Harty assures me. "They told her it was too far back the Inish, they didn't have enough wire or pipe, the field was too low or too high, too wet or too dry. What they didn't tell her just to get rid of her! Well and good if she believed them. But she kept after them, and they had to give in to her in the end."

My eyelids have suddenly become deathly heavy. Her ruddy countenance swims before me. I cannot tell whether she is smiling or leering at me.

A loud rasping noise at my ear makes me start. Con turns his head and coughs into his hand.

"She's expecting to have the place," Mrs. Harty persists. "God knows she has a right to it if anyone has, after all the work she had done."

She leans back with a satisfied air, then suddenly reaches forward again to touch my sleeve. "Where would you be yourself if she hadn't come in to look after him for you?"

I stare at her stupidly. I am choked by turf smoke, drenched in sweat, my knees burning in the proximity of the flames. I want to escape from here. I look longingly up the chimney — as though I could ascend to the tiny square of night that it frames and float away on the blessedly cool night air!

Con takes a gulp from his glass and slumps against me.

"If I don't get this house," he says dolefully, "the next wake on the island will be my own."

"Would you give over that kind of talk?" Mrs. Harty flings at him. "There's small fear of you."

"Don't you see I'm no more than a shadow?" he retorts. "If I had a place of my own now, to live out my days in, instead of that old room in the Cable that the Farrells want to turn me out of."

His voice is broken and wretched. I am afraid he is going to cry. I am at the bottom of a well, confined with shades who talk the language of nightmare. I feel sure that, as in a nightmare, if I attempt to move, my limbs will not obey me.

The woman with Christine's eyes is standing in front of me, holding the little boy in her arms. She gives me a sad apologetic smile, as though she has played a trick on me.

"Hello, Matt," she says, in Christine's voice. "Don't you remember me?"

I stand up slowly. I seem to have been transported out of the noise and the heat.

"I've been back for more than a year," she says matter-of-factly. "They told me you were in Dublin."

The woman Christine has become is wearing a curiously formal black dress, high at the neck, of limp black material, with panels of matching lace and a fringe about the hem. It seems out of keeping with her brown freckled face and unruly mass of curls, which are just as I remember them.

"How are you, Chrissie?" I say.

"I'm good. This is Jonty."

The child turns his head and peers at me. He is dressed in a tiny yellow oilskin with matching hat. Christine watches me out of her clear gray eyes. I have a moment of confusion, as though I have woken into another time.

"Do you want to go outside for a breath of air?" she says. "It's suffocating in here."

I follow her to the door. The cold air restores the real world to me. Christine is part of it, not a dream. I ought to be happy to see her again. But I feel distant, tired, and downcast. She walks ahead of me down the gravel path, elegant in her black dress, bearing her son. We sit on the seawall, and she cradles him in her arms.

"You're down for the funeral?" Christine says.

I nod. The night is calm, the silence seems accentuated by the noise of voices from the house. I *want* to be happy to see her. If only our reunion had taken place under different circumstances.

"You'll miss him," she prompts me.

"I hadn't seen him in two years. I didn't realize he was bad."

"I didn't know myself," she says with a little sob. "I was afraid to come and see him, after the way I left."

I cannot see her face, but I can tell that she is crying. It makes me terribly sad to hear that she did not see the old man before he died. The pain of it pierces my numbness. I want to find a way to comfort her — to comfort us both — but we are not children anymore, and I do not know how to do it.

She takes a breath and lets it out in a sigh. "I'm sorry, Matt."

"For what?"

"That I never wrote to you — or to himself. It wasn't because I didn't think of you over there. You know that.

"I know. It doesn't matter."

"It matters," she says.

There is something in her voice that makes me want to contradict her. We will be friends again, I want to say. The past doesn't matter. But I cannot say it. Her conviction depresses me.

"Where are you living?" I ask.

"Back the Inish, beyond Paris. Jer Leary's house — if you could call it a house. The family are letting me have it for nothing."

The child is sleeping. She shifts him in her arms, so that his head lies in the hollow of her arm and breast.

"Is your husband with you?"

"I'm not married," she says quickly. "Or anything."

My heart stops for an instant. What a calamity. To have an illegitimate child and to bring him back to the Inish. It is on the tip of my tongue to ask her why she came back, but I check myself. Her return is a failure, and we both know it. A sense of gloom descends upon me. I do not want to think that Christine could not escape.

"What about London?" I say.

Another sigh. I regret my tactlessness.

"It's a long story, Matt," she says.

The shaft of light from the open door behind us is blocked by a shadow. I hear someone crunching over the gravel.

"They're looking for you inside, Matt," Pat-Joe's voice says.

My body tenses. I stand up quickly. The child stirs and whimpers in Christine's arms.

"It's too late for him to be up," she says familiarly to Pat-Joe. "Would you ever give me a lift back the Inish?"

A terrible sound, of wailing and shouting commingled, cleaves the silence. It takes a moment for me to realize that it has come from the house. I run up the path and thrust open the door. I am surprised to find the crowd has thinned out into a number of small groups of people talking quietly together. A jumble of plates and glasses is stacked on the soiled tablecloth. Some of the candles are burned out, and the overhead bulb sheds a dim bleak light. It is no longer so hot in the room: the fire has been allowed to burn down.

As I stand there, the sound begins again, shockingly close. I rush to the door of the room. The coffin is open upon the bed, and a woman in a stylish suit is bent over it, her hands covering the old man's. She opens her mouth, and the strange unearthly sound comes out. Her eyes are closed, and a lock of gray hair falls loose upon her forehead. The sound goes on and on. She does not notice that I am here. It is my mother.

*　　*　　*

It rains for the funeral. I am ill and cold; my clothes are not warm enough. My mother is still distraught and has to be supported by Con. She wears a veil over her swollen face. I stand beside her with an umbrella. She plucks at my sleeve as though she has something to tell me, but she cannot get the words out.

Pat-Joe, looking chastened in a shirt and tie and a suit that is too small for him, holds an umbrella over Peg and Mrs. Harty. The crowd of mourners extends a little distance from the graveside, scattered among the closely packed tombstones. Out of the corner of my eye, I see Christine holding her son in her arms. She is bareheaded in the rain. I would stand beside her, but I know that my place is here with the family.

Father Carey cuts short the graveside service, and the coffin is lowered into the wet hole. The gravediggers toss in a few spadefuls of earth and then lean respectfully on their spades. My mother sags against me, her weight bearing down on my arm. I lead her to the gate, where Con helps her into the car. As I step in after her, Mrs. Harty takes my hand.

"Happy the corpse, love."

"I beg your pardon."

"Happy the corpse the rain falls on."

She squints up at me out of her puckered ageless face.

"I wonder if he's telling his old stories now to Saint Peter," she says.

In the car Con is hunched and silent in the front seat. My mother lifts her veil and dabs at her eyes with a tissue. I look out of the window to avoid the sight of her ravaged face. Her hand gropes for mine. I allow her to squeeze my hand, but I do not look at her.

"I should have brought the children to see him," she murmurs brokenly. "But it's a such a long way. I suppose they'll have to grow up now without ever knowing their grandfather. At least you knew him, Matthew. You're glad you knew him, aren't you?"

I turn to look at her, and our eyes meet. It is the same distracted pleading look she turns upon me; there is always something she wants of me. I am about to answer shortly, but she bites her lip and I am afraid she will start to cry.

"Yes, Mother," I say, and turn to the window.

There is the drumming of the rain on the car roof, the sound of my mother's sniffling. The sense of time erased, of an interminable present in which I travel about the Inish closed up in a car with my mother, contorted by feelings that I cannot express. The events of the wake seem remote. Tomorrow will find me here or back in Dublin, but I cannot imagine what I will do in either place. I have forgotten my life. I do not want to do anything. I am very tired. I want to sleep.

My mother sighs, rummages in her purse, and produces powder and lipstick.

"The priest will say I look a fright," she says peering into a little mirror.

She snaps her purse shut and places it on her knees.

"A death in the family brings people together," she tells me with pathetic gaiety. "I suppose it's an ill wind."

I look out the window and see that we are passing through the Foot. In another moment we will be at the priest's house.

"But we never see you or hear from you at all, Matthew," my mother says, a tearful note creeping into her voice. "Couldn't you drop us a line every now and then, if only to keep in touch?"

The parlor of the priest's house is full of large heavy furniture and smells of dampness, as though it is rarely used. My mother is escorted to an armchair. I take a chair by the door, where I do not have to meet her eye. The room is dark, with layers of lace curtains and heavy drapes half drawn. I can make out Peg's gaunt silhouette against one of the windows. Pat-Joe is standing in a corner. Con slumps on the couch, looking very much the worse for wear.

Father Carey has placed a chair for himself in the middle of the room. He clears his throat and begins to read in a stiff unnatural voice without preamble.

"Be it remembered that I, Bartholomew O'Donnell, of Reenglass, in the Barony of Iveragh, being of sound mind and memory, but knowing the uncertainty of this life, do make this my last will and testament, hereby revoking all former wills . . ."

A strange illusion comes over me. I seem to hear my grandfather's voice speaking the words.

"After the payment of my just debts and funeral charges, I do bequeath and devise as follows: To my sister, Peg Lynch, I do give the sum of One Hundred and Fifty Pounds. To my son Connor O'Donnell, I do give the sum of One Hundred and Fifty Pounds. To my daughter Maura O'Brien, I do give the sum of One Hundred and Fifty Pounds."

I stare feverishly at Father Carey. The old man's drawl grates maddeningly in my ears.

"To my grandchildren, Brendan O'Brien, Teresa O'Brien, Kathleen O'Brien, Vincent O'Brien, I do give to each the sum of Fifty Pounds."

My mother stifles a sob. I shut my eyes, but it is no use. I cannot escape him.

"To my great-nephew Pat-Joe Duggan, I do give the sum of Fifty Pounds."

I lean forward and put my burning face in my hands. I want to shut out the sound of his voice, to flee from its accusation. He has left me out; this is his judgment of me before them all.

"The house of Reenglass and all its appurtenances, the land appertaining thereto from the Lower Road to the strand, the currach *Puffin* and all its gear, all the rest and remainder of my estate, of whatever kind and nature, I do give to my grandson Matthew Quigley, to use and occupy for the rest of his days."

I open my eyes and lift my head There is no sound in the room. The people around me are motionless shadows. Father Carey's is the only face I can see. He is smiling, incongruously, as though with relief. He rises and comes toward me, hand extended.

"Congratulations, Matthew," he says, shaking my hand.

The trap has closed around me.

I trundle the Monster through the parking lot and bring it to a halt in an unmarked space facing the grim red-walled eminence of Carr. After I have turned off the engine, I sit for a while, thinking of nothing, while my eyes wander over the drab green upholstery and the uncomplicated configuration of the instrument panel. There is comfort here, the solidity of the familiar and the mundane. I have returned to it from a long way off, and my senses are scarcely my own. But with every passing moment I feel them more firmly anchored to the present. The past recedes, and I draw a breath of relief.

The day shift comes streaming from three doors in the red facade, down the steps, and into the lot. My muscles contract in anticipation. Noise, heat, exertion: I welcome them. My job is my lifeline — for in its deafening turmoil lies forgetfulness.

Fire and Ice

HEAT WAVE. Defined by the TV weatherman as three consecutive days of ninety degrees or more: today is day seven and counting. I've spent most of the week at Lily's house because it's cooler here — and because I think she wants me to. I sleep better here, in the guest room with the blinds drawn against the midday heat, soothed by the air of the fields. But perhaps it has been a couple of days too long. Today is Sunday, and although I have more than twenty-four hours until my first shift of the week, I feel a need to be alone.

"I'm going back to Cambridge," I tell Lily.

"Already?"

She is standing at the door of her darkroom. She seems unhappy, and for a moment I almost decide to stay.

"It looks like you're about to do some work," I say.

"I am. But I don't have to."

"I'd better go. I haven't been back for a week. There might be some mail."

There will be no mail. I have nothing to do there before I go to work tomorrow, save to get some sleep. But I have to go.

"Are you feeling all right today?" Lily wonders.

"Sure."

I am unable to articulate what I feel. She will surely misunderstand it. I do not understand it myself. Perhaps I'm becoming attached to my apartment, especially since I am now alone there. I have begun to transfer to it some of the feeling of security I derive from the Monster, so that it's no longer necessary for me to sit in my car instead of in my living room.

"I'll be out next Saturday, Lily."

Her quizzical look repeats her question. When I do not respond, she shrugs. "Have a good week."

She is worried about Sam, who has been hospitalized for more tests. Perhaps she is also worried about me.

"Give me a call if you hear from your father."

"OK."

I want to say something reassuring, but I have a bad feeling about Sam's tests. I have a bad feeling about this parting too. I stand there, on the verge of changing my mind.

"Bye," Lily says, and closes the darkroom door.

I say good-bye to Cooper and leave him watching me from the porch, ears raised in the hope that I'm not really serious about it. We have established a bond, Cooper and I: we sit together on the porch every night after Lily falls asleep, listening to the dark. I am becoming attached to him, in the way I was attached to old Finn.

I open the Monster's windows and doors, to release the overheated air from the interior. The day has been stifling, and the evening brings no abatement. The heat has finally gotten to me. This sort of weather is as strange as the ferocity of the winter's cold. The icy showers I take in my apartment are good for no more than half an hour of rest apiece, after which I toss and turn anew, while the midday traffic roars on Cambridge Street. Useless to place fans in the windows fore and aft. The weathermen say that this heat wave constitutes an emergency of sorts, and I believe them, though their advice is not particularly helpful: stay in an air-conditioned room, avoid strenuous activity, don't breath unhealthful air. I still have to go to work, and there are no air conditioners at Carr.

I pull out of the driveway and start to pick up speed. My imperative need for solitude makes me nervous. What's the matter with you, Matty? It is a grand life you have entirely. Why is it you cannot embrace it?

I drive with all windows open, but there is no more than a remembrance of coolness in the breeze. The Monster is equipped with air-conditioning, but it doesn't work, and my budget will cover only essential repairs. Verily, this is a climate of extremes. Yet I find it preferable to the mild rainy climate of Ireland, which seems to blur the distinctions between the seasons that are so striking here. Lily is planning to take me on a foliage trip come fall, and I look forward to this, since I grew up in a place that does not nourish trees. She will take photographs, and I will enjoy the clean cool air and the colors I have seen only in photographs. The New World seems full of colors, loud, brash, unnatural. The color of Ireland is gray, not green: the gray of lowering clouds, of chilly mists, of so-called soft rains that penetrate not only flesh and bone but the gray matter of the brain, the very pores of the soul. It is the uniformity of it, the unrelenting dampness, the lack of sharp cold or stable pleasurable warmth. The seasons will be like unto each other, according to the Prophecy of St. Columcille, when the end of the world is nigh. If this is the case, then the end of the world has been imminent in Ireland for a long time! The land breathes a sea air and exhales a miasma, partaking of the wetness and grayness and mildness of the sea. What is Ireland after all but an island differing only in scale from the Inish, no place throughout its length and breadth to which the salt spray of ocean does not penetrate? Who can say what influence the weather has had upon the sorry tale of its history? The Protestant winds blew English fleets to Ireland, and wintering out sapped the spirit of many a rebel. If climate is destiny, then I have truly escaped — or traded one fate for another.

Cambridge. The Charles. I take the turn before JFK Street, to avoid the Square, and drive through the maze of Harvard dorms. The shade of buildings and dusty sidewalk trees provides no relief. I turn onto Cambridge Street, pass the hospital, and approach the block in which my building is located. Something is different. My building looks darker than its neighbors. I have not noticed this before. None of the buildings is new or freshly painted, but mine now seems more dilapidated than the rest. Perhaps I have been living with delusions of grandeur. It's a rather unprepossessing part of Cambridge. But that's what I like about it, its lack of pretension, its functionality, the absence of any concession to the red-brick-and-ivy aesthetics of the Yard.

I succeed in parking opposite my door, and I do not notice the plywood wall in front of it until I am in the act of crossing the street. Still, it does not register. Someone has erected a barrier in front of my door. I assume it must have some function that has nothing to do with me. But when I reach the sidewalk, I am confounded. The plywood extends on both sides to the corners of the building, higher than the doorway and the windows of the first-floor apartment, blocking even the narrow alley that is my access to the basement. I step back into the street and look up. The building has undergone a remarkable change: it seems to have aged a hundred years during the week I spent at Lily's. Still without comprehending, I survey the warped asphalt siding, the battered drains, the ragged edge of the roof. Then my eyes come to rest upon the gaping windows of my own living room and the coal black stains above them. There has been a fire!

I feel quite calm. I am relieved to have discovered the cause of my strange impression of unfamiliarity. I feel a little foolish for not having realized it sooner, and I look around me sheepishly, as though someone may have witnessed my mistake. It seems to me that the spectacle of the fire-scarred building ought to excite some interest. But none of the people on the street pays any attention to it or to me. They merely step off the sidewalk to get around the plywood and continue on their way. I have the odd and frightening sense of having stumbled upon a calamity that no one else will acknowledge. And it is *my* calamity.

I step toward the plywood, determined to find a way around it. Through a gap I see the doorway. It is hardly recognizable. The porch with its columns is gone, as is the door itself. All that remains is a gaping hole with blackened edges. Within, it is all dark and black, but I can see far enough to realize that the staircase no longer exists.

I step away, appalled. If I can no longer mount the stairs, I am cut off from my apartment. Even if anything has survived the fire up there, it will remain forever suspended in space, inaccessible, until it falls into the rubble and is lost. I look up at the fire-blackened window frames. Nothing is left. I will never set foot in the place again.

I cross the street and sit in the car. I do not look up at the building. What to do? It occurs to me that I should seek some official confirmation of what my eyes have told me, that I should present myself at a police station lest they think me a fatality of the fire, or that I should at least talk to one of the storekeepers nearby and obtain an account of it. But how will it help to know? I *could* have been a victim, if I had been home at the time. The place was a firetrap, with no external fire escape. Perhaps someone *did* die in it. I should find out. But I do not move. I become aware that my clothes are drenched in sweat, that the air is virtually poisonous, the heat unabated. This increases my sense of helplessness and immobility. I do not even feel capable of driving. If it is help that I need, I do not know where to seek it. I am beyond help.

And now I begin to enumerate what I have lost. I discount my personal effects: a dozen books, a suitcase of clothes, nothing that can't be replaced. But what about a fragment of the chimney from the old man's house? His tobacco pouch, still faintly redolent. His gold pocket watch, so treasured that he never wore it, made in Waltham, a town not far from here, where I intended to have it repaired. One of his shoe lasts, an old brass bell he kept in the shop, a nickel coin embossed with the head of Wolfe Tone that I found under his bed. I regarded these things as a species of relic, containing a residue of his physical presence, distilled through long contact with his person. Nothing of real value — and yet all that I had of him, quite irreplaceable.

I know as surely as if a voice had spoken from a cloud that this calamity is a judgement on me, the final consequence of having given away the old man's house. I have repudiated what was rightfully mine, and now I am made to see the folly of it. I will never be able to have or to hold anything of value in this place because I did not respect and value my own.

Suddenly I am angry as I sit here, so angry that my hands clench about the steering wheel and stinging perspiration flows into my eyes. I am angry because a malignant fate will not let me be, because the past has come between me and the simple unambitious life I wish to live. Must I mourn my losses for the rest of my life, as though no one had ever survived such losses? Must I forever hold Lily at arm's length, must I repudiate her comfort and refuse her my support, must I bewilder and betray her with my scruples and my moods — when she is what I want and all I want?

I fold my arms upon the steering wheel and rest my forehead upon them. Waves of hopelessness and fatigue wash over me. I give myself up to them. I cease to struggle. I surrender to the shameful sensation of defeat.

I leave the Monster where it is parked and walk for a long time without aim or direction through streets I do not know. Eventually I come out on Memorial Drive. Night has brought no relief from the heat. I walk in the grass of the riverbank, as far as I can get from the traffic. The dark mass of the water is on my left, and I draw a little comfort from its presence. It is the only natural thing for miles. I must get out of this city or it will stifle me as sure as I live. I must escape.

I come to Rick's apartment building. I stand for a long time looking up, trying to distinguish his windows from the others. Rick will help me. He will know what to do. I walk impulsively into the lobby and press his bell. His voice comes on almost immediately, so he cannot have been asleep. He buzzes me up.

"Matty!" He chuckles, pumping my hand and literally pulling me inside.

The apartment consists mainly of one huge room, with floor-to-ceiling windows giving onto the river. The only light falls in a discreet cone from a slender floor lamp.

"I'm sorry it's so hot in here," Rick says. "I've got the AC off. When the weather's like this, the electricity bill is a killer. I might even have to move, the way things are going. You want a cold one?"

"Sure."

As in a dream, I approach the windows. The graceful curve of the river is evident from the height, and the headlights of cars flit through the heavy foliage of the sycamores lining the bank. I ease myself down onto the couch. I'm glad to be off the street. But now that I am here, I feel utterly drained of will. It is as though I want Rick to intuit that something has happened to me.

"I'm really glad you came by," he says. "I've been meaning to call you."

By the light from the fridge I see that he is wearing black silk boxer shorts patterned with what appear to be tiny red devils with tridents and pointed tails. A wide gold chain flops against his muscular neck. He tosses me a can, and I fumble it onto the couch. He pops a can for himself, drops into the armchair beside me, and puts his feet up on the oval glass coffee table.

"It's just that I've been so bummed out," he tells me ruefully. "Didn't Lily tell you?"

He runs his fingers through his hair. I notice that he has let it grow so that it covers his ears and curls at the back of his neck. He hasn't shaved either. He does look a little down in the mouth. My heart sinks. I need him to be his ebullient, can-do self.

"She said you'd lost some money in the market."

"Oh, man. That's the least of it. Remember that stock I bought into? It bombed. I bought on margin, and the market took a nosedive. I ended up owing money on it, and I had to borrow just to pay off the broker. Turned out not to be a very good tip. I should never have gone out with that woman who gave it to me, the one I sold the car to. She was out of my league. She probably makes a dozen deals like that every day; it's no sweat if one of them doesn't pan out. She turned out to be a complete bore too. All she could talk about was the market."

I've never seen him like this. I am confounded by his distress. I do not know what to say.

"I put my brother's life savings in this stock," he tells me. "And my cousin wanted in too. I feel terrible about it. The least I can do is pay them back what they put in. I have to sell a dozen cars next week! So how are *you* doing?"

"I'm OK," I hear myself say. "It's just that — my apartment burned down, and —"

"What! Your apartment? Tonight?"

Rick is on his feet, leaning over me, as though to assure himself that I am all in one piece.

"I don't know when it happened —"

"Christ! Why didn't you call me? Why didn't you *tell* me?"

His reaction induces a reprise of my shock. I close my eyes and sit quietly, trying to calm myself. When I open them, Rick is sitting in front of me on the coffee table, peering at me with an expression of earnest concern.

"Matt, are you all right?"

"I'm fine. I wasn't there when it happened."

"Thank God for that. Did you lose anything?"

"No," I say, absurdly self-deprecating. "I mean, everything I had. But that wasn't very much."

"What are you going to do?"

"I don't know, Rick."

"You can stay here, you know that. Until you find another place. And you can go through my closet. I have more clothes than I need. I'm planning a yard sale — I can use an extra few bucks — but I'll let you have your pick first."

I take a deep breath. "I appreciate it, Rick. But the way I feel right now, I don't know if I can start all over again. I don't have it in me. I'm out for the count. You asked me a couple of months ago if I'd be interested in driving cross-country with you. I'm interested now."

Rick's eyes widen with what appears to be delight. My spirits are lifted suddenly. I see the miles stretching out behind us, as we traverse a colossal road map of the continent, unseen new vistas opening every day, and no limit to our progress save the distant, inconceivable Pacific.

"I'd love to, Matty. But I don't have a car! I can't afford to own an Infiniti anymore. I'm still making monthly payments — to my brother! I'm taking the T to work."

"We could go in *my* car."

"What? In that old clunker? We wouldn't even get to the end of the Pike! Believe me, there's nothing I'd like better than to pack up and drive away from my life. But if I left town right now, my family would probably set the feds on me. And Erica could say she was right about me."

I feel ashamed of myself. I had forgotten about Erica. Or else I had assumed she didn't figure in Rick's plans.

"Lily told me you and Erica weren't getting along."

"That's the understatement of the year. She's dumped me!"

"You're joking."

But Rick's misery is written all over his face.

"It's no joke, Matt. Since her date with you, she's like a different person. I guess it's because she's sick. Used to be she went along with just about anything I suggested. But she's really pissed at me for going out with that woman who gave me the stock tip. She told me she has enough on her plate without me blowing hot and cold about the relationship. Made me feel like a complete jerk. I'd never have gone out with someone else if I'd known she was sick. But it's too late now. She doesn't want to hear it."

I'm sorry for Rick — but I cannot get over the extent of his collapse. I depend upon him to cut a suave and confident figure. I feel that the ground is shifting beneath my feet.

"Is Erica going to be OK?"

"She was doing great up until a week ago, when she had a setback. They tried to take her off the medication too quickly. But she's going to be fine. And the way she's dealing with it you wouldn't believe. I just had my head stuck up my ass. She'll probably never speak to me again."

I am glad Erica's prognosis is good. But my own hope of deliverance through Rick is crushed.

"I guess this means I'm going to have to go on my own."

Rick jumps up, suddenly animated. "Go where? What are you talking about? You can't drive cross-country on your own."

"Why not?"

"Come on, Matty. You know better than that. You can't run away from the man in the mirror. What does Lily say about this?"

"It's not going to work out for me and Lily. There's something in me I can't get over, something that's going to prevent us from ever living together."

"Bullshit!" Rick says. "You listen to me. I've heard it from both sides, and it seems to me that you and Lily are just made for each other. So you're having problems? Face them: don't run away. I speak from bitter experience here. If I'd only appreciated what I had with Erica, I wouldn't be in this mess. I wanted to keep my options open, in case something better turned up. Now I'm back to where I was before I got into having a fancy car and an expensive apartment. I don't even want to get out of bed in the morning. It won't do me any good to travel. Wherever you go, there you are."

I place my untasted beer carefully on the floor. I do not want to admit the extent of my own despair. Rick rises with a sigh. "You're just tired," he tells me. "I'm going to make up a bed for you on the couch. Let me get some sheets."

I become aware of my fatigue; it is almost a physical discomfort. But it does not mean that I will be able to sleep. I stand up and move to the window.

"And in the morning you'll drive out to Lily's house," Rick calls. "If it wasn't so late, I'd call her."

The towers of the city are visible on the horizon, bathed in an unearthly orange glow — and beyond the city, the unseen ocean. I have not really penetrated very far into America. And I am about to lose what little ground I have made.

"You're all set," Rick says. "We'll talk. Maybe you and I will look for a place together, if you decide not to live with Lily. I'll have to look for a cheaper apartment — and even then I'm going to need to share the rent."

"Thanks, Rick."

"For nothing. It's always darkest before the dawn, Matty. Think good thoughts, OK? Sleep tight."

So Rick has taken care of everything after all. I do not have to concern myself. I stretch out on the couch with my hands behind my head. I am beyond tiredness. My limbs ache, my temples throb, but I cannot close my eyes.

Rick is right. I should go back to Lily. I know I must do this — and yet I cannot, not under the cloud of this calamity, perhaps not ever. I have already failed to be happy with her, and I cannot bear to make her sick of me, of my incurable malady. No, there is only one thing for me to do. I must go back to Ireland, I must go home. God knows it is not much of a home — but it is the only home I know.

As soon as it is light, I get up from the couch and let myself out quietly. I walk the deserted length of Cambridge Street to where the Monster is parked, and drive off without a glance at the gutted building that was my home. I end up in the parking lot at Carr, and for part of the afternoon I undergo something that is not the waking state, but hardly deserves the name of sleep. I am standing by my machines before the day shift is ready to leave. During break, instead of going down to the food truck with Al, I sit alone on the stairs to the vacant fifth floor. By some miracle, I manage to get through the night without doing myself an injury.

I drive to Lily's. Cooper is sitting in the same place on the porch. He rushes to meet me excitedly, circling the car, barking. I step out, like a zombie. Cooper comes around the rear of the Monster and rushes at me. I bend down to him, holding him still. There is comfort in his greeting. Someone is glad to see me. There is something enviable about a dog's life — or at least about Cooper's. His great eloquent eyes are pools of dark, receptacles of a wisdom I cannot know.

I go in the house. Lily is not up yet, which is unusual. It occurs to me as I pass through the kitchen that I haven't eaten since dinner on Sunday, but it is more than my life is worth to do anything about it. I am like the victim of an accident. Messages still reach me from my everyday functions, but they are coming from a great distance, and I do not have the strength to respond to them.

I sit on the couch, neither asleep nor awake. After an indeterminate amount of time has elapsed, I hear footsteps on the stairs, and Lily appears in a short nightgown, walking toward me. Her face has the rapt serious look that I love, she carries herself carefully, almost formally, and she does not seem surprised to see me. Her bare feet make no sound on the floor. Her appearance has the uncanny quality of dream.

"I've been trying to call you," she says. "There's something wrong with your phone."

Her voice rouses me, restores me to a semblance of normality.

"I don't have a phone anymore. My house burned down."

She draws in her breath sharply. In an instant she is sitting beside me on the couch.

"Are you all right?"

"Sure. It must have happened Friday night or Saturday. I found out when I went back there yesterday. I mean, Sunday."

I am beginning to be confused about what day I'm in. I must get some more sleep, somehow.

"Were you able to save anything?" Lily murmurs.

"I couldn't even get into it."

"Oh, Matt," she says, putting her hand on mine. "I'm sorry."

Her touch, her ready understanding, moves me. Her comfort is there for me, if I can only accept it.

"Lily. I have to tell you something. I'm going home."

"Home?"

"To Ireland. To Dublin — or somewhere. It wasn't meant to be. My coming over here. This just proves it."

"What proves it? The fact that your house burned down?"

I nod, seeing the incomprehensibility of my position reflected in her tone, but unable to relinquish it.

"Matt," she says reasonably, "it was an accident. You lost all your belongings and you're upset. Who wouldn't be?"

"I can't live in this country. If I do, some part of me will die. I'll never be a whole person: I'll be a ghost. I feel torn between here and Ireland, and I can't live with it."

"You *have* been living with it."

"Sooner or later I'll have to go back. I'll spoil everything between us. And then you'll just hate me, and you'll be sorry you ever met me."

Lily sits without moving. Is she angry? She has a right to be.

"Perhaps it's for the best then," she says quietly. "I don't think you'll want to live here."

The finality of her tone is a painful wrench. I turn to her help-lessly — to find that the tears are streaming down her face. She puts her face down on her knees and begins to cry aloud, her shoulders shaking. I put my arm around her, but she does not seem to notice. She cries for a long time, with deep racking sobs, and I sit beside her, unable to speak, appalled by what I have wrought.

When she ceases, she draws quickly away from me, gets up, and goes into the kitchen. I hear her sighing vigorously. She comes back, drying her eyes with a paper towel. I stand up.

"I'm sorry, Lily," I begin.

"I had a phone call from my father last night," Lily says, looking past me. "He has a rare type of cancer of the prostate, and he's going to die very soon. It's too late for the treatments, and he doesn't want them anyway. He's coming here so that I can take care of him."

She breaks off and goes back in the kitchen. I follow her, my heart pounding. My fatigue has fallen from me. I am wakeful and alert. It is the sudden frightful proximity of death. I believe I am almost an-gry. Why must it happen to Sam? Why must it happen to Lily?

We sit at the table together, facing each other. I want to take her hand, but I do not dare.

"I'm sorry, Lily. I'm very fond of your father. And I feel bad for you. That this should happen now. Just when you've got the chance to work on your photos."

She gives me a wan smile. "Just when you've decided to go back to the old country. But that's your problem, Matt. I can't worry about it right now. My father is coming this week. I have to deal with that, with or without you."

I am impressed by her composure. She turns her head slightly, as though indicating something — and in the moment I see without the possibility of contradiction that this thing, this fatalism, this hopelessness, is truly mine. It is as though a fog upon the Head has parted, revealing the ocean and the Skelligs where a moment before there was only nothingness. I see that I have lived without hope from force of habit, not knowing any better, not really believing it. Up un-til this moment it has been a more or less plausible theory of Lily's, to which I subscribed for want of insight. But now the theory has become experience. The finger points at me: Thou art the man. I am the man whose element is hopelessness, who swims in it like a fish, knowing it no more than the fish knows the ocean — until now.

Lily gives me a steady unblinking look across the table.

"Do you *want* me here when your father comes?" I say.

"I want you to do what you have to do — for yourself."

I have to go home, a voice within me says. I cannot make a life here. I will never be able to live up to Lily's expectations. This is the voice of hopelessness. But even as it speaks I know that I do not *have* to believe it. I am separate from it, and I see it for what it is: a part of me, not the whole. I am raised to a height, the fog is rent before my eyes, and I have a vision of possibilities. There is a world of choice, of freedom, that I did not know existed, and I can act in this world. I am not fated to repeat a futile pattern, to react in the same ineffectual way to adversity. I know this with a conviction that is beyond all theory and explanation.

Lily is waiting for my answer. Suddenly I know what I have to do and what I want to do, and they are one and the same. I have an appointment with death.

The News from Ireland

I AWAKE IN THE DARK. Lily is beside me. I am still at her house — and not in Ireland. It is Tuesday night. Lily has persuaded me not to go to work, in order to get some sleep. I listen for a while to the sound of her breathing. I'm glad that *she* is sleeping; she probably needs it more than I do. Tomorrow we are going to Sam's office, to bring him back here to die.

A death in the house; I do not know how I can face it. But I have promised Lily.

I get up carefully and walk into the room next door, Lily's study. Below in the driveway the Monster gleams in the faint light from an occluded moon. I would like to drive around until I am tired enough to sleep or until it is time for us to leave for Boston. But I am afraid that Lily will wake and find me gone. I cannot leave her alone tonight.

I go downstairs and pass through the kitchen. Cooper is at my heels, alert, interested. We go out on the porch. Mild night air, a hint of coolness from the fields. It is not yet morning, but the darkness has somehow begun to recede. In the false dawn I see Cooper's ears raised in joyful anticipation.

I walk to the Monster and rest my arms upon the roof, which is wet with dew. Cooper whines, snuffles about my feet. I open the door, and he scrambles eagerly into the backseat. I stretch out in front. His head appears over the seat back, quizzically tilted to the side. I close my eyes. After a little while I hear him slump down in back with a disgruntled sigh. We lie there, man and dog, listening to each other's breathing, to the meditative note of the crickets. But memory does not sleep . . .

After the wake, the funeral, and the reading of the will, they all went about their own business — and left me alone in his house, which was now mine. It transpired that the old man had also left me the bulk of his savings: almost a thousand pounds. I wished he had given it to someone else. But I'd burned my bridges in Dublin. My scholarship at the college had surely been rescinded, and my flat was probably rented to someone else. I'd need the money if I couldn't find a way to earn a living.

I had to write to Lily, but I did not know what to say. I was supposed to go to her, and now there was no longer anything to prevent it. But I could not even think of leaving the Inish. It was as if I alone of all men had no business of my own — unless it was my grandfather's business, the care of his house and boat, of his two fallow fields, of the mountains outside his door and the stone huts beyond on the Great Skellig.

At first I worked about the house. I wanted to restore it to the way I remembered it, the way it was when I lived here with him. I swept out the shop, I moved the furniture about, I scraped flecks of whitewash off the windowpanes. I even started to chisel away the crumbling cement on the outside walls in order to reveal the slate. But that would have taken me the rest of my life! The house itself began to discourage me, being neither fish nor flesh. There was electricity in the kitchen, but not upstairs; a new toilet adjoining the house, but no shower or bath. I felt no nostalgia for the oil lamp, and I hated washing in the old man's tiny metal tub. But I couldn't carry on the renovations Peg had begun. I slept upstairs in my old room and kept a chamber pot underneath the bed. I learned to find my way around without a light, and when I wanted to read, I used a flashlight. I stopped trying to set the house in order and accommodated myself to it instead. I felt that it was crouched over me, a cheerless shelter, like the stone oratory on the Skellig that is shaped like an upturned boat.

*   *   *

Fog down on the channel, enclosing a semicircle of absolutely motionless water. I am on the strand looking for the old man's currach.
Everything is gray and wet. To breathe is to inhale moisture. My feet
make no sound on the shingle; even the smells of the strand are stifled.

The black hull looms up out of the fog. I go and stand beside it,
and put my hands on the wet gunwale. I want to take it out on the
channel. I think that I can row through the fog and come out into
the open air. I am bending over the gunwale in search of the oars
when I become aware that I am looking at the stones of the strand.
This gives me a little shock. It is as if the currach itself is not real.
Then I see that one side of the hull is open, like a gaping wound, the
canvas torn, the ribs of the frame rotted away. There is nothing anyone can do to salvage it.

I walk down to the edge of the water and stand there looking out.
There is no sound, almost no sensory stimulation of any kind, save
the dull film of the water. The fog advances, and the semicircle of
water dwindles. I try to look through it, to catch a glimpse of the
mountains of the mainland, but I can see nothing through the shifting gray veils.

I know I am back on the Inish, but I cannot take it in. I remember
Lily; I remember our plan, which seemed so substantial — and now
is nothing. What has happened to the time I spent with her in
Dublin, the time I was to be with her in Boston? All has vanished in
this wretched fog, and I stand here, stupidly surprised — while I am
drifting further away from her with the passage of every moment.

A nightmare. I wake sitting up in bed, as though torn from sleep.
Where am I? I am in my old room, the room where I have slept for
most of my life. There is no comfort in this. Frightful images of the
dream: a colossal cirque, the glacial valley of Mount Brandon, a pack
of dogs I have unchained, running in circles within it, harrying some
creature to death. The severed head of a pig, blood on the wet grass.

My body draws in deep gasping breaths. The bloody images fade.
I have slept only a few hours. But I have to get out of the house.

As soon as it is light, I walk along the strand, in order to avoid meeting anyone, facing away from the bridge. I am very tense and apprehensive, and I keep up a brisk pace, in the hope that physical exhaustion will relieve my distress. I pass below the Cable Station and the Foot and round the eastern tip of the Inish. The harbor is on my right, with the Knight's estate and the lighthouse at the end of it. There are great shelves of rock across my path, and I clamber up and down them recklessly. I stumble and slam my shoulder against one of them. This gives me a fright. I have to get off the shore, before I do myself an injury.

I cross the field behind the lightkeepers' houses with furtive haste, as if I were a trespasser. Christine's old house is empty, the windows dark and curtainless. I feel a sudden almost painful longing to see Christine. I haven't seen her since the funeral. Can it really be no more than a month? The thought bewilders and frightens me. It is an interminable time; it is the blink of an eye. A lost month. A hole in my life.

I will go to her, now, today. I need to see her. But suddenly I am afraid she will not be happy to see me. I am the only person who knows how much she wanted to leave the Inish, and now she is back here again, a failure like myself, a bird alone that can neither roost nor fly.

I take the road above the cove of Glan, with the mouth of the harbor below me and the sheer face of Doulus head beyond. Sunlight slashes the sea and the slopes, whitens the surf about the cliff base. Out by Doulus they saw the White Boat the night of the accident, when seven men from the Inish and from Port were drowned. I see something black among the surf. It is a boat, a person, a rock. It is nothing. Then why am I beside myself with fright? In broad daylight I am about to witness a spectral boat, herald of disaster, floating unscathed in treacherous waters.

I turn my head away from the ocean and pass into a copse of leafless trees. This is the glen where Diarmat and Grania hid from Finn the night they first were man and wife. I taste their fear, fugitives concealed in the fern, while to my ears are borne faintly the sounds of pursuit, the cries of hounds, the trampling of a company, harsh calls of men and the shrill horn. I shuffle on, hardly aware of my body, the wind dinning in my ears. Is this experience real — or the figment of a dream? I do not know what to think, and my confusion terrifies me.

Up over the spine of the Inish and away to the west along the Upper Road, like a creature pursued. I run between the high hedgerows, past farmhouses screened from the road by fuchsia and privet and huge outlandish clumps of flax.

A couple of cyclists overtake me and flash by, calling out a greeting. *"Dia is Muire duit,"* I respond, without looking to see who it is. "God and Mary be with you."

For an instant I am part of their world, whoever they may be. Then the sense of the other, uncanny world engulfs me again.

The hedgerows are gone, and the broad back of the Inish declines in a long gentle slope of bog to the extremities of Paris. A cluster of white cottages, tiny from my vantage, faces the cliff. Christine's is the outermost, above a little inlet, Diarmat's Cove. I come to the track that runs out into the bog and stop in the middle of the road. But I do not want her to see me in this state: exhausted, downcast, virtually out of my mind. I cannot go today. I will feel better by and by.

I climb to the top of the Head and sit on a heap of rocks protruding from the heather. The air is unseasonably mild, the clouds high, with patches of a very pale blue between them, an early morning sky, tender and remote. Stupefied, I watch the ocean far below me, where the channel broadens into the open sea. The movement of the tide seems to mesmerize me.

I shake my head and blink my eyes — and there are the Skelligs, piercing the horizon. Skellig Michael: burial ground of the ancients, great funeral ship. *Teach Duinn,* the old man called it, the House of Donn, his namesake, cursed by the De Danann and buried on the rock. To me, to my house, you shall all come after your death.

It occurs to me that the old man is out there on his beloved rock, if he is anywhere. Why not? If I believed such things — or allowed them as possible — perhaps I would feel less afraid. The sun emerges from a band of clouds, and the rocks stand out from the glittering sea. Granda used to say that all the madmen in Ireland are drawn to the Skelligs, there to live in perfect harmony among their own.

You're in good company out there, old man. I try to smile, to laugh aloud. But the Skelligs are gilded with a strange and precious light, and I am afraid that if I look at them too long I will see winged forms in the air above them, the souls of the dead, the transformed bodies of the lunatics, whirling in ecstasy.

I stand up in the heather. The sunlight strengthens until the sea is a deep rich blue. I turn to look west over Paris, across the empty plain of the Bay, toward Slea Head, the House of Mór, Queen of Munster, whom all the kings of Ireland sought and could not find. The old man pointed it out to me. When the sun shines on Slea, he said, Mór is on her throne.

Beyond that austere promontory, appearing joined to it though separated by a treacherous sound, the Great Blasket, an abandoned hulk upon the brilliant sea. The last few islanders, elderly, forsaken by children fleeing from loneliness, were relocated by the government and now live on the mainland, some within sight of their island. What kind of fate is that? To have to leave your home is bad enough, but to live with it forever in view and inaccessible, to watch the houses crumble into ruins, the fields lie fallow, the walls disintegrate stone by stone. 'Twere better to go to America.

Clouds move in, and the air is suddenly chilly. I stand there looking out, between two great Houses, of light and of dark. I do not want to go back to the house that is mine. Something is waiting for me there. It is not a physical threat, rather a knowledge I must not allow to enter me. But I have no choice.

I descend toward the channel and come to the Lower Road as a shower of rain commences. When I get to the house, I light a huge fire and huddle over it. I sit for a long time, motionless, dumbly absorbing the warmth. It occurs to me that this is all I have to look forward to now, the vicissitudes of the weather and the humdrum comforts of shelter and warmth. I am an animal, living an animal's life, shrinking from cold, clinging to warmth, unreflective and dull. And yet it is a life for all that, perhaps the only one that is possible for me.

I wake suddenly in the night, a question on my lips. What question? The wind is making a fiendish racket — unless there is someone in the house, throwing things about. I get out of bed and steal across the floor, straining to hear above the noise. I have turned into the child I used to be, afraid to walk abroad in the dark. At the head of the stairs I recall a fragment of dream: a ghostly hillside, peopled with specters, the famine dead, wailing voicelessly in the wind, hunger without end. God above, what next? If I should meet the hag that turns into a hideous crow to haunt the fields of battle and feed on severed limbs and gore! There *is* someone in the house.

Shouting aloud, I rush down the stairs and fumble frantically for the light switch, while a cold chill passes down my spine. The light comes on, and immediately the bulb pops and goes out. In the flash of light I see overturned chairs, a broken cup, scattered books on the floor — and the open door swinging back and forth in the gale.

I close and latch the door, light a candle, and build a fire among the embers. I feel its warmth upon my hands, but it does not stop me from shivering. I wedge myself into the chimney corner. The wind howls down the shaft. There is something personal and malevolent about its awful tumult. The wind is a woman, the old man used to say, an agent of death and destruction, whose names are many: Sigh, Sough, Storm, Rough Wind, Winter-Night, Cry, Wail, Groan. My head droops on my chest. I start awake again. I hear the inhuman shrieks of battle, the bleating of trumpets and horns, sounds of the chase that Diarmet heard, waking three times in the night before he rose to meet his death. Don't go to Finn, Grania said. She knew.

Cold sweat on my forehead. He tried to defend himself. Not by day or by night, not in softness or in hardness, neither within nor without, not in company or alone. But he had to go with her and leave behind kith and kin, he had to lie with her and betray Finn's trust, he had to rise out of her bed to meet the kinsman who turned against him, to pay for his pleasures with his death.

The fire is burning brightly, but I cannot get warm. Never to hear the baying of the hounds without rising to follow the hunt. Never to hunt a boar. His fate coming to meet him at every turn, a shattered weapon, a cupful of blood, a blood-soaked shirt. Death in the woman's fearful whisper, in the voices of the hounds, in the red eyes of the boar, in the suave request of the cuckold. Forbidden to hunt, obliged to follow. Compelled to love and break the tie of kinship. Compelled to break the tie of love — and die upon the tusks of the boar!

My body jerks involuntarily. I rise in a sudden fright and rush into the kitchen. I pace back and forth between the kitchen and the shop. I am at my wit's end.

The wretched man who breaks his *geasa* sees their force recoil upon him like a sprung trap. Death is the only atonement.

And then it comes to me. I know what I will do! I will write a book: the Book of the Inish. In this way will I reclaim it and pay my debt to the old man at the same time. I will take his knowledge of story and place and join it to my observation. I will walk the Inish step by step, I will describe it as accurately as I can, and I will set down every place name, every scrap of local story, every mythological association that I can recall from the old man's store of knowledge. I believe he always meant for me to have the stories, to keep them alive after he was gone.

But no more analysis, no more interpretation or explanation. My business is simply to record and to witness. This is what he would have wanted above all else.

I no longer feel any desire to sleep. I pace back and forth half the night, elaborating the Book of the Inish.

In the morning I feel drained and dull, as though after a night of serious drinking. I sweep up the pieces of the broken cup and make myself some tea. I put paper and a pen on the table. I must write to Lily today. I cannot put it off any longer. I sit at the table and put my head down on my hands.

Isn't it the thought of what I might still have with her in that un-imaginable country that poisons my life here, that makes it a bitter draft I can neither bear to my lips nor cast from me? I must make my choice. I do not think I will ever see that bright and happy place. I have unfinished business here. I thought while I was with her that I could leave the Inish behind me, but I was wrong. That belief was nourished by her presence, and I cannot sustain it any longer. I have responsibilities. I have come into house and land; more than that, I am custodian of a tradition. It if be an unhappy fate, I must make the best of it.

But I will do more than that. I will make sense of it. This is a poor enough place, as the world goes. Yet it is what I know, it is where I am, and I cannot give it up, not for love nor money.

What is a *geis*? What's bred in the bone.

I draw a breath and take up my pen.

December. I dread the approach of Christmas.

The postman comes to the door, and my heart pounds at the sight of him. It cannot be a letter from Lily — for the simple reason that my letter remains unsent and she does not know my address. I have made her unhappy, and I cannot bear for her to tell me so. But perhaps she has found me after all.

I take the letter with trembling fingers. It is postmarked London. I carry it into the shop and stand by the window, holding it to the light.

Dear Matthew, I was very surprised not to hear from you since Daddy passed away. I know you must be very busy with the house and all, but even so. I suppose you won't know us now that you have got the house and the land and we are still renting. I hope you will be happy now that you are set up for the rest of your life.

I haven't been myself since Daddy's funeral and the way he divided things up. It was all his to do what he wanted with, of course, and what would I want with that old house and a house of my own to look after? But you'd think he might have been more generous to myself and Con, his own children. I wouldn't mind it so much only Jack has been sick and out of work and I don't know what I'm going to do if his health goes bad on him. I told my friends here that we would surely get some help from the will, and I was embarrassed to have to tell them that he only left me a hundred and fifty pounds — and Pat-Joe Duggan to get fifty! Jack said that the will was a travesty, but I said that Matthew would not forget us. I know that Daddy was fond of you, but everyone said it was queer of him to leave everything to you, especially after the way you ran off on him and never even came back to visit.

If you can't remember us, I suppose we will manage somehow, but I only hope that you can live with it, Matthew, when we're all dead and gone like Daddy. You will always be welcome to visit us here no matter what, and we won't ask you any questions or tell you what to do with what you have.

Have a nice Christmas. Love as always, Mam

I drop the letter. I feel that it has injected some kind of poison into me, but I am beside myself with the sting of it, and I cannot muster any defense. I walk into the kitchen and start to move cups and plates from the sink to the counter without quite knowing what I am doing or why. I chip a plate on the side of the sink, and this makes me stop. I sit on the settle. But I cannot remain still. I rock back and forth in front of the fire, hunched over as though I am cold.

I should have known that the will would cause trouble. I haven't touched a penny of the old man's money, and I do not need it. I can always work behind the bar in Dennehy's again. Maybe I should give it to my mother, just to be shut of it. She needs it more than I.

A charge of anger courses through me. Why *should* I give it to her? She cannot even ask me for it without giving out to me. She went away herself and washed her hands of the Inish; that is why he didn't leave it to her. She could have had the house and the land too, if she'd wanted them. But she got what she wanted, as always, and I am left here to take care of the old man's business for him. I couldn't give her the money even if I wanted to, no more than I could give the house to Con, if that is what she is hinting at. The old man would turn in his grave.

This explanation calms me, but it does not relieve my distress. I sit here until the short day moves to its close and darkness draws in. It is utterly quiet and still within the house, apart from the faint sputtering of the fire. I raise my eyes and look at my grandfather's place in the chimney corner, in expectation — of what? There is no trace of him there — or anywhere. He is irrevocably absent, as though he had never lived here. This is what it will be like in this house from now on, a cheerless fireside, with *uaigneas* the sole guest. Everyone is gone from this place, and I alone am left. I do not understand it. I cannot bear it.

I get up suddenly and walk out of the door, leaving it open behind me. It is dark, but I am aware of the body of the channel and the vague shapes of mountains beyond. I make my way slowly along the strand and walk up the lane. It is pitch black between the hedges: only the faint white blur of the cart ruts guides me. I walk rapidly, with all the muscles of my upper body tensed, as though to repel an assault. I am in a terrible state. What am I afraid of? Everything — and nothing. Loneliness has unhinged me.

When I reach the road I breathe a little easier. The hedges are not so close, and I can see the shadow of the Head against the black sky. There is nothing the matter with me, save that I need some company. I cannot pass this night alone.

I follow the road up and over the flank of the Head and descend toward Paris. A misty rain starts up, wetting my face and shoulders. Out along the Paris road, past the warm lights of houses that seem to flicker in the rainy dark like the beacons of ships, to where the road peters out in the bog. I stand for a while, trying to orient myself. Christine's cottage is out there somewhere, but I cannot see a light. If I miss it in the dark I will go over the cliff, unless I fall head-first into a turf cutting and drown myself in bog water. I think of turning back, but the thought of that empty fireside unnerves me. It is *uaigneas* itself will choke and drown me if I do not press on. I make a rapid sign of the cross, the way the old man used to do before he stepped into a boat, and I walk out into the bog.

As I approach the ocean, the wind becomes stronger and wetter, cutting through my shirt. Then there is a lull, and I hear the sound of waves breaking on rock. It seems somehow to be above me, and suddenly I have the sense that the waves are sweeping toward me across an obstructed plain. A moment of panic — and then a squall of wind rushes past.

The darkness is complete. I am absorbed in trying to sense the absence of solid ground in front of me, and I lose all count of time.

Something is blocking my way: the blank gable wall of a cottage. My heart leaps with relief. It seems dark and empty from the outside, but as I come into the yard, I catch a faint glimmer of light on the drawn blind of one of the windows. I am drenched to the skin. The wind feels like ice, and I have to clench my teeth to keep them from chattering. But I am safe from harm now, for tonight at least.

As I approach the door, it opens, and Christine comes out. She steps to one side and peers into the dark. I walk over to her. It takes her a moment to recognize me. Then she takes my hands quickly and draws me into the house.

"Matt," she says. "God, your hands are cold."

She does not seem in the least surprised to see me. Her composure has a calming effect; the terrors of the dark recede. The house is filled with a delicious warmth.

"I meant to come and see you this long time," I say. I am trying to give my visit some semblance of normality.

"I'm glad you came," she says cheerily. "You picked a fine night for it."

I look around. The interior is cramped and dark. The fire is low, and the only light is a candle in an old-fashioned tin holder. I notice that Christine is wearing her nightgown, with a man's overcoat thrown about her shoulders.

"I'm sorry if I woke you," I say.

"It would have been a whole lot worse if you woke Jonathan," she says with a wry grin. "We go to bed early here."

She goes down on her knees, pokes the fire, and adds some fresh sods. Then she fetches some clothes from the back of the house and tosses them on a chair by the fire. She hands me a towel. All this without appearing to notice my wet and disheveled state, for which I am grateful.

There is a ladder leading to a little loft. She climbs the ladder and disappears from view. I strip next to the fire, towel myself dry, and put on the dry clothes, a man's flannel shirt and jeans, a thick pair of woolen socks, a worn sweater. To whom do these clothes belong? They're too big for me, and I am still shivering in them. I pull a chair closer to the fire. I suppose I will not catch my death.

Christine descends the ladder backwards. She has exchanged the overcoat for a dressing gown. She goes into the gloom at the back of the house. A gas jet flares on the stove. She stands with her back to me for a little while, and then she comes to the fire and hands me a bowl of soup. She draws up a chair and sits with me while I eat. The soup warms me. I haven't eaten all day. By the time I have finished, I feel almost normal again.

We sit together looking at the fire. I am sorry I did not come to see her sooner. We are two of a kind, Chrissie and I, misfits both. She has left the Inish and come back again; she knows what that means. Our silence is not uncomfortable. It is the silence of friends who share memories of childhood. But a great deal has happened that we have not shared. I do not know how to begin to talk to her again.

"How are you getting along in Reenglass?" she says.

"It's lonesome enough there," I tell her. "Though not as lonesome as this place."

"I don't mind it," she says brightly. "London can be lonely too."

I am afraid that it will be painful for her to talk about it, and I say nothing. She draws her feet up on the chair and turns to me.

"I was afraid of the city at first. I worked for Aunt Julia's friends for three years, looking after their children, and at the end of that time I didn't know a single English person. I spent Christmas and holidays with them and went to Brighton with them for two weeks in the summer, and that was my life. I got sick and tired of it. I started to go out on my own. Then I met Michael. He was ten years older than me, he'd already been married and divorced, and he had a little girl who lived with his former wife. He was a painter, and he had a flat off the Brompton Road, full of beautiful old things. I moved in with him — and left Aunt Julia's friends in the lurch."

She gives me a mischievous grin. I am glad to catch a glimpse of the Christine I used to know. She is in good spirits. But she seems almost too eager to tell me her story, as though she wants to get it over with.

"Michael and I were very happy at first," she says. "And then it just fell apart. I suppose it was an unlikely match. His friends were all much older than me, and they talked about books and paintings till you were blue in the face, and there I was going to night classes just to try to get my O levels. I was jealous of the time Michael spent with his daughter. It was terrible of me, but I couldn't help it. And then I got homesick! I was pining away for the Inish. I thought if I didn't come back I'd turn into an English person — a fate worse than death!"

She laughs softly, her eyes inviting me to share the joke. But her story has knotted something inside of me. I do not want it to happen to Christine. I want to rewrite it, to unravel the difficulties she seems to make light of, to relieve the pain of the ending.

"I made up my mind to go back, without telling Michael or anything. That was when I found out I was pregnant. I was supposed to meet him in Kensington Gardens after I got the results of the test. He was sitting on a park bench with his back to me, feeding the pigeons out of a little bag. I stood there and I looked at him. I knew he'd want me to get rid of it. I said to myself, I'm going to stand here for five minutes and if he turns around and sees me I'll go up to him and I'll tell him and I'll do whatever he wants."

She pauses, smiling, as though remembering a person she is not. It is like one of the old man's pauses, heavy with fatality. We could be gathered around the fire to hear one of *his* stories, save that he is dead and gone and our childhood no longer protects us from the world. But this is not just a story, and there is something incongruous and disturbing about Christine's smile.

"So I stood there and Michael lit a cigarette and smoked it and fed some more bread to the pigeons and he never looked around. After the five minutes were up I turned around and walked out of there —"

"No," I say involuntarily.

"I got a train to Swansea, and I walked onto the boat that night. I was in Port the following day. I'll say this for Aunt Julia: As soon as she heard I was pregnant, she stopped telling me how ungrateful I'd been and she couldn't do enough for me. I even heard her giving the edge of her tongue to someone who wondered where the father was. I stayed with her until I had Jonty."

"Have you been back to London since he was born?"

She shakes her head. "I thought I might go," she says wonderingly. "But I wanted to come back to the Inish. After I'd been here for a while, London began to seem very far away. It's hard to travel with a young baby. And I didn't have a penny to my name."

She tosses her head and laughs.

"Chrissie," I say, putting my hand on hers, "if it's only a matter of money — I'll give it to you. I have plenty of money since the old man died, more than I know what to do with. Why should you stay here and have to listen to people talking? Why should your son have to grow up without knowing his father? It's no small thing not to have a father. We both of us know that."

She gives me a quick serious look out of her gray eyes. I withdraw my hand, and we sit in silence. I shouldn't have said anything. It is none of my business.

"It's very nice of you, Matt," she murmurs. "I won't forget it. But I haven't seen Michael for more than two years."

"Didn't he try to get in touch with you?"

"He wouldn't have wanted another child."

She sighs and gives a little shrug.

"I never felt at home in London anyway," she says brightly. "I'd rather have Jonty grow up on the Inish, with the ocean and the fresh air and the plants and animals, than on the Brompton Road. He won't feel deprived. He's gotten very attached to Pat-Joe — and so have I."

Her look has a pleading quality, as though she is afraid I will disapprove. I do not speak. Something is beginning to dawn on me. I know what she is going to say.

"To tell you the truth, we're thinking of getting married."

"Well, well," I say, trying to feign pleasure. "Congratulations!"

"Don't tell a soul. We haven't announced it yet. I don't know what the priest will say to us. I'll have to start going to mass again."

I answer her smile, but I feel heavy and tired. Christine has made her peace with the Inish. 'Tis I'm the misfit of the two of us.

Christine rises, picks up the candle, and motions me to follow her.

"I'll be all right by the fire," I begin.

She puts her finger to her lips and glances toward the loft. I follow her up the ladder. The loft is in a windowless gable just big enough for a double mattress on the floor. The air is warmer up here than below, perhaps because it traps the heat of the fire.

Jonathan is asleep on the mattress. Christine lies down beside him, puts her arms underneath him, and draws him toward her. Then she points to the place where he has been. I lie down, and she blows out the candle.

I lie there with my eyes open. I am grateful to be warm and safe and out of the night. But I do not feel any less alone.

"Are you all right, Matt?" Christine's voice says.

"Not really, Chrissie. But I'm looking out for better weather."

"It must be hard, living on your own in the house after him."

"It's getting on my nerves," I say.

I want to tell her more, but I am afraid of what she will think. There is a kind of distance between us now. I do not begrudge Christine and Pat-Joe their happiness, but I can no longer think that she shares my predicament. I suspect that she hasn't really opened her heart to me. But why should she, after all this time?

"I thought you were going back to Dublin," she says.

"That was before I found out that he'd left me the house."

"Isn't it well for you?" she says. "But I suppose it needs a bit of fixing up."

She is trying to be sympathetic. I take this opportunity to change the subject.

"Where are you and Pat-Joe going to live?"

"God alone knows! He still lives with Peg and his sister. His parents are long gone from the Inish, and his brother is married in their old house. I suppose we'll have to live here, though the three of us will be like sardines in a can! Never mind. We'll soldier on," she finishes brightly.

Silence, then an unexpected sigh.

"I don't mind so much about a house," she says, "but I'd like to have a garden. A flower garden, like my mother had. But I can't get anything to grow out here. The soil is too poor for most plants, and the wind kills the rest."

There is something in her voice that arrests my attention, an echo of our past intimacy. I lift my head off the pillow and lean on one elbow.

"When I was in England," she says, "Michael told me about Vita Sackville-West's garden where everything was white or gray. Her house was called Sissinghurst. There are white roses there, and lilies, of course, and pansies and peonies and irises and white delphinium. Then there are plants like foamflower and silver mound and savior's flannel. But there are no colors at all: everything is white."

The past is restored. That awful day the old man sent me to see her mother. The quiet adult formality with which Christine named for me the flowers of her mother's neglected garden — and the whiteness of the sickroom walls, the brilliant curtains, the sunlit bedspread, the swollen face on the pillow.

"We were supposed to go see it, Michael and I, but we never did."

I feel her distress. Is there any place more unlike an English country garden than this godforsaken lump of rock and begrudging soil? I want to say something that will help her.

"Do you think it would have made any difference, to you and Michael?"

"Oh God, no," she says quickly. "But at least I would have *seen* it. I could have gone with *you,* if you'd come over. I kept thinking you'd come and look me up, even though I never wrote to you. You were angry with me," she murmurs, "on account of the way I left."

I open my mouth to deny it, but then I realize that there is no need. We are close in this moment, as of old. We do not need to pretend with each other.

"I would have gone over," I tell her, "but I had no money, no place to stay."

"I suppose it's all for the best," she murmurs.

I am listening intently, waiting for her to explain something to me. But this is the sum total of her knowledge.

"You know I went to London because I thought my father was there," she says suddenly. "I used to ride the Tube on my day off from one end of the line to the other, looking at people's faces. I had a feeling that I'd meet him somehow, that we'd recognize each other. But then one day I didn't have that feeling anymore. Either he'd gone away or he was never there at all. I knew that I wasn't going to find him, that I'd never know him."

"I'm sorry, Chrissie."

"It's all right, Matt," she says, trying to keep the tremor out of her voice. "I went to London to look for my father, and I came back with Jonathan. I left the Inish, and I found what was in store for me. It happens to everyone sooner or later."

It is a sad story, but I am grateful to Christine for telling it to me. It is my story too, a shared history, the only kind that matters. A little warmth has crept into my heart, the warmth of companionship, the knowledge that we are still close. For now, for tonight, this warmth will suffice.

"There's only one thing I regret," Christine says. "That I never went to see Mister O. before he died. But I just couldn't!"

"I didn't see him myself. I came too late."

A taut pause. A sharp inhalation.

"Did he take it bad, the way I left?"

The question catches me without a ready answer. I hesitate just a second too long before I reply.

"He missed you, Chrissie. But you know the way he was. Whenever anyone talked about leaving the Inish, he'd say, 'Sure what is there here.'"

Silence. Another, conclusive sigh.

"What are *you* going to do, Matt?"

I lie back on the pillow and stare into the dark. I am thinking of my own failed plans, of the New World, and of Lily.

"I don't know."

But even as I say the words, something within me hardens into certainty. I am going away from the Inish. I have no business here after all. Or rather, I cannot undertake the business with which I have been charged. I must pack my bag and leave, before it is too late.

Her fingers search for and grip my hand.

"I needed to talk to you," she says. "I'll be all right now. You will be too. I know it."

*   *   *

I sleep like the dead. When I wake, I am alone in the loft. In the moment of waking I feel free and light, cleansed of thought; I am examining without bewilderment my novel surroundings, the exposed beams of the roof, the weak light filtered from below; and then the events of last night reconstitute themselves in a single instant, and the recollection of my conversation with Christine is immediately present, whole and entire.

I hear Jonathan downstairs. I get up and climb down the ladder. He is playing on the floor, and Christine is at the stove. She looks up quickly when I appear and then goes back to what she is doing. I gather my own clothes and head for the outhouse, where I dress.

On my way back, I pause by the gable, looking out toward the Blaskets. It is a wild and bright day, the high white clouds chasing each other across a pale sky. The far peninsula and the islands are soft and ethereal, screened by a curtain of flying spray. I can taste this spray on the air and feel its chilly breath around me. The ocean is a deeper blue flecked with white, and it too seems to be hurrying in the direction of the wind, surging between the arms of the Bay.

A magnificent spectacle to be sure — but scarcely human. I do not like to think of leaving Christine in this bleak spot. There are no human sounds here, none of the friendly sounds of a garden, no rustle of leaves or birdsong, just the wearisome buffeting of the wind and the intermittent thunder of the waves. Nothing but — Nothing: the wet waste of the ocean, the end of the world. It could drive a person stone mad.

I walk back into the house, and Christine hands me a cup of tea. We sit at the table in the gloom. The windows are small and set high in the walls. It must be always dark in here, no matter what the weather. It is smoky too; the chimney does not draw properly. I don't know how she can stand it.

"I have to be going, Chrissie," I say.

"Sure I'll see you again," she says, smiling.

"I'm afraid not. I'm just going to take my things from the house and leave. I've had enough."

To hear myself say it gives me a wrench. To walk out and lock the door and leave the house empty after he intended for me to live there. How can I do it? I feel the trap closing about me again. My head throbs; my body squirms in the chair. I put my flushed face in my hands.

"Matt?"

It comes to me suddenly: the way out.

"I want you to have Granda's house, Chrissie. To live there."

Will I not incur his wrath for all eternity? I raise my head slowly. Christine's face is all lit up. The sight of it gives me heart.

"Oh, Matt," she says.

She reaches for my hand across the table. I look into her eyes for a long moment. She is serious again. We understand each other. I am grateful to her for being able to accept the house from me.

"We'll pay you a fair rent," she says conscientiously.

"No, Chrissie. The house will be yours. That way nobody in the family can do anything about it. I'll get all the paperwork done in Caher before I go."

"Won't you ever want to come back here?"

"I'll come back here to die," I joke with her. "There's plenty of room above in the graveyard."

Her eyes fill with tears. "You're a very generous person, Matt. It's a grand house."

"He would have wanted you to have it, Chrissie, if it couldn't be mine. You know how fond he was of you."

An expression of pain appears on her face. I get up hurriedly. I have a lump in my throat. It is important to have someone to say good-bye to, but now I want to flee as quickly as I can.

"Where will you go, Matt?"

"I have a friend in the States. I'm going to go to her."

Christine is smiling again. "A girlfriend in America. And you never told me."

"I don't know if she'll have me," I feel obliged to add. "I haven't written to her since Granda died."

"She'll be lucky to get you."

She picks up Jonathan and comes to the door with me. She leans toward me and kisses me carefully on the cheek. I put my arms around them both, and then I am out of the door and into the windy yard.

I look back once as I cross the bog. Christine is standing in the doorway, her face and hair almost white in a shaft of sunlight, behind her the dark of the door. I lift my hand. She is holding Jonathan in her arms, and she does not wave back.

Then I am running across the Inish. The sky seems very blue and high and wide, the bog black and stark in the cold sunlight. I take a deep clean salty breath. My way through the bog is clear, and the fears of the night are far from me. The wind pushes me from behind, and for a moment I feel light, of head and heart. It seems that if I run just a little faster, I will be torn free from this black earth.

You can take the man out of the bog, Granda loved to say, but you can't take the bog out of the man. So be it. I will live with it. If I can live with having given the house to Chrissie — to the certain consternation of all my family — I can live with anything.

The sun is burning the tops of the trees across the field. The house door opens, and Lily comes rushing down the porch steps. Seeing Cooper and me sitting together in the front seat of the Monster, she stops dead, stares at us, and walks over slowly. Cooper lashes his tail and squirms about. I open the driver's door, and he leaps across me. Lily leans into the car.

"Are you all right, Matt?"

"Right as the rain."

Cooper sticks his head in at the door, as though to give the lie to my response.

"Did you guys take a trip together?" Lily wants to know.

"He was keeping me company. I couldn't sleep."

"Maybe you want to go back to bed while I go and get Dad. I think I can manage him on my own."

"No," I say. "I'm coming with you. I was just waiting for you to wake up."

This is what is in store for me; there is no escaping it. I can lie here and wait for it to find me — or rise up and go out to meet it.

Shaking Hands with God

"Did I ever tell you about your great-uncle Arthur?" Sam's voice issues from the backseat.

"Yes, Dad," Lily says. She does not turn to look at him but stares straight ahead. Her face looks strained, taut.

"Well, Matt doesn't know the story," Sam continues. "Lily's great-uncle was originally called Herman, but he almost died when he was six months old so they renamed him *Alte*, that's *old*, you see, so the Lord would think he was an old man. Why bother with an *alte kaka*? Let him live another few years. And it worked — he lived to ninety-three and died fighting the Cossacks!"

"I guess it's better to die fighting at ninety-three than to die in your sleep at six months," I say, feeling that some response is required of me.

Sam's manner seems hopelessly out of tune with the seriousness of the occasion.

"Of course it is!" he proclaims. "And that's what I should have done for Lily. I should have said to God, That girl looks like she's set for life, but she's got her troubles. She had a good job, but she couldn't take the pressure. That Irishman she's shacked up with, he's no good, he'll run off and leave her. She lives in a nice house, but she's only renting, throwing good money after bad, and she can't afford a mortgage."

I feel his fingers jabbing my shoulder, and I glance back at him.

He's lying full length on the Monster's backseat, muffled up in a scarf and woolen hat.

"And that way, I would have outsmarted the Lord, you see. He'd have said to himself, Enough already! He wouldn't have remembered her health, he wouldn't have even thought to afflict her with a bad back, not for another forty years."

"My back is not so bad, Dad. You're the one who's sick."

A profound groan issues from the backseat.

"Who would have thought it?" Sam says, as though he'd actually forgotten. "Struck down. And after the way I've lived. For the past twenty years I've kept myself alive on cod-liver oil, bananas, and ice cream, with chicken soup every time the temperature in my office goes below fifty. I've never been sick a day in my life, never even had a common cold."

His voice expresses disdain for the rest of humanity, whose indulgence in minor ailments has drastically shortened their life span.

"Never drank, never smoked. A cup of coffee in the morning is my only vice. And now look at me. I haven't got the strength to hold a tennis racket, not to mind swing it and hit the ball. Oh . . . my . . . God."

I have been driving as slowly as I possibly can, to avoid causing him discomfort. I slow down some more and turn into the unpaved driveway to Lily's house.

"Where are we?" Sam says. "Well — what do I care? It doesn't matter to me where I die, so long as it's not in some hospital where they try to keep you alive against your will. I've had a good at bat. I'm ready to let someone else step up to the plate. But the way I feel — no zizzle, no interest in anything, no appetite for life. I don't mind saying I'm a dying man: you start to die the moment you're born. But to have to say I'm a *sick* man! It's embarrassing."

I squeeze the brakes and bring the Monster to a halt in front of the house. Both Lily and I jump from the car and rush to the back doors, as though haste were really necessary. Sam has already pulled himself into a sitting position, and I help him to swing his feet through the door.

"Let me sit here for a minute," he mutters.

The skin of his face is unnaturally pale and stretched tautly across his cheekbones and the bridge of his nose. He has become an old man in the space of a couple of months. Only his eyes retain their wicked youthful fire.

I believe that Lily and I have gone through the business of moving him out of his office in a state of collective shock. Throughout the morning, we have worked efficiently and silently to pack up his few possessions: a folder of papers, a briefcase full of first-issue postage stamps and unused checkbooks, a suitcase of clothes. Though hardly aware of each other, we share an unspoken distress, watching the procession of Sam's friends, tenants of the building, vendors from Haymarket, a couple of panhandlers from South Station, if I am not mistaken, come to say good-bye. He presides over the desolation of his office like a comic Lear, bequeathing tennis racket, bicycle, and television sets with reckless benevolence, fending off embarrassed emotion with irascibility. It's all up with me, he tells one and all self-deprecatingly. I'm going to my daughter's house to die.

I am almost embarrassed myself that his manner makes no concession to his imminent death. If only for Lily's sake, I think, he ought to be less blunt. But would that really make it any easier for her? Already I want to be alone with her, to talk to her, to know what she is going through. But there's too much to do.

"All right," Sam says. "Let's get the funeral over with."

With Lily and me guiding him, he negotiates the steps to the porch, where he halts to rest. He stands for a few moments in silence, and Lily and I exchange a look over the top of his head. Then we lead him into the house. We've prepared a bed for him downstairs, but he eases himself down on the couch in the living room next to the woodstove.

"This is my spot," he announces. "I'm not going to budge from here. Can you light a fire in that thing? I feel like I'm in an icehouse."

The heat wave is over. It has been pleasantly cool in the house since the weather broke. But it will not be cool if I light the stove. I glance at Lily.

"Don't you want to take off your muffler and your hat, Dad?"

"I'll take them off as soon as I warm up. But I may never be warm again. This must be what death feels like. It starts with a chill, then you get colder and colder until you freeze, you're like a block of ice. So don't waste the heat. It won't do me any good."

I light a roaring blaze in the stove, and Sam seems to revive a little. I take off my shirt, and Lily changes into shorts. We picnic on the floor between the couch and the stove, in an air of unnatural gaiety, orchestrated by Sam, who takes a couple of spoonfuls of the chicken soup Lily has made for him, just to keep us company.

"Who would have thought it?" He groans, raising his hands laboriously to clutch his head, in the true Dostoyevskian manner. "But it could be worse! A couple of weeks and I'll be out of here: I can tell. Look what happened to my sister. Poor Sarah, having to stick around like that for five years — *five years!* She was never very smart, but by the time she was ready to go, she didn't know whether she was coming or going. There was nothing left but skin and bone: they had to search the bed for her before they could perform the autopsy."

I cannot suppress a chuckle. Sam seizes upon it.

"And I told her, I told her," he proclaims hoarsely. "At my brother's funeral. She's tottering up the undertaker's steps, and I'm running after her ready to catch her if she falls. We come to the door and she stops to shed a few tears. Poor Eli, she says to me. She's standing there in the door of the funeral parlor, we're holding up the rest of the mourners, who probably want to get in and get it over with. After you, Sarah, I say. You're next. And she was!"

"That really wasn't a very nice thing to say to your sister, Dad."

"Anybody could see the woman was on her last legs. And besides, she was as deaf as a post! Bring me that folder, will you, Lily? Oh my God. Not to be able to do anything for yourself! Who would have thought it?"

He lifts his head and takes the folder that she hands him, spilling the contents on his chest.

"Here it is, the autopsy report the hospital sent me. Listen to this: My God, is there anything that poor woman didn't have? She was a virtual medical celebrity, doctors coming from all over just to take her pulse, everybody in the hospital except the elevator operator had been in to take a look at her! Peptic ulcer, diverticulosis, acute hem-

orrhagic esophagitis, coronary atherosclerosis, pulmonary conges-
tion, pleural effusions, arterial and arteriolar nephrosclerosis,
chronic cholecystitis."

He molds the words gleefully as his lips release them.

"Not to mention cancer, moderate; hepatitis, severe; paralysis of
the aged, general; atrophification of brain function, complete; cessa-
tion of heart throb, imminent. Good-bye, so long, end of story."

I glance at Lily and see that she is no longer smiling. I feel
ashamed that I have encouraged Sam. But who can stop him?

"And what kind of life did she have for the last seven, eight, nine
years?" he says disgustedly. "When that doctor told me I had the big
C, I said, That's it, that's the end. He was a good man, didn't pull his
punches, gave it to me straight up. I thought you were a fighter, Sam,
he said to me. What do you mean? I said. Who can fight God? I
didn't think you were the kind to throw in the towel, he said. There's
a treatment. A treatment! Excruciating torture — and for what? Six
to eight months. That's the best you could hope for after his treatment. Six to eight lousy months."

"It might have given your friends a little more time to say good-
bye," Lily says quietly.

"Who needs a long good-bye?" Sam sputters. "Every time I see
someone, I say good-bye for the last time. I don't want anyone coming by. To see me like this? After the way I've lived? Oh . . . my . . .
God."

He lays his head back and composes his hands upon his chest, as
though already laid out for his wake.

"Mother will want to come."

His eyes snap open, and his head darts up. "You didn't tell her I
was *sick?*"

"Well, what do you think, Dad?" Lily says with a wan smile. "I'm
going to say to Mother, Oh and by the way, Dad was here for a couple of weeks. He just died."

Sam lays his head back.

"Let her come if she wants," he murmurs. "There's nothing I can
do about it. She'd better hurry, or she'll go to all that trouble for
nothing."

We sit in silence in the dusk, the only light coming from the stove's tarnished window.

"I think I'm ready for another pill," Sam says.

Lily gets up quickly, gives him a pill, and holds a paper cup of water to his mouth while he swallows.

"I forgot you were due. Why didn't you tell me? Are you in pain?" Sam shrugs, lays back.

"When is the nurse coming?" he murmurs.

"Tomorrow."

"Is she going to bring more of the pills?"

"She'll have everything you need, Dad."

"How am I going to take them when I get to be non compos?"

"She's going to bring some liquid morphine. We'll continue to give it to you. If that's what you want."

Sam raises his head to peer at us, a tuft of hair in his left eyebrow like an indignant punctuation mark.

"If that's what I want!" he snorts. "Of course it's what I want. Who could put up with this pain? I want you to promise you'll give it to me. You too, Irishman. In case she gets squeamish."

"Sure," I say, under the pressure of his baleful look.

Lily says nothing. He flops back.

"Liquid morphine. What a relief. Now I can rest in peace."

Lily sighs.

"I hate to tell you this, Dad, but if you want to stay where you are, you have to get up to let me put on some sheets."

No answer. A faintly audible snore. I help Lily to spread a blanket over him, and then we tiptoe away. I am exhausted, a little dazed, grateful to be out of the range of the stove. At the foot of the stairs, Lily halts, takes my hand, and lays her head on my shoulder. We stand like this, listening to the soft noises of the fire, to Sam's breathing.

"You go on up," Lily says. "I'm going to sit with him for a while."

The hospice nurse is Irish American. She has close-cropped red hair, is slim and athletic-looking, and wears a short skirt. Her name, appropriately enough, is Kathleen.

"Is this the suicide lady?" Sam greets her. "Is this the lady with the morphine?"

Lily hastens to assure her that Sam is under a misimpression, but Kathleen doesn't seem to mind. She removes her large elegant spectacles, beneath which her face is soft and undefended, and bends over Sam.

"I'm pleased to meet you," she tells him with a confident smile.

"And I to meet you, Kathleen," Sam says, immediately on familiar terms. "Though you may be the last person I'll have the pleasure to meet this side of the Great Divide."

"I want to say, I hope not."

"Not at all, not at all," Sam says, grinning. "I'm through with meeting people. I deserve a rest. If you're to be the last, sure I couldn't wish for a nicer pair of smiling Irish eyes."

He gives her a few bars of "When Irish Eyes Are Smiling" in his best brogue. She stands by the couch, blushing prettily. He appears to have charmed her. But as soon as he is done, she goes to work with impressive efficiency. Tactfully she inquires about the welfare of the caretakers. How are we bearing up? She hands Lily a number of cardboard sheets with pills enclosed in little bubbles and explains the dosage in a discreet undertone. The important thing, she informs us, is to stay ahead of the pain. She tells Sam that the couch will not do and that a hospital bed will be delivered. He receives this news with remarkable equanimity.

"I wish you could have known me in my prime, Kathleen. It was just a couple of months ago. It's all up with me now. But I can tell you my secret, and maybe you'll live as long and die as happy. You look like a person who knows the value of exercise. Apart from the cigarettes."

"I'm trying to give them up, Sam," Kathleen says guiltily. "Tell me your secret and maybe it'll help me."

"Better never to have started, like me. You've got a tough row to hoe, I can tell. What's my secret? I'll give you a hint. The Eskimos are the only race of people on the face of the earth that don't suffer from heart disease. That ought to tell you something right there."

"I have to move to the North Pole?" Kathleen says, getting into the spirit of it, after an almost imperceptible hesitation.

"Would that it were so simple, Kathleen!" Sam raises himself on his elbows, his voice taut with conviction. "A judicious diet is the only route to health and longevity. Augmented by cod-liver oil. Two generous tablespoons, taken religiously every day, on an empty stomach."

"But I don't like the taste, Sam," Kathleen protests.

"A small price to pay for decades of health and happiness. If you don't like the taste, eat a slice of lemon afterwards. Or do like me: rub the lemon over your tongue and your gums. It'll take away the fishy taste."

"I'll give it a shot, Sam," Kathleen says, shouldering her pocket-book. "Now you take care."

"I always liked to take what's good for me straight up, no messing around. I refused to eat anything that came out of a can or a carton — or a cow's udder, as far as that goes. Americans eat like pigs: it's disgusting. When I saw these potbellied men with four jowls driving by in their Cadillacs, I used to pity them. I said to myself, They're headed for an early rendezvous with the Grim Reaper. I wouldn't be in their shoes for all the tea in China. But it just goes to show, clean living will only get you so far. Now I'm in the same fix."

Kathleen takes Sam's hand loosely in hers and stands by the couch patiently. "No, you're not, Sam," she says quietly. "You've still got your joie de vivre, which is more than you can say for most people, young or old."

There is an undertone of emotion in her voice, a minute crack in the professional facade.

"You're the salt of the earth, Kathleen," Sam tells her. "You're one of Nature's gentlewomen. But you've taken your knocks too. I can tell. You know that life is no bowl of cherries."

Kathleen catches my eye, and I can see immediately that this is true, that Sam has unerringly found a tender spot. But she takes his probing in good part.

"I'll be back this afternoon to check on the bed," she tells Lily.

"You can call me at the office in the meantime if you need anything. Bye, Sam."

Lily goes outside with her. Sam is singing in a remarkably tuneful voice. "All I want is a room somewhere. Far away from the cold night air."

"She certainly cheered you up, Dad," Lily says, coming back from the door.

"With one enormous chair. Ah, wouldn't it be lov-er-ly?"

I scan Lily's face. She looks a little less strained. I am glad. We have a long road ahead of us. I cannot imagine that Sam will actually die. He hardly seems sick to me, apart from his pallor and his lack of, as he puts it, zizzle.

"That Kathleen," he says. "She's better than any medication."

"She liked you too," Lily says.

"Which reminds me. Did she bring any fatal pills or powders?"

"She gave me some pills. She's bringing the liquid morphine this afternoon."

Another sigh, this time one of satisfaction.

"And by a sleep to say we end the heartache and the thousand natural shocks that flesh is heir to," Sam murmurs. " 'Tis a consummation devoutly to be wished."

The first week passes. I go to my job each evening, dubbed the night owl by Sam, as though he cannot quite believe that one can be gainfully employed at night. In the mornings, still wakeful, I spell Lily while she takes a shower. She has been up two or three times each night, Sam calling for a paper cup of root beer, his staple, or to initiate a rambling discussion on the advisability of taking another half a pill. True to his regimen, he has eaten only a couple of spoonfuls of ice cream and a negligible quantity of chicken soup. I bring him coffee in the morning, of which he does not take more than a couple of sips. He has submitted to the hospital bed, though he protests that it is an unnecessary expense.

"I've always lived within my means," he confides to me. "Why should I use up my daughter's inheritance on my deathbed?"

I tell him about Wilde's remark — I am dying beyond my means — and he chuckles appreciatively.

"It takes a special kind of person to crack a joke at a time like that."

"It sure does, Sam."

At every conceivable opportunity, it seems, the knowledge that he is dying flees from my mind: he's simply visiting us, he's confined to bed, he'll soon be up and about. I am almost ashamed at how lightly I appear to take it: the sufferings of others are easy to bear. But it is Sam who reminds me, time after time, as though in spite of his manner he is living with this knowledge moment by moment, turning it over in his mind, examining it from all angles, studying it, as it were, as he used to study the news.

On Saturday I sleep for a couple of restless hours and get up at lunchtime. I'm drawn to his bedside by a fascination I cannot name, even when he is sleeping. For dinner Lily and I eat scrambled eggs in silence in the kitchen, and then she troops wearily upstairs. I've volunteered to sleep downstairs, where I can hear him if he calls.

I leave the light off and sit in the armchair opposite the bed. All my attention is focused upon him, and my mind is empty and clear. It is strange how all of my concerns have withdrawn to a respectful distance, as it were. Living with Lily, living alone, leaving Ireland, remembering Ireland: nothing seems to matter save what is happening at this time, in this room. I have never in my life had this sure sense of knowing my place, of knowing what it is I have to do. Go to work, come home, spell Lily, sit by his bed. It sounds monotonous, but it feels incontrovertibly right.

Would it have been like this if I'd stayed behind to nurse the old man? Would my life now be whole instead of a tangle of unfinished business?

A stirring from the bed. A faint thoughtful murmur.

"To sleep. Perchance to dream. Ay, there's the rub."

He pauses, as though groping for the rest of the line.

"For in that sleep of death what dreams may come," I begin.

"When we have shuffled off this mortal coil, must give us pause!" Sam finishes eagerly, wide awake now. "It's all nonsense, of course. Have you ever seen a corpse?"

"Just once."

"Did you think that it was dreaming?"

"To tell you the truth, Sam —"

"Nonsense!" he insists. "There's nothing. I'm looking forward to it. I can hardly wait. When you've lost the use of your vital functions like I have and there's nothing left to feel but pain —"

"Do you want me to give you half a pill?"

"No, no. I'll wait. When you've never taken a pill in your life, not even an aspirin . . ." His voice trails off. I sit forward in the chair, listening to his breathing.

"It's hard to believe in something you can't see or touch," he says. "You'd have to be a fool to believe in it! And yet, and yet. How can you have a world like this, so complex, so detailed? A whole society beneath an anthill. The way bees produce honey within their hives, the division of labor they have. And there's a hummingbird whose beak can fit into only one species of flower. Only one flower, of all the flowers in the world!"

I sit back in the chair. There is no need to do anything, just to sit. There is nothing I can do for him, save keep him company.

"You should exercise your eyes," he tells me, "if you want to have the use of them when you're my age. Stand outside, hold your finger up, focus on the finger, focus on the stars. How can there be so many of them? How do we know what they are? Who can say that there isn't some other form of life out there, looking back at us? It's a poor universe if there isn't. To think that we're the best it has to offer. It's an insult to the creative powers of God."

"I thought you didn't believe."

"Bah," he says impatiently. "What does it matter whether I believe or not? Do you think that'll make any difference to the cancer that's eating away my insides? The universe is a big place. If you want to know what I think, my guess is that God is AWOL, absent without leave. He's off somewhere attending to his own affairs, and there's nobody minding the store. It's like Uncle Sam. He's supposed to be looking out for all of us, but where the hell is he when you need him, when your stock takes a nosedive or you can't get a mortgage? God is out to lunch. He's no slouch when it comes to dreaming up different kinds of plants and animals — and what are we all but animals anyway? — but when it comes to keeping the peace and running the show, forget it, He's gone fishing."

He pauses, as though for breath. I seize my chance and tell him the probably apocryphal story of Gertrude Stein's last words, how she asked those attending her deathbed, What is the answer? and when no one ventured a reply, she laughed and asked, What is the question?

"That was one smart lady," Sam murmurs, drifting off. "To know the question: that would be something. But I have another question. How *can* you know the question? That's the *real* question."

I doze in the armchair and on the couch, which has been moved to make way for the hospital bed. At 5:00 A.M. Sam asks for a pill. He does not seem to be entirely awake, and as soon as he has taken it he closes his eyes. I sit on the porch with Cooper in the pristine Sunday morning silence. Lily comes down in her nightgown and joins us. We sit for a while without speaking.

"How are you bearing up?" Lily says.

I am to help Lily nurse her father until he dies. Further than that I cannot see.

"I'm fine. What about you?"

She shakes her head, as though her feelings are too complex or too overwhelming to describe.

"Did he sleep?"

"Off and on. We talked."

"About what?"

"Death. Whether or not God exists — and if so where."

Lily shakes her head again.

"I can't believe this is happening," she says. "I'm all caught up in it, of course, and it's the only thing I want to do. But some part of me refuses to believe it. Some part of me is disengaged, just watching it all go by."

I feel her distress, but I do not know how to comfort her. Sam has taken the business of dying out of the realm of the special and tragic and into life. His caustic humor has made expressions of grief or sympathy seem absurd. Perhaps later it will be appropriate to mourn him. But not now.

For me it is an extraordinarily peaceful Sunday. Lily goes for a walk with Cooper, and I talk with Sam or lie on the couch reading. He is incontinent and needs to be changed. I have been tutored by the expert Kathleen, and I want to spare Lily this chore, which is hard for her. Sam submits to it with no loss of dignity. If anything, it serves to heighten his humorous appreciation of the irony of his predicament.

"If only my wife or my mother could see me now," he croaks. "Or those secretaries in the Federal Reserve. You remember that building across the street from me, looks like a big silver dollar. I used to work in the building that was on the lot next door, before they put that thing up. Fourteen stories my building was, the tallest building for miles. I'd sunbathe on the roof every day, summer, spring, and fall, even a few days during the January thaw. Then they put up the Financial Center, the one that looks like a giant egg carton. Then the Federal Reserve. Pretty soon there were a half dozen of them, all of them higher than mine. The superintendent of the building comes up to me one day and he says, 'I'm sorry, Sam, you've got to put on a pair of trunks or else find somewhere else to sunbathe. The secretaries in the Federal Reserve are complaining about you.' 'Those are my most vital parts,' I said. 'Those are the parts that need sun the most.' I bet it was the bosses who complained — because their secretaries were looking out the windows all the time!"

He's sitting on the edge of the hospital bed, one hand on my shoulder to steady himself, the other sawing the air.

"'Tell them to look the other way,' I said, 'and I'll turn the other cheek. This is a free country. I'll stand up for my right to let my pants down in private on my own roof without a fifty-story building full of peeping toms looking over my shoulder.'"

"Oh, my God," Lily says, coming in. "You're sitting up. How are you feeling today, Dad?"

Sam lets his hand fall lifelessly to his knee. He lowers his shoulder slowly to the bed and rolls upon his back. "Don't ask," he croaks, his face a mask of weariness.

I lift his feet back into the bed and draw the covers over his wasted flesh.

"Are you tired?" Lily persists.

A profound sigh. "I'm tired of everything. Except Kathleen! When is she coming back?"

"She'll be here tomorrow, Dad."

I notice Lily's lips tighten and set. She turns and walks into the kitchen.

"I can tell you this, Lily," Sam calls after her, suddenly animated. "Your Irishman here is better at this dirty business than anyone. Better than you, better than Kathleen even. When he changes me, I stay changed. He'd make someone a good mother, if he wasn't a man."

No reply from the kitchen. I am flattered that Sam appreciates my attentions, but something tells me that I must now attend to Lily. I go into the kitchen and find her weeping silently over the coffeepot. I shepherd her out onto the porch. She has a little spasm of weeping, and then she wipes the tears from her eyes with determination.

"It's just my father," she says. "That's the way he is and there's nothing I can do about it. I thought it would be different now that he's dying —"

She chokes on the word, bites her lips, and forces herself to continue. "But he's just the same about dying as he was about his health or his cod-liver oil or his stupid tennis racket: he's obsessed with it and you can't get his attention."

"Maybe I should let you spend more time alone with him. I just wanted to give you a break. And I like sitting with him."

"I know," Lily says, turning to look at me. "I appreciate it. I was alone with him every night last week while you were at work. It doesn't make any difference. He needs someone to perform for, like you and Kathleen, someone to laugh at his jokes. That's all he's ever needed. He doesn't want to see my mother — and he doesn't want to see me."

"Lily, he asked if he could come here."

"I know, I know. It's just so hard for me. I thought it'd be different. I thought —"

Sam's hoarse call comes to our ears, followed by the faltering strains of song: "All day I paced the barren waste without a trace of water . . ."

"I'm glad you're here, Matt," Lily tells me, squeezing my hand as she turns away. "I don't know what I'd do if I were all alone with him."

Monday. I sit with him in the afternoon while Lily is shopping, strangely unwilling to go to work for the first time since I started. For some reason, I find myself describing to him the scenario of *Breath,* one of Beckett's last and most minimal plays.

"There are no actors you can see," I tell him. "The stage is filled by a heap of rubbish, and the dialogue, if you can call it that, consists of a recording of a baby crying and the sound of someone breathing in and out."

"All of life," Sam declaims, "right there on the stage."

I fetch my copy of *Waiting for Godot,* sole survivor of the fire, unearthed from the Monster's glove compartment.

"Nothing to be done," I begin, reading aloud.

"Nothing to be done," Sam echoes from the bed. "You said it."

"I'm beginning to come round to that opinion."

"God!" comes indignantly from Sam. "How could you ever have thought otherwise?"

"All my life I've tried to put it from me, saying, Vladimir, be reasonable, you haven't tried everything."

"Ha! Be reasonable. What's the use? Does the big C listen to reason?"

I have some misgivings. Perhaps I am merely upsetting him. But he presses me to continue. I read the first page, with Sam interjecting his vehement approbation between the lines.

"It's too much for one man," I read.

"Oh! Don't I know it!"

"On the other hand what's the good of losing heart now, that's what I say. We should have thought of it a million years ago —"

"We should have thought of a lot of things," Sam muses quietly, as though to himself. "But who knew it would turn out like this?"

I am beginning to have an uncanny feeling of discomfort. Sam's responses are almost too convincing.

"Go on, go on," he urges.

He laughs so hard at Estragon's difficulties with his boot that I am afraid he will not be the better of it.

"Hurts!" I read. "He wants to know if it hurts!"

"Stop!" Sam sputters. "Enough! I can't take any more of it. It's too much. The man is a genius."

I hear Lily come in, and I slip the book under the bedclothes. I am afraid I have overstepped my brief. But Sam is lying quietly, his chin tilted up, eyes closed. Lily puts her head in the door and gives me a questioning look.

"What a time we've had while you were out," Sam says, without opening his eyes.

"What were you guys doing?" she says, advancing into the room. She's smiling. She seems more relaxed.

"We were performing in a play," Sam tells her. "Now I can't tell whether my life is a play or the play is my life. What difference does it make? All the world's a stage."

When I come to leave for work, I stop by Sam's bed. He reaches up, and I shake his hand. His grip is remarkably strong. He holds on to my hand, peering at me over the edge of the sheet, his eyes bright and birdlike.

"It's been peculiarly wonderful, Matt," he tells me, drawing out and savoring the adverb.

This strikes me as a sort of valediction. I get a catch in my throat. I want to tell him it isn't true, he will be here a good while yet, we will have more good times, read the entire play perhaps. But looking at his pinched features, at the wasted flesh of his face, the taut yellowed old man's skin, I know it is not true. Death is near at hand already. But it is a discreet, almost a benign presence, patient, unassuming, nothing harsh or terrible about it. And yet it means absence, irrevocable loss, regret. It gives me a turn to be so at ease with it.

"I'll talk to you in the morning, Sam," I say, trying to cast a cold eye.

"I'll talk to you when I talk to you," is his rejoinder.

* * *

The second week. Sam rambles, in and out of clarity. He will not even look at food. When I get home on Wednesday morning, bleary-eyed, longing for sleep, Kathleen is already there. She and Lily are standing in the living room, where Sam cannot see them from the bed. They hardly look up when I come in, so absorbed are they in their conversation. I stand by the bed. Sam appears to be sleeping. I move away, intending to slip upstairs to bed.

"If a cat has nine lives," Sam murmurs, without opening his eyes, "I must have had ninety-nine. I ought to write the book — a hundred ways to shuffle off your mortal coil. I've tried them all."

Kathleen comes over and stands by the bedside, looking grave.

"I'm saying this for his benefit, Kathleen," Sam continues, still with his eyes closed. "He wants to know what it's like to die." A dry chuckle, almost inaudible. "Who can know what it's like to die? God is saving that for last."

Is that what I want? Is that why I feel drawn to his bedside? Or is it simply my attachment to him? The realization of this attachment steals over me, and I feel the void that will take its place when he is gone.

"And for your benefit too, Kathleen, since helping people to die is your business. What a business! But that's what you do, and you're good at it. There must be a lot of *alte kakas* hanging by their finger-nails from a trestle, just for another look into those Irish eyes are smiling. And you're supposed to be helping them to die!"

He gives her a couple of weak snatches of "I've Grown Accustomed to Her Face." I catch Lily's eye across the room. She seems preoccupied, aloof. I wonder why she doesn't approach the bed.

"Death by drowning," Sam announces. "They tell you it's the easiest way to go. What do they know? That undiscovered country from whose bourn no traveler returns. The time I fell into the East River — lucky it wasn't winter — went under one barge, then another. Keelhauled they would've called it in the navy. I had spots before my eyes and I was starting to pass out and all I could think of was, How is your mother ever going to find someone as interesting as me? Her own words: the most interesting man I ever met."

Lily walks quietly out of the room.

"Death by misadventure. The time two hoods chased me into Kenmore Square at three o'clock in the morning, one of them with a stiletto in his hand, not another soul in sight. I tripped on something and I thought to myself, This is it, this is the end, it's all going to come down to the point of that stiletto. But at exactly the same moment, the nearest guy fell down, just like he'd been shot, and the stiletto slid along the pavement, right to where I was lying. And the guy behind fell over him. This is a sign from God, I said to myself. I picked up the stiletto — a nasty piece of work it was — I threw it into the subway, and I ran. I didn't look back until I came to the Common. Here I was a fifty-year-old man — ah, to be fifty again! — and these were two youngsters, and I outran them."

"I'm going to check your blood pressure, Sam," Kathleen says.

She lifts his wasted arm and rolls the cuff around it. She inflates the cuff and scrutinizes the little dial. Her face is impassive.

"Death from iatrogenic causes," Sam says delightedly. "It's a good job I conceived an aversion for the medical profession as a young man. That's the real secret of my longevity. You risk your life every time you go to see a doctor. And if you get yourself committed to the hospital your risks are quadrupled. All those sick people. Take my advice: Don't be sick. Eat right and let nature take its course."

Kathleen gives a little shake of her head, removes the cuff, and lays Sam's arm gently by his side.

"I'll see you tomorrow, Sam."

"Don't be too sure, Kathleen. I've used up all my lives."

"You'll be here tomorrow."

"Today, tomorrow, what's the difference?" Sam mumbles, closing his eyes. "I'm not really here right now."

I go upstairs to find Lily sleeping in her clothes, face down on the bed. I cover her with a blanket, not because it is cold, but simply in order to do something for her; I can see that Sam's appreciation of Kathleen is getting on her nerves. She sighs in her sleep but does not stir. I come downstairs again and stretch out on the couch opposite Sam.

I am woken out of the sleep of exhaustion by Sam's voice. "Isn't she a wonderful girl?"

"She's certainly competent," I manage, still groggy.

"Ho, ho," Sam chuckles. "I'm talking about my daughter. Kathleen is a good nurse, but she's not in the same class as Lily. Doesn't have her sensitivity, her perspicacity."

I stretch, rub my eyes, sit on the edge of the couch.

"It might not be a bad idea for you to tell Lily that," I say in a rush, getting it out before I have time to change my mind about it.

"I know, I know," Sam says. "You don't have to tell me. I know what's on her mind. But you see it wouldn't do any good. She wouldn't believe me. She'd think you put me up to it. I'd end up doing more harm than good. It doesn't matter what anybody says to you if you don't believe in yourself. No, she's just going to have to find out for herself that her father loves her. She'll realize it, sooner or later."

Sam is regarding me intently, wide awake and present, a gleam of mischief in his eyes. Perhaps I should have stayed out of it.

"I know what she thinks," Sam informs me. "I wasn't a model father. She's perfectly right. But where are you going to find a model father? It's like old Diogenes looking for an honest man with a lantern in the middle of the day. Good luck. But it was nothing personal. That's what she doesn't understand. If I was somebody else, she might have had an easier time, but she wouldn't be the same person either, so who's to say? I wasn't exactly a model husband either, but that's another story . . ."

He closes his eyes. I am in such an odd state of exhaustion that I do not know if I am touched by his confidence, impressed by his profundity, or offended on Lily's behalf.

"You can tell her what I said," he murmurs, "if you can find a way to put it that won't upset her. You're a lucky man to end up with Lily."

"I know, Sam," I whisper, my insides in a knot of fear and hope.

Surely this communion with her father will forge an unbreakable bond between Lily and me. This is what I hope for, this is what I fear.

"But the thing is," Sam says loudly, waking up momentarily. "She's a lucky woman too. And don't let her forget it!"

He sleeps. I dash the tears from my eyes and leave the room on tiptoe. I walk slowly upstairs and lie beside Lily on the bed. She is still sleeping. I think that I will tell her everything, but when I wake, she is already gone.

Lily's mother arrives on Saturday. When I come downstairs after three or four hours of sleep — it is as though I am afraid Sam will die if I leave his room — she is sitting quietly in the kitchen with Lily. I like Rachel immediately. She has Lily's warmth and unforced friendliness without the energy. She is diffident and unassuming, and there is a trace of melancholy in her manner. But that must be because her husband is dying. They are still married, in spite of a long-standing separation.

"Mother is here, Dad," Lily announces.

Sam's eyes pop open and dart about in agitation.

"No tears!" he orders, catching sight of Rachel standing meekly in the doorway.

She draws a chair up to the bed and sits there without saying anything, biting her lip.

"Oh well, what's the use?" Sam says. "I'm dying beyond my brains, as Oscar Wilde, or somebody very like him, once said. I'm on my penultimate legs. Or maybe I should say, postpenultimate. I can't even feel them anymore."

"I always thought you'd outlive me, Sam —"

"If there was any justice in the world, I would have, Rachel, with the way you eat. But it's never too late to turn over a new leaf."

Lily and I leave them alone. We sit on the porch and watch Cooper romp about the field, the white ruff at his throat catching the brilliant light. We are too exhausted to talk — or else it is that everything that might be said is self-evident. I doze off with my head against one of the columns.

Rachel's voice wakes me. "What about the service?" she wonders plaintively. "What about the funeral?"

"I don't want a rabbi," Sam trumpets. "I don't want a roomful of people weeping and gnashing their teeth over me. Going to all that trouble for a stiff."

"Oh my God," Lily says.

She gets up and goes into the house. I follow her and stand in the doorway. Rachel is standing at the foot of the bed, pocketbook clasped to her chest, as though beating a strategic retreat.

"The service isn't for your sake, Sam," she tells him. "It's for people in the family to come and pay their respects."

"There's no need. I know what those people think of me — and they know my opinion of them, because I've told them to their faces, many times. There's no need for them to come. And they don't *want* to come. It's just an inconvenience, even for the few friends I have left. Some of them may be glad to hear of my demise, but they won't thank me for taking up their time. Why give them an excuse to bad-mouth me when I'm not around to defend myself?"

Lily is standing between them, looking from one to the other. She seems unsure which of them to appeal to.

"There's never been a cremation in the family," Rachel begins.

"There's never been a lot of common sense either, Rachel, if the truth be known. I've been signed up with this company for years, got a fifty percent discount for booking in advance. I'll save the expense of the rabbi and the funeral home and the food — and the coffin. Instead of chopping down another tree and putting it in the ground to rot or burning it up in the oven, they send you into the fire in a cardboard box."

"A cardboard box!"

"There's not even a lid on it." Sam chortles.

"It's a disgrace," Rachel says. "I believe you're doing this just to humiliate me."

"Mother. Dad," Lily pleads.

"Humiliate you?" Sam sputters, tossing his head back and forth on the pillow. "I've never knowingly humiliated another human being in my life! I don't understand why people want to make such a fuss about a dead person. It's a crazy country. They have the right idea over there in India: make a big pile of your possessions, hoist you up on top, and put a match to it. But here we're saving all the dead people who ever lived, dressing them in fancy clothes and putting them in silk-lined boxes and building little houses for them in cemeteries all over the land. What are we saving them for, do you think? Are we hoping that medical science will find a way to revive them? How would you like to meet all the members of your family that ever lived? What a family reunion that would be! But that will never happen because once the soul leaves the body you can never recall it. Pretty soon the U.S. will be one huge cemetery and you won't be able to turn around without falling over a tombstone. But mine won't be one of them. I'm going to go up in smoke for the sake of future generations —"

"That man is impossible," Rachel says.

She has withdrawn to the door while Sam is expostulating, and now she slips out quickly. Lily follows her.

"I don't know what she's complaining about," Sam remarks to me. "She's going to be the beneficiary of my parsimony."

He subsides with a moan. I am embarrassed to have witnessed this scene, and I do not know what to say to him. I walk out onto the porch. Rachel is going down the steps toward her rented car.

"I'll call you from the motel, dear," she tells Lily. "Bye, Matt."

Lily slumps onto the couch. We watch the car drive away.

"She's going back to Florida," Lily tells me with a catch in her voice. "She'll call me tomorrow and say she just has to get back to her apartment."

I put my arm around her.

"In a way I don't blame her," she says. "What's the point in her staying here? She'll only argue with my father. But that's my mother: whenever I need her, she's out of town."

I sit with Sam in the evening. He sleeps, and I read. In the middle of the night, he startles me with the following question: "Who is the third person in the room with us?"

I am instantly alert. I feel the skin of my arms prickling with fear and excitement. In the diffused light from my reading lamp, his face is terribly drawn, the closed eyes deeply sunken.

"The third person in the room," he pronounces, "is Godot."

Is there a trace of a smile about the corners of his mouth? Or does he perceive something that I cannot? The same uncanny feeling I experienced in the presence of my grandfather's corpse comes over me, the sense of a reality beyond the purely material. I put down my book, draw a chair close to the bed, and compose myself to wait.

Toward morning he becomes restless and agitated, trying weakly to turn himself in the bed and muttering incoherently. I wake Lily. It seems that we have fallen behind the pain, in spite of Kathleen's warning. He hasn't taken a pill for some twelve hours; he can't swallow because his throat is so dry. I take the dropper from Lily's trembling hand and squeeze the drops between his lips. His eyes open, and he gives me an alert and irate stare. Then he is no longer looking at me, and his lids slowly close, as though from extreme exhaustion.

He sleeps for most of Sunday. I look in on him and stand by the bed listening to his breathing, wondering whether I should ask Lily to call Kathleen. I am in the kitchen when I hear his astonished voice.

"Where am I?"

I stand at the foot of the bed where he can see me without moving. "You're in Lily's house, Sam."

The vehement spark in his eyes, the dry chuckle. Hope is helplessly evoked in me, in defiance of what I know.

"What a wonderful sleep I had," he crows. "The sleep of death. Great God, I could be bounded within a nutshell and count myself a king of infinite space, but that I have bad dreams. I had *no* dreams. That stuff you gave me. I was as good as dead. As good as dead. I think I'm going to like it."

Lily comes in and stands behind him, her eyes watching me.

"Is that you, Lily?"

He lifts his hand from the covers, and she takes it.

"I'm right here, Dad."

"What a way to go," he murmurs, drifting off again. "All the comforts of home. The two of you. Kathleen. Not a doctor in sight. And such a sleep I had — in the arms of Morpheus!"

We stand there, a motionless tableau. I feel that I have drawn close to the brink of something, that in another moment I will be able to look over.

"The inside of my mouth feels like the Gobi desert," Sam informs us.

"I'm going to get you a Popsicle, Dad," Lily says, almost cheerfully. "It'll be easier for you to handle."

"No, I don't want anything. What's the use?"

Lily goes in the kitchen and comes back with a long pink Popsicle. She leans over Sam, who has his eyes closed again.

"Just try it, Dad."

Slowly he raises his hand and wraps his bony fingers around the Popsicle.

"The stiletto of death," he murmurs.

Lily draws in a quick breath.

"Or maybe I'm shaking the icy hand of God."

The third week: a blur. Sam is almost never awake now, and the room is dark and curtained during the day because the light hurts his eyes. Kathleen comes and goes, a silent indomitable presence. His blood pressure is down below the gauge, she informs us with a meaningful look. He refuses all attention, even medication. Lily cannot bring herself to administer the liquid morphine, so the task falls to me. I slip the dropper into the corner of his mouth when he is asleep or dozing. I feel like a criminal, but I reassure myself by recalling our promise not to discontinue the drugs. Perhaps he is someplace where pain no longer matters, where its significance is revealed, its intensity mitigated by some marvelous expansion of consciousness. I am here in this world and must live by its promises only.

The worst of it is that he no longer seems to recognize me. My sense of loss has deepened, I am longing helplessly for the "good old days" of last week, for our conversations, our intimacy, our comfortable conspiracy against death. For a week we managed to keep it at bay. But now Sam's humor has been quenched, and without it I feel the imponderable weight of death pressing in upon me, the blank walls of the unknown. For a week we were fellow travelers, but now he has gone on ahead and left me to my uncertainty.

I am miserable at work, incompetent and distracted, waiting for Lily's phone call. I confide in Al, who advises me to call in sick. On Friday evening I take his advice. I dread having to tell Ed Lunt, but Al picks up the phone as though by prearrangement and promises to take care of it. I am sorry to spoil my perfect record, but I cannot leave the house tonight. I have enough to regret in my life. Let me not add one more thing.

Lily opens the curtains to let in the cool night air, and we sit in the dark beside the bed. The dog is restless, and Lily puts him out. He watches us through the porch window, his ears raised at the slightest noise.

"The stocks and bonds are in the toaster oven, Rachel," Sam murmurs. "Take my advice and sell while you still have the chance. The crash is coming. There'll be so many grown men jumping off those tall buildings it won't be safe to walk in the streets. It was all predicted back in 1917 by a fellow called Kondratieff. They sent him to Siberia with chains around his ankles."

He sleeps for a while, then he becomes agitated and restless.

"How *could* I have stayed in school when my mother was on her feet from morning till night?" he protests. "So it was off to the Lamartine Screw Factory for little Shmuel. But I owed it to that woman and all she did for me. Three months in steerage, with three young children and a newborn baby. What a woman."

He is quiet for a while, as though contemplating the enormity of it.

"You're a good boy, Sam," he comes out with. "That was the last thing she said to me. I'd waited all my life to hear her say that. You're a good boy, Sam."

I hear Lily's stifled sob, and I rise and put my arm around her. We stay like this — for how long? Sam becomes increasingly agitated. He seems to be asking for something, but I cannot make out what it is.

"Give him the morphine," Lily says. "I keep hoping he'll say something to me. But I feel like we're just torturing him."

I ply the dropper once more, and after a while Sam sleeps. I touch his hand and find that it is remarkably cold. There is nothing to do but listen to the sound of his breathing. It is alternately faint and scratchy, like a signal that is moving beyond the range of its reception. For an indeterminate time I am unnaturally alert, following the progress of this breathing, attuned to its vicissitudes, feeling it in my own lungs. Then I realize that I have been asleep. Lily is slumped over in her chair. I stand by the bed. Sam is breathing without difficulty. I feel that some emergency is past. It is all right to let down my guard, for a little while at any rate. I wake Lily, and we grope our way upstairs to bed.

It is bright when I wake. Lily is lying on her side, with her head pillowed on an arm. I feel that I am coming back to myself from a great distance; there is a sense of novelty, of strangeness about the day. I get up and go downstairs, without thought or intention. I stand by the head of Sam's bed and see without surprise that his eyes are open and that he is staring at a point above the lintel of the door that leads to the kitchen. I touch his hand, as in a dream. It is quite cold. I stand there, keeping him company, as it were. In this moment I feel no grief, no pity. What is there to be sad about? I never knew that death could be such a clean and noble thing.

Lily is standing in the doorway. She is very solemn and beautiful. I have never been more aware of my love for her, not as a thought or even as a feeling of the heart, but as a total experience of all my being. She comes forward slowly, leans across me, and closes her father's eyes.

Kathleen arrives and verifies Sam's passing. Instead of calling the cremation service right away, she leaves us alone with the body, to say our good-byes. Lily reads from the mourners' kaddish in Hebrew. At her request, I find and read some favorite lines from Ecclesiastes: The heart of the wise is in the house of mourning. I still have a lively sense of Sam's presence and of the ironic satisfaction he would derive from these proceedings. He still looks like himself, as I have come to know him in the past three weeks. Can it really be that someone will now come and remove him from the house? I find that I am dreading this moment, as much for its effect upon me as upon

Lily. I want our little service to continue. There is comfort in imposing a certain order on the inconceivable.

Lily leaves the room and comes back wearing an old denim work shirt over her blouse. She stands beside the bed and looks down at Sam.

"The rending of garments signifies the grief of the mourners," she intones carefully, "the parting of the soul and the body — and the separation of my father from my heart."

She tears the shirt deliberately and firmly. I go and put my arms around her. She cries for a little while, deep, profound sobs. Then she steps back and wipes her face with the torn shirt.

"I feel so alone," she murmurs, as though to herself. "So terribly alone."

A Night of My Life

ICOME TO THE intersection, swing across three empty lanes, and plunge onto the ramp to the Pike. The bleak gorge of the highway appears, lit from above by ghostly streetlights, not a car in sight.

I told Lily I was going to work. Why not? she said. It's probably best to keep busy. Will you be all right? I said. I'm fine, she said. I just want to sleep.

But I am not going to work. I am not even going to call Al. He will have to operate my machines or share them out among the rest of the floor. I cannot help it. I cannot wait. I have to drive.

I ease into the middle lane and start to accelerate. A sheer concrete retaining wall flies by on my right; I'm below street level. The tunnel beneath the Prudential Center rushes toward me, and I'm suddenly underground. Walls and columns stream past, and my headlights flee across the ceiling. The Monster is the only car in here, beneath the unconscionable mass of the Pru, the tons of streets, bridges, and pavements, burrowing beneath the nighttime city, like a mole shunning the light. There is comfort in this reckless headlong motion. But will it hold my thoughts at bay?

When they laid Sam in the body bag, his limbs thumped on the floor, as if he were a piece of wood. Lily tearing her shirt: I feel so alone, she said.

I do not want to be touched by her grief. It will render her helpless and dependent — and I will have to look after her.

I press down the accelerator, as though crazed. The Monster flies out of the tunnel, and a gentle curve of the roadway to the right takes me into the outside lane. Heedless, I press down. My legs and arms are fully extended, and I'm gripping the wheel as though it is pulling me along after it, as though my life depends upon flight.

The speedometer needle crawls toward seventy — and suddenly there's a rhythmic vibration coming through the sole of my foot from the accelerator pedal. I pull my foot away as though I'd been burned; the vibration ceases. Again I apply tentative pressure. As soon as the needle passes sixty-five, the vibration begins anew. Aghast, I pull over to the right lane and cruise along at fifty. Everything seems OK; there's no vibration. Maybe I imagined it. I accelerate to sixty-five, and it starts up again, a pulsing that makes my entire leg tremble, accompanied by a drumming sound that seems to come from directly underneath my seat, though it's hard to tell for certain because of the noise of the engine and the wheels on the roadway. My heart sinks. The Monster is maimed.

I slow down again and crawl along at forty, utterly sobered and aware of my exhaustion. A police cruiser passes in the left lane, lights flashing, but I'm not even thankful to have missed getting a ticket. I am a thief in the night, stealing away from Lily, from Rick, from my workmates at Carr. But providence has served notice that it's not going to be a party to such folly. I see myself standing in the road beside the smoking corpse of the Monster. Night is falling, the road runs to both horizons, and there's nothing to be seen in either direction, save for the gray and blighted land.

The yellow buffer dividing the exit ramp from the highway comes toward me, and I pass to the left of it and keep on going. The toll plaza looms ahead, a ruined temple strung with gaudy flares. I point the Monster toward a single gate with a green light and roll down the window. In a booth on the incoming side, a solitary toll collector in blue stands with his broad back to me, staring down the darkened highway. I take the ticket that the machine spits at me, hold it between my lips, and roll up the window while I accelerate away from the gate. Facing the highway, I gun the Monster up to sixty. I don't feel any vibration, and I balance my foot on the accelerator and hold the speedometer needle as steady as I can.

But as I roll past the state police station in Weston, in the comfortable dark of the Monster's cab, it comes to me — the very taste of the Inish, the wet salty night air with its savor of the wastes of the sea, the unsteady flickering of the mainland lights threatened by the great ocean of night, the sound close at hand of the tide worrying the stones of the beach below the Cable as I pass its friendly lights on my way home from the flicks and proceed past the darkened houses of the terrace into an almost palpable darkness: from far away across the dim channel a faint clanking, a cart on the road beneath the shrouded wall of mountains, its ungreased axle grating in the hubs of the wheels — or is it the sound of rowlocks knocking against the gunwales of a punt, some oarsman out there on the water on a midnight errand?

I hold my breath, waiting for it to disappear. I think of Lily and hope that she is sleeping. But the Inish grows stronger and more uncannily convincing to the senses. Unnerved, I speed up a little, to outdistance it, but the knocking commences beneath my feet, and I ease off the gas. I have the unutterably strange sensation of going in two directions at once, forward at speed into the great body of America, displacing space and thrusting it behind me, driving myself into the future with the power of the Monster's horses — and backward in time to a fixed point in the immensity of the ocean, a dot of rock and poor soil, a kidney-shaped medallion upon the morning sea, touched now by the revolving disk of dawn.

Silence gathers around me, an extraterrestrial silence, independent of time and space, a silence full of the old man's unmistakable presence. In this moment I am possessed by *eagla an domhain,* the great fear of the world, the fear of reproach from beyond the grave. I am like that child whom he all but convinced by his unbending seriousness that it is possible to communicate with the dead. I remember the silence with which he enforced this conviction — and the one occasion upon which he was moved to speak.

For almost a week after my mother's visit — during which she had asked me to rejoin the family in London and I had refused, for reasons that were unclear to me — the old man and I hardly spoke. I would look up from a book or a chore to find his eyes upon me. For an instant he would continue to stare, and then he would simply turn his head. This gesture maddened me. It confirmed my suspicion that he thought me an unnatural child to refuse my mother's invitation — and to remain where I wasn't wanted. Both of them had turned away from me, and I felt increasingly alone, as though the very air I breathed was growing thin and cold. My only source of comfort was old Finn. But I sensed that there was something within my grandfather struggling for expression; beneath his inscrutability it was turning this way and that, painfully seeking a way out.

He has been in and out of the shop all evening, stumping across the house from one door to the other, peering out windows as though expecting someone. Finally he confronts me where I am sitting in the corner of the chimney.

"'Tis high time you learned to manage the boat," he says.

It's a relief to hear him speak. I have grown almost rigid with the tension his silence has created. He has been promising to take me out since Christine and I swam the channel from Port. A week ago I would have been elated. But now there is nothing that matters to me because I know that he doesn't really want me.

"Isn't it getting late, Granda?"

" 'Tis early enough."

We proceed gingerly over the stones, myself with the heavy narrow-bladed oars balanced together on one shoulder, the old man placing the end of his stick with slow care, keeping a wary distance from the swaying oars, the dog prancing about us, filling up the silence with the sound of his barking that echoes about the strand like the clatter of footsteps in an empty hall.

"I was a fisherman like my father," the old man informs me. "And his father before him. It's a hard way to earn your bread, and I wouldn't wish it on anyone. A bookish lad like yourself would never go in for the fishing. You'll be off to Dublin again before very much more water passes under Butt Bridge, believe you me. But while you're here, you might as well know how to take the boat out without coming to grief."

I am glad he's decided to speak to me. Being outdoors seems to have lifted his spirits. But how can I go back to Dublin? There is nowhere I can go.

"I'll show you how to take up the scallops with the net," he tells me in an almost conspiratorial tone. "So long as you don't breathe a word to your mother."

This mention of my mother recalls my responsibility. That is all that is left me: I am good for nothing else. I want to drag the bow of the currach out of the water so that the old man will not get his feet wet, but before I can put the oars down he has taken off his shoes, waded in, and rolled himself clumsily over the gunwale. He retrieves his cap and hunkers down in the stern, holding on with his good hand. I stow the oars quickly, trying to forestall his ineffectual efforts to help me. I push off and clamber in after him. It's surprising how little weight he makes in the boat. Finn regards us mournfully from the strand while we drift out slowly on an absolutely calm tide, still carried by the momentum of my thrust. I watch the water deepening beneath us, the stones of the bottom still visible at what seems a great depth. I feel a little tremor of apprehension. I look up at the old man. He sprawls in the stern, shoulders hunched, leaning to one side and supporting himself upon the crippled hand. The position looks uncomfortable, not to say painful, and I want to do something for him. But his face is stiff and expressionless: the tiny piercing eyes, narrow line of the mouth, stiff inflexible lips. There is nothing that he needs — and he has no use for me.

"Take the net," he says, "and put it over the side."

The net is stretched on a frame and attached to the end of a long pole. I work it over the side and force it down through the resistance of the water until the frame touches the bottom.

"How do I do it, Granda?"

"You have to move it along the bottom and get the scallops into it."

"Are there any scallops down there?"

"I couldn't tell you. Aren't your eyes better than mine?"

I peer over the side. The declining sun is glancing off the surface of the water, and it's hard to tell a scallop shell from a stone. The pole is bent crazily where it enters the water, and I have to lean out of the boat in order to move the frame along the bottom.

"Mind you don't capsize us now!"

My first attempt produces a net full of stones — and two scallops. I am not making much of a fist of it. I toss the stones back and watch them wiggling their way to the bottom. I'll never be any good at it. But the old man doesn't seem to be impatient.

"There's a knack to it, boyeen," he tells me. "Put it back in the water, and wait till the ripples are gone. Then you'll be able to see. You need a very calm day for it. That's what I was waiting for."

I put the net over again and rest my chin on the gunwale, the better to make out what is below. The stones are a golden coppery color, the scallops pale against the mud. I move the pole very slowly in order not to disturb the water — and draw up a half dozen scallops!

"That'll put a few extra pennies in your old tin back at the house," the old man tells me, "and your mother will be none the wiser!"

The sun is behind him, and I cannot see his face. His voice seems to float on the water. With the mention of my mother it has become harsh again. Something is growing within me: a sense of loneliness and loss.

"Put the oars in the pins, let you."

I ease one long heavy oar between the thole pins and pass the end of it to him to hold while I struggle with the other one, afraid in case I drop it overboard or strike him a glancing blow in my awkwardness. I shift into the middle of the thwart, and he places the smooth and worn handles in my hands. Fortunately, the currach has turned on the tide so that the bow is facing the channel. I lean forward with the oars and pull back in my first stroke. I scrape the skin off the knuckles of one hand with the oar in the other — but I scarcely feel the pain in my amazement at the currach's swift and silky movement through the water. I lean upon the oars, watching the wake silently unfold behind us. Finn whines and wades into the water. He is not supposed to go in the water. My stomach contracts in fear.

"Go back, Finn!" the old man calls. "Go home! Go on now! — Pull away, let you!"

Finn withdraws up the shore, his tail drooping, stopping to look back over his shoulder. I pull away reluctantly, watching the dog and the shore recede behind the old man. But I cannot help taking pleasure in the movement of the boat. On the strand it is a dead and awkward thing, but in the water it seems to move with a life of its own. And it is mine to use now. If old Finn goes in the water, I will be able to follow him. I will not let him drown.

The sun is settling upon the heights of the Inish, and there is scarcely a puff of wind on the water. The atmosphere — the still air, the slanting golden light — is like that of a church: hushed, solemn, unspeakably sad. I pull out into the deeper water, where I begin to feel the set of the tide toward the strait that leads out into the open sea. I glance at the old man. He has fumbled pipe and tobacco from his pockets and is staring down at them. I lift one oar and maneuver with the other until the currach is pointed toward the shore again. A few more strokes and we are protected from drifting by a nearby point of land. I look to the old man for approval. He is still looking down at his hands. I lean on the oars. It is odd that he doesn't light up his pipe. Is there something the matter?

"Did your mother ever tell you how I came to fall out with Peg?" he says suddenly.

"My mother would never tell me anything."

He looks up sideways at the paling sky. The crippled hand gives a little involuntary jerk. Placing the pipe and pouch on the thwart beside him, he grips it with the other hand, as though to hold it still.

" 'Tis a long story, and not fit for the ears of a child, most of it. But the gist of it is this: I took Peg's husband Pat — that was Alice's older brother — away in my seine boat with me one night. And didn't I lose him out of it."

I am puzzled — and appalled. How can you lose someone out of a boat like an oar or a net?

"Of course it was no fault of mine!" he says vehemently, as though answering a charge. "He went over the side to try could he save his father, whose boat had foundered with the great weight of fish they had in it. I didn't see him go. It was a wild night, and they were all in the water with the upturned boat. We took up as many of them as we could, and we had to throw our catch overboard to make room for them. I knew we didn't have them all. But we weren't safe from harm ourselves with hardly an inch of freeboard and two crews in the boat. I didn't even know Pat was lost until I met Peg beyond on the pier. He wasn't the only one. There was hardly a family in the Foot didn't lose someone that night. But Peg never forgave me, that I didn't take her husband out of the water. The rest of them were thrown ashore when the storm was finished with them, but poor Pat was never found."

He stops there and looks at me. But it is not the sort of look you give a child. It is a bewildered look, a look that requires an explanation or an answer of me, a look that doesn't seem to recognize me. Inside of me the feeling of *uaigneas* is growing stronger, swelling like a balloon, filling me with emptiness.

"I used to hear Pat's voice whenever there was a sea," he murmurs, "moaning and groaning, unquiet in his watery grave. I had no heart for the fishing anymore after that."

The currach is drifting onto the shallows of the point. I want to bring the old man's attention to this; if we run aground we will have to leave the currach and walk through the mud to get to the shore. But my mind is filled with the image of a drowned man, lost out of my grandfather's boat, streaming water, blue from the cold. I cannot utter a word.

The old man gives a short forced sigh, as though expelling something unpleasant.

"That was a night of my life," he says. "Your grandmother lost father and brother that night. And that was the night your mother was born."

I feel the swelling inside my chest. I can hardly breathe.

"And weren't we all awarded bronze medals for gallantry by the great Winston Churchill himself." The old man snorts. "And a pound a piece for drink! I have his letter still above in the house. 'It affords me much gratification, Sir, to forward this medal to you — from His Majesty the King!' So you see, boyeen, that a man may please the king of a foreign country — and turn his own family against him forever."

The currach touches bottom, wheels about, sticks.

"Merciful hour!" the old man exclaims.

"We're aground on the point, Granda," I inform him.

I take a breath and wait for his reaction. But it does not come. He is sitting quite motionless, his head tilted to one side, like a bird listening for a sound. It has gotten almost dark; I cannot see his face clearly. My shoulders ache. I realize that I've been holding the oars out of the water all this time, and I ease them through the pins now and allow them to rest upon the mud. The tide is gone. We're stranded. A lump comes suddenly in my throat.

"Is my mother ever coming back?" I blurt out.

The shape of the old man is hunched in the stern like an old bundle of sacks.

"Haven't you myself to look after you, boyeen?" he says quietly.

I bite my lip. My eyes are brimming with tears.

"We are not our own men," he tells me. "We must take whatever life brings us and put up with it the best we can."

Silence. Not even the sound of the tide. Then I hear the planks creak, and the currach rolls awkwardly to one side. The shape of his head looms up suddenly in front of me, and I feel his arm about my waist. Without a word he drags me roughly off the thwart and into the bottom of the boat. Nestled up against him, held by his arm that is as hard and unyielding as a stick, I can smell the dust of his clothes and the sharp tobacco smell of his yellowed fingers. But there is warmth in his unfamiliar closeness for all of that. The pressure on my chest is miraculously relieved. My tears flow silently and painlessly.

I sit quietly beside him. My body is at ease; it feels remote, far away. After what seems an age, his voice again out of the dark:

"They said I was always a bit odd after that — as well they might. I took a job outside on the Skellig, looking after the monks' cells, and I spent ten years there. Alice wasn't pleased to be left on her own from May to October. But it was your mother took it the worst."

My head is tilted back against the gunwale, and I am looking up. The sky is clear, spattered with the first stars. I am sitting in a puddle of water, but I do not want to move for fear the old man will withdraw.

"She was only a child of four or five," he says, "but she'd know by the weather when it was time for me to go to the Skellig, and she'd catch on to my leg, the way she'd stop me from leaving the house. She was a willful young thing, not quiet like yourself, a handful for her mother."

He does not ever tell me what I am like — or talk to me about my mother. The novelty of it amazes me. I hardly dare to breathe for fear he will cease.

"I caught a pair of linnets for songbirds and I put their cages up on either side of the door, for company for Maura while I'd be away. If the weather was fine they'd sing till their hearts would burst! But I came home one year from the Skellig to find the empty cages thrown in the corner of the shed. Didn't Maura open the cages the day after I left, to spite me, Alice said, because I wouldn't stop at home? I told her the hawks had got them, and away out of the house with her, crying and bawling. After that, when I had to go to the Skelligs, I used to steal away on her and not tell her I was going at all. I didn't want to have her crying after me."

"Why did you go, Granda?"

"Didn't I have to put food on the table? What else was there for me to do without the fishing?"

He starts forward and gives me a little shake. For a moment I am afraid he will be angry. But then he settles back again and grips me more tightly to himself. The night air drifts about me, chilling my face. But I am warm inside so long as he holds me.

"However it was, your mother and I never got along," he says. "When she was a young woman, she'd want me to put on a shirt and tie of a Sunday and to take her to mass at the Foot. So the neighbors could see her decked out in her finery. But if I sat in to the fire of an evening and began to give out one of the stories, she'd stand up and walk out of the door. She could never sit quiet and listen — not like yourself now. If it wasn't for yourself, there's no one would have the stories after me."

"And Chrissie," I murmur.

"And Christy," he allows. "Your mother had no time for them anyhow. All she wanted was to be walking the road to the Foot or to be off gallivanting in Port. She wanted to go to a dance in Dingle one night, and she was supposed to come home afterwards in some boat from the Foot. But I didn't want her crossing the Bay at night with some fellows who might have drink taken. Hadn't I trouble enough from the sea? Well, she commenced to keen and moan and tear her hair and to tell the world how she was going to go and I couldn't stop her. There were words spoken in anger between us, and the upshot was that she went to live with her cousins in Port that very night, and the next I heard she was getting married to Matthew Quigley — your father that was."

The old man is trembling. Is he cold? Then I hear his quiet dry chuckle in the dark.

"Didn't your father come to the house to ask for her hand — like they used to do in the old days! I remember him standing on the hearth above. He was afraid of his life I'd show him the door. Hasn't she a mind of her own? I said to him. If she wants you, take her, for she'll never be said by me. But he was a decent poor soul, your father, not a bit of harm in him at all. He used to come back the road when your mother was still not speaking to me and sit quiet by the fire, just like yourself. He liked to listen to the stories too; he might have picked them up himself, if he'd only lived."

I am looking at the stars and thinking of my father. The stars seem friendly and familiar, like stones on the beach or the scallops in the net. I do not feel so alone.

"He was a better man than that fellow she's married to now," he informs me. "But sure there's no use talking. It isn't *your* fault that she married him — or that she sent you back to look after a contrary old man like myself. I don't know whose fault it was. But you'll have to put up with me for a while more."

"Are you going to die soon, Granda?"

"Oh, not yet, not yet!" he cries. "Not yet awhile. Don't mind it at all. And I won't be going far anyhow. Only to the Skelligs outside there. You'll come and visit me."

This reassures me, in spite of its improbability. The Skelligs are close and familiar. And they will always be there. Even in the dark I am aware that his attention is fixed upon me. And that is all I want.

He squeezes my shoulder and gently withdraws.

"What about an old story?" he says. "It will pass the time till the moon comes up."

An old story! In a stranded boat in the middle of a mudflat! The idea of it makes me want to laugh out loud.

"The voyage of Bran, son of Ferbal, to the land of the living," he intones. "A blessing on everyone who will commit it faithfully to memory. A year's protection from harm for all to whom it is recited."

The voice is full of light and pleasure; its very sound is warming. Issuing from the darkness it seems to cast a protective spell around me, excluding my fears.

"It was a clear cold night, very calm and still. The sea was like a beaten shield of silver and the sky a riddle of stars —"

Suddenly the Monster's interior is as bright as day, its shadow long and stark upon the road ahead. I swerve into the right lane, and a car goes past at shocking speed, flinging water across the windscreen like a whip. My heart is in my mouth. I am gripping the wheel tightly, in expectation of a blow. Little charges of shock pass through my body.

I hunch over the wheel. There is a tightness about my chest, like the embrace of a drowning man. Then I am weeping without restraint, giving forth great sobs and sighs, the way Lily cried at her father's deathbed. I can hardly see the highway through the tears that sting and blind me. It is all I can do to keep my hands on the wheel.

But I am still on the road, in one piece. I let the Monster coast. I turn on the wipers, and the highway reappears. Another car streams by me in the eastbound lane, its headlights flickering through the divider like a strobe.

The Inish is no longer present, not even as a dream. The highway is gray, and the headlights have ceased to cut a swath through the night. I am alone with America.

I guide the Monster onto the exit ramp and pull over on a little rise within sight of the tollbooth. The sign says STOCKBRIDGE. My skin feels chilled, and my hands are unsteady. I turn off the engine.

"Good-bye, old man," I say.

I open the door and step out. It's light, though the sun has not yet cleared the trees lining the highway. A cool morning breeze blows around my neck. I'm unsteady on my feet; I rest my elbows on the cold roof of the Monster. Below me the highway curves behind a hill; ahead a stand of aspens flickers with preternatural intensity.

That was a night of *my* life. I let its emotion drain away out of my body into the solid earth. Here I am, at a solitary tollbooth on a westbound highway, the whole of this great continent before me. But I have come far enough.

I stand here until I am quite steady on my feet. Then I drive through the tollbooth and pay my toll. I cross the highway, take a new ticket, and enter the eastbound ramp. A few cars zip by as I approach the merge lane: the first commuters. I bring the Monster up to speed.

I am wondering if Lily has passed a good night. It pleases me to know that I will arrive at the time she expects me. I have missed a night of work; I must call Al to apologize, though I have no idea what I will say to him. My eye lights on the fuel gauge: almost out. If I call Al from a pay phone when I stop for gas, I will catch him before the shift ends. So much to do: the responsibilities of the living.

I roll down the windows and let the wind rush through the Monster, to ward off sleep. I drive with two fingers lightly guiding the lower arc of the steering wheel. I have weathered a hard night. No doubt there will be others. But for now I know where I am going, and I have no hesitation. The Pike is the straight and narrow: it leads to Boston, to Lily, to day.

Walden

DEATH ENDS A LIFE, Lily says. "But it doesn't end a relationship."

A sunny Saturday in September. We are driving west out of the city on Route 2. Here the highway is wide and spacious, houses rise steeply from the top of a sheer embankment, and the towers of downtown are visible in the rearview mirror, between Cooper's shaggy head and the protruding end of Lily's canoe, which is roped to the Monster's roof through the open windows.

"I wish I'd known him a little better before he got sick," I say.

"So do I. But you can never know the truth about another person's experience. I realized that after they took him away. I thought he might open up to me at the end. But I'm never going to know how he felt about me or my mother — or about his mistress. The only thing I can hope to know is how *I* feel about it."

The highway passes over water and suddenly narrows to four lanes. There are closely packed trees on both sides, and the oncoming cars seem to be moving too fast. I slow down involuntarily.

"You're still angry with him."

"I didn't feel angry while I was taking care of him," she says. "I was glad to do what had to be done. And he rose to the occasion too, in his own way. But he didn't tell me what I wanted to hear. You have to turn left."

I turn onto a narrow two-lane road and drive for a moment into the woods.

"This is it," Lily announces. "You can drive down to the water."

There is a parking lot on one side and a fence on the other, where the ground falls away steeply. I had imagined a sort of virgin wilderness — or at least that the pond itself would not be visible from the road. Still, the view from the top of the steep bank is impressive: the flat bright plane of the pond, the sense of open space, the deep, beckoning shadows of the trees at the far end.

I pay a uniformed attendant, drive down a steep dirt road, and park in a shady lot.

"Lily," I say. "He told me how he felt about you one night when I was sitting up with him. He even said he knew he wasn't a model father. But when I suggested that he should talk to you, he said it wouldn't do any good. He said you'd have to find out for yourself that he loved you."

I glance at her. She's sitting quietly with her hands in her lap, apparently unimpressed. The dog pokes his nose between our heads, lashing his tail impatiently.

"He was just too stubborn to say it," she says. "My father was witty, charming, full of life, with a great sense of humor. Everybody knew that. But he couldn't express the love he felt, he put his own pleasure before anything else — and he didn't take any interest in me when I was growing up. This is what *I* know. Even though it's painful, it's also a great relief to acknowledge it, to try to bring together the good and the bad."

She turns to me, suddenly animated. "That's my work in progress. Grief is a hard teacher. But it's made a tremendous difference for me to know what I feel about him, now that I can't hope for anything more from him. I feel that I'm emerging from my family, that I'm finally coming into my own."

She gets out of the car and walks over to the water. Cooper is after her in a mad dash; he wades into the pond, barking. I untie the canoe and carry it to the water. Its buoyancy reminds me of my grandfather's currach, though it could not look more different, all varnished wood, the hull a bright green. We are here today because it is the anniversary of the old man's death. My mother, no doubt, has paid a priest to celebrate mass for the repose of his soul. But I want to remember him by water.

A wet Cooper jumps into the bow, and I follow him, balancing myself with the paddle. Lily takes off her shoes, rolls up the legs of her jeans, and pushes off. We glide upon the shadows of old trees whose branches overhang the water, out into the sunlight that ricochets off the surface of the pond. The air is warm for September — for all the Septembers I have ever known. I am grateful to be here, to be with Lily, safe and well in Concord.

We pass the beach. There are some boys swimming in front of a bathhouse, laughing and splashing each other. Lily turns the head of the canoe toward the far end of the pond, and we paddle together until the shouts of the bathers are no longer audible. The canoe glides into a small cove. The water is still, with dark rich reflections of the trees and pieces of vegetation scattered upon the surface. The forward motion ceases. We turn slowly in a circle, while Cooper strains toward the bank, neck and tail extended in a line.

"Did you want to say something about your grandfather?" Lily murmurs.

I want to remember him. I want to retain some continuity with what was, not the numbing proximity of living year after year in his house, but a kind of continuity that transcends time, linking the critical epochs of my life, the New World and the Old, that now like the planets of an expanding universe seem to become daily more remote from each other.

I turn in my seat to face Lily. In the middle of the pond, the sun makes a brilliant path of light on the surface, and another canoe passes in and out of this light, appearing and disappearing, a bright, otherworldly bark of light.

"Let me tell you a story," I say. "One of his stories."

"I'd love to hear a story."

She sits on the floor of the canoe, and I get down beside her, propped against the edge of the seat. I let my fingers trail in the warm water. The reflections of branches ripple on the surface — and in an instant I see the weed-fringed face of the Inish pier, the shadow of the moored ferry, the dark sleek forms of mullet as they hover and dart beneath it. Strange visitation — that vanishes as soon as I try to hold it.

"The voyage of Bran, son of Ferbal, to the land of the living," I intone. "A blessing on everyone who will commit it faithfully to memory. A year's protection from harm for all to whom it is recited."

"Amen," Lily murmurs.

But I stop dead. Surely this is impossible. The old man's stories cannot be dismembered or abridged, they must be told only at night, and there's a certain propriety to be observed in the telling that only he could know.

But the world in which those constraints have meaning is dead and gone. I need only evoke an echo, not stand against time and tide. I try to recall how he used to tell this story, the manner and the conviction of his delivery. But it is no use. I am on my own. I must try to make a fist of it for myself.

"It was a cold clear night, very calm and still. The sea was like a beaten shield or a plain of silver, and the sky a riddle of stars. Bran was walking on the cliffs by the Head and he heard the crying of the seals on the rocks below him and it seemed to him the voices of women singing. He fell asleep listening to them, and when he woke he found a silver branch with white blossoms, the like of which he had never seen before. He took it home to his people, and he found a strange woman in the house before him. She spoke to Bran alone and told him that the branch had come from a marvelous island where there was nothing but sweet friendly women and pleasant music and drink that intoxicates without drunkenness and unfailing youthfulness, nothing of grief, sorrow, sickness, or death. Then the branch sprang from his hand to hers and she went out of the house with it and was never seen again. Nothing would do but for Bran to go in his boat in search of this marvelous island, and the very next morning he took a company of his kinsmen and sailed out of the harbor westward."

I hear in my voice the accent of the Inish, and the notes and inflections that I preserve of *his* voice. It gives me a little shock, the past contained in the present. Are you still within hearing, old man?

"They traveled for two days and nights upon the face of the ocean like murderers cast adrift for their crimes, but before the sun went down upon the third day, they came to an island, and the woman who spoke to Bran was waiting to make them welcome. She had a company of women equal to the number of men who came with Bran, and she drew Bran aside and took him to bed and bolster. It was truly an island of delight, but after a time Bran began to think of home. When he told the woman he was going to leave, she said he would regret it, but nothing would stop him. As he sailed away, she threw a ball of thread after him, and it stuck to his hand and she hauled the boat back to land and detained him another long time. This happened twice more, and twice Bran tore himself from her arms. The third time she threw her ball of thread after him, he let another man catch it, and when she tried to draw them back to land, Bran cut off the man's hand and they escaped."

Grisly image of a severed hand! What part of myself must I sever in order to leave that which threatens to ensnare me — and go toward Lily and a new life?

"They found the Inish again, and they sailed into the harbor and there were people waiting for them on the strand. Bran told them he was the son of Ferbal, but they didn't know him nor he them and everything about them seemed strange. His brother jumped ashore — and as soon as he touched the earth his flesh withered and his bones crumbled into dust, as though he had been dead for hundreds of years."

There is no going back. Learn that once and for all. I cannot repay my debt by repudiating the world and burying myself alive on the Inish. The debt of existence can never be repaid, save by living, by taking what I have and trying to make something of it. The old man gave me what love he had to spare. It was less than I needed, but it will have to do.

"Bran stood up in the boat and told them his story, so that some among them might remember him. Then he turned his face from the island where he was born. And from that hour his wanderings are not known."

Lily puts her hand in mine, closes her eyes, and leans her head back against the seat. I breathe a sigh of relief. I have faced his death, and the loss is not fatal. What parting can there be without loss? But perhaps Lily is right: a relationship can continue beyond the grave. In time I may learn that my legacy is more than hopelessness and *uaigneas,* that I also have from him qualities that will help me in the New World: his stubborn persistence, his loyalty — and his love of a good story.

Together we turn the canoe and paddle toward the parking lot.

"I'm ready to move back to Cambridge," Lily says behind me.

This gives me a little shock. I've been living with her in Walpole since Sam died, on an unquestioned day-to-day basis. What am I going to do now?

I ship the paddle and turn in my seat to look at her. I become aware of a warm feeling in the vicinity of my heart. I am attached to Lily, for good or ill. This means that I am vulnerable: what affects her in turn affects me. But I no longer wish to run away from her: she is my hope of love. Lily is a person who bears her trouble with dignity. I will have to learn to do the same.

"I want to move with you."

She shades her eyes with her hand to look at me.

"Are you sure?"

"Yes! I'm making a plan — for the first time in my life! — and my plan is to live with you."

She lets her hand fall, and I see her tears. I try to get up and go to her, but the canoe rocks alarmingly and I drop back on my seat. We grin at each other across its length. We are ready, for whatever will come. I have made no promises that I cannot keep; I have simply given my assent to what already exists.

Cooper turns in the bow to face me, long pink tongue lolling, his coat a blaze of white and gold.

"You're going to have to walk him every other night in Cambridge," Lily says behind me. "It's love me, love my dog."

Cooper is looking at me out of his dark eloquent eyes — and all of a sudden I see old Finn, I smell his wet black coat, hear his unmistakable panting, the rattle of the strand beneath his paws. In this instant, without the slightest warning, I am both there and here, on the strand below the house, facing a channel flat as milk, inhaling sea-weed and salt air, and sitting on the warm varnished bench of the ca-noe, with the bright jewel of the pond around me. Time seems no longer to move in a horizontal succession of moments; it is suddenly deep and still, infinite in extent. This experience is accompanied by a feeling of unassailable well-being, and I want to prolong it, to in-habit this infinitude, to hold the sense of continuity: the Inish and Walden, my own presence, parts of a single whole.

The experience is past, and time is restored. But I know now that the two worlds are one and that I cannot be cast out of either. I have not severed myself from the past; the lines of communication are not down. A faint but insistent signal, trapped in the blood and the nerves, the ghost of the Cable's obsolete pulse, still finds me here across an ocean of change.

The canoe glides on soundlessly toward the shore. But what will I *do* here? Who will I *be?*

I become aware that Lily is no longer paddling. I turn my head to meet her brilliant smile — and the black eye of her camera.

Rick's new car is a refurbished 1969 Ford Fairlane. The upholstery is spotless, and the paintwork — a flamboyant turquoise with a wide white stripe — gleams like new. It's a birthday present from Erica, he tells me. I know from Lily that they've had a rapprochement. They are virtually living together in Rick's apartment, where Rick is look-ing after her. But this is quite a present.

We drive through the rural lanes of Dover, a town southwest of the city. The very landscape — green fields, manicured hedgerows, tree-screened estates — exudes affluence. What are we doing here? I had thought Rick was just showing off his new car, but it transpires that he has something else to show me, which he's being quite mys-terious about.

He pulls off the road into a gravel driveway, by a for sale sign that has been pasted over with the word *sold*. We emerge from shrubs and trees before a large three-story house flanked by flower beds and lawns. The house is white clapboard with black shutters and faded red-brick gables; there is an elegant fanlight over the spacious entry.

Behind it there is a huge barn, a building with a quaint little bell tower that looks like a stable, and a vista of level fields and fences.

Rick parks in a corner of the driveway, leaving the engine running.

"What do you think?" he says, grinning. "It's supposed to look traditional, but it's only ten years old. The interior is completely modern."

"Very nice. Who lives here?"

"Rick Cozzolino from Medfo'd. But I don't get to take possession until after the wedding."

"Wedding? You and Erica?"

He nods his head, eyes wide with glee.

"Congratulations!" I say, reaching across and pumping his hand. "I'm happy for you."

"So am I, Matty. The last time I saw you I really hit bottom. I called up Erica and we had a heart-to-heart. She'd missed me too! But she wanted a commitment. She said we owed it to each other to make up our minds what we wanted. It really made me think. I decided I'd been barking up the wrong tree, trying to get ahead and make a lot of money. I couldn't believe Erica was really interested in someone like me. I thought I had to impress her, to put on a show. But that isn't me. That's not where I'm coming from. I want my piece of the pie, but I also want to come home to someone I care about: *that's* the bottom line. Erica doesn't care what I do, so long as I'm there for her. It's a shame that she had to get sick for me to come to my senses. But it's all going to work out."

Rick has turned it all around. I was afraid that he would lose his job, sink into depression, never see Erica again. But that is just my fatalism, my instinctive reaction to adversity. In the New World, there is no reason to give up hope. It ain't over till it's over.

"It's a wedding present from Erica's parents," Rick says, nodding at the house. "She's going to keep horses, maybe even run a stable of her own. And I'm going to have a high-class body shop in the barn there. I'm retiring from sales. I was never cut out to be a salesman. I'm a hands-on sort of guy at heart. I've always messed around with cars, ever since high school, but I was too proud to be a grease monkey. I'm going into restoring, bodywork and upholstery, classics like this one right here, and one of my old buddies from the neighborhood is going to fix things under the hood."

I have always admired Rick's competence, but now it is his flexibility that impresses me. There is a lesson here. If your plan doesn't work out, try something else. It is possible to adapt to circumstances. Difficulty does not invariably mean defeat.

"Speaking of cars," Rick says. "Yours is first on my list. It's not exactly an antique, like this one. But it's got a real classic shape."

"What are you going to do to it?" I ask warily.

"Bodywork. Paint job. Chrome. Upholstery. But that's it. I'm strictly a cosmetics man. You'll have to talk to my buddy about that knocking you've been hearing."

My heart leaps. A vision of the Monster transformed, a stately black — or stunning white! — gleaming hubcaps, whitewall tires, carpet underfoot instead of the worn rubber mats, new seat covers, the works. But it sounds too good to be true, too good for Matthew Quigley.

"I'm not sure I can afford you, Rick."

He laughs.

"You can't! But don't worry about it. This one is on the house."

I am waiting at a light on Cambridge Street on my way to my shift at Carr when a hand emerges from the car beside me and shakes my shoulder roughly. "Hello, Irishman!"

It is George, the Monster's erstwhile owner. He is in the passenger seat of a shabby old Citroën, almost as big as the Monster. I cannot see who is driving, because the bulk of his substantial frame fills the window. He has gained weight since I saw him last — and shaved his head, to reveal an impressive shining dome.

"Where did you get that car?" is all I can think to say to him.

His blue eyes twinkle merrily.

"I get from my brother," he informs me. "Where he gets, I don't ask."

"I thought your wife wanted a new car."

"My wife is French. This car is French. Right? She is very happy.

And I have room enough for mother and sister and sister's family —
all in backseat. So I am happy too."

He regards me casually, yet with attention. There is something regal about his bearing, the way his arm rests on the window, the unhurried clarity of his look. I want to tell him everything that has
happened to me since I bought the Monster from him. At the same
time, his composure unnerves me. I remember that I have not kept
my part of the bargain.

"I haven't been to your brother's restaurant yet," I admit. "But I'm
going to go. Maybe I'll go today."

"Too late," George says. "Sold. You can still go, but not the same."

"I'm sorry," I feel obliged to say. "I really wanted to."

"They say in Ireland, Have to make hay while the sun shines?"

He fixes his steady look upon me, and I squirm a little in my seat.
I find myself wishing for the light to change.

"But you get another chance," George says. "He's got a garage
now. In Allston. This is his card."

He swiftly passes me a thumb-marked business card with the
name Peter Hagopian and a telephone number.

"How are the brakes?" he wants to know.

"The brakes? They're fine. I mean, as far as I know."

George shakes a plump finger in admonition. "So you still don't
look under the hood? You forget about the old horse. Got to look after horse. If you don't, he let you fall."

I haven't heard the ominous knocking since my night drive on the
Pike — because I don't dare to exceed fifty. But I should have had it
looked at. Perhaps I have caused some damage that could have been
prevented.

"I don't drive it as much," I tell George, "since I live with my girlfriend. But I'm having some bodywork done."

He shakes his head seriously.

"Same girlfriend?"

"That's right."

He blinks his great inscrutable eyes.

"Go see my brother," he intones. "Got to look after horse. Then do
bodywork."

He turns his head slowly as though the conversation is over. The left-turn light changes to green. I feel a sudden impulse of gratitude toward him.

"I'm very happy with the car," I say. "I think it's a lucky car."

The regal head turns slowly, the eyes engage mine.

"No such thing as luck. You're an Irishman and you not know that? If you think you're lucky, maybe you earn. If not, not."

Someone behind him honks. George places a restraining hand on the driver's sleeve.

"You go home yet?"

"I like it here," I say. "I think I'll stay."

George shrugs.

"They say in Ireland, Home is where the heart is?"

He lifts his hand. The Citroën surges forward. I sit there watching his massive head through the rear window until he rounds the corner, and then I put the Monster in drive and pull away from the light, urged on by a fanfare of horns.